Acclaim for THE GIRL FROM HOLLYWOOD

This Hollywood story of 1924 by the creator of *Tarzan* reflects the tensions between the agrarian dream of California — utopian life on the bountiful land — and the tawdry modernity of the Jazz Age represented by Los Angeles: a cesspit of rapacious directors, the sex trade, drug addiction, alcoholism, and crime. Most interesting is the novel's moral conundrum — in a utopia, what outlet is there for youth's restlessness and ambition, besides out and, most likely, down?

— Janet Fitch, author of *White Oleander*
& *The Revolution of Marina M.*

Mr. Burroughs, having exhausted the apes and the Martians, has now brought his pen to bear on one of the most interesting and sordid sections of mere humanity. The interest of Hollywood is natural enough; its sordidness, according to accounts, is mainly due to the herding together of actors and actresses whose salaries are, for the most part, grotesquely disproportionate to their abilities. Mr. Burroughs keeps away from personalities but spares us no detail of the general scene: drug fiends and vampires advance from his pages almost as realistically as, in their professional moments, they loom from the screen. A powerful foil is needed for these distressing disclosures; the dramatic values and the popular voice alike demand one. Mr. Burroughs obliges by importing into the milieu of his story a palpably healthy breeze from the adjacent West, an indisputably strong man, and an ingénue whose "innocence," though it might captivate Tarzan, would certainly seem suspect to Freud. It will be interesting to see if "The Girl from Hollywood," which, like its predecessors, has obvious merits as a *succès de sujet*, will come to share their enormous vogue. The path is clear, and it would be as unfair as futile to attempt any further influence on the popular verdict.

— *The Spectator*, London, April 5, 1924

"How wonderful that the *Los Angeles Review of Books* has resurrected this forgotten classic set in 1920s L.A. that rings with timeless truth about Hollywood's twisted allure but also waxes lyrical about the rolling hills and canyons that Edgar Rice Burroughs, creator of *Tarzan* and Tarzana, once called home. The naïve starlets, dodgy directors, morphine addicts, cowboys, rum-runners, aspiring writers, and gentlemen ranchers of a century past are vivid, flawed characters, and the precise, poetic descriptions of open land now ravaged by development and forest fires will make you weep. This is a melodramatic page-turner that by turns enthralls and shocks while presenting a keyhole into a vanished era with haunting resonance to our own. Drop everything and buy *The Girl From Hollywood*. This is an imprint to watch, and as a student of L.A. history, I can't wait to see what *LARB* publishes next."

—Denise Hamilton, former *LA Times* reporter, crime novelist, and editor of the award-winning *Los Angeles Noir I* and *Los Angeles Noir 2: The Classics* short story anthologies

THE GIRL FROM HOLLYWOOD

THE GIRL FROM HOLLYWOOD

EDGAR RICE BURROUGHS

Introduction by Steph Cha

LARB
CLASSICS

This is a LARB Classics publication
Published by The Los Angeles Review of Books
6671 Sunset Blvd., Suite 1521, Los Angeles, CA 90028
www.larbbooks.org

Introduction copyright © 2019 by Steph Cha

ISBN 978-1-940660-47-9

Library of Congress Control Number 2018965704

Designed by Tom Comitta

INTRODUCTION

EDGAR RICE BURROUGHS is best known for his many adventure novels set in the jungles of Africa and the alien landscapes of Mars, but one could argue — if one were just a little bit of a smartass — that he left a bigger footprint on Los Angeles than any other writer. Chandler got Raymond Chandler Square at the intersection of Hollywood and Cahuenga, marked by a few inconspicuous signs pinned to traffic lights; John Fante got the corner of 5th and Grand downtown. Burroughs got all of Tarzana, an 8.79 square mile neighborhood in the San Fernando Valley, named for his most famous creation, the feral child/British lord Tarzan.

His books may not have aged quite as well as those of his contemporaries, but Burroughs was enormously successful in his time. Born in Chicago to a Mayflower-white family (his great-great-etc.-grandfather was the Puritan settler Edmund Rice), he was a wholesaler of pencil sharpeners before trying his hand at writing. He spent a lot of time reading pulp magazines and decided he "could write stories just as rotten." He started his Barsroom series in 1912, and published *Tarzan of the Apes* in October of the same year. His Tarzan books became a big enough sensation that he moved to California in 1919, where he bought 550 acres of land from the estate of General Harrison Gray Otis, president and general manager of the *Los Angeles Times*, for $125,000. (When was the last time, I wonder, that a novelist bought major real estate from a newspaper publisher? I'll bet it was closer to 1919 than 2019.) He built a huge ranch house on the property and called it Tarzana Ranch. Over the next several years, he subdivided and sold off the surrounding land for development, and in 1930, the residents of the new community chose to name their home Tarzana.

I didn't know anything about Burroughs's business or legacy when I started reading *The Girl from Hollywood*, serialized in *Munsey's Magazine* from June to November, 1922 (it was later published in book form in August 1923, by The Macaulay Company). Burroughs wrote only a handful of contemporary novels — all anyone wanted from him was sci-fi and Tarzan — and this one offers rare insight into his life in California and his relationship with Los Angeles.

Unlike some other big-name novelists who moved to Los Angeles, Burroughs was not a screenwriter, but he had ploenty of interaction with Hollywood: his books were adapted into movies at a furious pace, seven of them between 1917 and 1921 alone. (His daughter Joan married James Pierce, the fourth actor to play Tarzan, in the 1927 silent film *Tarzan and the Golden Lion*. They were married for over 40 years, until her death in 1972 — pretty sweet for a Hollywood romance, nothing this book would have predicted.) Tarzan took on a cinematic life of his own, and Burroughs wasn't always pleased with the results.

The Girl from Hollywood paints a rather nasty picture of Hollywood and city life, which stand in opposition to "the country," where most of the novel takes place. The fictional Ganado is a rural idyll:

> It was the first day of early spring. The rains were over. The California hills were green and purple and gold. The new leaves lay softly fresh on the gaunt boughs of yesterday. A blue jay scolded from a clump of sumac across the trail.

The Rancho del Ganado, Ganado's largest ranch, is owned and occupied by the Pennington family: Colonel and Mrs. Julia Pennington, their adult son Custer, and their teenage daughter Eva. Their neighbors, the Evans family — the widowed Mrs. Mae Evans and her son and daughter, Guy and Grace — live a half-mile away. The two families seem to be the only residents of Ganado, other than various employees and one new neighbor — a widow named Mrs. George Burke, whose daughter Shannon is the titular girl from Hollywood. The Penningtons and the Evanses are close and almost incestuously intertwined. The children grew up together and fell in love: Custer with Grace, Eva with Guy.

They spend their days doing wholesome things like riding horses at the crack of dawn and having dinner parties with their parents that end with chaste dancing. Burroughs doesn't hide his admiration for their simple, pastoral way of life:

> Unlike city dwellers, these people had never learned to conceal the lovelier emotions of their hearts behind a mask of assumed indifference. Perhaps the fact that they were not forever crowded shoulder to shoulder with strangers permitted them an enjoyable naturalness which the dweller in the wholesale districts of humanity can never know.

They aren't without troubles, of course. There are bootleggers in the hills, for one. For another, the children, now grown, start longing for city life.

Their little world starts falling apart when Grace decides to move to Hollywood to seek stardom before settling down and marrying Custer:

> Why, I haven't lived yet, Custer! I want to live. I want to do something outside of the humdrum life that I have always led and the humdrum life that I shall live as a wife and mother. I want to live a little, Custer, and then I'll be ready to settle down. You all tell me that I am beautiful, and down, away down in the depth of my soul, I feel that I have talent. If I have, I ought to use the gifts God has given me.

She leaves to follow her dreams, upsetting the quiet happiness of Ganado. At first, her letters are frequent and hopeful, but as the weeks and months go on, she writes less and less, fading into her new life. She doesn't visit, and the Penningtons and the other Evanses more or less lose track of her — it's like she lives in a different world entirely.

There's so much made of this country/city divide, I was shocked and delighted to learn that Ganado is in fact Tarzana. According to John Taliaferro, who wrote the Burroughs biography *Tarzan Forever* (1999), "Rancho del Ganado is Tarzana to the last detail; the description of roads, trails, topography, and architecture verge on the encyclopedic — and thus have great historical value for anyone trying to picture the original Tarzana before it became suburbia."

I pictured Ojai or Temecula or at least Malibu, but Tarzana is a relatively close-in suburb, less than half an hour from Hollywood unless traffic is heavy (which, I suppose, it often is). I thought maybe it took longer to get around in Burroughs's time, but when he was selling his ranch in 1936, he placed an ad in *Script* magazine describing the property: "I want to sell it to somebody looking for a beautiful estate only 20 minutes drive from Hollywood."

I've made that drive more times than I can reliably estimate. I grew up in Encino, just one neighborhood east of Tarzana, where Burroughs lived in his later years. He died in his home at 5565 Zelzah Avenue. That house no longer exists, but if it did, it would be just a couple blocks away from the Trader Joe's with the terrible parking lot (I know all Trader Joe's have bad parking lots, but I think Valley dwellers will agree with me that this is by far the worst one), and only minutes away from my childhood home.

I spent a lot of time in Tarzana. I went to a Saturday school on the Portola Middle School campus, where I learned Korean and took classes in taekwondo and abacus. One of my best friends lived in Tarzana and got rejected from a job at the Coldstone on Reseda and Ventura (he ended up working at a Jamba Juice instead); we hung out there all the time anyway, and he'd exchange awkward greetings with the manager while we ordered our ice cream, which we ate on the concrete patio adjoining the parking lot, shared with a Panda Express. We didn't do much horseback riding.

We went into central Los Angeles often, particularly after we learned to drive. Mostly Koreatown and the area near the

Grove, and sometimes, we bummed around Hollywood — the Amoeba and the ArcLight being great places to waste time when you're not yet old enough to drink.

Of course for Burroughs, the distance between Tarzana and Hollywood was more conceptual than physical (though you wouldn't know it from the book). And the idea that neighborhood shapes your character and determines your fate is, as they say, "very L.A." Downtown and Beverly Hills are only about 11 miles apart, but drive between them on Wilshire or 3rd or Beverly, and you run through dozens of distinct communities, with widely varying characters and demographics. Tarzana may no longer qualify as "country," but it does offer the relative quiet and seclusion of suburbia, which is what seemed to appeal to Burroughs.

This craving for peaceful escape from the chaos and danger of city life is part of what created suburbia in the first place. Of course, another way to describe that drive is "white flight." The Ganado of the Penningtons and the Evanses is an enclave of whiteness. There are Mexicans hiding in the hills, but they are criminals, bootleggers and murderers; the land is not for them. Where there are non-whites in this book, there is corruption, and it would be unduly generous — the text in no way demands it — to chalk this up to coincidence. The only characters of color are the Mexican criminals and a "Japanese 'schoolboy' of 35," sometimes referred to as "the Jap," who works as a housekeeper at an actor/director/drug dealer's bungalow. The only one with a name is a Mexican murderer who tries to blackmail, rape, and kill Shannon Burke: "She knew how lightly the criminal Mexican esteems life — especially the life of the hated gringo."

Burroughs was a product of his time, etc. etc., but *The Girl from Hollywood* does have plenty of resonance with ours — it is a novel about the sordidness of Hollywood, after all. When Grace makes her move to the big, bad L.A., Shannon Burke is already there, using the stage name Gaza de Lure:

> Two years ago she came to Hollywood from a little town in the Middle West [...] She was fired by high purpose then. Her child's heart, burning with lofty ambition, had

set its desire upon a noble goal. The broken bodies of a
thousand other children dotted the road to the same goal,
but she did not see them, or seeing, did not understand.

The girl from Hollywood was originally a girl from the Midwest, brought down low by the corrupting influence of the city and the film industry. Her career stagnated due to her resistance to the advances of powerful men. As one sleazy assistant director put it, "The trouble with you is you ain't enough of a good fellow. You got to be a good fellow to get on in pictures." Grace runs into the same obstacles when she starts making her rounds:

If she could only have a chance! In the weeks of tramping from studio to studio she had learned much. For one thing, she had come to know the ruthlessness of a certain type of man that must and will some day be driven from the industry — that is, in fact, even now being driven out, though slowly, by the stress of public opinion and by the example of the men of finer character who are gradually making a higher code of ethics for the studios.

How optimistic, in retrospect, and how heartbreaking. Burroughs wrote those lines 30 years before Harvey Weinstein was even born, and almost a century before he and others like him were held to account for their decades of misconduct.

Burroughs's outrage is strong and apparent. He recognizes the vulnerability of young naïve women trying to make it in Hollywood, and condemns the industry men who abuse their position and power. Unsurprisingly, though, his attitudes are far from feminist. He wants men to behave honorably and protect women: "It brought the tears to her eyes — tears of happiness, for every woman wants to feel that she belongs to some man — a father, a brother, or a husband — who loves her well enough to order her about for her own good," and for women to maintain their sexual purity.

Shannon manages to stay chaste, even in the clutches of the wily, villainous Wilson Crumb, the aforementioned actor/

director/drug dealer, who tricked her into becoming a drug addict (he tells her the white powder is crushed aspirin; not the brightest, our Shannon). She spends her days with him at his bungalow, helping him sling cocaine, heroin, and morphine. When we meet her — and we do meet her, in a brief, brilliant passage that makes rare good use of second-person narration — she's in poor shape, as are we:

> At sight of you she rises, a bit unsteadily, and, smiling with her lips, extends a slender hand in greeting. The fingers of the hand tremble and are stained with nicotine. Her eyes do not smile — ever [...]

> Probably you have not noticed that she is wild-eyed and haggard, or that her fingers are stained and trembling, for you, too, are wild-eyed and haggard, and you are trembling worse than she.

It takes her mother's death to pull her from her wretched Hollywood life by bringing her to Ganado, and under the benevolent influence of the Penningtons. She falls in love with Custer, but his engagement and her shame — more about her close association with Crumb, which most would wrongly assume was sexual, than her two years of being a straight-up drug dealer — pose major problems for their romance.

Burroughs has a lot of sympathy for Shannon, and that sympathy makes her a substantial protagonist, a flawed female character who is easy to root for — a bit of a feat for a pulp writer in the 1920s. He doesn't judge her too harshly for her criminal activity, and he portrays her fight against addiction with real humanity: "Already she could feel her will weakening. It was the old, old story that she knew so well." She has more depth and courage than any of the male characters, and she does more to protect Custer than even he, the noble, selfless hero, does to protect her.

The Girl from Hollywood has many of the trappings of a standard morality tale — heroes and villains, virtue and vice, astonishing levels of coincidence — but it has enough shadows and ambiguity to keep things interesting. There are moments in the book that seem to predict the coming age of hardboiled detective fiction. Both Shannon and Guy Evans — on the side of good, decent people — find themselves entangled with criminals and illicit activity. Guy works with the bootleggers in the hills:

> Young Evans, while scarcely to be classed as a strong character, was more impulsive than weak, nor was he in any sense of the word vicious. While he knew that he was breaking the law, he would have been terribly shocked at the merest suggestion that his acts placed upon him the brand of criminality. Like many another, he considered the Volstead Act the work of an organized and meddlesome minority, rather than the real will of the people. There was, in his opinion, no immorality in circumventing the 18th Amendment whenever and wherever possible.

He gets in way over his head, of course, but it all starts because the Prohibition placed him and others like him on the other side of the law. "Every one's breaking the damned old 18th Amendment," he says, "and it's got so it don't seem like committing a crime, or anything like that." This is classic noir territory, slippery slopes and shades of gray, many of them introduced by the strictures of Prohibition, which created a large, fresh class of booze-running criminals.

Burroughs still comes off as pretty prudish in his values (even as some of his characters engage in treachery and violence and snort copious amounts of cocaine), but *The Girl from Hollywood* is a departure from the tales of male heroism that formed his reputation. Shannon has sinned and suffered, and is therefore forgiving and flexible: "Her own misfortune had made her generously ready to seek excuses for wrongdoing in others," which is good because even Custer has a bit of a drinking problem. *The Girl from Hollywood* is an entertaining book and a fascinating study of Los Angeles in the 1920s: a decade before

Chandler tied the city's identity to the tradition of noir and almost a century before the reckoning of #MeToo. Enjoy the morphine and blackmail and romance, and the rustic paradise of old Tarzana.

Steph Cha
Los Angeles
2019

THE GIRL FROM HOLLYWOOD

CHAPTER I

THE TWO HORSES picked their way carefully downward over the loose shale of the steep hillside. The big bay stallion in the lead sidled mincingly, tossing his head nervously and flecking the flannel shirt of his rider with foam. Behind the man on the stallion, a girl rode a clean-limbed bay of lighter color whose method of descent, while less showy, was safer, for he came more slowly, and in the very bad places, he braced his four feet forward and slid down, sometimes almost sitting upon the ground.

At the base of the hill, there was a narrow level strip; then, an eight-foot wash with steep banks barred the way to the opposite side of the cañon, which rose gently to the hills beyond. At the foot of the descent, the man reined in and waited until the girl was safely down; then, he wheeled his mount and trotted toward the wash. Twenty feet from it, he gave the animal its head and a word. The horse broke into a gallop, took off at the edge of the wash, and cleared it so effortlessly as almost to give the impression of flying.

Behind the man came the girl, but her horse came at the wash with a rush — not the slow, steady gallop of the stallion — and, at the very brink, he stopped to gather himself. The dry bank caved beneath his front feet, and into the wash he went, head first.

The man turned and spurred back. The girl looked up from her saddle, making a wry face.

"No damage?" he asked, an expression of concern upon his face.

"No damage," the girl replied. "Senator is clumsy enough at jumping, but no matter what happens, he always lights on his feet."

"Ride down a bit," said the man. "There's an easy way out just below."

She moved off in the direction he indicated, her horse picking his way among the loose boulders in the wash bottom.

"Mother says he's part cat," she remarked. "I wish he could jump like the Apache!"

The man stroked the glossy neck of his own mount.

"He never will," he said. "He's afraid. The Apache is absolutely fearless; he'd go anywhere I'd ride him. He's been mired with me twice, but he never refuses a wet spot; and that's a test, I say, of a horse's courage."

They had reached a place where the bank was broken down, and the girl's horse scrambled from the wash.

"Maybe he's like his rider," suggested the girl, looking at the Apache; "brave, but reckless."

"It was worse than reckless," said the man. "It was asinine. I shouldn't have led you over the jump when I know how badly Senator jumps."

"And you wouldn't have, Custer" — she hesitated — "if —"

"If I hadn't been drinking," he finished for her. "I know what you were going to say, Grace; but I think you're wrong. I never drink enough to show it. No one ever saw me that way — not so that it was noticeable."

"It is always noticeable to me and to your mother," she corrected him gently. "We always know it, Custer. It shows in little things like what you did just now. Oh, it isn't anything, I know, dear; but we who love you wish you didn't do it quite so often."

"It's funny," he said, "but I never cared for it until it became a risky thing to get it. Oh, well, what's the use? I'll quit it if you say so. It hasn't any hold on me."

Involuntarily, he squared his shoulders — an unconscious tribute to the strength of his weakness.

Together, their stirrups touching, they rode slowly down the cañon trail toward the ranch. Often, they rode thus, in the restful silence that is a birthright of comradeship. Neither spoke until after they reined in their sweating horses beneath the cool shade of the spreading sycamore that guards the junction of El Camino Largo and the main trail that winds up Sycamore Cañon.

It was the first day of early spring. The rains were over. The California hills were green and purple and gold. The new leaves lay softly fresh on the gaunt boughs of yesterday. A blue jay scolded from a clump of sumac across the trail.

The girl pointed up into the cloudless sky where several great birds circled majestically, rising and falling upon motionless wings.

"The vultures are back," she said. "I am always glad to see them come again."

"Yes," said the man. "They are bully scavengers, and we don't have to pay 'em wages."

The girl smiled up at him.

"I'm afraid my thoughts were more poetic than practical," she said. "I was only thinking that the sky looked less lonely now that they have come. Why suggest their diet?"

"I know what you mean," he said. "I like them, too. Maligned as they are, they are really wonderful birds and sort of mysterious. Did you ever stop to think that you never see a very young one or a dead one? Where do they die? Where do they grow to maturity? I wonder what they've found up there! Let's ride up. Martin said he saw a new calf up beyond Jackknife Cañon yesterday. That would be just about under where they're circling now."

They guided their horses around a large, flat slab of rock that some camper had contrived into a table beneath the sycamore and started across the trail toward the opposite side of the cañon. They were in the middle of the trail when the man drew in and listened.

"Someone is coming," he said. "Let's wait and see who it is. I haven't sent any one back into the hills today."

"I have an idea," remarked the girl, "that there is more going on up there"— she nodded toward the mountains stretching to the south of them — "than you know about."

"How is that?" he asked.

"So often, recently, we have heard horsemen passing the ranch late at night. If they weren't going to stop at your place, those who rode up the trail must have been headed into the high hills; but I'm sure that those whom we heard coming down weren't coming from the Rancho del Ganado."

"No," he said, "not late at night — or not often, at any rate."

The footsteps of a cantering horse drew rapidly closer, and, presently, the animal and its rider came into view around a turn in the trail.

"It's only Allen," said the girl.

The newcomer reined in at sight of the man and the girl. He was evidently surprised, and the girl thought that he seemed ill at ease.

"Just givin' Baldy a workout," he explained. "He ain't been out for three or four days, an' you told me to work 'em out if I had time."

Custer Pennington nodded.

"See any stock back there?"

"No. How's the Apache today — forgin' as bad as usual?"

Pennington shook his head negatively.

"That fellow shod him yesterday just the way I want him shod. I wish *you'd* take a good look at his shoes, Slick, so you can see that he's always shod this same way."

His eyes had been traveling over Slick's mount whose heaving sides were covered with lather. "Baldy's pretty soft, Slick; I wouldn't work him too hard all at once. Get him up to it gradually."

He turned and rode off with the girl at his side. Slick Allen looked after them for a moment and then moved his horse off at a slow walk toward the ranch. He was a lean, sinewy man of medium height. He might have been a cavalryman once. He sat his horse, even at a walk, like one who has sweated and bled under a drill sergeant in the days of his youth.

"How do you like him?" the girl asked of Pennington.

"He's a good horseman, and good horsemen are getting rare these days," replied Pennington; "but I don't know that I'd choose him for a playmate. Don't you like him?"

"I'm afraid I don't. His eyes give me the creeps — they're like a fish's."

"To tell the truth, Grace, I don't like him," said Custer. "He's one of those rare birds — a good horseman who doesn't love horses. I imagine he won't last long on the Rancho del Ganado; but we've got to give him a fair shake — he's only been with us a few weeks."

They were picking their way toward the summit of a steep hogback. The man, who led, was seeking carefully for the safest footing, shamed out of his recent recklessness by the thought of how close the girl had come to a serious accident through his thoughtlessness. They rode along the hogback until they could look down into a tiny basin where a small bunch of cattle was grazing, and then, turning and dipping over the edge, they dropped slowly toward the animals.

Near the bottom of the slope, they came upon a white-faced bull standing beneath the spreading shade of a live oak. He turned his woolly face toward them, his red-rimmed eyes observing them dispassionately for a moment. Then, he turned away again and resumed his cud, disdaining further notice of them.

"That's the King of Ganado, isn't it?" asked the girl.

"Looks like him, doesn't he? But he isn't. He's the King's likeliest son, and unless I'm mistaken, he's going to give the old fellow a mighty tough time of it this fall if the old boy wants to hang on to the grand championship. We've never shown him yet. It's an idea of Father's. He's always wanted to spring a new champion at a great show and surprise the world. He's kept this fellow hidden away ever since he gave the first indication that he was going to be a fine bull. At least a hundred breeders have visited the herd in the past year, and not one of them has seen him. Father says he's the greatest bull that ever lived and that his first show is going to be the International."

"I just know he'll win," exclaimed the girl. "Why look at him! Isn't he a beauty?"

"Got a back like a billiard table," commented Custer proudly.

They rode down among the heifers. There were a dozen beauties — three-year-olds. Hidden to one side, behind a small bush, the man's quick eyes discerned a little bundle of red and white.

"There it is, Grace," he called, and the two rode toward it.

One of the heifers looked fearfully toward them, then at the bush and finally walked toward it, lowing plaintively.

"We're not going to hurt it, little girl," the man assured her.

As they came closer, there arose a thing of long, wobbly legs, big joints, and great, dark eyes, its spotless coat of red and white shining with health and life.

"The cunning thing!" cried the girl. "How I'd like to squeeze it! I just love 'em, Custer!"

She had slipped from her saddle and, dropping her reins on the ground, was approaching the calf.

"Look out for the cow!" cried the man as he dismounted and moved forward to the girl's side with his arm through the Apache's reins. "She hasn't been up much, and she may be a little wild."

The calf stood its ground for a moment and then, with tail erect, cavorted madly for its mother behind whom it took refuge.

"I just love 'em! I just love 'em!" repeated the girl.

"You say the same thing about the colts and the little pigs," the man reminded her.

"I love 'em all!" she cried, shaking her head, her eyes twinkling.

"You love them because they're little and helpless, just like babies," he said. "Oh, Grace, how you'd love a baby!"

The girl flushed prettily. Quite suddenly, he seized her in his arms and crushed her to him, smothering her with a long kiss. Breathless, she wriggled partially away, but he still held her in his arms.

"Why won't you, Grace?" he begged. "There'll never be anybody else for me or for you. Father and Mother and Eva love you almost as much as I do, and, on your side, your mother and Guy have always seemed to take it as a matter of course that we'd marry. It isn't the drinking, is it, dear?"

"No, it's not that, Custer. Of course, I'll marry you — someday; but not yet. Why, I haven't lived yet, Custer! I want to live. I want to do something outside of the humdrum life that I have always led and the humdrum life that I shall live as a wife and mother. I want to live a little, Custer, and then I'll be ready to settle down. You all tell me that I am beautiful, and down, away down in the depth of my soul, I feel that I have talent. If I have, I ought to use the gifts God has given me."

She was speaking very seriously, and the man listened patiently and with respect, for he realized that she was revealing for the first time a secret yearning that she must have long held locked in her bosom.

"Just what do you want to do, dear?" he asked gently.

"I — oh, it seems silly when I try to put it in words, but, in dreams, it is very beautiful and very real."

"The stage?" he asked.

"It is just like you to understand!" Her smile rewarded him. "Will you help me? I know Mother will object."

"You want me to help you take all the happiness out of my life?" he asked.

"It would only be for a little while — just a few years, and then I would come back to you — after I had made good."

"You would never come back, Grace, unless you failed," he said. "If you succeeded, you would never be contented in any other life or atmosphere. If you came back a failure, you couldn't help but carry a little bitterness always in your heart. It would never be the same dear, carefree heart that went away so gayly. Here, you have a real part to play in a real drama — not make-believe upon a narrow stage with painted drops." He flung out a hand in broad gesture. "Look at the setting that God has painted here for us to play our parts in — the parts that He has chosen for us! Your mother played upon the same stage, and mine. Do you think them failures? And both were beautiful girls — as beautiful as you."

"Oh, but you don't understand after all, Custer!" she cried. "I thought you did."

"I do understand that, for your sake, I must do my best to persuade you that you have as full a life before you here as upon the stage. I am fighting first for your happiness, Grace, and then for mine. If I fail, then I shall do all that I can to help you realize your ambition. If you cannot stay because you are convinced that you will be happier here, then I do not want you to stay."

"Kiss me," she demanded suddenly. "I am only thinking of it, anyway, so let's not worry until there is something to worry about."

CHAPTER II

THE MAN BENT his lips to hers again, and her arms stole about his neck. The calf, in the meantime, perhaps disgusted by such absurdities, had scampered off to try his brand-new legs again with the result that he ran into a low bush, turned a somersault, and landed on his back. The mother, still doubtful of the intentions of the newcomers, to whose malevolent presence she may have attributed the accident, voiced a perturbed low; whereupon there broke from the vicinity of the live oak a deep note not unlike the rumbling of distant thunder.

The man looked up.

"I think we'll be going," he said. "The Emperor has issued an ultimatum."

"Or a bull, perhaps," Grace suggested as they walked quickly toward her horse.

"Awful!" he commented as he assisted her into the saddle.

Then he swung to his own.

The Emperor moved majestically toward them, his nose close to the ground. Occasionally, he stopped, pawing the earth and throwing dust upon his broad back.

"Doesn't he look wicked?" cried the girl. "Just look at those eyes!"

"He's just an old bluffer," replied the man. "However, I'd rather have you in the saddle, for you can't always be sure just what they'll do. We must call his bluff, though; it would never do to run from him — might give him bad habits."

He rode toward the advancing animal, breaking into a canter as he drew near the bull and striking his booted leg with a quirt:

"Hi there, you old reprobate! Beat it!" he cried.

The bull stood his ground with lowered head and rumbled threats until the horseman was almost upon him; then, he turned quickly aside as the rider went past.

"That's better," remarked Custer as the girl joined him.

"You're not a bit afraid of him, are you, Custer? You're not afraid of anything."

"Oh, I wouldn't say that," he demurred. "I learned a long time ago that most encounters consist principally of bluff. Maybe I've just grown to be a good bluffer. Anyhow, I'm a better bluffer than the Emperor. If the rascal had only known it, he could have run me ragged."

As they rode up the side of the basin, the man's eyes moved constantly from point to point, now noting the condition of the pasture grasses or again searching the more distant hills. Presently, they alighted upon a thin, wavering line of brown, which zigzagged down the opposite side of the basin from a clump of heavy brush that partially hid a small ravine, and crossed the meadow ahead of them.

"There's a new trail, Grace, and it don't belong there. Let's go and take a look at it."

They rode ahead until they reached the trail at a point where it crossed the bottom of the basin and started up the side they had been ascending. The man leaned above his horse's shoulder and examined the trampled turf.

"Horses," he said. "I thought so, and it's been used a lot this winter. You can see even now where the animals slipped and floundered after the heavy rains."

"But you don't run horses in this pasture, do you?" asked the girl.

"No; and we haven't run anything in it since last summer. This is the only bunch in it, and they were just turned in about a week ago. Anyway, the horses that made this trail were mostly shod. Now what in the world is anybody going up there for?" His eyes wandered to the heavy brush into which the trail disappeared upon the opposite side of the basin. "I'll have to follow that up to-morrow — it's too late to do it today."

"We can follow it the other way toward the ranch," she suggested.

They found the trail wound up the hillside and crossed the hogback in heavy brush, which, in many places, had been cut away to allow the easier passage of a horseman.

"Do you see," asked Custer as they drew rein at the summit of the ridge, "that although the trail crosses here in plain sight of the ranch house, the brush would absolutely conceal a horseman from the view of any one at the house? It must run right down into Jackknife Cañon. Funny none of us have noticed it, for there's scarcely a week that that trail isn't ridden by some of us!"

As they descended into the cañon, they discovered why that end of the new trail had not been noticed. It ran deep and well marked through the heavy brush of a gully to a place where the brush commenced to thin, and, there, it branched into a dozen dim trails that joined and blended with the old, well-worn cattle paths of the hillside.

"Somebody's mighty foxy," observed the man; "but I don't see what it's all about. The days of cattle runners and bandits are over."

"Just imagine!" exclaimed the girl. "A real mystery in our lazy, old hills!"

The man rode in silence and in thought. A herd of pure-bred Herefords, whose value would have ransomed half the crowned heads remaining in Europe, grazed in the several pastures that ran far back into those hills; and back there somewhere that trail led, but for what purpose? No good purpose, he was sure, or it had not been so cleverly hidden.

As they came to the trail which they called the Camino Corto, where it commenced at the gate leading from the old goat corral, the man jerked his thumb toward the west along it.

"They must come and go this way," he said.

"Perhaps they're the ones mother and I have heard passing at night," suggested the girl. "If they are, they come right through your property below the house — not this way."

He opened the gate from the saddle and they passed through, crossing the *barranco* and stopping for a moment to look at the pigs and talk with the herdsman. Then, they rode on toward the ranch house a half mile farther down the widening cañon. It stood upon the summit of a low hill, the declining sun transforming its plastered walls, its cupolas, the sturdy arches of its arcades into the semblance of a Moorish castle.

At the foot of the hill, they dismounted at the saddle-horse stable, tied their horses, and ascended the long flight of rough concrete steps toward the house. As they rounded the wild sumac bush at the summit, they were espied by those sitting in the patio around three sides of which the house was built.

"Oh, here they are now!" exclaimed Mrs. Pennington. "We were so afraid that Grace would ride right on home, Custer. We had just persuaded Mrs. Evans to stay for dinner. Guy is coming, too."

"Mother, you here, too?" cried the girl. "How nice and cool it is in here! It would save a lot of trouble if we brought our things, Mother."

"We are hoping that at least one of you will, very soon," said Colonel Pennington, who had risen and now put an arm affectionately about the girl's shoulders.

"That's what I've been telling her again this afternoon," said Custer; "but instead she wants to —"

The girl turned toward him with a little frown and shake of her head.

"You'd better run down and tell Allen that we won't use the horses until after dinner," she said.

He grimaced good-naturedly and turned away.

"I'll have him take Senator home," he said. "I can drive you and your mother down in the car when you leave."

As he descended the steps that wound among the umbrella trees taking on their new foliage, he saw Allen examining the Apache's shoes. As he neared them, the horse pulled away from the man, his suddenly lowered hoof striking Allen's instep. With an oath, the fellow stepped back and swung a vicious kick to the animal's belly. Almost simultaneously, a hand fell heavily upon his shoulder. He was jerked roughly back, whirled about, and sent spinning a dozen feet away where he stumbled and fell. As he scrambled to his feet, white with rage, he saw the younger Pennington before him.

"Go to the office and get your time," ordered Pennington.

"I'll get you first, you son of a —"

A hard fist connecting suddenly with his chin put a painful period to his sentence before it was completed and stopped his mad rush.

"I'd be more careful of my conversation, Allen, if I were you," said Pennington quietly. "Just because you've been drinking is no excuse for *that*. Now go on up to the office as I told you to."

He had caught the odor of whisky as he jerked the man past him.

"You goin' to can me for drinkin' — *you!*" demanded Allen.

"You know what I'm canning you for. You know that's the one thing that don't go on Ganado. You ought to get what you gave the Apache, and you'd better beat it before I lose my temper and give it to you!"

The man rose slowly to his feet. In his mind, he was revolving his chances of successfully renewing his attack; but, presently, his judgment got the better of his desire and his rage. He moved off slowly up the hill toward the house. A few yards, and he turned.

"I ain't a goin' to ferget this, you — you —"

"Be careful!" Pennington admonished.

"Nor you ain't goin' to ferget it, neither, you fox-trottin' dude!"

Allen turned again to the ascent of the steps. Pennington walked to the Apache and stroked his muzzle.

"Old boy," he crooned, "there don't anybody kick you and get away with it, does there?"

Halfway up, Allen stopped and turned again.

"You think you're the whole cheese, you Penningtons, don't you?" he called back. "With all your money an' your fine friends! Fine friends, yah! I can put one of 'em where he belongs any time I want — the darn bootlegger! That's what he is. You wait — you'll see!"

"A-ah, beat it!" sighed Pennington wearily.

Mounting the Apache, he led Grace's horse along the foot of the hill toward the smaller ranch house of their neighbor some half mile away. Humming a little tune, he unsaddled Senator, turned him into his corral, saw that there was water in his trough, and emptied a measure of oats into his manger — for the horse had cooled off since the afternoon ride. As neither of the Evans ranch hands appeared, he found a piece of rag and wiped off the Senator's bit, turned the saddle blankets wet side up to dry, and then, leaving the stable, crossed the yard to mount the Apache.

A young man in riding clothes appeared simultaneously from the interior of the bungalow, which stood a hundred feet away. Crossing the wide porch, he called to Pennington.

"Hello there, Penn! What you doing?" he demanded.

"Just brought Senator in — Grace is up at the house. You're coming up there, too, Guy."

"Sure, but come in here a second. I've got something to show you."

Pennington crossed the yard and entered the house behind Grace's brother who conducted him to his bedroom. Here, young Evans unlocked a closet and, after rummaging behind some clothing, emerged with a bottle the shape and dimensions of which were once as familiar in the land of the free as the benign countenance of Lydia E. Pinkham.

"It's the genuine stuff, Penn, too!" he declared. Pennington smiled.

"Thanks, old fellow, but I've quit," he said.

"Quit!" exclaimed Evans.

"Yep."

"But think of it, man — aged eight years in the wood and bottled in bond before July 1, 1919. The real thing and as cheap as moonshine — only six beans a quart. Can you believe it?"

"I cannot," admitted Pennington. "Your conversation listens phony."

"But it's the truth. You may have quit, but one little snifter of this won't hurt you. Here's this bottle already open — just try it"; and he proffered the bottle and a glass to the other.

"Well, it's pretty hard to resist anything that sounds as good as this does," remarked Pennington. "I guess one won't hurt me any." He poured himself a drink and took it. "Wonderful!" he ejaculated.

"Here," said Evans, diving into the closet once more. "I got you a bottle, too, and we can get more."

Pennington took the bottle and examined it almost caressingly.

"Eight years in the wood!" he murmured. "I've got to take it, Guy. Must have something to hand down to posterity." He drew a bill fold from his pocket and counted out six dollars.

"Thanks," said Guy. "You'll never regret it."

CHAPTER III

AS THE TWO young men climbed the hill to the big house a few minutes later, they found the elder Pennington standing at the edge of the driveway that circled the hilltop looking out toward the wide cañon and the distant mountains. In the nearer foreground lay the stable and corrals of the saddle horses, the henhouse with its two long alfalfa runways, and the small dairy barn accommodating the little herd of Guernseys that supplied milk, cream, and butter for the ranch. A quarter of a mile beyond, among the trees, was the red-roofed "cabin" where the unmarried ranch hands ate and slept near the main corrals with their barns, outhouses, and sheds.

In a hilly pasture farther up the cañon, the black and iron gray of Percheron brood mares contrasted with the greening hillsides of spring. Still farther away, the white and red of the lordly figure of the Emperor stood out boldly upon the summit of the ridge behind Jackknife Cañon.

The two young men joined the older, and Custer put an arm affectionately about his father's shoulders.

"You never tire of it," said the young man.

"I have been looking at it for 22 years, my son," replied the elder Pennington, "and each year it has become more wonderful to me. It never changes, and yet it is never twice alike. See the purple sage away off there and the lighter spaces of wild buckwheat and here and there among the scrub oak the beautiful pale green of the manzanita — scintillant jewels in the diadem of the hills! And the faint haze of the mountains that seems to throw them just a little out of focus to make them a perfect background for the beautiful hills which the Supreme Artist is placing on his canvas today. An hour from now, He will paint another masterpiece, and tonight another, and forever others, with never two alike, nor ever one that mortal man can duplicate; and all for us, boy, all for us, if we have the hearts and the souls to see!"

"How you love it!" said the boy.

"Yes, and your mother loves it; and it is our great happiness that you and Eva love it, too."

The boy made no reply. He did love it; but his was the heart of youth, and it yearned for change and for adventure and for what lay beyond the circling hills and the broad, untroubled valley that spread its level fields below "the castle on the hill."

"The girls are dressing for a swim," said the older man after a moment of silence. "Aren't you boys going in?"

"The girls" included his wife and Mrs. Evans as well as Grace, for the colonel insisted that youth was purely a physical and mental attribute independent of time. If one could feel and act in accord with the spirit of youth, one could not be old.

"Are you going in?" asked his son.

"Yes, I was waiting for you two."

"I think I'll be excused, sir," said Guy. "The water is too cold yet. I tried it yesterday and nearly froze to death. I'll come and watch."

The two Penningtons moved off toward the house to get into swimming things while young Evans wandered down into the water gardens. As he stood there, idly content in the quiet beauty of the spot, Allen came down the steps, his check in his hand. At sight of the boy, he halted behind him, an unpleasant expression upon his face.

Evans, suddenly aware that he was not alone, turned and recognized the man. "Oh, hello, Allen!" he said.

"Young Pennington just canned me," said Allen with no other return of Evans's greeting.

"I'm sorry," said Evans.

"You may be sorrier!" growled Allen, continuing on his way toward the cabin to get his blankets and clothes.

For a moment, Guy stared after the man, a puzzled expression knitting his brows. Then, he slowly flushed, glancing quickly about to see if anyone had overheard the brief conversation between Slick Allen and himself.

A few minutes later, he entered the enclosure west of the house where the swimming-pool lay. Mrs. Pennington and her guests were already in the pool swimming vigorously to keep warm, and, a moment later, the colonel and Custer ran from the house and dived in simultaneously. Though there was 26 years' difference in their ages, it was not evidenced by any lesser vitality or agility on the part of the older man.

Colonel Custer Pennington had been born in Virginia 50 years before. Graduated from the Virginia Military Institute and West Point, he had taken a commission in the cavalry branch of the service. Campaigning in Cuba, he had been shot through one lung, and, shortly after the close of the war, he was retired for disability with rank of lieutenant colonel. In 1900, he had come to California on the advice of his physician in the forlorn hope that he might prolong his sufferings a few years more.

For 200 years, the Penningtons had bred fine men, women, and horses upon the same soil in the state whose very existence was inextricably interwoven with their own. A Pennington leave Virginia? Horrors! Perish the thought! But Colonel Custer Pennington had had to leave it or die, and, with a young wife and a two-year-old boy, he couldn't afford to die. Deep in his heart, he meant to recover his health in distant California and then return to the land of his love; but his physician had told a mutual friend, who was also Pennington's attorney, that "poor old Cus" would almost undoubtedly be dead inside of a year.

And so, Pennington had come West with Mrs. Pennington and little Custer, Jr., and had found the Rancho del Ganado run down, untenanted, and for sale. A month of loafing had left him almost ready to die of stagnation — without any assistance from his poor lungs; and when, in the course of a drive to another ranch, he had happened to see the place and had learned that it was for sale, the germ had been sown.

He judged from the soil and the water that Ganado was not well suited to raise the type of horse that he knew best and that he and his father and his grandfathers before them had bred in

Virginia; but he saw other possibilities. Moreover, he loved the hills and the cañons from the first; and so, he had purchased the ranch, more to have something that would temporarily occupy his mind until his period of exile was ended by a return to his native state — or by death — than with any idea that it would prove a permanent home.

The old Spanish-American house had been remodeled and rebuilt. In four years, he had found that Herefords, Berkshires, and Percherons may win a place in a man's heart almost equal to that which a thoroughbred occupies. Then, a little daughter had come, and the final seal that stamps a man's house as his home was placed upon "the castle on the hill."

His lung had healed — he could not tell by any sign it gave that it was not as good as ever — and still he stayed on in the land of sunshine, which he had grown to love without realizing its hold upon him. Gradually, he had forgotten to say "when we go back home"; and when, at last, a letter came from a younger brother saying that he wished to buy the old place in Virginia if the Custer Penningtons did not expect to return to it, the colonel was compelled to face the issue squarely.

They had held a little family council — the colonel and Julia, his wife, with seven-year-old Custer and little one-year-old Eva. Eva, sitting in her mother's lap, agreed with everyone. Custer, Jr. burst into tears at the very suggestion of leaving dear old Ganado.

"And what do you think about it, Julia?" asked the colonel.

"I love Virginia, dear," she had replied; "but I think I love California even more, and I say it without disloyalty to my own state. It's a different kind of love."

"I know what you mean," said her husband. "Virginia is a mother to us, California a sweetheart."

And so, they stayed upon the Rancho del Ganado.

CHAPTER IV

WORK AND PLAY were inextricably entangled upon Ganado, the play being of a nature that fitted men better for their work, while the work, always in the open and usually from the saddle, they enjoyed fully as much as the play. While the tired businessman of the city was expending a day's vitality and nervous energy in an effort to escape from the turmoil of the mad rush hour and find a strap from which to dangle homeward amid the toxic effluvia of the melting pot, Colonel Pennington plunged and swam in the cold, invigorating waters of his pool after a day of labor fully as constructive and profitable as theirs.

"One more dive!" he called, balancing upon the end of the springboard, "and then I'm going out. Eva ought to be here by the time we're dressed, hadn't she? I'm about famished."

"I haven't heard the train whistle yet, though it must be due," replied Mrs. Pennington. "You and Boy make so much noise swimming that we'll miss Gabriel's trump if we happen to be in the pool at the time!"

The colonel, Custer, and Grace Evans dived simultaneously and, coming up together, raced for the shallow end where Mrs. Evans and her hostess were preparing to leave the pool. The girl, reaching the hand rail first, arose laughing and triumphant.

"My foot slipped as I dived," cried the younger Pennington, wiping the water from his eyes, "or I'd have caught you!"

"No alibis, Boy!" laughed the colonel. "Grace beat you fair and square."

"Race you back for a dollar, Grace!" challenged the young man.

"You're on," she cried. "One, two, three — go!"

They were off. The colonel, who had preceded them leisurely into the deep water, swam close to his son as the latter was passing a yard in the lead. Simultaneously, the young man's progress ceased. With a Comanche-like yell, he turned upon his father, and the two men grappled and went down. When they came up, spluttering and laughing, the girl was climbing out of the pool.

"You win, Grace!" shouted the colonel.

"It's a frame-up!" cried Custer. "He grabbed me by the ankle!"

"Well, who had a better right?" demanded the girl. "He's referee."

"He's a fine mess for a referee!" grumbled Custer good-naturedly.

"Run along and get your dollar and pay up like a gentleman," admonished his father.

"What do you get out of it? What do you pay him, Grace?"

They were still bantering as they entered the house and sought their several rooms to dress.

Guy Evans strolled from the walled garden of the swimming pool to the open arch that broke the long pergola beneath which the driveway ran along the north side of the house. Here, he had an unobstructed view of the broad valley stretching away to the mountains in the distance.

Down the center of the valley, a toy train moved noiselessly. As he watched it, he saw a puff of white rise from the tiny engine. It rose and melted in the evening air before the thin, clear sound of the whistle reached his ears. The train crawled behind the green of trees and disappeared.

He knew that it had stopped at the station and that a slender, girlish figure was alighting with a smile for the porter and a gay word for the conductor who had carried her back and forth for years upon her occasional visits to the city a hundred miles away. Now, the chauffeur was taking her bag and carrying it to the roadster that she would drive home along the wide, straight boulevard that crossed the valley — utterly ruining a number of perfectly good speed laws.

Two minutes elapsed, and the train crawled out from behind the trees and continued its way up the valley — a little black caterpillar with spots of yellow twinkling along its sides. As twilight deepened, the lights from ranch houses and villages sprinkled the floor of the valley. Like jewels scattered from a careless hand, they fell singly and in little clusters; and then, the stars, serenely superior, came forth to assure the glory of a perfect California night.

The headlights of a motor car turned in at the driveway. Guy went to the east porch and looked in at the living room door where some of the family had already collected.

"Eva's coming!" he announced.

She had been gone since the day before, but she might have been returning from a long trip abroad if every one's eagerness to greet her was any criterion. Unlike city dwellers, these people had never learned to conceal the lovelier emotions of their hearts behind a mask of assumed indifference. Perhaps the fact that they were not forever crowded shoulder to shoulder with strangers permitted them an enjoyable naturalness which the dweller in the wholesale districts of humanity can never know; for what a man may reveal of his heart among friends he hides from the unsympathetic eyes of others — though it may be the noblest of his possessions. With a rush, the car topped the hill, swung up the driveway, and stopped at the corner of the house. A door flew open, and the girl leaped from the driver's seat.

"Hello, everybody!" she cried.

Snatching a kiss from her brother as she passed him, she fairly leaped upon her mother, hugging, kissing, laughing, dancing, and talking all at once. Espying her father, she relinquished a disheveled and laughing mother and dived for him.

"Most adorable Pops!" she cried as he caught her in his arms. "Are you glad to have your little nuisance back? I'll bet you're not. Do you love me? You won't when you know how much I've spent, but oh, Popsy, I had *such* a good time! That's all there was to it, and oh, Momsie, who, who, *who* do you suppose I met? Oh, you'd never guess — never, never!"

"Whom did you meet?" asked her mother.

"Yes, little one, *whom* did you meet?" inquired her brother.

"And he's perfectly *gorgeous*," continued the girl, as if there had been no interruption; "and I danced with him — oh, such *divine* dancing! Oh, Guy Evans! Why how do you do? I never saw you."

The young man nodded glumly.

"How are you, Eva?" he said.

"Mrs. Evans is here, too, dear," her mother reminded her.

The girl curtsied before her mother's guest and then threw her arm about the older woman's neck.

"Oh, Aunt Mae!" she cried. "I'm *so* excited; but you should have *seen* him, and, Momsie, I got the *cutest* riding hat!" They were moving toward the living room door, which Guy was holding open. "Guy, I got you the splendiferousest Christmas present!"

"Help!" cried her brother, collapsing into a porch chair. "Don't you know that I have a weak heart? Do your Christmas shopping early — do it in April! Oh, Lord, can you beat it?" he demanded of the others. "Can you beat it?"

"I think it was mighty nice of Eva to remember me at all," said Guy, thawing perceptibly.

"What is it?" asked Custer. "I'll bet you got him a pipe."

"However in the world did you guess?" demanded Eva.

Custer rocked from side to side in his chair, laughing. "What are you laughing at? Idiot!" cried the girl. "How did you guess I got him a pipe?"

"Because he never smokes anything but cigarettes."

"You're horrid!"

He pulled her down onto his lap and kissed her. "Dear little one!" he cried. Taking her head between his hands, he shook it. "Hear 'em rattle!"

"But I love a pipe," stated Guy emphatically. "The trouble is, I never had a really nice one before."

"There!" exclaimed the girl triumphantly. "And you know Sherlock Holmes always smoked a pipe."

Her brother knitted his brows.

"I don't quite connect," he announced.

"Well, if you need a diagram, isn't Guy an author?" she demanded.

"Not so that anyone could notice it — yet," demurred Evans.

"Well, you're going to be!" said the girl proudly.

The Girl from Hollywood / 25

"The light is commencing to dawn," announced her brother. "Sherlock Holmes, the famous author who wrote Conan Doyle!"

A blank expression overspread the girl's face to be presently expunged by a slow smile.

"You are perfectly horrid!" she cried. "I'm going in to dapper up a bit for dinner — don't wait."

She danced through the living room and out into the patio toward her own rooms.

"Rattle, rattle, little brain; rattle, rattle round again," her brother called after her. "Can you beat her?" he added to the others.

"She can't even be approximated," laughed the colonel. "In all the world there is only one of her."

"And she's ours, bless her!" said the brother. The colonel was glancing over the headlines of an afternoon paper that Eva had brought from the city.

"What's new?" asked Custer.

"Same old rot," replied his father. "Murders, divorces, kidnappers, bootleggers, and they haven't even the originality to make them interesting by evolving new methods. Oh, hold on — this isn't so bad!"

"'200,000 dollars's worth of stolen whisky landed on coast,'" he read. "'Prohibition enforcement agents, together with special agents from the Treasury Department, are working on a unique theory that may reveal the whereabouts of the fortune in bonded whisky stolen from a government warehouse in New York a year ago. All that was known until recently was that the whisky was removed from the warehouse in trucks in broad daylight, compassing one of the boldest robberies ever committed in New York. Now, from a source which they refuse to divulge, the government sleuths have received information which leads them to believe that the liquid loot was loaded aboard a sailing vessel and, after a long trip around the Horn, is lying somewhere off the coast of Southern California. That it is being lightered ashore in launches and transported to some hiding place in the mountains is one theory upon which the government is working. The whisky is eleven years old, was bottled in bond three years ago, just before the Eighteenth Amendment became a harrowing reality. It will go hard with the traffickers in this particular parcel of wet goods if they are apprehended since the theft was directly from a government bonded warehouse, and all government officials concerned in the search are anxious to make an example of the guilty parties.'"

"Eleven years old!" sighed the colonel. "It makes my mouth water! I've been subsisting on homemade grape wine for over a year. Think of it — a Pennington! Why, my ancestors must be writhing in their Virginia graves!"

"On the contrary, they're probably laughing in their sleeves. They died before July 1, 1919," interposed Custer. "Eleven years old — eight years in the wood," he mused aloud, shooting a quick glance in the direction of Guy Evans who suddenly became deeply interested in a novel lying on a table beside his chair — notwithstanding the fact that he had read it six months before and hadn't liked it. "And it will go hard with the traffickers, too," continued young Pennington. "Well, I should hope it would. They'll probably hang 'em, the vile miscreants!"

Guy had risen and walked to the doorway opening upon the patio.

"I wonder what is keeping Eva," he remarked.

"Getting hungry?" asked Mrs. Pennington. "Well, I guess we all are. Suppose we don't wait any longer? Eva won't mind."

"If I wait much longer," observed the colonel, "someone will have to carry me into the dining room."

As they crossed the library toward the dining room, the two young men walked behind their elders.

"Is your appetite still good?" inquired Custer.

"Shut up!" retorted Evans. "You give me a pain."

They had finished their soup before Eva joined them, and, after the men were reseated, they took up the conversation where it had been interrupted. As usual, if not always brilliant, it was at least diversified, for it included many subjects from grand opera to the budding of English walnuts on the native wild stock and from the latest novel to the most practical method of earmarking pigs. Paintings, poems, plays, pictures, people, horses, and home brew — each came in for a share of the discussion, argument, and raillery that ran round the table.

During a brief moment when she was not engaged in conversation, Guy seized the opportunity to whisper to Eva who sat next to him.

"Who was that bird you met in L.A.?" he asked.

"Which one?"

"Which one! How many did you meet?"

"Oodles of them."

"I mean the one you were ranting about."

"Which one was I ranting about? I don't remember."

"You're enough to drive anybody to drink, Eva Pennington!" cried the young man disgustedly.

"Radiant man!" she cooed. "What's the dapper little idea in that talented brain — jealous?"

"I want to know who he is," demanded Guy.

"Who who is?"

"You know perfectly well who I mean — the poor fish you were raving about before dinner. You said you danced with him. Who is he? That's what I want to know."

"I don't like the way you talk to me; but, if you must know, he was the most dazzling thing you ever saw. He —"

"I never saw him, and I don't want to, and I don't care how dazzling he is. I only want to know his name."

"Well, why didn't you say so in the first place? His name's Wilson Crumb." Her tone was as of one who says: "Behold Alexander the Great!"

"Wilson Crumb! Who's he?"

"Do you mean to sit there and tell me that you don't know who Wilson Crumb is, Guy Evans?" she demanded.

"Never heard of him," he insisted.

"Never heard of Wilson Crumb, the famous actor-director? Such ignorance!"

"Did you ever hear of him before this trip to L.A.?" inquired her brother from across the table. "I never heard you mention him before."

"Well, maybe I didn't," admitted the girl; "but he's the most dazzling dancer you ever saw — and such eyes! And maybe he'll

28 \ Edgar Rice Burroughs

come out to the ranch and bring his company. He said they were often looking for just such locations."

"And I suppose you invited him?" demanded Custer accusingly.

"And why not? I had to be polite, didn't I?"

"You know perfectly well that father has never permitted such a thing," insisted her brother, looking toward the colonel for support.

"He didn't ask father — he asked me," returned the girl.

"You see," said the colonel, "how simply Eva solves every little problem."

"But you know, Popsy, how perfectly superb it would be to have them take some pictures right here on our very own ranch where we could watch them all day long.

"Yes," growled Custer; "watch them wreck the furniture and demolish the lawns! Why, one bird of a director ran a troop of cavalry over one of the finest lawns in Hollywood. Then, they'll go up in the hills and chase the cattle over the top into the ocean. I've heard all about them. I'd never allow one of 'em on the place."

"Maybe they're not all inconsiderate and careless," suggested Mrs. Pennington.

"You remember there was a company took a few scenes at my place a year or so ago," interjected Mrs. Evans. "They were very nice indeed."

"They were just wonderful," said Grace Evans. "I hope the colonel lets them come. It would be piles of fun!"

"You can't tell anything about them," volunteered Guy. "I understand they pick up all sorts of riffraff for extra people — IWWs[1] and all sorts of people like that. I'd be afraid."

He shook his head dubiously.

"The trouble with you two is," asserted Eva, "that you're afraid to let us girls see any nice-looking actors from the city. That's what's the matter with you!"

"Yes, they're jealous," agreed Mrs. Pennington, laughing.

---

1 IWW — Industrial Workers of the World. A former international labor union and radical labor movement in the United States; founded in Chicago in 1905 and dedicated to the overthrow of capitalism. — R-G.]

"Well," said Custer, "if there are leading men, there are leading ladies, and from what I've seen of them, the leading ladies are better looking than the leading men. By all means, now that I consider the matter, let them come. Invite them at once, for a month — wire them!"

"Silly!" cried his sister. "He may not come here at all. He just mentioned it casually."

"And all this tempest in a teapot for nothing," said the colonel.

Wilson Crumb was forthwith dropped from the conversation and forgotten by all, even by impressionable little Eva.

As the young people gathered around Mrs. Pennington at the piano in the living room, Mrs. Evans and Colonel Pennington sat apart, carrying on a desultory conversation while they listened to the singing.

"We have a new neighbor," remarked Mrs. Evans, "on the 10-acre orchard adjoining us on the west."

"Yes — Mrs. Burke. She has moved in, has she?" inquired the colonel.

"Yesterday. She is a widow from the East — has a daughter in Los Angeles, I believe."

"She came to see me about a month ago," said the colonel, "to ask my advice about the purchase of the property. She seemed rather a refined, quiet little body. I must tell Julia — she will want to call on her."

"I insisted on her taking dinner with us last night," said Mrs. Evans. "She seems very frail and was all worn out. Unpacking and settling is trying enough for a robust person, and she seems so delicate that I really don't see how she stood it all."

Then the conversation drifted to other topics until the party at the piano broke up and Eva came dancing over to her father.

"Gorgeous Popsy!" she cried, seizing him by an arm. "Just one dance before bedtime — if you love me, just one!"

Colonel Pennington rose from his chair, laughing.

"I know your one dance, you little fraud — five foxtrots, three one-steps, and a waltz."

With his arms about each other, they started for the ballroom — really a big playroom, which adjoined the garage. Behind them, laughing and talking, came the two older women, the two sons, and Grace Evans. They would dance for an hour and then go to bed, for they rose early and were in the saddle before sunrise, living their happy, care-free life far from the strife and squalor of the big cities and yet with more of the comforts and luxuries than most city dwellers ever achieve.

CHAPTER V

THE BUNGALOW at 1421 Vista del Paso was of the new school of Hollywood architecture, which appears to be a hysterical effort to combine Queen Anne, Italian, Swiss chalet, Moorish, Mission, and Martian. Its plaster walls were of a yellowish rose, the outside woodwork being done in light blue while the windows were shaded with striped awnings of olive and pink. On one side of the entrance rose a green pergola — the ambitious atrocity that marks the meeting place of landscape gardening and architecture and that outrages them both. Culture has found a virus for the cast-iron dogs, deer, and rabbits that ramped in immobility upon the lawns of yesteryear, but the green pergola is an incurable disease.

Connecting with the front of the house, a plaster wall continued across the narrow lot to the property line at one side and from there back to the alley, partially inclosing a patio — which is Hollywood for backyard. An arched gateway opened into the patio from the front. The gate was of rough redwood boards, and, near the top, there were three auger holes arranged in the form of a triangle — this was art. Upon the yellow-rose plaster above the arch a design of three monkeys was stenciled in purple — this also was art.

As you wait in the three-foot-square vestibule, you notice that the floor is paved with red brick set in black mortar and that the Oregon pine door, with its mahogany stain, would have been beautiful in its severe simplicity but for the little square of plate glass set in the upper right hand corner, demonstrating conclusively the daring originality of the artist-architect.

Presently, your ring is answered, and the door is opened by a Japanese "schoolboy" of 35 in a white coat. You are ushered directly into a living room, whereupon you forget all about architects and art, for the room is really beautiful, even though a trifle heavy in an Oriental way, with its Chinese rugs, dark hangings, and ponderous, overstuffed furniture. The Japanese schoolboy, who knows you, closes the door behind you and then tiptoes silently from the room.

Across from you, on a divan, a woman is lying, her face buried among pillows. When you cough, she raises her face toward you, and you see that it is very beautiful even though the eyes are a bit wide and staring and the expression somewhat haggard. You see a mass of black hair surrounding a face of perfect contour. Even the plucked and penciled brows, the rouged cheeks, and carmined lips cannot hide a certain dignity and sweetness.

At sight of you, she rises, a bit unsteadily, and, smiling with her lips, extends a slender hand in greeting. The fingers of the hand tremble and are stained with nicotine. Her eyes do not smile — ever.

"The same as usual?" she asks in a weary voice.

Your throat is very dry. You swallow before you assure her eagerly, almost feverishly, that her surmise is correct. She leaves the room. Probably, you have not noticed that she is wild-eyed and haggard or that her fingers are stained and trembling, for you, too, are wild-eyed and haggard, and you are trembling worse than she.

Presently, she returns. In her left hand is a small glass phial containing many little tablets. As she crosses to you, she extends her right hand with the palm up. It is a slender, delicate hand, yet there is a look of strength to it for all its whiteness. You lay a bill in it, and she hands you the phial. That is all. You leave, and she closes the Oregon pine door quietly behind you.

As she turns about toward the divan again, she hesitates. Her eyes wander to a closed door at one side of the room. She takes a half step toward it and then draws back, her shoulders against the door. Her fingers are clenched tightly, the nails sinking into the soft flesh of her palms; but, still, her eyes are upon the closed door. They are staring and wild like those of a beast at bay. She is trembling from head to foot.

For a minute, she stands there, fighting her grim battle alone and without help. Then, as with a last mighty effort, she drags her eyes from the closed door and glances toward the divan. With unsteady step, she returns to it and throws herself down among the pillows.

Her shoulders move to dry sobs, she clutches the pillows frantically in her strong fingers, she rolls from side to side as people do who are suffering physical torture; but, at last, she relaxes and lies quiet.

A clock ticks monotonously from the mantel. Its sound fills the whole room, growing with fiendish intensity to a horrid din that pounds upon taut, raw nerves. She covers her ears with her palms to shut it out, but it bores insistently through. She clutches her thick hair with both hands; her fingers are entangled in it. For a long minute, she lies thus, prone, and then her slippered feet commence to fly up and down as she kicks her toes in rapid succession into the unresisting divan.

Suddenly, she leaps to her feet and rushes toward the mantel.

"Damn you!" she screams and, seizing the clock, dashes it to pieces upon the tiled hearth.

Then, her eyes leap to the closed door; and now, without any hesitation, almost defiantly, she crosses the room, opens the door, and disappears within the bathroom beyond.

Five minutes later, the door opens again, and the woman comes back into the living room. She is humming a gay little tune. Stopping at a table, she takes a cigarette from a carved wooden box and lights it. Then, she crosses to the baby grand piano in one corner and commences to play. Her voice, rich and melodious, rises in a sweet old song of love and youth and happiness.

Something had mended her shattered nerves. Upon the hearth lies the shattered clock. It can never be mended.

If you should return now and look at her, you would see that she was even more beautiful than you had at first suspected. She has put her hair in order once more and has arranged her dress. You see now that her figure is as perfect as her face, and, when she crossed to the piano, you could not but note the easy grace of her carriage.

Her name — her professional name — is Gaza de Lure. You may have seen her in small parts on the screen and may have wondered why someone did not star her. Of recent months, you have seen her less and less often, and you have been sorry, for you had learned to admire the sweetness and purity that were reflected in her every expression and mannerism. You liked her, too, because she was as beautiful as she was good — for you knew that she was good just by looking at her in the pictures; but, above all, you liked her for her acting, for it was unusually natural and unaffected, and something told you that here was a born actress who would someday be famous.

Two years ago, she came to Hollywood from a little town in the Middle West — that is, two years before you looked in upon her at the bungalow on the Vista del Paso. She was fired by high purpose then. Her child's heart, burning with lofty ambition, had set its desire upon a noble goal. The broken bodies of a thousand other children dotted the road to the same goal, but she did not see them, or seeing, did not understand.

Stronger, perhaps, than her desire for fame was an unselfish ambition that centered about the mother whom she had left behind. To that mother, the girl's success would mean greater comfort and happiness than she had known since a worthless husband had deserted her shortly after the baby came — the baby who was now known as Gaza de Lure.

There had been the usual rounds of the studios, the usual disappointments followed by more or less regular work as an extra girl. During this period, she had learned many things — some of which she had never thought as having any possible bearing upon her chances for success.

For example, a director had asked her to go with him to Vernon one evening for dinner and dancing, and she had refused for several reasons — one being her certainty that her mother would disapprove and another the fact that the director was a married man. The following day, the girl who had accompanied him was cast for a part which had been promised to Gaza and for which Gaza was peculiarly suited. As she was leaving the lot that day, greatly disappointed, the assistant director had stopped her.

"Too bad, kid," he said. "I'm mighty sorry; for I always liked you. If I can ever help you, I sure will."

The kindly words brought the tears to her eyes. Here, at least, was one good man; but he was not in much of a position to help her.

"You're very kind," she said; "but I'm afraid there's nothing you can do."

"Don't be too sure of that," he answered. "I've got enough on that big stiff so's he has to do about as I say. The trouble with you is you ain't enough of a good fellow. You got to be a good fellow to get on in pictures. Just step out with me some night, an' I promise you you'll get a job!"

The suddenly widening childish eyes meant nothing to the shallow mind of the callow little shrimp, whose brain pan would doubtless have burst under the pressure of a single noble thought. As she turned quickly and walked away, he laughed aloud. She had not gone back to that studio.

In the months that followed, she had had many similar experiences until she had become hardened enough to feel the sense of shame and insult less strongly than at first.

She could talk back to them now and tell them what she thought of them; but she found that she got fewer and fewer engagements. There was always enough to feed and clothe her and to pay for the little room she rented; but there seemed to be no future, and that had been all that she cared about.

She would not have minded hard work — she had expected that. Nor did she fear disappointments and a slow, tedious road; for though she was but a young girl, she was not without character, and she had a good head on those trim shoulders of hers. She was unsophisticated yet mature, too, for her years; for she had always helped her mother to plan the conservation of their meager resources.

Many times, she had wanted to go back to her mother, but she had stayed on because she still had hopes and because she shrank from the fact of defeat admitted. How often she cried herself to sleep in those lonely nights after days of bitter disillusionment! The great ambition that had been her joy was now her sorrow. The vain little conceit that she had woven about her screen name was but a pathetic memory.

She had never told her mother that she had taken the name of Gaza de Lure, for she had dreamed of the time when it would leap into national prominence overnight in some wonderful picture, and her mother, unknowing, would see the film and recognize her. How often she had pictured the scene in their little theater at home — her sudden recognition by her mother and their friends — the surprise, the incredulity, and then the pride and happiness in her mother's face! How they would whisper! And after the show, they would gather around her mother all excitedly talking at the same time.

And then, she had met Wilson Crumb. She had had a small part in a picture in which he played lead and which he also directed. He had been very kind to her, very courteous. She had thought him handsome, notwithstanding a certain weakness in his face; but what had attracted her most was the uniform courtesy of his attitude toward all the women of the company. Here at last, she thought, she had found a real gentleman whom she could trust implicitly; and, once again, her ambition lifted its drooping head.

She thought of what another girl had once told her — an older girl who had been in pictures for several years.

"They are not all bad, dear," her friend had said. "There are good and bad in the picture game, just as there are in any sort of business. It's been your rotten luck to run up against a lot of the bad ones."

The first picture finished, Crumb had cast her for a more important part in another, and she had made good in both. Before the second picture was completed, the company that employed Crumb offered her a five-year contract. It was only for 50 dollars a week; but it included a clause which automatically increased the salary to 100 a week, 250, and then 500 dollars in the event that they starred her. She knew that it was to Crumb that she owed the contract — Crumb had seen to that.

Very gradually, then — so gradually and insidiously that the girl could never recall just when it had started — Crumb commenced to make love to her. At first, it took only the form of minor attentions — little courtesies and thoughtful acts; but, after a while, he spoke of love — very gently and very tenderly, as any man might have done.

She had never thought of loving him or any other man; so, she was puzzled at first, but she was not offended. He had given her no cause for offense. When he had first broached the subject, she had asked him not to speak of it as she did not think that she loved him, and he had said that he would wait; but the seed was planted in her mind, and it came to occupy much of her thoughts.

She realized that she owed to him what little success she had achieved. She had an assured income that was sufficient for her simple wants while permitting her to send something home to her mother every week, and it was all due to the kindness of Wilson Crumb. He was a successful director, he was more than a fair actor, he was good-looking, he was kind, he was a gentleman, and he loved her. What more could any girl ask?

She thought the matter out very carefully, finally deciding that, though she did not exactly love Wilson Crumb, she probably would learn to love him and that, if he loved her, it was in a way her duty to make him happy when he had done so much for her happiness. She made up her mind, therefore, to marry him whenever he asked her; but Crumb did not ask her to marry him. He continued to make love to her; but the matter of marriage never seemed to enter the conversation.

Once, when they were out on location and had had a hard day, ending by getting thoroughly soaked in a sudden rain, he had followed her to her room in the little mountain inn where they were stopping.

"You're cold and wet and tired," he said. "I want to give you something that will brace you up."

He entered the room and closed the door behind him. Then, he took from his pocket a small piece of paper folded into a package about an inch and three-quarters long by half an inch wide with one end tucked ingeniously inside the fold to form a fastening. Opening it, he revealed a white powder, the minute crystals of which glistened beneath the light from the electric bulbs.

"It looks just like snow," she said.

"Sure!" he replied with a faint smile. "It is snow. Look, I'll show you how to take it."

He divided the powder into halves, took one in the palm of his hand, and snuffed it into his nostrils.

"There!" he exclaimed. "That's the way — it will make you feel like a new woman."

"But what is it?" she asked. "Won't it hurt me?"

"It'll make you feel bully. Try it."

So, she tried it, and it made her "feel bully." She was no longer tired but deliriously exhilarated.

"Whenever you want any, let me know," he said as he was leaving the room. "I usually have some handy."

"But I'd like to know what it is," she insisted.

"Aspirin," he replied. "It makes you feel that way when you snuff it up your nose."

After he left, she recovered the little piece of paper from the waste basket where he had thrown it, her curiosity aroused. She found it a rather soiled bit of writing paper with a "C" written in lead pencil upon it.

"'C,'" she mused. "Why aspirin with a C?"

She thought she would question Wilson about it.

The next day, she felt out of sorts and tired, and, at noon, she asked him if he had any aspirin with him. He had, and again she felt fine and full of life. That evening she wanted some more, and Crumb gave it to her. The next day, she wanted it oftener, and, by the time they returned to Hollywood from location, she was taking it five or six times a day. It was then that Crumb asked her to come and live with him at his Vista del Paso bungalow; but he did not mention marriage.

He was standing with a little paper of the white powder in his hand, separating half of it for her, and she was waiting impatiently for it.

"Well?" he asked.

"Well, what?"

The Girl from Hollywood / 39

"Are you coming over to live with me?" he demanded.

"Without being married?" she asked.

She was surprised that the idea no longer seemed horrible. Her eyes and her mind were on the little white powder that the man held in his hand.

Crumb laughed.

"Quit your kidding," he said. "You know perfectly well that I can't marry you yet. I have a wife in San Francisco."

She did not know it perfectly well — she did not know it at all; yet it did not seem to matter so very much. A month ago, she would have caressed a rattlesnake as willingly as she would have permitted a married man to make love to her; but now, she could listen to a plea from one who wished her to come and live with him without experiencing any numbing sense of outraged decency.

Of course, she had no intention of doing what he asked; but, really, the matter was of negligible import — the thing in which she was most concerned was the little white powder. She held out her hand for it, but he drew it away.

"Answer me first," he said. "Are you going to be sensible or not?"

"You mean that you won't give it to me if I won't come?" she asked.

"That's precisely what I mean," he replied. "What do you think I am, anyway? Do you know what this bundle of 'C' stands me? Two-fifty, and you've been snuffing about three of 'em a day. What kind of a sucker do you think I am?"

Her eyes, still upon the white powder, narrowed.

"I'll come," she whispered. "Give it to me!"

She went to the bungalow with him that day, and she learned where he kept the little white powders hidden in the bathroom. After dinner, she put on her hat and her fur and took up her vanity case while Crumb was busy in another room. Then, opening the front door, she called:

"Goodbye!"

Crumb rushed into the living room. "Where are you going?" he demanded.

"Home," she replied.

"No, you're not!" he cried. "You promised to stay here."

"I promised to come," she corrected him. "I never promised to stay, and I never shall until you are divorced, and we are married."

"You'll come back," he sneered, "when you want another shot of snow!"

"Oh, I don't know," she replied. "I guess I can buy aspirin at any drug store as well as you."

Crumb laughed aloud.

"You little fool, you!" he cried derisively. "Aspirin! Why, it's cocaine you're snuffing, and you're snuffing about three grains of it a day!"

For an instant a look of horror filled her widened eyes.

"You beast!" she cried. "You unspeakable beast!"

Slamming the door behind her, she almost ran down the narrow walk and disappeared in the shadows of the palm trees that bordered the ill-lighted street.

The man did not follow her. He only stood there laughing, for he knew that she would come back. Craftily, he had enmeshed her. It had taken months, and never had quarry been more wary or difficult to trap. A single false step earlier in the game would have frightened her away forever; but he had made no false step. He was very proud of himself, was Wilson Crumb, for he was convinced that he had done a very clever bit of work.

Rubbing his hands together, he walked toward the bathroom — he would take a shot of snow; but when he opened the receptacle, he found it empty.

"The little devil!" he ejaculated.

Frantically, he rummaged through the medicine cabinet but in vain. Then, he hastened into the living room, seized his hat, and bolted for the street.

Almost immediately, he realized the futility of search. He did not know where the girl lived. She had never told him. He did not know it, but she had never told anyone. The studio had a post office box number to which it could address communications to Gaza de Lure; the mother addressed the girl by her own name at the house where she had roomed since coming to Hollywood. The woman who rented her the room did not know her screen name. All she knew about her was that she seemed a quiet, refined girl who paid her room rent promptly in advance every week and who was always home at night, except when on location.

Crumb returned to the bungalow, searched the bathroom twice more, and went to bed. For hours, he lay awake, tossing restlessly.

"The little devil!" he muttered, over and over. "Fifty dollars' worth of cocaine — the little devil!"

The next day, Gaza was at the studio, ready for work, when Crumb put in his belated appearance. He was nervous and irritable. Almost immediately, he called her aside and demanded an accounting; but when they were face to face, and she told him that she was through with him, he realized that her hold upon him was stronger than he had supposed. He could not give her up. He was ready to promise anything, and he would demand nothing in return, only that she would be with him as much as possible. Her nights should be her own — she could go home then. And so, the arrangement was consummated, and Gaza de Lure spent the days when she was not working at the bungalow on the Vista del Paso.

Crumb saw that she was cast for small parts that required but little of her time at the studio yet raised no question at the office as to her salary of 50 dollars a week. Twice, the girl asked why he did not star her, and, both times, he told her that he would — for a price; but the price was one that she would not pay. After a time, the drugs, which she now used habitually, deadened her ambition so that she no longer cared. She still managed to send a little money home, but not so much as formerly.

As the months passed, Crumb's relations with the source of the supply of their narcotic became so familiar that he could obtain considerable quantities at a reduced rate, and the plan of peddling the drug occurred to him.

Gaza was induced to do her share, and so it came about that the better class "hypes" of Hollywood found it both safe and easy to obtain their supplies from the bungalow on the Vista del Paso. Cocaine, heroin, and morphine passed continually through the girl's hands, and she came to know many of the addicts, though she seldom had further intercourse with them than was necessary to the transaction of the business that brought them to the bungalow.

From one, a woman, she learned how to use morphine, dissolving the white powder in the bowl of a spoon by passing a lighted match beneath and then drawing the liquid through a tiny piece of cotton into a hypodermic syringe and injecting it beneath the skin. Once she had experienced the sensation of well-being it induced, she fell an easy victim to this more potent drug.

One evening, Crumb brought home with him a stranger whom he had known in San Francisco — a man whom he introduced as Allen. From that evening, the fortunes of Gaza de Lure improved. Allen had just returned from the Orient as a member of the crew of a freighter, and he had succeeded in smuggling in a considerable quantity of opium. In his efforts to dispose of it, he had made the acquaintance of others in the same line of business and had joined forces with them. His partners could command a more or less steady supply of morphine and cocaine from Mexico while Allen undertook to keep up their stock of opium and to arrange a market for their drugs in Los Angeles.

If Crumb could handle it all, Allen agreed to furnish morphine at 50 dollars an ounce — Gaza to do the actual peddling. The girl agreed on one condition — that half the profits should be hers. After that, she had been able to send home more money than ever before and, at the same time, to have all the morphine she wanted at a low price. She began to put money in the bank, made a first payment on a small orchard about a hundred miles from Los Angeles, and sent for her mother.

The day before you called on her in the "art" bungalow at 1421 Vista del Paso, she had put her mother on a train bound for her new home with the promise that the daughter would visit her "as soon as we finish this picture." It had required all the girl's remaining willpower to hide her shame from those eager mother eyes; but she had managed to do it, though it had left her almost a wreck by the time the train pulled out of the station.

To Crumb, she had said nothing about her mother. This was a part of her life that was too sacred to be revealed to the man whom she now loathed even as she loathed the filthy habit he had tricked her into; but she could no more give up the one than the other.

There had been a time when she had fought against the domination of these twin curses that had been visited upon her, but that time was over. She knew now that she would never give up morphine — that she could not if she wanted to and that she did not want to. The little bindles of cocaine, morphine, and heroin that she wrapped so deftly with those slender fingers and marked "C," "M," or "H," according to their contents, were parts of her life now. The sallow, trembling creatures who came for them, or to whom she sometimes delivered them, and who paid her two dollars and a half a bindle, were also parts of her life. Crumb, too, was a part of her life. She hated the bindles, she hated the sallow, trembling people, she hated Crumb; but still she clung to them, for how else was she to get the drug without which she could not live?

CHAPTER VI

IT WAS MAY. The rainy season was definitely over. A few April showers had concluded it. The Ganado hills showed their most brilliant greens. The March pigs were almost ready to wean. White-faced calves and black colts and gray colts surveyed this beautiful world through soft, dark eyes and were filled with the joy of living as they ran beside their gentle mothers. A stallion neighed from the stable corral, and from the ridge behind Jackknife Cañon, the Emperor of Ganado answered him.

A girl and a man sat in the soft grass beneath the shade of a live-oak upon the edge of a low bluff in the pasture where the brood mares grazed with their colts. Their horses were tied to another tree nearby. The girl held a bunch of yellow violets in her hand and gazed dreamily down the broad cañon toward the valley. The man sat a little behind her and gazed at the girl. For a long time, neither spoke.

"You cannot be persuaded to give it up, Grace?" he asked at last.

She shook her head.

"I should never be happy until I had tried it," she replied.

"Of course," he said, "I know how you feel about it. I feel the same way. I want to get away — away from the deadly stagnation and sameness of this life; but I am going to try to stick it out for father's sake, and I wish that you loved me enough to stick it out for mine. I believe that together we could get enough happiness out of life here to make up for what we are denied of real living, such as only a big city can offer. Then, when father is gone, we could go and live in the city — in any city that we wanted to live in — Los Angeles, Chicago, New York, London, Paris — anywhere."

"It isn't that I don't love you enough, Custer," said the girl. "I love you too much to want you to marry just a little farmer girl. When I come to you, I want you to be proud of me. Don't talk about the time when your father will have gone. It seems wicked. He would not want you to stay if he knew how you felt about it."

"You do not know," he replied. "Ever since I was a little boy, he has counted on this — on my staying on and working with him. He wants us all to be together always. When Eva marries, he will build her a home on Ganado. You have already helped with the plan for ours. You know it is his dream, but you cannot know how much it means to him. It would not kill him if his dream was spoiled, but it would take so much happiness out of his life that I cannot bring myself to do it. It is not a matter of money but of sentiment and love. If Ganado were wiped off the face of the earth tomorrow, we would still have all the money that we need; but he would never be happy again, for his whole life is bound up in the ranch and the dream that he has built around it. It is peculiar, too, that such a man as he should be so ruled by sentiment. You know how practical he is, and sometimes hard — yet I have seen the tears come to his eyes when he spoke of his love for Ganado."

"I know," she said, and they were silent again for a time. "You are a good son, Custer," she said presently. "I wouldn't have you any different. I am not so good a daughter. Mother does not want me to go. It is going to make her very unhappy, and yet I am going. The man who loves me does not want me to go. It is going to make him very unhappy, and yet I am going. It seems very selfish; but, oh, Custer, I cannot help but feel that I am right! It seems to me that I have a duty to perform and that this is the only way I can perform it. Perhaps I am not only silly, but sometimes I feel that I am called by a higher power to give myself for a little time to the world, that the world may be happier and, I hope, a little better. You know I have always felt that the stage was one of the greatest powers for good in all the world, and now I believe that someday the screen will be an even greater power for good. It is with the conviction that I may help toward this end that I am so eager to go. You will be very glad and very happy when I come back that I did not listen to your arguments."

"I hope you are right, Grace," Custer Pennington said.

On a rustic seat beneath the new leaves of an umbrella tree, a girl and a boy sat beside the upper lily pond on the south side of the hill below the ranch house. The girl held a spray of Japanese quince blossoms in her hand and gazed dreamily at the water splashing lazily over the rocks into the pond. The boy sat beside her and gazed at the girl. For a long time neither spoke.

"Won't you please say yes?" whispered the boy presently.

"How perfectly, terribly silly you are!" she replied.

"I am not silly," he said. "I am 20, and you are almost 18. It's time that we were marrying and settling down."

"On what?" she demanded.

"Well, we won't need much at first. We can live at home with mother," he explained, "until I sell a few stories."

"How perfectly gorgeristic!" she cried.

"Don't make fun of me! You wouldn't if you loved me," he pouted.

"I *do* love you, silly! But whatever in the world put the dapper little idea into your head that I wanted to be supported by my mother-in-law?"

"Mother-in-law!" protested the boy. "You ought to be ashamed to speak disrespectfully of my mother."

"You quaint child!" exclaimed the girl, laughing gayly. "Just as if I would speak disrespectfully of Aunt Mae, when I love her so splendiferously! Isn't she going to be my mother-in-law?"

The boy's gloom vanished magically.

"There!" he cried. "We're engaged! You've said it yourself. You've proposed, and I accept you. Yes, sure — she's going to be your mother-in-law!"

Eva flushed.

"I never said anything of the kind. How perfectly idiotical!"

"But you did say it. You proposed to me. I'm going to announce the engagement — 'Mrs. Mae Evans announces the engagement of her son, Guy Thackeray, to Miss Eva Pennington.'"

"Funeral notice later," snapped the girl, glaring at him.

"Aw, come now, you needn't get mad at me. I was only fooling; but wouldn't it be great, Ev? We could always be together then, and I could write, and you could — could —"

"Wash dishes," she suggested.

The light died from his eyes, and he dropped them sadly to the ground.

"I'm sorry I'm poor," he said. "I didn't think you cared about that, though."

She laid a brown hand gently over his.

"You know I don't care," she said. "I am a catty old thing. I'd just love it if we had a little place all our very own — just a teeny, weeny bungalow. I'd help you with your work and keep hens and have a little garden with onions and radishes and everything, and we wouldn't have to buy anything from the grocery store, and a bank account, and one sow; and when we drove into the city, people would say, 'There goes Guy Thackeray Evans, the famous author, but I wonder where his wife got that hat!'"

"Oh, Ev!" he cried laughing. "You never can be serious more than two seconds, can you?"

"Why should I be?" she inquired. "And anyway, I was. It really would be elegantiferous if we had a little place of our own; but my husband has got to be able to support me, Guy. He'd lose his self-respect if he didn't; and then, if he lost his, how could I respect him? You've got to have respect on both sides or you can't have love and happiness."

His face grew stern with determination.

"I'll get the money," he said; but he did not look at her. "But now that Grace is going away, mother will be all alone if I leave, too. Couldn't we live with her for a while?"

"Papa and Mama have always said that it was the worst thing a young married couple could do," she replied. "We could live near her and see her every day; but I don't think we should all live together. Really, though, do you think Grace is going? It seems just too awful."

"I am afraid she is," he replied sadly. "Mother is all broken up about it; but she tries not to let Grace know."

"I can't understand it," said the girl. "It seems to me a selfish thing to do, and yet, Grace has always been so sweet and generous. No matter how much I wanted to go, I don't believe I could bring myself to do it knowing how terribly it would hurt Papa. Just think, Guy — it is the first break, except for the short time we were away at school, since we have been born. We have all lived here always, it seems, your family and mine, like one big family; but after Grace goes, it will be the beginning of the end. It will never be the same again."

There was a note of seriousness and sadness in her voice that sounded not at all like Eva Pennington. The boy shook his head.

"It is too bad," he said, "but Grace is so sure she is right — so positive that she has a great future before her and that we shall all be so proud of her — that sometimes I am convinced myself."

"I hope she is right," said the girl, and then, with a return to her joyous self: "Oh, wouldn't it be spiffy if she really does become famous! I can see just now puffed up we shall all be when we read the reviews of her pictures, like this — 'Miss Grace Evans, the famous star, has quite outdone her past successes in the latest picture, in which she is ably supported by such well-known actors as Thomas Meighan, Wallace Reid, Gloria Swanson, and Mary Pickford.'"

"Why slight Douglas Fairbanks and Charlie Chaplin?" suggested Guy.

The girl rose.

"Come on!" she said. "Let's have a look at the pools — it isn't a perfect day unless I've seen fish in every pool. Do you remember how we used to watch and watch and watch for the fish in the lower pools and run as fast as we could to be the first up to the house to tell if we saw them and how many?"

"And do you remember the little turtles and how wild they got?" he put in. "Sometimes we wouldn't see them for weeks, and then we'd get just a glimpse so that we knew they were still there. Then, after a while, we never saw them again, and how we used to wonder and speculate as to what had become of them!"

"And do you remember the big water snake we found in the upper pool, and how Cus used to lie in wait for him with his little 22?"

"Cus was always the hunter. How we used to trudge after him up and down those steep hills there in the cow pasture while he hunted ground squirrels, and how mad he'd get if we made any noise! Gee, Ev, those were the good old days!"

"And how we used to fight, and what a nuisance Cus thought me; but he always asked me to go along, just the same. He's a wonderful brother, Guy!"

"He's a wonderful man, Ev," replied the boy. "You don't half know how wonderful he is. He's always thinking of someone else. Right now, I'll bet he's eating his heart out because Grace is going away; and he can't go, just because he's thinking more of someone else's happiness than his own."

"What do you mean?" she asked.

"He wants to go to the city. He wants to get into some business there; but he won't go because he knows your father wants him here."

"Do you really think that?"

"I know it," he said.

They walked on in silence along the winding pathways among the flower-bordered pools to stop at last beside the lower one. This had originally been a shallow wading pool for the children when they were small, but it was now given over to water hyacinth and brilliant fantails.

"There!" said the girl, presently. "I have seen fish in each pool."

"And you can go to bed with a clear conscience tonight," he laughed.

To the west of the lower pool, there were no trees to obstruct their view of the hills that rolled down from the mountains to form the western wall of the cañon in which the ranch buildings and cultivated fields lay. As the two stood there, hand in hand, the boy's eyes wandered lovingly over the soft, undulating lines of these lower hills with their parklike beauty of greensward dotted with wild walnut trees. As he looked, he saw, for a brief moment, the figure of a man on horseback passing over the hollow of a saddle before disappearing upon the southern side.

Small though the distant figure was and visible but for a moment, the boy recognized the military carriage of the rider. He glanced quickly at the girl to note if she had seen, but it was evident that she had not.

"Well, Ev," he said, "I guess I'll be toddling."

"So early?" she demanded.

"You see, I've got to get busy if I'm going to get the price of that teeny, weeny bungalow," he explained. "Now that we're engaged, you might kiss me goodbye — eh?"

"We're not engaged, and I'll not kiss you goodbye or good anything else. I don't believe in people kissing until they're married."

"Then why are you always raving about the wonderful kisses Antonio Moreno, or Milton Sills, or some other poor prune gives the heroine at the end of the last reel?" he demanded.

"Oh, that's different," she explained. "Anyway, they're just going to get married. When we are just going to get married, I'll let you kiss me — once a week, *maybe!*"

"Thanks!" he cried.

A moment later, he swung into the saddle, and, with a wave of his hand, cantered off up the cañon.

"Now what," said the girl to herself, "is he going up there for? He can't make any money back there in the hills. He ought to be headed straight for home and his typewriter!"

CHAPTER VII

ACROSS THE RUSTIC BRIDGE, and once behind the sycamores at the lower end of the cow pasture, Guy Evans let his horse out into a rapid gallop. A few minutes later, he overtook a horseman who was moving at a slow walk farther up the cañon. At the sound of the pounding hoofbeats behind him, the latter turned in his saddle, reined about, and stopped. The boy rode up and drew in his blowing mount beside the other.

"Hello, Allen!" he said.

The man nodded.

"What's eatin' you?" he inquired.

"I've been thinking over that proposition of yours," explained Evans.

"Yes?"

"Yes, I've been thinking maybe I might swing it; but are you sure it's safe? How do I know you won't double-cross me?"

"You don't know," replied the other. "All you know is that I got enough on you to send you to San Quentin. You wouldn't get nothin' worse if you handled the rest of it, an' you stand to clean up between twelve and fifteen thousand bucks on the deal. You needn't worry about me double-crossin' you. What good would it do me? I ain't got nothin' against you, kid. If you don't double-cross me, I won't double-cross you; but look out for that cracker-fed dude your sister's goin' to hitch to. If he ever butts in on this, I'll croak him an' send you to San Quentin, if I swing for it. Do you get me?"

Evans nodded.

"I'll go in on it," he said, "because I need the money; but don't you bother Custer Pennington — get that straight. I'd go to San Quentin and I'd swing myself before I'd stand for that. Another thing, and then we'll drop that line of chatter — you couldn't send me to San Quentin or anywhere else. I bought a few bottles of hooch from you, and there isn't any judge or jury going to send me to San Quentin for that."

"You don't know what you done," said Allen, with a grin. "There's a thousand cases of bonded whisky hid back there in the hills, an' you engineered the whole deal at this end. Maybe you didn't have nothin' to do with stealin' it from a government bonded warehouse in New York; but you must 'a' knowed all about it, an' it was you that hired me and the other three to smuggle it off the ship and into the hills."

Evans was staring at the man in wide-eyed incredulity.

"How do you get that way?" he asked derisively.

"They's four of us to swear to it," said Allen; "an' how many you got to swear you didn't do it?"

"Why, it's a rotten frame-up!" exclaimed Evans.

"Sure, it's a frame-up," agreed Allen; "but we won't use it if you behave yourself properly."

Evans looked at the man for a long minute — dislike and contempt unconcealed upon his face.

"I guess," he said presently, "that I don't need any twelve thousand dollars that bad, Allen. We'll call this thing off as far as I am concerned. I'm through, right now. Goodbye!"

He wheeled his horse to ride away.

"Hold on there, young feller!" said Allen. "Not so quick! You may think you're through, but you're not. We need you, and, anyway, you know too damned much for your health. You're goin' through with this. We got some other junk up there that there's more profit in than what there is in booze, and it's easier to handle. We know where to get rid of it; but the booze we can't handle as easy as you can, and so you're goin' to handle it."

"Who says I am?"

"*I* do," returned Allen with an ugly snarl. "You'll handle it,

The Girl from Hollywood / 53

or I'll do just what I said I'd do, and I'll do it *pronto*. How'd you like your mother and that Pennington girl to hear all I'd have to say?"

The boy sat with scowling, thoughtful brows for a long minute. From beneath a live oak on the summit of a low bluff, a man discovered them. He had been sitting there talking with a girl. Suddenly he looked up.

"Why, there's Guy," he said. "Who's that with — why, it's that fellow Allen! What's he doing up here?" He rose to his feet. "You stay here a minute, Grace. I'm going down to see what that fellow wants. I can't understand Guy."

He untied the Apache and mounted, while below, just beyond the pasture fence, the boy turned sullenly toward Allen.

"I'll go through with it this once," he said. "You'll bring it down on burros at night?"

The other nodded affirmatively.

"Where do you want it?" he asked.

"Bring it to the west side of the old hay barn — the one that stands on our west line. When will you come?"

"Today's Tuesday. We'll bring the first lot Friday night about twelve o'clock; and, after that, every Friday the same time. You be ready to settle every Friday for what you've sold during the week — *sabe*?"

"Yes," replied Evans. "That's all, then"; and he turned and rode back toward the rancho.

Allen was continuing on his way toward the hills when his attention was again attracted by the sound of hoofbeats. Looking to his left, he saw a horseman approaching from inside the pasture. He recognized both horse and rider at once but kept sullenly on his way.

Pennington rode up to the opposite side of the fence along which ran the trail that Allen followed.

"What are you doing here, Allen?" he asked in a not unkindly tone.

"Mindin' my own business, like you better!" retorted the ex-stableman.

"You have no business back here on Ganado," said Pennington. "You'll have to get off the property."

"The hell I will!" exclaimed Allen.

At the same time, he made a quick movement with his right hand; but Pennington made a quicker.

"That kind of stuff don't go here, Allen," said the younger man, covering the other with a forty-five. "Now, turn around and get off the place and don't come on it again. I don't want any trouble with you."

Without a word, Allen reined his horse about and rode down the cañon; but there was murder in his heart. Pennington watched him until he was out of revolver range and then turned and rode back to Grace Evans.

CHAPTER VIII

BENEATH THE COOL SHADOWS of the north porch, the master of Ganado, booted and spurred, rested after a long ride in the hot sun sipping a long, cool glass of peach brandy and orange juice and talking with his wife. A broad barley field lay below them, stretching to the state highway half a mile to the north. The yellowing heads of the grain stood motionless beneath the blazing sun. Inside the myriad kernels, the milk was changing into dough. It would not be long now, barring fogs, before that gorgeous pageant of prosperity would be falling in serried columns into the maw of the binder.

"We're going to have a bully crop of barley this year, Julia," remarked the colonel, fishing a small piece of ice from his glass. "Do you know, I'm beginning to believe this is better than a mint julep!"

"Heavens, Custer — whisper it!" admonished his wife. "Just suppose the shades of some of your ancestors, or mine, should overhear such sacrilege!"

The colonel chuckled.

"Is it old age, or has this sunny land made me effeminate?" he queried. "It's quite a far cry from an old-fashioned mint julep to this homemade wine and orange juice. You can't call it brandy — it hasn't enough of what the boys call 'kick' to be entitled to that honor; but I like it. Yes, sir, that's bully barley — there isn't any better in the foothills!"

"The oats look good, too," said Mrs. Pennington. "I haven't noticed the slightest sign of rust."

"That's the result of the boy's trip to Texas last summer," said the colonel proudly. "Went down there himself and selected all the seed — didn't take anybody's word for it. Genuine Texas rustproof oats was what he went for and what he got. I don't know what I'd do without him, Julia. It's wonderful to see one's dreams come true! I've been dreaming for years of the time when my boy and I would work together and make Ganado even more wonderful than it ever was before; and now my dream's a reality. It's great, I tell you — it's great! Is there another glass of this Ganado elixir in that pitcher, Julia?"

They were silent then for a few minutes, the colonel sipping his "elixir" and Mrs. Pennington, with her book face down upon her lap, gazing out across the barley and the broad valley and the distant hills — into the future, perhaps, or back into the past.

It had been an ideal life that they had led here — a life of love and sunshine and happiness. There had been nothing to vex her soul as she reveled in the delight of her babies, watching them grow into sturdy children and then develop into clean young manhood and womanhood. But growing with the passing years had been the dread of that day when the first break would come, as come she knew it must.

She knew the dream that her husband had built, and that, with it, he had purposely blinded his eyes and dulled his ears to the truth which the mother heart would have been glad to deny but could not. Someday, one of the children would go away and then the other. It was only right and just that it should be so, for as they two had built their own home and their own lives and their little family circle, so their children must do even as they.

It was going to be hard on them both — much harder on the father — because of that dream that had become an obsession. Mrs. Pennington feared that it might break his spirit, for it would leave him nothing to plan for and hope for as he had planned and hoped for this during the 22 years that they had spent upon Ganado.

Now that Grace was going to the city, how could they hope to keep their boy content upon the ranch? She knew he loved the old place, but he was entitled to see the world and to make his own place in it — not merely to slide spinelessly into the niche that another had prepared for him.

"I am worried about the boy," she said presently.

"How? In what way?" he asked.

"He will be very blue and lonely after Grace goes," she said.

"Don't talk to me about it!" cried the colonel, banging his glass down upon the table and rising to his feet. "It makes me mad just to think of it. I can't understand how Grace can want to leave this beautiful world to live in a damned city! She's crazy! What's her mother thinking about, to let her go?"

"You must remember, dear," said his wife soothingly, "that everyone is not so much in love with the country as you and that these young people have their own careers to carve in the way they think best. It would not be right to try to force them to live the way we like to live."

"Damned foolishness, that's what it is!" he blustered. "An actress! What does she know about acting?"

"She is beautiful, cultured, and intelligent. There is no reason why she should not succeed and make a great name for herself. Why shouldn't she be ambitious, dear? We should encourage her now that she has determined to go. It would help her, for she loves us all — she loves you as a daughter might, for you have been like a father to her ever since Mr. Evans died."

"Oh, pshaw, Julia!" the colonel exclaimed. "I love Grace — you know I do. I suppose it's because I love her that I feel so about this. Maybe I'm jealous of the city, to think that it has weaned her away from us. I don't mean all I say, sometimes; but, really, I am broken up at the thought of her going. It seems to me that it may be just the beginning of the end of the beautiful life that we have all led here for so many years."

"Have you ever thought that someday our own children may want to go?" she asked.

"I won't think about it!" he exploded.

"I hope you won't have to," she said; "but it's going to be pretty hard on the boy after Grace goes."

"Do you think he'll want to go?" the colonel asked. His voice sounded suddenly strange and pleading, and there was a suggestion of pain and fear in his eyes that she had never seen there before in all the years that she had known him. "Do you think he'll want to go?" he repeated in a voice that no longer sounded like his own.

"Stranger things have happened," she replied, forcing a smile, "than a young man wanting to go out into the world and win his spurs!"

"Let's not talk about it, Julia," the colonel said presently. "You are right, but I don't want to think about it. When it comes will be time enough to meet it. If my boy wants to go, he shall go — and he shall never know how deeply his father is hurt!"

"There they are now," said Mrs. Pennington. "I hear them in the patio. Children!" she called. "Here we are on the north porch!"

They came through the house together, brother and sister, their arms about each other.

"Cus says I am too young to get married," exclaimed the girl.

"Married!" ejaculated the colonel. "You and Guy talking of getting married? What are you going to live on, child?"

"On that hill back there."

She jerked her thumb in a direction that was broadly south by west.

"That will give them two things to live on," suggested the boy, grinning.

"What do you mean — two things?" demanded the girl.

"The hill and father," her brother replied, dodging.

She pursued him, and he ran behind his mother's chair; but, at last, she caught him and, seizing his collar, pretended to chastise him until he picked her up bodily from the floor and kissed her.

"Pity the poor goof she ensnares!" pleaded Custer, addressing his parents. "He will have three avenues of escape — being beaten to death, starved to death, or talked to death."

Eva clapped a hand over his mouth.

"Now listen to me," she cried. "Guy and I are going to build a teeny, weeny bungalow on that hill all by ourselves with a white tile splash board in the kitchen and one of those broom closets that turn into an ironing board and a very low, overhanging roof, almost flat, and a shower and a great big living room where we can take the rugs up and dance and a spiffy little garden in the backyard and chickens and Chinese rugs and he is going to have a study all to himself where he writes his stories and —"

At last, she had to stop and join in the laughter.

"I think you are all mean," she added. "You always laugh at me!"

"With you, little jabberer," corrected the colonel; "for you were made to be laughed with and kissed."

"Then kiss me," she exclaimed and sprang into his lap at the imminent risk of deluging them both with "elixir"— a risk which the colonel, through long experience of this little daughter of his, was able to minimize by holding the glass at arm's length as she dived for him.

"And when are you going to be married?" he asked.

"Oh, not for ages and ages!" she cried.

"But are you and Guy engaged?"

"Of course not!"

"Then why in the world all this talk about getting married?" he inquired, his eyes twinkling.

"Well, can't I talk?" she demanded.

"Talk? I'll say she can!" exclaimed her brother.

CHAPTER IX

TWO WEEKS LATER, Grace Evans left for Hollywood and fame. She would permit no one to accompany her, saying that she wanted to feel that from the moment she left home, she had made her own way unassisted toward her goal.

Hers was the selfish egotism that is often to be found in otherwise generous natures. She had never learned the sweetness and beauty of sharing — of sharing her ambitions, her successes, and her failures, too, with those who loved her. If she won to fame, the glory would be hers; nor did it once occur to her that she might have shared that pride and pleasure with others by accepting their help and advice. If she failed, they would not have even the sad sweetness of sharing her disappointment.

Over two homes, there hovered that evening a pall of gloom that no effort seemed able to dispel. In the ranch house on Ganado, they made a brave effort at cheerfulness on Custer Pennington's account. They did not dance that evening, as was their custom, nor could they find pleasure in the printed page when they tried to read. Bridge proved equally impossible.

Finally, Custer rose, announcing that he was going to bed. Kissing them all good night, as had been the custom since childhood, he went to his room, and tears came to the mother's eyes as she noted the droop in the broad shoulders as he walked from the room.

The girl came then and knelt beside her, taking the older woman's hand in hers and caressing it.

"I feel so sorry for Cus," she said. "I believe that none of us realize how hard he is taking this. He told me yesterday that it was going to be just the same as if Grace was dead, for he knew she would never be satisfied here again, whether she succeeded or failed. I think he has definitely given up all hope of their being married."

"Oh, no, dear, I am sure he is wrong," said her mother. "The engagement has not been broken. In fact, Grace told me only a few days ago that she hoped her success would come quickly so that she and Custer might be married the sooner. The dear girl wants us to be proud of our new daughter."

"My God!" ejaculated the colonel, throwing his book down and rising to pace the floor. "Proud of her! Weren't we already proud of her? Will being an actress make her any dearer to us? Of all the damn fool ideas!"

"Custer! Custer! You mustn't swear so before Eva," reproved Mrs. Pennington.

"Swear?" he demanded. "Who in hell is swearing?"

A merry peal of laughter broke from the girl nor could her mother refrain from smiling.

"It isn't swearing when Popsy says it," cried the girl. "My gracious, I've heard it all my life, and you always say the same thing to him as if I'd never heard a single little cuss word. Anyway, I'm going to bed now, Popsy, so that you won't contaminate me. According to Momsy's theory, she should curse like a pirate by this time, after 25 years of it!"

She kissed them, leaving them alone in the little family sitting room.

"I hope the boy won't take it too hard," said the colonel after a silence.

"I am afraid he has been drinking a little too much lately," said the mother. "I only hope his loneliness for Grace won't encourage it."

"I hadn't noticed it," said the colonel.

"He never shows it much," she replied. "An outsider would not know that he had been drinking at all when I can see that he has had more than he should."

"Don't worry about that, dear," said the colonel. "A Pennington never drinks more than a gentleman should. His father and his grandsires, on both sides, always drank, but there has never been a drunkard in either family. I wouldn't give two cents for him if he couldn't take a man's drink like a man; but he'll never go too far. My boy couldn't!"

The pride and affection in the words brought the tears to the mother's eyes. She wondered if there had ever been father and son like these before — each with such implicit confidence in the honor, the integrity, and the manly strength of the other. *His boy* couldn't go wrong!

Custer Pennington entered his room, lighted a reading lamp beside a deep, wide-armed chair, selected a book from a rack, and settled himself comfortably for an hour of pleasure and inspiration. But he did not open the book. Instead, he sat staring blindly at the opposite wall.

Directly in front of him hung a water color of the Apache done by Eva and given to him the previous Christmas; a framed enlargement of a photograph of a prize Hereford bull; a pair of rusty Spanish spurs; and a frame of ribbons won by the Apache at various horse shows. Custer saw none of these but only a gloomy vista of dreary years stretching through the dead monotony of endless ranch days that were all alike — years that he must travel alone.

She would never come back, and why should she? In the city, in that new life, she would meet men of the world — men of broader culture than his, men of wealth — and she would be sought after. They would have more to offer her than he, and, sooner or later, she would realize it. He could not expect to hold her.

Custer laid aside his book.

"What's the use?" he asked himself.

Rising, he went to the closet and brought out a bottle. He had not intended drinking. On the contrary, he had determined very definitely not to drink that night; but, again, he asked himself the old question, which, under certain circumstances of life and certain conditions of seeming hopelessness, appears unanswerable:

"What is the use?"

It is a foolish question, a meaningless question, a dangerous question. What is the use of what? Of combating fate — of declining to do the thing we ought not to do — of doing the thing we should do? It is not even a satisfactory means of self-justification; but amid the ruins of his dreams, it was sufficient excuse for Custer Pennington's surrender to the craving of an appetite which was daily becoming stronger.

The next morning, he did not ride before breakfast with the other members of the family, nor, in fact, did he breakfast until long after they.

On the evening of the day of Grace's departure, Mrs. Evans retired early, complaining of a headache. Guy Evans sought to interest himself in various magazines, but he was restless and too ill at ease to remain long absorbed. At frequent intervals, he consulted his watch, and as the evening wore on, he made numerous trips to his room where he had recourse to a bottle like the one with which Custer Pennington was similarly engaged.

It was Friday — the second Friday since Guy had entered into an agreement with Allen; and, as midnight approached, his nervousness increased.

Young Evans, while scarcely to be classed as a strong character, was more impulsive than weak, nor was he in any sense of the word vicious. While he knew that he was breaking the law, he would have been terribly shocked at the merest suggestion that his acts placed upon him the brand of criminality. Like many another, he considered the Volstead Act the work of an organized and meddlesome minority rather than the real will of the people. There was, in his opinion, no immorality in circumventing the 18th Amendment whenever and wherever possible.

The only fly in the ointment was the fact that the liquor in which he was at present trafficking had been stolen; but he attempted to square this with his conscience by the oft reiterated thought that he did not know it to be stolen goods — they couldn't prove that he knew it. However, the fly remained. It must have been one of those extremely obnoxious, buzzy flies if one might judge by the boy's increasing nervousness.

Time and again, during that long evening, he mentally reiterated his determination that once this venture was concluded, he would never embark upon another of a similar nature. The several thousand dollars which it would net him would make it possible for him to marry Eva and settle down to a serious and uninterrupted effort at writing — the one vocation for which he believed himself best fitted by inclination and preparation; but, never again, he assured himself repeatedly, would he allow himself to be cajoled or threatened into such an agreement.

He disliked and feared Allen, whom he now knew to be a totally unscrupulous man, and his introduction, the preceding Friday, to the confederates who had brought down the first consignment of whisky from the mountains had left him fairly frozen with apprehension as he considered the type of ruffians with whom he was associated. During the intervening week, he had been unable to concentrate his mind upon his story-writing even to the extent of a single word of new material. He had worried and brooded, and he had drunk more than usual.

As he sat waiting for the arrival of the second consignment, he pictured the little cavalcade winding downward along hidden trails through the chaparral of dark, mountain ravines. His nervousness increased as he realized the risk of discovery sometime during the six months that it would take to move the contraband to the edge of the valley in this way — 36 cases at a time packed out on six burros.

He had little fear of the failure of his plan for hiding the liquor in the old hay barn and moving it out again the following day.

For three years, there had been stored in one end of the barn some 50 tons of baled melilotus. It had been sown as a cover crop by a former foreman and allowed to grow to such proportions as to render the plowing of it under a practical impossibility. As hay, it was in little or no demand, but there was a possibility of a hay shortage that year. It was against this possibility that Evans had had it baled and stored away in the barn where it had lain ever since, awaiting an offer that would at least cover the cost of growing, harvesting, and baling. A hard day's work had so rearranged the bales as to form a hidden chamber in the center of the pile, ingress to which could readily be had by removing a couple of bales near the floor.

A little after 11 o'clock, Guy left the house and made his way to the barn where he paced nervously to and fro in the dark interior. He hoped that the men would come early and get the thing over, for it was this part of the operation that seemed most fraught with danger.

The disposal of the liquor was affected by daylight, and the very boldness and simplicity of the scheme seemed to assure its safety. A large motor truck — such trucks are constantly seen upon the roads of southern California loaded with farm and orchard products and bound cityward — drove up to the hay barn on the morning after the receipt of the contraband. It backed into the interior, and, half an hour later, it emerged with a small load of baled melilotus. That there were 36 cases of bonded whisky concealed by the innocent-looking bales of melilotus Mr. Volstead himself could not have guessed; but such was the case.

Where it went to after it left his hands, Guy Evans did not know or want to know. The man who bought it from him owned and drove the truck. He paid Evans six dollars a quart in currency and drove away taking, besides the load on the floor of the truck, a much heavier burden from the mind of the young man.

The whisky was in Guy's possession for less than 12 hours a week; but, during those 12 hours, he earned the commission of a dollar a bottle that Allen allowed him, for his great fear was that, sooner or later, someone would discover and follow the six burros as they came down to the barn. There were often campers in file hills. During the deer season, if they did not have it all removed by that time, they would be almost certain of discovery since every courageous ribbon-counter clerk in Los Angeles hied valiantly to the mountains with a high-powered rifle to track the ferocious deer to its lair.

At a quarter past 12, Evans heard the sounds for which he had been so expectantly waiting. He opened a small door in the end of the hay barn through which there filed in silence six burdened burros led by one swarthy Mexican and followed by another. Quietly, the men unpacked the burros and stored the 36 cases in the chamber beneath the hay. Inside this same chamber, by the light of a flash lamp, Evans counted out to one of them the proceeds from the sale of the previous week. The whole transaction consumed less than half an hour and was carried on with the exchange of less than a dozen words. As silently as they had come, the men departed with their burros into the darkness toward the hills, and young Evans made his way to his room and to bed.

CHAPTER X

AS THE WEEKS passed, the routine of ranch life weighed more and more heavily on Custer Pennington. The dull monotony of it took the zest from the things that he had formerly regarded as the pleasures of existence. The buoyant Apache no longer had power to thrill. The long rides were but obnoxious duties to be performed. The hills had lost their beauty.

Custer attributed his despondency to an unkind fate that had thwarted his ambitions. He thought that he hated Ganado; and he thought, too — he honestly thought — that freedom to battle for success in the heart of some great city would bring happiness and content. For all that, he performed his duties and bore himself as cheerfully as ever before the other members of his family, though his mother and sister saw that when he thought he was alone and unobserved, he often sat with drooping shoulders, staring at the ground in an attitude of dejection, which their love could scarce misinterpret.

The frequent letters that came from Grace during her first days in Hollywood had breathed a spirit of hopefulness and enthusiasm that might have proven contagious but for the fact that he saw in her success a longer and probably a permanent separation. If she should be speedily discouraged, she might return to the foothills and put the idea of a career forever from her mind; but if she received even the slightest encouragement, Custer was confident that nothing could wean her from her ambition. He was the more sure of this because in his own mind he could picture no inducement sufficiently powerful to attract anyone to return to the humdrum existence of the ranch. Better be a failure in the midst of life, he put it to himself, than a success in the unpeopled spaces of its outer edge.

Ensuing weeks brought fewer letters, and there was less of enthusiasm, though hope was still unquenched. She had not yet met the right people, Grace said, and there was a general depression in the entire picture industry. Universal had a new manager, and there was no guessing what his policy would be; Goldwyn had laid off half their force; Robertson-Cole had shut down. She was sure, though, that things would brighten up later and that she would have her chance. Would they please tell her how Senator was and give him her love and kiss the Apache for her? There was just a note, perhaps, of homesickness in some of her letters; and, gradually, they became fewer and shorter.

The little gatherings of the neighbors at Ganado continued. Other young people of the valley and the foothills came and danced or swam or played tennis. Their elders came, too, equally enjoying the hospitality of the Penningtons; and among these was the new owner of the little orchard beyond the Evans ranch.

The Penningtons had found Mrs. Burke a quiet woman of refined tastes and the possessor a quiet humor that made her always a welcome addition to the family circle. That she had known more of sorrow than of happiness was evidenced in many ways, but that she had risen above the petty selfishness of grief was strikingly apparent in her thoughtfulness for others, her quick sympathy, and the kindliness of her humor. Whatever ills fate had brought her, they had not left her soured.

As she came oftener and came to know the Penningtons better, she depended more and more on the colonel for advice in matters pertaining to her orchard and her finances. Of personal matters, she never spoke. They knew that she had a daughter living in Los Angeles; but of the girl, they knew nothing, for deep in the heart of Mrs. George Burke, who had been born Charity Cooper, was a strain of Puritanism that could not look with aught but horror upon the stage and its naughty little sister, the screen — though in her letters to that loved daughter, there was no suggestion of the pain that the fond heart held because of the career the girl had chosen.

Charity Cooper's youth had been so surrounded by restrictions that at 18 she was as unsophisticated as a child of 12. As a result, she had easily succumbed to the blandishments of an unscrupulous young Irish adventurer who had thought that her fine family connections indicated wealth. When he learned the contrary, shortly after their marriage, he promptly deserted her, nor had she seen or heard aught of him since. Of him, she never spoke, and, of course, the Penningtons never questioned her.

At 39, Mrs. George Burke still retained much of the frail and delicate beauty that had been hers in girlhood. The effort of moving from her old home and settling the new, followed by the responsibilities of the unfamiliar and highly technical activities of orange culture, had drawn heavily upon her always inadequate vitality. As the Penningtons became better acquainted with her, they began to feel real concern as to her physical condition; and this concern was not lessened by the knowledge that she had been giving the matter serious thought as was evidenced by her request that the colonel would permit her to name him as executor of her estate in a will that she was making.

While life upon Ganado took its peaceful way, outwardly unruffled, the girl whose image was in the hearts of them all strove valiantly in the face of recurring disappointment toward the high goal upon which her eyes were set.

If she could only have a chance! How often that half prayer, half cry of anguish was in the silent voicing of her thoughts! If she could only have a chance! In the weeks of tramping from studio to studio, she had learned much. For one thing, she had come to know the ruthlessness of a certain type of man that must and will someday be driven from the industry — that is, in fact, even now being driven out, though slowly, by the stress of public opinion and by the example of the men of finer character who are gradually making a higher code of ethics for the studios.

She had learned even more from the scores of chance acquaintances who, through repeated meetings in the outer offices of casting directors, had become almost friends. Indeed, when she found herself facing the actuality of one of the more repulsive phases of studio procedure, it appeared more in the guise of habitude through the many references to it that she had heard from the lips of her more experienced fellows.

She was interviewing, for the dozenth time, the casting director of the KKS Studio who had come to know her by sight and perhaps to feel a little compassion for her — though there are those who will tell you that casting directors, having no hearts, can never experience so human an emotion as compassion.

"I'm sorry, Miss Evans," he said; "but I haven't a thing for you today." As she turned away, he raised his hand. "Wait!" he said. "Mr. Crumb is casting his new picture himself. He's out on the lot now. Go out and see him — he might be able to use you."

The girl thanked him and made her way from the office building in search of Crumb. She stepped over light cables and picked her way across stages that were littered with the heterogeneous jumble of countless interior sets. She dodged the assistants of a frantic technical director who was attempting to transform an African water hole into a Roman bath in an hour and 45 minutes. She bumped against a heavy shipping crate through the iron-barred end of which a savage lioness growled and struck at her. Finally, she discovered a single individual who seemed to have nothing to do and who therefore might be approached with a query as to where Mr. Crumb might be found. This resplendent idler directed her to an Algerian street-set behind the stages, and, as he spoke, she recognized him as the leading male star of the organization, the highest salaried person on the lot.

A few minutes later, she found the man she sought. She had never seen Wilson Crumb before, and her first impression was a pleasant one, for he was courteous and affable. She told him that she had been to the casting director and that he had said that Mr. Crumb might be able to use her. As she spoke, the man watched her intently, his eyes running quickly over her figure without suggestion of offense.

"What experience have you had?" he asked.

"Just a few times as an extra," she replied.

He shook his head.

"I am afraid I can't use you," he said; "unless"— he hesitated — "unless you would care to work in the seminude, which would necessitate making a test — in the nude."

He waited for her reply. Grace Evans gulped. She could feel a scarlet flush mounting rapidly until it suffused her entire face. She could not understand why it was necessary to try her out in any less garmenture than would pass the censors; but then, that is something which no one can understand.

Here, possibly, was her opportunity. She had read in the papers that Wilson Crumb was preparing to make the greatest picture of his career. She thought of her constant prayer for a chance. Here was a chance, and yet she hesitated. The brutal, useless condition he had imposed outraged every instinct of decency and refinement inherent in her just as it has outraged the same characteristics in countless other girls — just as it is doing in other studios in all parts of the country every day.

"Is that absolutely essential?" she asked.

"Quite so," he replied.

Still she hesitated. Her chance! If she let it pass, she might as well pack up and return home. What a little thing to do, after all, when one really considered it!

It was purely professional. There would be nothing personal in it if she could only succeed in overcoming her self-consciousness; but *could* she do it?

Again, she thought of home. A hundred times, of late, she had wished that she was back there; but she did not want to go back a failure. It was that which decided her.

"Very well," she said; "but there will not be many there, will there?"

"Only a camera-man and myself," he replied. "If it is convenient, I can arrange it immediately."

Two hours later, Grace Evans left the KKS lot. She was to start work on the morrow at 50 dollars a week for the full period of the picture. Wilson Crumb had told her that she had a wonderful future and that she was fortunate to have fallen in with a director who could make a great star of her. As she went, she left behind all her self-respect and part of her natural modesty.

Wilson Crumb, watching her go, rubbed the ball of his right thumb to and fro across the back of his left hand and smiled.

The Apache danced along the wagon trail that led back into the hills. He tugged at the bit and tossed his head impatiently, flecking his rider's shirt with foam. He lifted his feet high and twisted and wriggled like an eel. He wanted to be off, and he wondered what had come over his old pal that there were no more swift, gay gallops and that washes were crossed sedately by way of their gravelly bottoms instead of being taken with a flying leap.

Presently, he cocked an eye ahead as if in search of something. A moment later, he leaped suddenly sidewise, snorting in apparent terror.

"You old fool!" said Pennington affectionately.

The horse had shied at a large white boulder lying beside the wagon trail. For nearly three years, he had shied at it religiously every time he had passed it. Long before they reached it, he always looked ahead to see if it was still there, and he would have been terribly disappointed had it been missing. The man always knew that the horse was going to shy — he would have been disappointed if the Apache had not played this little game of make-believe. To carry the game to its conclusion, the rider should gather him and force him snorting and trembling right up to the boulder, talking to him coaxingly and stroking his arched neck, but at the same time not neglecting to press the spurs against his glossy sides if he hesitated.

The Apache loved it. He loved the power that was his as exemplified by the quick, wide leap aside, and he loved the power of the man to force his nose to the boulder — the power that gave him such confidence in his rider that he would go wherever he was asked to go; but today he was disappointed. His pal did not force him to the boulder. Instead, Custer Pennington merely reined him into the trail again beyond it and rode on up Jackknife Cañon.

Custer was looking over the pasture. It was late July. The hills were no longer green except where their sides and summits were clothed with chaparral. The lower hills were browning beneath the hot summer sun, but they were still beautiful, dotted as they were with walnut and live oak.

As Pennington rode, he recalled the last time he had ridden through Jackknife with Grace. She had been gone two months now — it seemed as many years. She no longer wrote often, and, when she did write, her letters were short and unsatisfying. He recalled all the incidents of that last ride, and they reminded him again of the new-made trail they had discovered and of his oft-repeated intention of following it to see where it led. He had never had the time — he did not have the time today. The heifers with their calves were still in this pasture. He counted them, examined the condition of the feed, and rode back to the house.

It was Friday. From the hill beyond Jackknife, a man had watched through binoculars his every move. Three other men had been waiting below the watcher along the new-made trail. It was well for Pennington that he had not chosen that day to investigate.

After he had turned back toward the ranch, the man with the binoculars descended to the others.

"It was young Pennington," he said. The speaker was Allen. "I was thinking that it would be a fool trick to kill him unless we have to. I have a better scheme. Listen — if he ever learns anything that he shouldn't know, this is what you are to do, if I am away."

Very carefully and in great detail he elaborated his plan.

"Do you understand?" he asked. They did, and they grinned.

The following night, after the Penningtons had dined, a ranch hand came up from Mrs. Burke's to tell them that their new neighbor was quite ill and that the woman who did her housework wanted Mrs. Pennington to come down at once as she was worried about her mistress.

"We will be right down," said Colonel Pennington. They found Mrs. Burke breathing with difficulty, and the colonel immediately telephoned for a local doctor.

After the physician had examined her, he came to them in the living room.

"You had better send for Jones of Los Angeles," he said. "It is her heart. I can do nothing. I doubt if he can; but he is a specialist. And," he added, "if she has any near relatives, I think I should notify them — at once."

The housekeeper had joined them and was wiping tears from her face with her apron.

"She has a daughter in Los Angeles," said the colonel; "but we do not know her address."

"She wrote her today just before this spell," said the housekeeper. "The letter hasn't been mailed yet — here it is."

She picked it up from the center table and handed it to the colonel.

"Miss Shannon Burke, 1580 Panizo Circle, Hollywood," he read. "I will take the responsibility of wiring both Miss Burke and Dr. Jones. Can you get a good nurse locally?"

The doctor could, and so it was arranged.

CHAPTER XI

GAZA DE LURE was sitting at the piano when Crumb arrived at the bungalow at 1421 Vista del Paso at a little after six in the evening of the last Saturday in July. The smoke from a half-burned cigarette lying on the ebony case was rising in a thin, indolent column above the masses of her black hair. Her fingers idled through a dreamy waltz.

Crumb gave her a surly nod as he closed the door behind him. He was tired and cross after a hard day at the studio. The girl, knowing that he would be alright presently, merely returned his nod and continued playing. He went immediately to his room, and, a moment later, she heard him enter the bathroom through another doorway.

Half an hour later, he emerged shaved, spruce, and smiling. A tiny powder had effected a transformation just as she had known that it would. He came and leaned across the piano close to her. She was very beautiful. It seemed to the man that she grew more beautiful and more desirable each day. The fact that she had been unattainable had fed the fires of his desire, transforming infatuation into as near a thing to love as a man of his type can ever feel.

"Well, little girl!" he cried gayly. "I have good news for you."

She smiled a crooked little smile and shook her head.

"The only good news that I can think of would be that the government had established a comfortable home for superannuated hopheads where they would be furnished, without cost, with all the snow they could use."

The effects of her last shot were wearing off. He laughed good-naturedly.

"Really," he insisted; "on the level, I've got the best news you've heard in moons."

"Well?" she asked wearily.

"Old Battle-Ax has got her divorce," he announced, referring, thus, affectionately to his wife.

"Well," said the girl, "that's good news — for her — if it's true."

Crumb frowned.

"It's good news for you," he said. "It means that I can marry you now."

The girl leaned back on the piano bench and laughed aloud. It was not a pleasant laugh. She laughed until the tears rolled down her cheeks.

"What is there funny about that?" growled the man. "It would mean a lot to you — respectability, for one thing, and success, for another. The day you become Mrs. Wilson Crumb I'll star you in the greatest picture that was ever made."

"Respectability!" she sneered. "Your name would make me respectable, would it? It would be the insult added to all the injury you have done me. And as for starring — poof!" She snapped her fingers. "I have but one ambition, thanks to you, you dirty hound, and that is snow!" She leaned toward him, her two clenched fists almost shaking in his face. "Give me all the snow I need," she cried, "and the rest of them may have their fame and their laurels!"

He thought he saw his chance then. Turning away with a shrug, he walked to the fireplace and lighted a cigarette.

"Oh, very well!" he said. "If you feel that way about it, alright; but"— he turned suddenly upon her — "you'll have to get out of here and stay out — do you understand? From this day on, you can only enter this house as Mrs. Wilson Crumb, and you can rustle your own dope if you don't come back — understand?"

She looked at him through narrowed lids. She reminded him of a tigress about to spring, and he backed away.

"Listen to me," she commanded in slow, level tones. "In the first place, you're lying to me about your wife getting her divorce. I'd have guessed as much if I hadn't known, for a hophead can't tell the truth; but I do know. You got a letter from your attorney today telling you that your wife still insists not only that she never will divorce you but that she will never allow you a divorce."

"You mean to say that you opened one of my letters?" he demanded angrily.

"Sure, I opened it! I open 'em all — I steam 'em open. What do you expect," she almost screamed, "from the thing you have made of me? Do you expect honor and self-respect, or any other virtue, in a hype?"

"You get out of here!" he cried. "You get out now — this minute!"

She rose from the bench and came and stood quite close to him.

"You'll see that I get all the snow I want if I go?" she asked. He laughed nastily.

"You don't ever get another bindle," he replied.

"Wait!" she admonished. "I wasn't through with what I started to say a minute ago. You've been hitting it long enough, Wilson, to know what one of our kind will do to get it. You know that either you or I would sacrifice soul and body if there was no other way. We would lie, or steal, or — murder! Do you get that, Wilson —*murder*? There is just one thing that I won't do, but that one thing is not murder, Wilson. Listen!" She lifted her face close to his and looked him straight in the eyes. "If you ever try to take it away from me or keep it from me, Wilson, I shall kill you."

Her tone was cold and unemotional, and because of that, perhaps, the threat seemed very real. The man paled.

"Aw, come!" he cried. "What's the use of our scrapping? I was only kidding, anyway. Run along and take a shot — it'll make you feel better."

"Yes," she said, "I need one; but don't get it into your head that I was kidding. I wasn't. I'd just as soon kill you as not — the only trouble is that killing's too damned good for you, Wilson!"

She walked toward the bathroom door.

"Oh, by the way," she said, pausing, "Allen called up this afternoon. He's in town and will be up after dinner. He wants his money."

She entered the bathroom and closed the door. Crumb lighted another cigarette and threw himself into an easy chair where he sat scowling at a temple dog on a Chinese rug.

The Japanese "schoolboy" opened a door and announced dinner, and, a moment later, Gaza joined Crumb in the little dining room. They both smoked throughout the meal, which they scarcely tasted. The girl was vivacious and apparently happy. She seemed to have forgotten the recent scene in the living room. She asked questions about the new picture.

"We're going to commence shooting Monday," he told her. Momentarily, he waxed almost enthusiastic. "I'm going to have trouble with that boob author, though," he said. "If they'd kick him off the lot and give me a little more money, I'd make 'em the greatest picture ever screened!" Then, he relapsed into brooding silence.

"What's the matter?" she asked. "Worrying about Allen?"

"Not exactly," he said. "I'll stall him off again."

"He isn't going to be easy to stall this time," she observed, "if I gathered the correct idea from his line of talk over the phone today. I can't see what you've done with all the coin, Wilson."

"You got yours, didn't you?" he growled.

"Sure, I got mine," she answered, "and it's nothing to me what you did with Allen's share; but I'm here to tell you that you've pulled a boner if you've double-crossed him. I'm not much of a character reader, as proved by my erstwhile belief that you were a high-minded gentleman; but it strikes me the veriest boob could see that that man Allen is a bad actor. You'd better look out for him."

"I ain't afraid of him," blustered Crumb.

"No, of course you're not," she agreed sarcastically. "You're a regular little lion-hearted Reginald, Wilson — that's what you are!"

The doorbell rang.

"There he is now," said the girl.

Crumb paled.

"What makes you think he's a bad man?" he asked.

"Look at his face — look at his eyes," she admonished. "Hard? He's got a face like a brickbat."

They rose from the table and entered the living room as the

Japanese opened the front door. The caller was Slick Allen. Crumb rushed forward and greeted him effusively.

"Hello, old man!" he cried. "I'm mighty glad to see you. Miss de Lure told me that you had phoned. Can't tell you how delighted I am!"

Allen nodded to the girl, tossed his cap upon a bench near the door, and crossed to the center of the room.

"Won't you sit down, Mr. Allen?" she suggested.

"I ain't got much time," he said, lowering himself into a chair. "I come up here, Crumb, to get some money." His cold, fishy eyes looked straight into Crumb's. "I come to get all the money there is comin' to me. It's a trifle over 10 thousand dollars, as I figure it."

"Yes," said Crumb; "that's about it."

"An' I don't want no stallin' this time, either," concluded Allen.

"Stalling!" exclaimed Crumb in a hurt tone. "Who's been stalling?"

"You have."

"Oh, my dear man!" cried Crumb deprecatingly. "You know that in matters of this kind, one must be circumspect. There were reasons in the past why it would have been unsafe to transfer so large an amount to you. It might easily have been traced. I was being watched — a fellow even shadowed me to the teller's window in my bank one day. You see how it is? Neither of us can take chances."

"That's alright, too," said Allen; "but I've been taking chances right along, and I ain't been taking them for my health. I been taking them for the coin, and I want that coin — I want it *pronto*!"

"You can most certainly have it," said Crumb.

"Alright!" replied Allen, extending a palm. "Fork it over."

"My dear fellow, you don't think that I have it here, do you?" demanded Crumb. "You don't think I keep such an amount as that in my home, I hope!

"Where is it?"

"In the bank, of course."

"Gimme a check."

"You must be crazy! Suppose either of us was suspected; that check would link us up fine. It would be as bad for you as for me. Nothing doing! I'll get the cash when the bank opens on Monday. That's the very best I can do. If you'd written and let me know you were coming, I could have had it for you."

Allen eyed him for a long minute. "Very well," he said, at last. "I'll wait till noon Monday."

Crumb breathed an inward sigh of profound relief.

"If you're at the bank Monday morning at half past ten, you'll get the money," he said. "How's the other stuff going? Sorry I couldn't handle that, but it's too bulky."

"The hooch? It's goin' fine," replied Allen. "Got a young high-blood at the edge of the valley handlin' it — fellow by the name of Evans. He moves 36 cases a week. The kid's got a good head on him — worked the whole scheme out himself. Sells the whole batch every week for cash to a guy with a big truck. They cover it with hay, and this guy hauls it right into the city in broad daylight, unloads it in a warehouse he's rented, slips each case into a carton labeled somebody-or-other's soap, and delivers it a case at a time to a bunch of drug stores. This second guy used to be a drug salesman, and he's personally acquainted with every grafter in the business."

As he talked, Allen had been studying the girl's face. She had noticed it before; but she was used to having men stare at her and thought little of it. Finally, he addressed her.

"Do you know, Miss de Lure," he said, "there's something mighty familiar about your face? I noticed it the first time I came here, and I been studyin' over it since. It seems like I'd known you somewhere else or someone you look a lot like; but I can't quite get it straight in my head. I can't make out where it was, or when, or if it was you or someone else. I'll get it someday, though."

"I don't know," she replied. "I'm sure I never saw you before you came here with Mr. Crumb the first time."

"Well, I don't know, either," replied Allen, scratching his head; "but it's mighty funny." He rose. "I'll be goin'," he said. "See you Monday at the bank — ten thirty sharp, Crumb!"

"Sure, ten thirty sharp," repeated Crumb, rising. "Oh, say, Allen, will you do me a favor? I promised a fellow I'd bring him a bindle of 'M' tonight, and if you'll hand it to him, it'll save me the trip. It's right on your way to the car line. You'll find him in the alley back of the Hollywood Drug Store just west of Cahuenga on the south side of Hollywood Boulevard."

"Sure, glad to accommodate," said Allen; "but how'll I know him?"

"He'll be standin' there, and you walk up and ask him the time. If he tells you and then asks if you can change a five, you'll know he's the guy alright. Then, you hand him these two ones and a 50 cent piece, and he hands you a five-dollar bill. That's all there is to it. Inside these two ones I'll wrap a bindle of 'M.' You can give me the five Monday morning when I see you."

"Slip me the junk," said Allen.

The girl had risen and was putting on her coat and hat.

"Where are you going — home so early?" asked Crumb.

"Yes," she replied. "I'm tired, and I want to write a letter."

"I thought you lived here," said Allen.

"I'm here nearly all day, but I go home nights," replied the girl.

Slick Allen looked puzzled as he left the bungalow.

"Goin' my way?" he asked of the girl as they reached the sidewalk.

"No," she replied. "I go in the opposite direction. Goodnight!"

"Goodnight!" said Allen and turned toward Hollywood Boulevard.

Inside the bungalow, Crumb was signaling central for a connection.

"Give me the police station on Cahuenga, near Hollywood," he said. "I haven't time to look up the number. Quick — it's important!"

There was a moment's silence and then:

"Hello! What is this? Listen! If you want to get a hophead with the goods on him — right in the act of peddling — send a dick to the back of the Hollywood Drug Store and have him wait there until a guy comes up and asks what time it is. Then have the dick tell him and say, 'Can you change a five?' That's the cue for the guy to slip him a bindle of morphine rolled up in a couple of one-dollar bills. If you don't send a dummy, he'll know what to do next — and you'd better get him there in a hurry. What? No — oh, just a friend — just a friend."

Wilson Crumb hung up the receiver. There was a grin on his face as he turned away from the instrument.

"It's too bad, Allen, but I'm afraid you won't be at the bank at half past 10 on Monday morning!" he said.

CHAPTER XII

AS GAZA DE LURE entered the house in which she roomed, her landlady came hastily from the living room.

"Is that you, Miss Burke?" she asked. "Here is a telegram that came for you just a few minutes ago. I do hope it's not bad news!"

The girl took the yellow envelope and tore it open. She read the message through very quickly and then again slowly, her brows puckered into a little frown as if she could not quite understand the meaning of the words she read.

"Your mother ill," the telegram said. "Possibly not serious — doctor thinks best you come — will meet you morning train." It was signed "Custer Pennington."

"I do hope it's not bad news," repeated the landlady.

"My mother is ill. They have sent for me," said the girl. "I wonder if you would be good enough to call up the SP and ask the first train I can get that stops at Ganado while I run upstairs and pack my bag?"

"You poor little dear!" exclaimed the landlady. "I'm so sorry! I'll call right away, and then I'll come up and help you."

A few minutes later, she came up to say that the first train left at nine o'clock in the morning. She offered to help pack, but the girl said there was nothing that she could not do herself.

"I must go out first for a few minutes," Gaza told her. "Then I will come back and finish packing the few things that it will be necessary to take."

When the landlady had left, the girl stood staring dully at the black traveling bag that she had brought from the closet and placed on her bed; but she did not see the bag or the few pieces of lingerie that she had taken from her dresser drawers. She saw only the sweet face of her mother and the dear smile that had always shone there to soothe each childish trouble — the smile that had lighted the girl's dark days even after she had left home.

For a long time, she stood there thinking — trying to realize what it would mean to her if the worst should come. It could make no difference, she realized, except that it might perhaps save her mother from a still greater sorrow. It was the girl who was dead, though the mother did not guess it; she had been dead for many months. This hollow, shaking husk was not Shannon Burke — it was not the thing that the mother had loved. It was almost a sacrilege to take it up there into the clean country and flaunt it in the face of so sacred a thing as mother love.

The girl stepped quickly to a writing desk and, drawing a key from her vanity case, unlocked it. She took from it a case containing a hypodermic syringe and a few small phials; then, she crossed the hall to the bathroom. When she came back, she looked rested and less nervous. She returned the things to the desk, locked it, and ran downstairs.

"I will be back in a few minutes," she called to the landlady. "I shall have to arrange a few things tonight with a friend."

She went directly to the Vista del Paso bungalow. Crumb was surprised and not a little startled as he heard her key in the door. He had a sudden vision of Allen returning, and he went white; but, when he saw who it was, he was no less surprised, for the girl had never before returned after leaving for the night.

"My gracious!" he exclaimed. "Look who's here!"

She did not return his smile.

"I found a telegram at home," she said, "that necessitates my going away for a few days. I came over to tell you and to get a little snow to last me until I come back. Where I am going they don't have it, I imagine."

He looked at her through narrowed, suspicious lids.

"You're going to quit me!" he cried accusingly. "That's why you went out with Allen! You can't get away with it. I'll never let you go. Do you hear me? I'll never let you go!"

"Don't be a fool, Wilson," she replied. "My mother is ill, and I have been sent for."

"Your mother? You never told me you had a mother."

"But I have, though I don't care to talk about her to you. She needs me, and I am going."

He was still suspicious.

"Are you telling me the truth? Will you come back?"

"You know I'll come back," she said. "I shall have to," she added with a weary sigh.

"Yes, you'll have to. You can't get along without it. You'll come back all right — I'll see to that!"

"What do you mean?" she asked.

"How much snow you got home?" he demanded.

"You know I keep scarcely any there. I forgot my case today — left it in my desk, so I had a little there — a couple of shots, maybe."

"Very well," he said. "I'll give you enough to last a week — then you'll have to come home."

"You say you'll give me enough to last a week?" the girl repeated questioningly. "I'll take what I want — it's as much mine as yours!"

"But you don't get any more than I'm going to give you. I won't have you gone more than a week. I can't live without you — don't you understand? I believe you have a wooden heart or none at all!"

"Oh," she said, yawning, "you can get some other poor fool to peddle it for you if I don't come back; but I'm coming, never fear. You're as bad as the snow — I hate you both, but I can't live without either of you. I don't feel like quarreling, Wilson. Give me the stuff — enough to last a week, for I'll be home before that."

He went to the bathroom and made a little package up for her.

"Here!" he said, returning to the living room. "That ought to last you a week."

She took it and slipped it into her case.

"Well, goodbye," she said, turning toward the door.

"Aren't you going to kiss me goodbye?" he asked

"Have I ever kissed you since I learned that you had a wife?" she asked.

"No," he admitted; "but you might kiss me goodbye now, when you're going away for a whole week."

"Nothing doing, Wilson!" she said with a negative shake of the head. "I'd as soon kiss a Gila monster!"

He made a wry face.

"You're sure candid," he said.

She shrugged her shoulders in a gesture of indifference and moved toward the door.

"I can't make you out, Gaza," he said. "I used to think you loved me, and the Lord knows I certainly love you! You are the only woman I ever really loved. A year ago, I believe you would have married me, but now you won't even let me kiss you. Sometimes, I think there is someone else. If I thought you loved another man, I'd — I'd —"

"No, you wouldn't. You were going to say that you'd kill me, but you wouldn't. You haven't the nerve of a rabbit. You needn't worry — there isn't any other man, and there never will be. After knowing you, I could never respect any man much less love one of 'em. You're all alike — rotten! And let me tell you something — I never did love you. I liked you at first before I knew the hideous thing that you had done to me. I would have married you, and I would have made you a good wife, too — you know that. I wish I could believe that you do love me. I know of nothing, Wilson, that would give me more pleasure than to *know* that you loved me madly; but, of course, you're not capable of loving anything madly except yourself."

"I do love you, Gaza," he said seriously. "I love you so that I would rather die than live without you."

She cocked her head on one side and eyed him quizzically.

"I hope you do," she told him; "for if it's the truth, I can repay you some measure of the suffering you have caused me. I can be around where you can never get a chance to forget me, or to forget the fact that you want me, but can never have me. You'll see me every day, and every day you will suffer vain regrets for the happiness that might have been yours if you had been a decent, honorable man; but you are not decent, you are not honorable, you are not even a man!"

He tried to laugh derisively, but she saw the slow red creep to his face and knew that she had scored.

"I hope you'll feel better when you come back from your mother's," he said. "You haven't been very good company lately. Oh, by the way, where did you say you are going?"

"I didn't say," she replied.

"Won't you give me your address?" he demanded.

"No."

"But suppose something happens? Suppose I want to get word to you?" Crumb insisted.

"You'll have to wait until I get back," she told him.

"I don't see why you can't tell me where you're going," he grumbled.

"Because there is a part of my life that you and your sort have never entered," she replied. "I would as soon take a physical leper to my mother as a moral one. I cannot even discuss her with you without a feeling that I have besmirched her."

On her face was an expression of unspeakable disgust as she passed through the doorway of the bungalow and closed the door behind her. Wilson Crumb simulated a shudder.

"I sure was a damn fool," he mused. "Gaza would have made the greatest emotional actress the screen has ever known if I'd given her a chance. I guessed her wrong and played her wrong. She's not like any woman I ever saw before. I should have made her a great success and won her gratitude — that's the way I ought to have played her. Oh, well, what's the difference? She'll come back!"

He rose and went to the bathroom, snuffed half a grain of cocaine, and then collected all the narcotics hidden there and every vestige of contributory evidence of their use by the inmates of the bungalow. Dragging a small table into his bedroom closet, he mounted it and opened a trap leading into the air space between the ceiling and the roof. Into this he clambered, carrying the drugs with him.

They were wrapped in a long, thin package to which a light, strong cord was attached. With this cord, he lowered the package into the space between the sheathing and the inner wall, fastening the end of the cord to a nail driven into one of the studs at arm's length below the wall plate.

"There!" he thought, as he clambered back into the closet. "It'll take some dick to uncover that junk!"

Hidden between plaster and sheathing of the little bungalow was a fortune in narcotics. Only a small fraction of their stock had the two peddlers kept in the bathroom, and Crumb had now removed that in case Allen should guess that he had been betrayed by his confederate and direct the police to the bungalow or the police themselves should trace his call and make an investigation on their own account. He realized that he had taken a great risk; but his stratagem had saved him from the deadly menace of Allen's vengeance, at least for the present. The fact that there must ultimately be an accounting with the man he put out of his mind. It would be time enough to meet that contingency when it arose.

As a matter of fact, the police came to the bungalow that very evening; but through no clue obtained from Allen, who, while he had suspicions that were tantamount to conviction, chose to await the time when he might wreak his revenge in his own way. The desk sergeant had traced the call to Crumb, and after the arrest had been made a couple of detective sergeants called upon him. They were quiet, pleasant-spoken men with an ingratiating way that might have deceived the possessor of a less suspicious brain than Crumb's.

"The lieutenant sent us over to thank you for that tip," said the spokesman. "We got him alright, with the junk on him."

Not for nothing was Wilson Crumb a talented actor. None there was who could better have registered polite and uninterested incomprehension.

"I am afraid," he said, "that I don't quite get you. What tip? What are you talking about?"

"You called up the station, Mr. Crumb. We had central trace the call. There is no use —"

Crumb interrupted him with a gesture. He didn't want the officer to go so far that it might embarrass him to retract.

"Ah!" he exclaimed, a light of understanding illuminating his face. "I believe I have it. What was the message? I think I can explain it."

"We think you can, too," agreed the sergeant, "seem you phoned the message."

"No, but I didn't," said Crumb, "although I guess it may have come over my phone alright. I'll tell you what I know about it. A car drove up a little while after dinner, and a man came to the door. He was a stranger. He asked if I had a phone and if he could use it. He said he wanted to phone an important and confidential message to his wife. He emphasized the 'confidential,' and there was nothing for me to do but go in the other room until he was through. He was only a minute or two talking, and then he called me. He wanted to pay for the use of the phone. I didn't hear what he said over the phone, but I guess that explains the matter. I'll be careful next time a stranger wants to use my phone."

"I would," said the sergeant dryly. "Would you know him if you saw him again?"

"I sure would," said Crumb.

They rose to go.

"Nice little place you have here," remarked one of them, looking around.

"Yes," said Crumb, "it is very comfortable. Wouldn't you like to look it over?"

"No," replied the officer. "Not now — maybe some other time."

Crumb grinned after he had closed the door behind them.

"I wonder," he mused, "if that was a threat or a prophecy!"

A week later Slick Allen was sentenced to a year in the county jail for having morphine in his possession.

CHAPTER XIII

AS SHANNON BURKE alighted from the Southern Pacific train at Ganado the following morning, a large, middle-aged man in riding clothes approached her.

"Is this Miss Burke?" he asked. "I am Colonel Pennington."

She noted that his face was grave, and it frightened her.

"Tell me about my mother," she said. "How is she?"

He put an arm about the girl's shoulders. "Come," he said. "Mrs. Pennington is waiting over at the car."

Her question was answered. Numb with dread and suffering, she crossed the station platform with him, the kindly, protecting arm still about her. Beside a closed car, a woman was standing. As they approached, she came forward, put her arms about the girl, and kissed her.

Seated in the tonneau between the colonel and Mrs. Pennington, the girl sought to steady herself. She had taken no morphine since the night before, for she had wanted to come to her mother "clean," as she would have expressed it. She realized now that it was a mistake, for she had the sensation of shattered nerves on the verge of collapse. Mastering all her resources, she fought for self-control with an effort that was almost physically noticeable.

"Tell me about it," she said at length in a low voice.

"It was very sudden," said the colonel. "It was a heart attack. Everything that possibly could be done in so short a time was done. Nothing would have changed the outcome, however. We had Dr. Jones of Los Angeles down — he motored down and arrived here about half an hour before the end. He told us that he could have done nothing."

They were silent for a while as the fast car rolled over the smooth road toward the hills ahead. Presently, it slowed down, turned in between orange trees, and stopped before a tiny bungalow a hundred yards from the highway.

"We thought you would want to come here first of all, dear," said Mrs. Pennington. "Afterward we are going to take you home with us."

They accompanied her to the tiny living room where they introduced her to the housekeeper and to the nurse who had remained at Colonel Pennington's request. Then, they opened the door of a sunny bedroom and, closing it after her as she entered, left her alone with her dead.

Beyond the thin panels they could hear her sobbing; but when she emerged fifteen minutes later, though her eyes were red, she was not crying. They thought then that she had marvelous self-control; but could they have known the hideous battle that she was fighting against grief and the insistent craving for morphine and the raw, taut nerves that would give her no peace and the shattered will that begged only to be allowed to sleep — could they have known all this, they would have realized that they were witnessing a miracle.

They led her back to the car where she sat with wide eyes staring straight ahead. She wanted to scream, to tear her clothing, to do anything but sit there quiet and rigid. The short drive to Ganado seemed to the half-mad girl to occupy hours. She saw nothing, not even the quiet, restful ranch house as the car swung up the hill and stopped at the north entrance. In her mind's eye was nothing but the face of her dead mother and the little black case in her traveling bag.

The colonel helped her from the car and a sweet-faced young girl came and put her arms about her and kissed her, as Mrs. Pennington had done at the station.

In a dazed sort of way, Shannon understood that they were telling her the girl's name — that she was a daughter of the Penningtons. The girl accompanied the visitor to the rooms she was to occupy.

Shannon wished to be alone — she wanted to get at the black case in the traveling bag. Why didn't the girl go away? She wanted to take her by the shoulders and throw her out of the room; yet outwardly she was calm and self-possessed.

Very carefully, she turned toward the girl. It required a supreme effort not to tremble and to keep her voice from rising to a scream.

"Please," she said, "I should like to be alone."

"I understand," said the girl and left the room, closing the door behind her.

Shannon crept stealthily to the door and turned the key in the lock. Then she wheeled and almost fell upon the traveling bag in her eagerness to get the small black case within it. She was trembling from head to foot, her eyes were wide and staring, and she mumbled to herself as she prepared the white powder and drew the liquid into the syringe.

Momentarily, however, she gathered herself together. For a few seconds, she stood looking at the glass and metal instrument in her fingers — beyond it she saw her mother's face.

"I don't want to do it," she sobbed. "I don't want to do it, mother!"

Her lower lip quivered, and tears came. "My God, I can't help it!" Almost viciously she plunged the needle beneath her skin. "I didn't want to do it today, of all days, with you lying over there all alone — dead!"

She threw herself across the bed and broke into uncontrolled sobbing; but her nerves were relaxed, and the expression of her grief was normal. Finally she sobbed herself to sleep, for she had not slept at all the night before.

It was afternoon when she awoke, and again she felt the craving for a narcotic. This time she did not fight it. She had lost the battle — why renew it? She bathed and dressed and took another shot before leaving her rooms — a guest suite on the second floor. She descended the stairs, which opened directly into the patio, and almost ran against a tall, broad-shouldered young man in flannel shirt and riding breeches with boots and spurs. He stepped quickly back.

"Miss Burke, I believe?" he inquired. "I am Custer Pennington."

"Oh, it was you who wired me," she said.

"No — that was my father."

"I am afraid I did not thank him for all his kindness. I must have seemed very ungrateful."

"Oh, no, indeed, Miss Burke," he said, with a quick smile of sympathy. "We all understand, perfectly — you have suffered a severe nervous shock. We just want to help you all we can, and we are sorry that there is so little we can do."

"I think you have done a great deal, already, for a stranger."

"Not a stranger exactly," he hastened to assure her. "We were all so fond of your mother that we feel that her daughter can scarcely be considered a stranger. She was a very lovable woman, Miss Burke — a very fine woman."

Shannon felt tears in her eyes and turned them away quickly. Very gently, he touched her arm.

"Mother heard you moving about in your rooms, and she has gone over to the kitchen to make some tea for you. If you will come with me, I'll show you to the breakfast room. She'll have it ready in a jiffy."

She followed him through the living room and the library to the dining room beyond which a small breakfast room looked out toward the peaceful hills. Young Pennington opened a door leading from the dining room to the butler's pantry and called to his mother.

"Miss Burke is down," he said.

The girl turned immediately from the breakfast room and entered the butler's pantry.

"Can't I help, Mrs. Pennington? I don't want you to go to any trouble for me. You have all been so good already!"

Mrs. Pennington laughed.

"Bless your heart, dear, it's no trouble. The water is boiling, and Hannah has made some toast. We were just waiting to ask if you prefer green tea or black."

"Green, if you please," said Shannon, coming into the kitchen.

Custer had followed her and was leaning against the door frame.

"This is Hannah, Miss Burke," said Mrs. Pennington.

"I am so glad to know you, Hannah," said the girl. "I hope you won't think me a terrible nuisance."

"Hannah's a brick," interposed the young man. "You can muss around her kitchen all you want, and she never gets mad."

"I'm sure she doesn't," agreed Shannon; "but people who are late to meals *are* a nuisance, and I promise that I shan't be again. I fell asleep."

"You may change your mind about being late to meals when you learn the hour we breakfast," laughed Custer.

"No — I shall be on time."

"You shall stay in bed just as late as you please," said Mrs. Pennington. "You mustn't think of getting up when we do. You need all the rest you can get."

They seemed to take it for granted that Shannon was going to stay with them instead of going to the little bungalow that had been her mother's — the truest type of hospitality because, requiring no oral acceptance, it suggested no obligation.

"But I cannot impose on you so much," she said. "After dinner I must go down to — to —"

Mrs. Pennington did not permit her to finish. "No, dear," she said, quietly but definitely. "You are to stay here with us until you return to the city. Colonel Pennington has arranged with the nurse to remain with your mother's housekeeper until after the funeral. Please let us have our way. It will be so much easier for you, and it will let us feel that we have been able to do something for you."

Shannon could not have refused if she had wished to, but she did not wish to. In the quiet ranch house, surrounded by these strong, kindly people, she found a restfulness and a feeling of security that she had not believed she was ever to experience again. She had these thoughts when, under the influence of morphine, her nerves were quieted and her brain clear. After the effects had worn off, she became restless and irritable. She thought of Crumb then, and of the bungalow on the Vista del Paso with its purple monkeys stenciled over the patio gate. She wanted to be back where she could be free to do as she pleased — free to sink again into the most degrading and abject slavery that human vice has ever devised.

The Girl from Hollywood / 95

On the first night, after she had gone to her rooms, the Penningtons, gathered in the little family living room, discussed her as people are wont to discuss a stranger beneath their roof.

"Isn't she radiant?" demanded Eva. "She's the most beautifulest creature I ever saw!"

"She looks much as her mother must have looked at the same age," commented the colonel. "There is a marked family resemblance."

"She *is* beautiful," agreed Mrs. Pennington; "but I venture to say that she is looking her worst right now. She doesn't appear at all well to me. Her complexion is very sallow, and sometimes there is the strangest expression in her eyes — almost wild. The nervous shock of her mother's death must have been very severe; but she bears up wonderfully, at that, and she is so sweet and appreciative!"

"I sized her up over there in the kitchen today," said Custer. "She's the real article. I can always tell by the way people treat a servant whether they are real people or only counterfeit. She was as sweet and natural to Hannah as she is to mother."

"I noticed that," said his mother. "It is one of the hallmarks of good breeding; but we could scarcely expect anything else of Mrs. Burke's daughter. I know she must be a fine character."

In the room above them, Shannon Burke, with trembling hands and staring eyes, was inserting a slender needle beneath the skin above her hip. In the movies, one does not disfigure one's arms or legs.

CHAPTER XIV

THE DAY OF THE FUNERAL had come and gone. It had been a very hard one for Shannon. She had determined that on this day, at least, she would not touch the little hypodermic syringe. She owed that much respect to the memory of her mother. And she had fought — God, how she had fought! — with screaming nerves that would not be quiet, with trembling muscles, and with a brain that held but a single thought — morphine, morphine, morphine!

She tried to shut the idea from her mind. She tried to concentrate her thoughts upon the real anguish of her heart. She tried to keep before her a vision of her mother; but her hideous, resistless vice crowded all else from her brain, and the result was that on the way back from the cemetery, she collapsed into screaming, incoherent hysteria.

They carried her to her room — Custer Pennington carried her, his father and mother following. When the men had left, Mrs. Pennington and Eva undressed her and comforted her and put her to bed; but she still screamed and sobbed — frightful, racking sobs, without tears. She was trying to tell them to go away. How she hated them! If they would only go away and leave her! But she could not voice the words she sought to scream at them, and so they stayed and ministered to her as best they could. After a while she lost consciousness, and they thought that she was asleep and left her.

Perhaps she did sleep, for later, when she opened her eyes, she lay very quiet and felt rested and almost normal. She knew, though, that she was not entirely awake — that when full wakefulness came the terror would return unless she quickly had recourse to the little needle.

In that brief moment of restfulness she thought quickly and clearly and very fully of what had just happened. She had never had such an experience before. Perhaps she had never fully realized the frightful hold the drug had upon her. She had known that she could not stop — or, at least, she had said that she knew; but whether she had any conception of the pitiful state to which enforced abstinence would reduce her is to be doubted. Now she knew, and she was terribly frightened.

"I must cut it down," she said to herself. "I must have been hitting it up a little too strong. When I get home, I'll let up gradually until I can manage with three or four shots a day."

When she came down to dinner that night, they were all surprised to see her, for they had thought her still asleep. Particularly were they surprised to see no indications of her recent breakdown. How could they know that she had just taken enough morphine to have killed any one of them? She seemed normal and composed, and she tried to infuse a little gayety into her conversation, for she realized that her grief was not theirs. She knew that their kind hearts shared something of her sorrow, but it was selfish to impose her own sadness upon them.

She had been thinking very seriously, had Shannon Burke. The attack of hysteria had jarred her loose, temporarily at least, from the selfish rut that her habit and her hateful life with Crumb had worn for her. She recalled every emotion of the ordeal through which she had passed, even to the thoughts of hate that she had held for those two sweet women at the table with her. How could she have hated them? She hated herself for the thought.

She compared herself with them, and a dull flush mounted to her cheek. She was not fit to remain under the same roof with them, and here she was sitting at their table, a respected guest! What if they should learn of the thing she was? The thought terrified her; and yet, she talked on, oftentimes gaily, joining with them in the laughter that was a part of every meal.

She really saw them, that night, as they were. It was the first time that her grief and her selfish vice had permitted her to study them. It was her first understanding glimpse of a family life that was as beautiful as her own life was ugly.

As she compared herself with the women, she compared Crumb with these two men. They might have vices — they were strong men, and few strong men are without vices, she knew — but she was sure they were the vices of strong men, which, by comparison with those of Wilson Crumb, would become virtues. What a pitiful creature Crumb seemed beside these two with his insignificant mentality and his petty egotism!

Suddenly it came to her, almost as a shock, that she had to leave this beautiful place and go back to the sordid life that she shared with Crumb. Her spirit revolted, but she knew that it must be. She did not belong here — her vice must ever bar her from such men and women as these. The memory of them would haunt her always, making her punishment the more poignant to the day of her death.

That evening she and Colonel Pennington discussed her plans for the future. She had asked him about disposing of the orchard — how she should proceed and what she might ask for it.

"I should advise you to hold it," he said. "It is going to increase in value tremendously in the next few years. You can easily get someone to work it for you on shares. If you don't want to live on it, Custer and I will be glad to keep an eye on it and see that it is properly cared for; but why don't you stay here? You could really make a very excellent living from it. Besides, Miss Burke, here in the country you can really *live*. You city people don't know what life is."

"There!" said Eva. "Popsy has started. If he had his way, we'd all have to move to the city to escape the maddening crowd. He'd move the maddening crowd into the country!"

"It may be that Shannon doesn't care for the country," suggested Mrs. Pennington. "There *are* such foolish people," she added, laughing.

"Oh, I would love the country!" exclaimed Shannon.

"Then why don't you stay?" urged the colonel.

"I had never thought of it," she said hesitatingly.

It was indeed a new idea. Of course, it was an absolute impossibility, but it was a very pleasant thing to contemplate.

"Possibly Miss Burke has ties in the city that she would not care to break," suggested Custer, noting her hesitation.

Ties in the city! Shackles of iron, rather, she thought bitterly; but, oh, it was such a nice thought! To live here, to see these people daily, perhaps be one of them, to be like them — ah, that would be heaven!

"Yes," she said, "I have ties in the city. I could not remain here, I am afraid, much as I should like to. I —? I think I had better sell."

"Rubbish!" exclaimed the colonel. "You'll not sell. You are going to stay here with us until you are thoroughly rested, and then you won't want to sell."

"I wish that I might," she said; "but —"

"But nothing!" interrupted the colonel. "You are not well, and I shan't permit you to leave until those cheeks are the color of Eva's."

He spoke to her as he might have spoken to one of his children. She had never known a father, and it was the first time that any man had talked to her in just that way. It brought the tears to her eyes — tears of happiness, for every woman wants to feel that she belongs to some man — a father, a brother, or a husband — who loves her well enough to order her about for her own good.

"I shall have to think it over," she said. "It means so much to me to have you all want me to stay! Please don't think that I don't want to; but — but — there are so many things to consider, and I want to stay so very, very much!"

"All right," said the colonel. "It's decided — you stay. Now run off to bed, for you're going to ride with us in the morning, and that means that you'll have to be up at half past five."

"But I can't ride," she said. "I don't know how, and I have nothing to wear."

"Eva'll fit you out, and as for not knowing how to ride, you can't learn any younger. Why, I've taught half the children in the foothills to ride a horse, and a lot of the grown-ups. What I can't teach you, Cus and Eva can. You're going to start in tomorrow, my little girl, and learn how to live. Nobody who has simply survived the counterfeit life of the city knows anything about living. You wait — we'll show you!"

She smiled up into his face.

"I suppose I shall have to mind you," she said. "I imagine everyone does."

Seated in an easy chair in her bedroom, she stared at the opposite wall. The craving that she was seldom without was growing in intensity, for she had been without morphine since before dinner. She got up, unlocked her bag, and took out the little black case. She opened it and counted the powders remaining. She had used half her supply — she could stay but three or four days longer at the outside; and the colonel wanted her to stay until her cheeks were like Eva's!

She rose and looked in the mirror. How sallow she was! Something — she did not know what — had kept her from using rouge here. During the first days of her grief, she had not even thought of it, and then, after that evening at dinner, she knew that she could not use it here. It was a make-believe, a sham, which didn't harmonize with these people or the life they led — a clean, real life, in which any form of insincerity had no place. She knew that they were broad people, both cultured and traveled, and so she could not understand why it was that she felt that the harmless vanity of rouge might be distasteful to them. Indeed, she guessed that it would not. It was something fine in herself, long suppressed, seeking expression.

It was this same thing, perhaps, that had caused her to refuse a cigarette that Custer had offered her after dinner. The act indicated that they were accustomed to having women smoke there, as women nearly everywhere smoke today; but she had refused, and she was glad she had, for she noticed that neither Mrs. Pennington nor Eva smoked. Such women didn't have to smoke to be attractive to men. She had smoked in her room several times, for that habit, too, had a strong hold on her; but she had worked assiduously to remove the telltale stains from her fingers.

"I wonder," she mused, looking at the black case, "if I could get through the night without you! It would give me a few more hours here if I could — a few more hours of life before I go back to *that*!"

Until midnight she fought her battle — a losing battle — tossing and turning in her bed; but she did her best before she gave up in defeat — no, not quite defeat; let us call it compromise, for the dose she took was only half as much as she ordinarily allowed herself. The three-hour fight and the half dose meant a partial victory, for it gained for her, she estimated, an additional six hours.

At a quarter before six, she was awakened by a knock on her door. It was already light, and she awoke with mingled surprise that she had slept so well and vague forebodings of the next hour or two, for she was unaccustomed to horses and a little afraid of them.

"Who is it?" she asked as the knock was repeated.

"Eva. I've brought your riding things."

Shannon rose and opened the door. She was going to take the things from the girl, but the latter bounced into the room, fresh and laughing.

"Come on!" she cried. "I'll help you. Just pile your hair up anyhow — it doesn't matter — this hat'll cover it. I think these breeches will fit you — we are just about the same size; but I don't know about the boots — they may be a little large. I didn't bring any spurs — Papa won't let anyone wear spurs until they ride fairly well. You'll have to win your spurs, you see! It's a beautiful morning — just spiffy! Run in and wash up a bit. I'll arrange everything, and you'll be in 'em in a jiffy."

She seized Shannon around the waist and danced off toward the bathroom.

"Don't be long," she admonished as she returned to the dressing room from where she laid down a barrage of conversation before the bathroom.

Shannon washed quickly. She was excited at the prospect of the ride. That and the laughing, talking girl in the adjoining room gave her no time to think. Her mind was fully occupied, and her nerves were stimulated. For the moment, she forgot about morphine, and then it was too late, for Eva had her by the hand and she was being led, almost at a run, down the stairs, through the patio, and out over the edge of the hill down toward the stable.

At first, the full-foliaged umbrella trees through which the walk wound concealed the stable and corrals at the foot of the hill, but presently they broke upon her view, and she saw the horses saddled and waiting, and the other members of the family. The colonel and Mrs. Pennington were already mounted. Custer and a stableman held two horses while the fifth was tied to a ring in the stable wall. It was a pretty picture — the pawing horses with arched necks eager to be away; the happy, laughing people in their picturesque and unconventional riding clothes; the new day upon the nearer hills; the haze upon the farther mountains.

"Fine!" cried the colonel, as he saw her coming. "Really never thought you'd do it! I'll wager this is the earliest you have been up in many a day. 'Barbarous hour'— that's what you're saying. Why, when my cousin was on here from New York, he was really shocked — said it wasn't decent. Come along — we're late this morning. You'll ride Baldy — Custer'll help you up."

She stepped to the mounting block as the young man led the dancing Baldy close beside it.

"Ever ridden much?" he asked.

"Never in my life."

"Take the reins in your left hand — so. Like this — lefthand rein coming in under your little finger, the other between your first and second fingers, and the bight out between your first finger and thumb — there, that's it. Face your horse, put your left hand on the horn, and your right hand on the cantle — this is the cantle back here. That's the ticket. Now, put your left foot in the stirrup and stand erect — no, don't lean forward over the saddle — good! Swing your right leg, knee bent, over the cantle, at the same time lifting your right hand. When you come down, ease yourself into the saddle by closing on the horse with your knees — that takes the jar off both of you. Ride with a light rein. If you want him to slow down or stop, pull him in — don't jerk."

He was holding Baldy close to the bit as he helped her and explained. He saw that her right foot found the stirrup and that she had the reins properly gathered, and then he released the animal. Immediately, Baldy began to curvet, raising both fore feet simultaneously and, as they were coming down, raising his hind feet together so that all four were off the ground at once.

Shannon was terrified. Why had they put her on a bucking horse? They knew she couldn't ride. It was cruel!

But she sat there with tight-pressed lips and uttered no sound. She recalled every word that Custer had said to her, and she did not jerk, though some almost irresistible power urged her to. She just pulled, and as she pulled, she glanced about to see if they were rushing to her rescue. Great was her surprise when she discovered that no one was paying much attention to her or to the mad actions of her terrifying mount.

Suddenly it dawned upon her that she had neither fallen off nor come near falling off. She had not even lost a stirrup. As a matter of fact, the motion was not even uncomfortable. It was enjoyable, and she was in about as much danger of being thrown as she would have been from a rocking chair as violently self-agitated. She laughed then, and in the instant, all fear left her.

She saw Eva mount from the ground and noted that the stableman was not even permitted to hold her restive horse much less to assist her in any other way. Custer swung to the saddle with the ease of long habitude. The colonel reined to her side.

"We'll let them go ahead," he said, "and I'll give you your first lesson. Then I'll turn you over to Custer — he and Eva can put on the finishing touches."

"He wants to see that you're started right," called the younger man, laughing.

"Popsy just wants to add another feather to his cap," said Eva. "Someday he'll 'point with pride' and say, 'Look at her ride! I gave her her first lesson.'"

"Here come Mrs. Evans and Guy!"

As Mrs. Pennington spoke, they saw two horses rounding the foot of the hill at a brisk canter, their riders waving a cheery long-distance greeting.

That first morning ride with the Penningtons and their friends was an event in the life of Shannon Burke that assumed the proportions of adventure. The novelty, the thrill, the excitement filled her every moment. The dancing horse beneath her seemed to impart to her a full measure of its buoyant life. The gay laughter of her companions, the easy fellowship of young and old, the generous sympathy that made her one of them gave her but another glimpse of the possibilities for happiness that requires no artificial stimulus.

She loved the hills. She loved the little trail winding through the leafy tunnel of a cool barranco. She loved the thrill of the shelving hillside where the trail clung precariously in its ascent toward some low summit. She tingled with the new life and a new joy as they broke into a gallop along a grassy ridge.

Custer, in the lead, reined in, raising his hand in signal for them all to stop.

"Look, Miss Burke," he said, pointing toward a near hillside. "There's a coyote. Thought maybe you'd never seen one on his native heath."

"Shoot it! Shoot it!" cried Eva. "You poor boob, why don't you shoot it?"

"Baldy's gun shy," he explained.

"Oh!" said Eva. "Yes, of course — I forgot"

"One of the things you do best," returned Custer loftily.

"I was just going to say that you were not a boob at all, but now I won't!"

Shannon watched the gray, wolfish animal turn and trot off dejectedly until it disappeared among the brush; but she was not thinking of the coyote. She was considering the thoughtfulness of a man who could remember to forego a fair shot at a wild animal because one of the horses in his party was gun shy and was ridden by a woman unaccustomed to riding. She wondered if this was an index to young Pennington's character — so different from the men she had known. It bespoke a general attitude toward women with which she was unfamiliar — a protective instinct that was chiefly noticeable in the average city man by its absence.

The Girl from Hollywood / 105

Interspersed with snatches of conversation and intervening silences were occasional admonitions directed at her by the colonel, instructing her to keep her feet parallel to the horse's sides, not to lean forward, to keep her elbows down and her left forearm horizontal.

"I never knew there was so much to riding!" she exclaimed, laughingly. "I thought you just got on a horse and rode, and that was all there was to it."

"That *is* all there is to it to most of the people you see riding rented horses around Los Angeles," Colonel Pennington told her. "It is all there can ever be to the great majority of people anywhere. Horsemanship is inherent in some; by others, it can never be acquired. It is an art."

"Like dancing," suggested Eva.

"And thinking," said Custer. "Lots of people can go through the motions of riding, or dancing, or thinking, without ever achieving any one of them."

"I can't even go through the motions of riding," said Shannon ruefully.

"All you need is practice," said the colonel. "I can tell a born rider in half an hour, even if he's never been on a horse before in his life. You're one."

"I'm afraid you're making fun of me. The saddle keeps coming up and hitting me, and I never see any of you move from yours."

Guy Evans was riding close to her.

"No, he's not making fun of you," he whispered, leaning closer to Shannon. "The colonel has paid you one of the greatest compliments in his power to bestow. He always judges people first by their morals and then by their horsemanship; but if they are good horsemen, he can make generous allowance for minor lapses in their morals."

They both laughed.

"He's a dear, isn't he?" said the girl.

"He and Custer are the finest men I ever knew," replied the boy eagerly.

That ride ended in a rushing gallop along a quarter mile of straight road leading to the stables where they dismounted, flushed, breathless, and laughing. As they walked up the winding concrete walk toward the house, Shannon Burke was tired, lame, and happy. She had adventured into a new world and found it good.

"Come into my room and wash," said Eva as they entered the patio. "We're late for breakfast now, and we all like to sit down together."

For just an instant, and for the first time that morning, Shannon thought of the hypodermic needle in its blade case upstairs. She hesitated and then resolutely turned into Eva's room.

CHAPTER XV

DURING THE HOUR following breakfast that morning, while Shannon was alone in her rooms, the craving returned. The thought of it turned her sick when she felt it coming. She had been occupying herself making her bed and tidying the room as she had done each morning since her arrival; but when that was done, her thoughts reverted by habit to the desire that had so fatally mastered her.

While she was riding, she had had no opportunity to think of anything but the thrill of the new adventure. At breakfast, she had been very hungry for the first time in many months; and this new appetite for food and the gay conversation of the breakfast table had given her nerves no chance to assert their craving. Now that she was alone and unoccupied, the terrible thing clutched at her again.

Once again, she fought the fight that she had fought so many times of late — the fight that she knew she was ordained to lose before she started fighting. She longed to win it so earnestly that her defeat was the more pitiable. She was eager to prolong this new-found happiness to the uttermost limit. Though she knew that it must end when her supply of morphine was gone, she was determined to gain a few hours each day in order that she might add at least another happy day to her life. Again, she took but half her ordinary allowance; but with what anguished humiliation she performed the hated and repulsive act. Always had she loathed the habit, but never had it seemed nearly so disgusting as when performed amid these cleanly and beautiful surroundings under the same roof with such people as the Penningtons.

There crept into her mind a thought that had found its way there more than once before during the past two years the thought of self-destruction. She put it away from her; but in the depth of her soul, she knew that never before had it taken so strong a hold upon her. Her mother, her only tie, was gone, and no one would care. She had looked into heaven and found that it was not for her. She had no future except to return to the hideous existence of the Hollywood bungalow and her lonely boarding house and to the hated Crumb.

It was then that Eva Pennington called her.

"I am going to walk up to the Berkshires," she said. "Come along with me!"

"The Berkshires!" exclaimed Shannon. "I thought they were in New England."

She was descending the stairs toward Eva, who stood at the foot, holding open the door that led into the patio. She welcomed the interruption that had broken in upon her morbid thoughts. The sight of the winsome figure smiling up at her dispelled them as the light of the sun sweeps away miasmatic vapors.

"In New England?" repeated Eva. Her brows puckered, and then suddenly she broke into a merry laugh. "I meant pigs, not hills!"

Shannon laughed, too. How many times she had laughed that day — and it was yet far from noon. Close as was the memory of her mother's death, she could laugh here with no consciousness of irreverence — rather, perhaps, with the conviction that she was best serving the ideals that had been dear to that mother by giving and accepting happiness when opportunity offered it.

"I'm only sorry it's not the hills," she said; "for that would mean walking, walking, walking — doing something in the open, away from people who live in cities and who can find no pleasures outside four walls."

Shannon's manner was tense, her voice had suddenly become serious. The younger girl looked up at her with an expression of mild surprise.

"My gracious!" cried Eva. "You're getting almost as bad as Popsy, and you've been here only half a week; but how radiant, if you really love it!"

"I do love it, dear, though I didn't mean to be quite so tragic; but the thought that I shall have to go away and can never enjoy it again *is* tragic."

"I hope you won't have to go," said Eva simply, slipping an arm about the other's waist. "We all hope that you won't have to."

They walked down the hill, past the saddle-horse barn, and along the graveled road that led to the upper end of the ranch. The summer sun beat hotly upon them, making each old sycamore and oak and walnut a delightful oasis of refreshing shade. In a field at their left, two mowers were clicking merrily through lush alfalfa. At their right, beyond the pasture fence, gentle Guernseys lay in the shade of a wide-spreading sycamore, a part of the pastoral allegory of content that was the Rancho del Ganado; and over all were the blue California sky and the glorious sun.

"Isn't it wonderful?" breathed Shannon, half to herself. "It makes one feel that there cannot be a care or sorrow in all the world!"

They soon reached the pens and houses where sleek, black Berkshires dozed in every shaded spot. Then they wandered farther up the cañon into the pasture where the great brood sows sprawled beneath the sycamores or wallowed in a concrete pool shaded by overhanging boughs. Eva stooped now and then to stroke a long, deep side.

"How clean they are!" exclaimed Shannon. "I thought pigs were dirty."

"They are when they are kept in dirty places — the same as people."

"They don't smell badly; even the pens didn't smell of pig. All I noticed was a heavy, sweet odor. What was it — something they feed them?"

Eva laughed.

"It was the pigs themselves. The more you know pigs, the better you love 'em. They're radiant creatures!"

"You dear! You love everything, don't you?"

"Pretty nearly everything, except prunes and washing dishes."

They swung up then through the orange grove and along the upper road back toward the house. It was noon and lunch time when they arrived. Shannon was hot and tired and dusty and delighted as she opened the door at the foot of the stairs that led up to her rooms above.

There she paused. The old, gripping desire had seized her. She had not once felt it since she had passed through that door more than two hours before. For a moment, she hesitated, and then, fearfully, she turned toward Eva.

"May I clean up in your room?" she asked.

There was a strange note of appeal in Shannon's voice that the other girl did not understand.

"Why, certainly," she said; "but is there anything the matter? You are not ill?"

"Just a little tired."

"There! I should never have walked you so far. I'm so sorry!"

"I want to be tired. I want to do it again this afternoon — all afternoon. I don't want to stop until I am ready to drop!"

Then, seeing the surprise in Eva's expression, she added: "You see, I shall be here such a short time that I want to crowd every single moment full of pleasant memories."

Shannon thought that she had never eaten so much before as she had that morning at breakfast; but at luncheon she more than duplicated her past performance. There was cold chicken — delicious Rhode Island Reds raised on the ranch; there was a salad of homegrown tomatoes — firm, deep-red beauties — and lettuce from the garden; Hannah's bread, with butter fresh from the churn, and tall, cool pitchers filled with rich Guernsey milk; and then a piece of Hannah's famous apple pie with cream so thick that it would scarce pour.

"My!" Shannon exclaimed at last. "I have seen the pigs and I have become one."

"And I see something, dear," said Mrs. Pennington, smiling.

"What?"

"Some color in your cheeks."

"Not *really*!" she cried, delighted.

"Yes, really."

"And it's mighty becoming," offered the colonel. "Nothing like a brown skin and rosy cheeks for beauty. That's the way God meant girls to be, or He wouldn't have given 'em delicate skins and hung the sun up there to beautify 'em. Here, He's gone to a lot of trouble to fit up the whole world as a beauty parlor, and what do women do? They go and find some stuffy little shop poked away where the sun never reaches it and pay some other woman who knows nothing about art to paint a mean imitation of a complexion on their poor skins. They wouldn't think of hanging a chromo in their living rooms; but they wear one on their faces when the greatest Artist of them all is ready and willing to paint a masterpiece there for nothing!"

"Popsy should have been a poet."

"Or an ad writer for a cosmetic manufacturer," suggested Custer. "Oh, by the way, not changing the subject or anything, but did you hear about Slick Allen?"

No, they had not. Shannon pricked up her ears, metaphorically. What did these people know of Slick Allen?

"He's just been sent up in L.A. for having narcotics in his possession. Got a year in the county jail."

"I guess he was a bad one," commented the colonel; "but he never struck me as being a drug addict."

"Nor me; but I guess you can't always tell them," said Custer.

"It must be a terrible habit," said Mrs. Pennington.

"It's about as low as anyone can sink," said Custer.

"I hear that there's been a great increase in it since prohibition," remarked the colonel. "Personally, I'd have more respect for a whisky drunkard than for a drug addict; or perhaps I should better say that I'd feel less disrespect. A police official told me not long ago at a dinner in town that if drug-taking continues to increase as it has recently, it will constitute a national menace by comparison with which the whisky evil will seem paltry."

Shannon Burke was glad when they rose from the table, putting an end to the conversation. She had plumbed the uttermost depths of humiliation. She had felt herself go hot and cold in shame and fear. At first, her one thought had been to get away —

to find some excuse for leaving the Penningtons at once. If they knew the truth, what would they think of her? Not because of her habit alone, but because she had imposed upon their hospitality in the guise of decency, knowing that she was unclean, and practicing her horrid vice beneath their very roof; associating with their daughter and bringing them all in contact with her moral leprosy.

She was hastening to her room to pack. She knew there was an evening train for the city, and while she packed, she could be framing some plausible excuse for leaving thus abruptly.

Custer Pennington called to her.

"Miss Burke!"

She turned, her hand upon the knob of the door to the upstairs suite.

"I'm going to ride over the back ranch this afternoon. Eva showed you the Berkshires this morning; now I want to show you the Herefords. I told the stableman to saddle Baldy for you. Will half an hour be too soon?"

He was standing in the north arcade of the patio a few yards from her waiting for her reply. How fine and straight and clean he was! If fate had been less unkind, she might have been worthy of the friendship of such a man as he.

Worthy? Was she unworthy, then? She had been just as fine and clean as Custer Pennington until a beast had tricked her into shame. She had not knowingly embraced a vice. It had already claimed her before she knew it for what it was. Must she then forego all hope of happiness because of a wrong of which she herself was innocent?

She wanted to go with Custer. Another day would make no difference, for the Penningtons would never know. How could they? By what chance might they ever connect Shannon Burke with Gaza de Lure? She well knew that her screen days were over, and there was no slightest likelihood that any of these people would be introduced into the bungalow on the Vista del Paso. Who could begrudge her just this little afternoon of happiness before she went back to Crumb?

"Don't tell me you don't want to come," cried Custer. "I won't take no for an answer!"

"Oh, but I do want to come — ever so much! I'll be down in just a minute. Why wait half an hour?"

She was in her room no more than five minutes, and during that time she sought bravely to efface all thought of the little black case; but with diabolic pertinacity it constantly obtruded itself, and with it came the gnawing hunger of nerves starving for a narcotic.

"I won't!" she cried, stamping her foot. "I won't! I won't!"

If only she could get away from the room before she succumbed to the mounting temptation, she was sure that she could fight it off for the rest of the afternoon. She had gained that much, at least; but she must keep occupied, constantly occupied, where she could not have access to it or see the black case in which she kept the morphine.

She triumphed by running away from it. She almost hurled herself down the stairs and into the patio. Custer Pennington was not there. She must find him before the craving dragged her back to the rooms above. Already she could feel her will weakening. It was the old, old story that she knew so well.

"What's the use?" the voice of the tempter asked. "Just a little one! It will make you feel so much better. What's the use?"

She turned toward the door again; she had her hand upon the knob, and then she swung back and called him. "Mr. Pennington!"

If he did not hear, she knew that she would go up into her rooms defeated.

"Coming!" he answered from beyond the arched entrance of the patio, and then he stepped into view.

She almost ran to him.

"Was I very long?" she asked. "Did I keep you waiting?"

"Why, you've scarcely been gone any time at all," he replied.

"Let's hurry," she said breathlessly. "I don't want to miss any of it!"

He wondered why she should be so much excited at the prospect of a ride into the hills, but it pleased him that she was, and it flattered him a little, too. He began to be a little enthusiastic over the trip, which he had planned only as part of the generous policy of the family to keep Shannon occupied so that she might not brood too sorrowfully over her loss.

114 \ Edgar Rice Burroughs

And Shannon was pleased because of her victory. She was too honest at heart to attempt to deceive herself into thinking that it was any great triumph; but even to have been strong enough to have run away from the enemy was something. She did not hope that it augured any permanent victory for the future, for she did not believe that such a thing was possible. She knew that scarce three in a hundred slaves of morphine definitely cast off their bonds this side of the grave, and she had gone too far to be one of the three. If she could keep going forever as she had that day, she might do it; but that, of course, was impossible. There must be hours when she would be alone with nothing to do but think, think, think, and what would she think about? Always the same things — the little white powder and the peace and rest that it would give her.

Custer watched her as she mounted, holding Baldy beside the block for her, and again, he was pleased to note that she did not neglect a single detail of the instructions he had given her.

"Some girl, this!" the young man soliloquized mentally.

He knew she must be at least a little lame and sore after the morning ride, but though he watched her face, he saw no sign of it registered there.

"Game!"

He was going to like her. Stirrup to stirrup, they rode slowly up the lane toward the cañon road. Her form was perfect. She seemed to recall everything his father had told her, and she sat easily with no stiffness.

"Don't you want to ride faster?" she asked. "You needn't poke along on my account."

"It's too hot," he replied; but the real reason was that he knew she was probably suffering, even at a walk.

For a long time, they rode in silence, the girl taking in every beauty of meadow, ravine, and hill, that she might store them all away for the days when they would be only memories. The sun beat down upon them fiercely, for it was an early August day, and there was no relieving breeze; but she enjoyed it. It was all so different from any day in her past and so much happier than anything in the last two years or anything she could expect in the future.

Custer Pennington, never a talkative man, was always glad of a companionship that could endure long silences. Grace had been like that with him. They could be together for hours with scarce a dozen words exchanged; and yet both could talk well when they had anything to say. It was the knowledge that conversation was not essential to perfect understanding and comradeship that had rendered their intimacy delightful.

The riders had entered the hills and were winding up Jackknife Cañon before either spoke.

"If you tire," he said, "or if it gets too hot, we'll turn back. Please don't hesitate to tell me."

"It's heavenly!" she said.

"Possibly a few degrees too hot for heaven," he suggested; "but it's always cool under the live oaks. Any time you want to rest, we'll stop for a bit."

"Which are the live oaks?" she asked.

He pointed to one.

"Why are they called *live* oaks?"

"They're evergreen — I suppose that's the reason. Here's a big old fellow — shall we stop?"

"And get off?"

"If you wish."

"Do you think I could get on again?"

Pennington laughed.

"I'll get you up alright. Still feel a little lame?"

"Who said I was lame?" she demanded.

"I know you must be, but you're mighty game!"

"I was when I started, but not anymore. I seem to have limbered up. Let's try it. I want to see if I can get on from the ground as Eva does. What are you smiling at? That's the second time in the last few seconds."

"Was I smiling? I didn't know it. I didn't mean to."

"What did I do?"

"You didn't do anything — it was something you said. You won't mind, will you, as long as you are learning to ride a horse, if I teach you the correct terminology at the same time?"

"Why, of course not! What did I say? Was it very awful?"

"Oh, no; but it always amuses me when I hear it. It's about getting on and off. You get on or off a street car, but you mount or dismount if you're riding a horse."

"But I don't!" she exclaimed, laughing. "Falling on and off would suit my method better."

"No, you mount very nicely. Now watch, and I'll show you how to dismount. Put your left hand on the horn; throw your right leg over the cantle, immediately grasping the cantle with the right hand; stand erect in the left stirrup, legs straight and heels together — you see, I'm facing right across the horse. Now, support the weight of the body with your arms, like this; remove the left foot from the stirrup and drop to the ground, alighting evenly on both feet. That's the correct form and a good plan to follow while you're learning to ride. Afterward, one gets to swing off almost any old way."

"I thought one always *dismounted*," she suggested, "from a horse!"

Her eyes twinkled. He laughed.

"I'll have to be careful, won't I? You scored that time!"

"Now watch me," she said.

"Splendid!" he exclaimed, as she dropped lightly to the ground.

They led their horses beneath the spreading tree and sat down with their backs to the huge bole.

"How cool it is here!" remarked the girl. "I can feel a breeze, though I hadn't noticed one before."

"There always is a breeze beneath the oaks. I think they make their own. I read somewhere that an oak evaporates about 180 gallons of water every day. That ought to make a considerable change of temperature beneath the tree on a hot day like this, and in that way, it must start a circulation of air about it."

"How interesting! How much there is to know in the world, and how little of it most of us know! A tree is a tree, a flower is a flower, and the hills are the hills — that much knowledge of them satisfies nearly all of us. The how and the why of them we never consider; but I should like to know more. We should know all about things that are so beautiful — don't you think so?"

The Girl from Hollywood / 117

"Yes," he said. "In ranching, we do learn a lot that city people don't need to know — about how things grow and what some plants take out of the soil and what others put into it. It's part of our business to know these things, not only that we may judge the food value of certain crops, but also to keep our soil in condition to grow good crops every year."

He told her how the tree beneath which they sat drew water and various salts from the soil, and how the leaves extracted carbon dioxide from the air, taking it in through myriads of minute mouths on the undersides of the leaves, and how the leaves manufactured starch and the sap carried it to every growing part of the tree, from deepest root to the tip of loftiest twig.

The girl listened, absorbed. As she listened, she watched the man's face, earnest and intelligent, and mentally she could not but compare him and his conversation with the men she had known in the city and their conversation. They had talked to her as if she was a mental cipher, incapable of understanding or appreciating anything worthwhile — small talk, that subverter of the ancient art of conversation. In a brief half hour, Custer Pennington had taught her things that would help to make the world a little more interesting and a little more beautiful; for she could never look upon a tree again as just a tree — it would be for her a living, breathing, almost a sentient creature.

She tried to recall what she had learned from two years' association with Wilson Crumb, and the only thing she could think of was that Crumb had taught her to snuff cocaine.

After a while, they started on again, and the girl surprised the man by mounting easily from the ground. She was very much pleased with her achievement, laughing happily at his word of approval.

They rode on until they found the Herefords. They counted them as they searched through the large pasture that ran back into the hills; and when the full number had been accounted for, they turned toward home. As he had told her about the trees, Custer told her also about the beautiful white-faced cattle, of their origin in the English county whose name they bear, and of their unequaled value as beef animals. He pointed out various prize winners as they passed them.

"There you are, smiling again," she said accusingly, as they followed the trail homeward. "What have I done now?"

"You haven't done anything but be very patient all afternoon. I was smiling at the idea of how thrilling the afternoon must have been for a city girl, accustomed, I suppose, to a constant round of pleasure and excitement!"

"I have never known a happier afternoon," she said.

"I wonder if you really mean that?"

"Honestly!"

"I am glad," he said; "for sometimes I get terribly tired of it here, and I think it always does me good to have an outsider enthuse a little. It brings me a realization of the things we have here that city people can't have and makes me a little more contented."

"You couldn't be discontented! Why, there are just thousands and thousands of people in the city who would give everything to change places with you! We don't all live in the city because we want to. You are fortunate that you don't have to."

"Do you think so?"

"I know it."

"But it seems such a narrow life here! I ought to be doing a man's work among men where it will count."

"You *are* doing a man's work here and living a man's life, and what you do here *does* count. Suppose you were making stoves or selling automobiles or bonds in the city. Would any such work count for more than all this — the wonderful swine and cattle and horses that you are raising? Your father has built a great business, and you are helping him to make it greater. Could you do anything in the city of which you could be half so proud? No, but in the city, you might find a thousand things to do of which you might be terribly ashamed. If I were a man, I'd like your chance!"

"You're not consistent. You have the same chance, but you tell us that you are going back to the city. You have your grove here and a home and a good living, and yet you want to return to the city you inveigh against."

"I do *not* want to," she declared.

"I hope you don't, then," Custer said simply.

The Girl from Hollywood / 119

They reached the house in time for a swim before dinner; but after dinner, when they started for the ballroom to dance, Shannon threw up her hands in surrender.

"I give up!" she cried laughingly. "I tried to be game to the finish, and I want ever so much to come and dance; but I don't believe I could even walk as far as the ballroom much less dance after I got there. Why, I doubt whether I'll be able to get upstairs without crawling!"

"You poor child!" exclaimed Mrs. Pennington. "We've nearly killed you, I know. We are all so used to the long rides and walking and swimming and dancing that we don't realize how they tire unaccustomed muscles. You go right to bed, my dear, and don't think of getting up for breakfast."

"Oh, but I want to get up and ride, if I may, and if Eva will wake me."

"She's got the real stuff in her," commented the colonel, after Shannon had bid them good night and gone to her rooms.

"I'll say she has," agreed Custer. "She's a peach of a girl!"

"She's simply divine," added Eva.

In her room, Shannon could barely get into bed before she was asleep.

CHAPTER XVI

IT WAS FOUR O'CLOCK the following morning before she awoke. The craving awoke with her. It seized her mercilessly; yet even as she gave in to it, she had the satisfaction of knowing that she had gone without the little white powders longer this time than since she had first started to use them. She took but a third of her normal dose.

When Eva knocked at half past five, Shannon rose and dressed in frantic haste that she might escape a return of the desire. She did not escape it entirely, but she was able to resist it until she was dressed and out of reach of the little black case.

That day she went with Custer and Eva and Guy to the country club, returning only in time for a swim before dinner; and again she fought off the craving while she was dressing for dinner. After dinner they danced, and once more she was so physically tired when she reached her rooms that she could think of nothing but sleep. The day of golf had kept her fully occupied in the hot sun, and in such good company, her mind had been pleasantly occupied, too, so that she had not been troubled by her old enemy.

Again, it was early morning before she was forced to fight the implacable foe. She fought valiantly this time, but she lost.

And so it went, day after day as she dragged out her dwindling supply and prolonged the happy hours of her all-too-brief respite from the degradation of the life to which she knew she must soon return. Each day it was harder to think of going back — of leaving these people, whom she had come to love as she loved their lives and their surroundings, and taking her place again in the stifling and degraded atmosphere of the Vista del Paso bungalow. They were so good to her and had so wholly taken her into their family life that she felt as one of them. They shared everything with her. There was not a day that she did not ride with Custer out among the brown hills. She knew that she was going to miss these rides — that she was going to miss the man, too. He had treated her as a man would like other men to treat his sister, with a respect and deference that she had never met with in the City of Angels.

Three weeks had passed. She had drawn out the week's supply that Crumb had doled out to her to this length, and there was even enough for another week, to such small quantities had she reduced the doses and to such lengths had she increased the intervals between them. She had gone two whole days without it; yet she did not once think that she could give it up entirely, for when the craving came in full force, she was still powerless to withstand it, and she knew that she would always be so.

Without realizing it, she was building up a reserve force of health that was to be her strongest ally in the battle to come. The sallowness had left her; her cheeks were tanned and ruddy; her eyes sparkled with the old fire and were no longer wild and staring. She could ride and walk and swim and dance with the best of them. She found interest in the work of her orchard where she went almost daily to talk with the caretaker to question him and to learn all that she could of citrus culture. She even learned to drive the light tractor and steer it in and out about the trees without barking them.

Every day that she was there, she went to the sunny bedroom in the bungalow — the bedroom that had been her mother's — and knelt beside the bed and poured forth her heart in blind faith that her mother heard. She did not grieve, for she held that sublime faith in the hereafter which many profess and few possess — the faith which taught her that her mother was happier than she had ever been before. Her sorrow had been in her own loss, and this she fought down as selfishness. She realized that her greatest anguish lay in vain regrets; and such thoughts she sought to stifle, knowing their uselessness.

Sometimes she prayed there — prayed for strength to cast off the bonds of her servitude. Ineffectual prayers she knew them to be, for the only power that could free her had lain within herself, and that power the drug had undermined and permanently weakened. Her will had degenerated to impotent wishes.

And now the time had come when she must definitely set a date for her departure. She had determined to retain the orchard, not alone because she had seen that it would prove profitable but because it would always constitute a link between her and the people whom she had come to love. No matter what the future held, she could always feel that a part of her remained here, where she would that all of her might be; but she knew that she must go, and she determined to tell them on the following day that she would return to the city within the week.

It was going to be hard to announce her decision, for she was not blind to the fact that they had grown fond of her and that her presence meant much to Eva, who, since Grace's departure, had greatly missed the companionship of a girl near her own age. Mrs. Pennington and the colonel had been a mother and father to her and Custer a big brother and a most charming companion.

She passed that night without recourse to the white powders, for she must be frugal of them if they were to last through the week. The next morning she rode with the Penningtons and the Evanses as usual. She would tell them at breakfast.

When she came to the table, she found a pair of silver spurs beside her plate, and when she looked about in astonishment, they were all smiling.

"For me?" she cried.

"From the Penningtons," said the colonel. "You've won 'em, my dear. You ride like a trooper already."

The girl choked, and the tears came to her eyes.

"You are all so lovely to me!" she said. Walking around the table to the colonel, she put her arms about his neck and, standing on tiptoe, kissed his cheek. "How can I ever thank you?'

"You don't have to, child. The spurs are nothing."

"They are everything to me. They are a badge of honor that — that — I don't deserve!"

The Girl from Hollywood / 123

"But you do deserve them. You wouldn't have got them if you hadn't. We might have given you something else — a vanity case or a book, perhaps; but no one gets spurs from the Penningtons who does not *belong*."

After that she simply couldn't tell them then that she was going away. She would wait until tomorrow; but she laid her plans without reference to the hand of fate.

That afternoon, immediately after luncheon, they were all seated in the patio, lazily discussing the chief topic of thought — the heat. It was one of those sultry days that are really unusual in southern California. The heat was absolutely oppressive, and even beneath the canvas canopy that shaded the patio, there was little relief.

"I don't know why we sit here," said Custer. "It's cooler in the house. This is the hottest place on the ranch on a day like this!"

"Wouldn't it be nice under one of those oaks up the cañon?" suggested Shannon.

He looked at her and smiled.

"Phew! It's too hot even to think of getting there."

"*That* from a Pennington!" she cried in mock astonishment and reproach.

"Do you mean to say that you'd ride up there through this heat?" he demanded.

"Of course I would. I haven't christened my new spurs yet."

"I'm game, then, if you are," Custer announced. She jumped to her feet.

"Come on, then! Who else is going?" Shannon looked around at them questioningly. Mrs. Pennington shook her head, smiling.

"Not I. Before breakfast is enough for me in the summertime."

"I have to dictate some letters," said the colonel.

"And I suppose little Eva has to stay at home and powder her nose," suggested Custer, grinning at his sister.

"Little Eva is going to drive over to Ganado with Guy Thackeray Evans, the famous author," said the girl. "He expects an express package — his story's coming back again. Horrid, stupid old editors! They don't know a real story when they see one. I'm in it — Guy put me in. You all ought to read it — oh, it's simply radiant! I'm *Hortense* — tall and willowy and very dignified —" Eva made a grimace.

"Yes, that's you, unmistakably," said Custer. "Tall and willowy and very dignified — Guy's some hot baby at character delineation!"

Eva ignored the interruption.

"I swoon when the villain enters my room and carries me off. Then the hero — he's *Bruce Bellinghame*, tall and slender with curly hair —"

"Is he very dignified, too?"

"And then the hero pursues and rescues me just as the villain is going to hurl me off a cliff — oh, it's gorgeristic!"

"It must be," commented Custer.

"You're horrid," said Eva. "You ought to have been an editor."

"Tall and slender with curly hair," gibed Custer. "Or was it tall and curly with slender hair? Come on, Shannon! I see we are the only real sports in the family."

"Hot sports is what you're going to be!" Eva called after them.

"The only real sports in the family — in the family!" The words thrilled her. They had taken her in — they had made her a part of their life. It was wonderful. Oh, God, if it could only last forever!

It was very hot. The dust rose from the shuffling feet of their horses. Even the Apache shuffled today. His head was low, and he did not dance. The dust settled on sweating neck and flank and filled the eyes of the riders.

"Lovely day for a ride," commented Custer.

"But think how nice it will be under the oak," she reminded him.

"I'm trying to."

Suddenly, he raised his head as his wandering eyes sighted a slender column of smoke rising from behind the ridge beyond Jackknife Cañon. He reined in the Apache.

"Fire!" he said to the girl. "Wait here. I'll notify the boys, and then we'll ride on ahead and have a look at it. It may not amount to anything."

He wheeled about and was off at a run — the heat and the dust forgotten. She watched him go, erect in the saddle, swinging easily with every motion of his mount — a part of the horse. In less than five minutes, he was back.

"Come on!" he cried.

She swung Baldy in beside the Apache, and they were off. The loose stones clattered from the iron hooves, the dust rose far behind them now, and they had forgotten the heat. A shortcut crossed a narrow wash that meant a jump.

"Grab the horn!" he cried to her. "Give him his head!"

They went over almost stirrup to stirrup, and he smiled broadly, for she had not grabbed the horn. She had taken the jump like a veteran.

She thrilled with the excitement of the pace. The horses flattened out — their backs seemed to vibrate in a constant plane — it was like flying. The hot wind blew in her face and choked her; but she laughed and wanted to shout aloud and swing a hat.

More slowly they climbed the side of Jackknife, and just beyond the ridge they saw the flames leaping in a narrow ravine below them. Fortunately there was no wind — no more than what the fire itself was making; but it was burning fiercely in thick brush.

"There isn't a thing to do," he told her, "till the boys come with the teams and plows and shovels. It's in a mean place — too steep to plow, and heavy brush; but we've got to stop it!"

Presently the "boys"— a wagon full of them — came with four horses, two walking plows, shovels, a barrel of water, and burlap sacks. They were of all ages, from 18 to 70. Some of them had been twenty years on the ranch and had fought many a fire. They did not have to be told what to bring or what to do with what they brought.

The wagon had to be left in Jackknife Cañon. The horses dragged the plows to the ridge, and the men carried the shovels and wet burlaps and buckets of water from the barrel. Custer dismounted and turned the Apache over to an old man to hold.

"Plow down the east side of the ravine. Try to get all the way around the south side of the fire and then back again," he directed the two men with one of the teams. "I'll take the other with Jake, and we'll try to cut her off across the top here!"

"You can't do it, Cus," said one of the older men.

"It's too steep."

"We've got to try it," said Pennington. "Otherwise we'd have to go back so far that it would get away from us on the east side before we made the circle. Jake, you choke the plow handles — I'll drive!"

Jake was a short, stocky, red-headed boy of 20 with shoulders like a bull. He grinned good-naturedly.

"I'll choke the tar out of 'em!" he said.

"The rest of you shovel and beat like hell!" ordered Custer.

Shannon watched him as he took the reins and started the team forward, slowly, quietly. There was no yelling.

They were horsemen, these men of Ganado. The great Percherons moved ponderously forward. The plow point bit deep into the earth, but the huge beasts walked on as if dragging an empty wagon.

When the girl saw where Custer was guiding them she held her breath. No, she must be mistaken! He would turn them up toward the ridge. He could not be thinking of trying to drive them across the steep, shelving side of the ravine!

But he was. They slipped and caught themselves. Directly below them the burning brush had become a fiery furnace. If ever they failed to catch themselves, nothing could save them from that hell of heat.

Jake, clinging to the plow handles, stumbled and slid, but the plow steadied him, and the furrow saved his footing a dozen times in as many yards. Custer, driving, walked just below the plow. How he kept the team going was a miracle to the girl.

The steep sides of the ravine seemed almost perpendicular in places, with footing fit only for a goat. How those heavy horses clung there was beyond her. Only implicit confidence in these men of Ganado, who had handled them from the time they were foaled, and great courage could account for it.

What splendid animals they were! The crackling of burning brush, the roaring of the flames, the almost unbearable heat that swept up to them from below must have been terrifying; and yet, only by occasional nervous side glances and uppricked ears did they acknowledge their instinctive fear of fire.

At first it had seemed to Shannon a mad thing to attempt, but as she watched and realized what Custer sought to accomplish, she understood the wisdom of it. If he could check the flames here with a couple of furrows, he might gain time to stop its eastward progress to the broad pastures filled with the tinder-dry grasses and brush of late August.

Already some of the men were working with shovels, just above the furrow that the plow was running, clearing away the brush and throwing it back. Shannon watched these men, and there was not a shirker among them. They worked between the fierce heat of the sun and the fierce heat of the fire, each one of them as if he owned the ranch. It was fine proof of loyalty; and she saw an indication of the reason for it in Custer's act when he turned the Apache over to the oldest man in order that the veteran might not be called upon to do work beyond his strength while young Pennington himself undertook a dangerous and difficult part in the battle.

The sight thrilled her; and beside this picture she saw Wilson Crumb directing a Western scene, sending mounted men over a steep cliff while he sat in safety beside the camera man hurling taunts and insults at the poor devils who risked their lives for five dollars a day. He had killed one horse that time and sent two men to hospital, badly injured — and the next day he had bragged about it!

Now they were across the ravine and moving along the east side on safer footing. Shannon realized the tension that had been upon her nerves when reaction followed the lessening of the strain — she felt limp and fagged.

The smoke hid them from her occasionally as it rose in cloud-like puffs. Then there would be a break in it, and she would see the black coats of the Percherons and the figures of the sweating men. They rounded well down the east side of the ravine and then turned back again; for the other team, with easier going, would soon be up on that side to join its furrow with theirs. They were running the second furrow just above the first, and this time the work seemed safer, for the horses had the first furrow below them should they slip — a ridge of loose earth that would give them footing.

They were more than halfway back when it happened. The off horse must have stepped upon a loose stone, so suddenly did he lurch to the left, striking the shoulder of his mate just as the latter had planted his left forefoot. The ton of weight hurled against the shoulder of the near horse threw him downward against the furrow. He tried to catch himself on his right foot, crossed his forelegs, stumbled over the ridge of newly turned earth, and rolled down the hill, dragging his mate and the plow after him toward the burning brush below.

Jake at the plow handles and Custer on the lines tried to check the horses' fall, but both were jerked from their hands, and the two Percherons rolled over and over into the burning brush. A groan of dismay went up from the men. It was with difficulty that Shannon stifled a scream; and then her heart stood still as she saw Custer Pennington leap deliberately down the hillside, drawing the long, heavy trail-cutting knife that he always wore on the belt with his gun.

The horses were struggling and floundering to gain their feet. One of them was screaming with pain. The girl wanted to cover her eyes with her palms to shut out the heart-rending sight, but she could not take them from the figure of the man.

She saw that the upper horse was so entangled with the harness and the plow that he could not rise and that he was holding the other down. Then she saw the man leap into the midst of the struggling, terrified mass of horseflesh, seeking to cut the beasts loose from the tangled traces and the plow. It seemed impossible that he could escape the flying hooves or the tongued flames that licked upward as if in hungry greed to seize this new prey.

As Shannon watched, a great light awoke within her, suddenly revealing the unsuspected existence of a wondrous thing that had come into her life — a thing which a moment later dragged her from her saddle and sent her stumbling down the hill into the burning ravine to the side of Custer Pennington.

He had cut one horse free, seized its headstall, dragged it to its feet, and then started it scrambling up the hill. As he was returning to the other, the animal struggled up, crazed with terror and pain, and bolted after its mate. Pennington was directly in its path on the steep hillside. He tried to leap aside, but the horse struck him with its shoulder, hurling him to the ground, and before he could stop his fall he was at the edge of the burning brush, stunned and helpless.

Every man of them who saw the accident leaped down the hillside to save him from the flames; but quick as they were, Shannon Burke was first to his side, vainly endeavoring to drag him to safety. An instant later strong hands seized both Custer and Shannon and helped them up the steep acclivity, for Pennington had already regained consciousness, and it was not necessary to carry him.

Custer was badly burned, but his first thought was for the girl, and his next, when he found she was uninjured, for the horses. They had run for only a short distance and were standing on the ridge above Jackknife where one of the men had caught them. One was burned about the neck and shoulder; the other had a bad cut above the hock, where he had struck the plow point in his struggles.

"Take them in and take care of those wounds, Jake," said Pennington after examining them. "You go along," he told another of the men, "and bring out Dick and Dave. I don't like to risk them in this work, but none of the colts are steady enough for this."

Then he turned to Shannon.

"Why did you go down into that?" he asked. "You shouldn't have done it — with all the men here."

"I couldn't help it," she said. "I thought you were going to be killed."

Custer looked at her searchingly for a moment.

"It was a very brave thing to do," he said, "and a very foolish thing. You might have been badly burned."

"Never mind that," she said. "*You* have been badly burned, and you must go to the house at once. Do you think you can ride?"

He laughed.

"I'm all right," he said. "I've got to stay here and fight this fire."

"You are not going to do anything of the kind." She turned and called to the man who held Pennington's horse. "Please bring the Apache over here," she said. "These men can fight the fire without you," she told Custer. "You are going right back with me. You've never seen anyone badly burned, or you'd know how necessary it is to take care of your burns at once."

He was not accustomed to being ordered about, and it amused him. Grace would never have thought of questioning his judgment in this or any other matter; but this girl's attitude implied that she considered his judgment faulty and his decisions of no consequence. She evidently had the courage of her convictions, for she caught up her own horse and rode over to the men who had resumed their work to tell them that Custer was too badly burned to remain with them.

"I told him that he must go back to the house and have his burns dressed; but he doesn't want to. Maybe he would pay more attention to you if you told him."

"Sure, we'll tell him," cried one of them. "Here comes Colonel Pennington now. He'll make him go, if it's necessary."

Colonel Pennington reined in a dripping horse beside his son, and Shannon rode over to them. Custer was telling him about the accident to the team.

"Burned, was he?" exclaimed the colonel. "Why damn it, man, *you're* burned!"

"It's nothing," replied the younger man.

"It *is* something, colonel," cried Shannon. "Please make him go back to the house. He won't pay any attention to me, and he ought to be cared for right away. He should have a doctor just as quickly as we can get one."

"Can you ride?" snapped the colonel at Custer.

"Of course I can ride!"

"Then get out of here and take care of yourself. Will you go with him, Shannon? Have them call Dr. Baldwin."

His rough manner did not conceal the father's concern or his deep love for his boy. That he could be as gentle as a woman was evidenced, when he dismounted, in the way that he helped Custer to his saddle.

"Take care of him, my dear," he said to Shannon. "I'll stay here and help the boys. Ask Mrs. Pennington to send the car out with some iced water or lemonade for them. Take care of yourself, boy!" he called after them as they rode away.

As the horses moved slowly along the dusty trail, Shannon, riding a pace behind the man, watched his profile for signs of pain that she knew he must be suffering. Once, when he winced, she almost gave a little cry as if it had been she who was tortured. They were riding very close, and she laid her hand gently upon his right arm in sympathy.

"I am so sorry!" she said. "I know it must pain you terribly."

He turned to her with a smile on his face, now white and drawn.

"It does hurt a little now," he said.

"And you did it to save those two dumb brutes. I think it was magnificent, Custer!"

He looked at her in mild surprise.

"What was there magnificent about it? It was my duty. My father has always taught me that the ownership of animals entails certain moral obligations which no honorable man can ignore — that it isn't sufficient merely to own them and feed them and house them; but to serve and protect them, even if it entailed sacrifices to do so."

"I don't believe he meant that you should give your life for them," she said.

"No, of course not; but I am not giving my life."

"You might have."

"I really didn't think there would be any danger to me," he said. "I guess I didn't think anything about it. I saw those two beautiful animals, who had been working there for me so bravely, helpless at the edge of that fire, and I couldn't have helped doing what I did under any circumstances. You don't know, Shannon, how we Penningtons love our horses. It's been bred in the bone for generations. Perhaps it's silly; but we don't think so."

"Neither do I. It's fine."

By the time they reached the house, she could see that the man was suffering excruciating pain. The stableman had gone to help the firefighters, as had every able-bodied man on the ranch, so that she had to help Custer from the Apache. After tying the two horses at the stable, she put an arm about him and assisted him up the long flight of steps to the house. There, Mrs. Pennington and Hannah came at her call and took him to his room while she ran to the office to telephone for the doctor.

When she returned, they had Custer undressed and in bed and were giving such first aid as they could. She stood in the doorway for a moment, watching him as he fought to hide the agony he was enduring. He rolled his head slowly from side to side as his mother and Hannah worked over him; but he stifled even a faint moan, though Shannon knew that his tortured body must be goading him to screams. He opened his eyes and saw her and tried to smile.

Mrs. Pennington turned then and discovered her.

"Please let me do something, Mrs. Pennington, if there is anything I can do."

"I guess we can't do much until the doctor comes. If we only had something to quiet the pain until then!"

If they only had something to quiet the pain. The horror of it! She had something that would quiet the pain; but at what a frightful cost to herself must she divulge it! They would know, then, the sordid story of her vice. There could be no other explanation of her having such an outfit in her possession. How they would loathe her. To see disgust in the eyes of these friends, whose good opinion was her one cherished longing, seemed a punishment too great to bear.

And then there was the realization of that new force that had entered her life with the knowledge that she loved Custer Pennington. It was a hopeless love, she knew; but she might at least have had the happiness of knowing that he respected her. Was she to be spared nothing? Was her sin to deprive her of even the respect of the man whom she loved?

She saw him lying there and saw the muscles of his jaws tensing as he battled to conceal his pain; and then she turned and ran up the stairway to her rooms. She did not hesitate again but went directly to her bag, unlocked it, and took out the little black case. Carefully she dissolved a little of the white powder — a fraction of what she could have taken without danger of serious results but enough to allay his suffering until the doctor came. She knew that this was the end — that she might not remain under that roof another night.

She drew the liquid through the needle into the glass barrel of the syringe, wrapped it in her handkerchief, and descended the stairs. She felt as if she moved in a dream. She felt that she was not Shannon Burke at all but another whom Shannon Burke watched with pitying eyes; for it did not seem possible that she could enter that room and before his eyes and Mrs. Pennington's and Hannah's reveal the thing that she carried in her handkerchief.

Ah, the pity of it! To realize her first love and in the same hour to slay the respect of its object with her own hand! Yet she entered the room with a brave step, fearlessly. Had he not risked his life for the two dumb brutes he loved? Could she be less courageous? Perhaps though, she was braver, for she was knowingly surrendering what was dearer to her than life.

Mrs. Pennington turned toward her as she entered.

"He has fainted," she said. "My poor boy!"

Tears stood in his mother's eyes.

"He is not suffering, then?" asked Shannon, trembling.

"Not now. For his sake, I hope he won't recover consciousness until after the doctor comes."

Shannon Burke staggered and would have fallen had she not grasped the frame of the door.

It was not long before the doctor came, and then she went back up the stairs to her rooms, still trembling. She took the filled hypodermic syringe from her handkerchief and looked at it. Then she carried it into the bathroom.

"You can never tempt me again," she said aloud, as she emptied its contents into the lavatory. "Oh, dear God, I love him!"

CHAPTER XVII

THAT NIGHT, Shannon insisted upon taking her turn at Custer's bedside, and she was so determined that they could not refuse her. He was still suffering, but not so acutely. The doctor had left morphine with explicit directions for its administration should it be required. The burns, while numerous and reaching from his left ankle to his cheek, were superficial and, though painful, not necessarily dangerous.

He slept but little, and when he was awake, he wanted to talk. He told her about Grace. It was his first confidence — a sweetly sad one — for he was a reticent man concerning those things that were nearest his heart and consequently the most sacred to him. He had not heard from Grace for some time, and her mother had had but one letter — a letter that had not sounded like Grace at all. They were anxious about her.

"I wish she would come home!" he said wistfully. "You would like her, Shannon. We could have such bully times together! I think I would be content here if Grace were back; but without her, it seems very different and very lonely. You know we have always been together, all of us, since we were children — Grace, Eva, Guy, and I; and now that you are here, it would be all the better, for you are just like us. You seem like us, at least — as if you had always lived here, too."

"It's nice to have you say that; but I haven't always been here, and, really, you know I don't *belong*."

"But you do belong!"

"And I'm going away again pretty soon. I must go back to the city."

"Please don't go back. You don't really have to, do you?"

"I had intended telling you all this morning; but after the spurs, I couldn't."

"Do you *really* have to go?" Custer insisted.

"I don't have to, but I think I ought to. Do you want me to stay — honestly?"

"Honest Injun!" he said, smiling.

"Maybe I will."

He reached over with his right hand and took hers.

"Oh, will you?" he exclaimed. "You don't know how much we want you — all of us."

It was precisely what he might have done or said to Eva in boyish affection and comradeship.

"I'm going to stay," she announced. "I've made up my mind. As soon as you are well I'm going to move down to my own place and really learn to work it. I'd love it!"

"And I'll come down and help you with what little I know about oranges. Father will, too. We don't know much — citrus-growing is a little out of our line, though we have a small orchard here; but we'll give you the best we've got. And it'll be fine for Eva — she loves you. She cried the other day — the last time you mentioned in earnest that you might not stay."

"She's a dear!"

"She is all of that," he said. "We have always had our fights — I suppose all brothers and sisters do — and we kid one another a lot; but there never was a sister like Eva. Just let anyone else say anything against me! They'd have a fight on their hands right there if Eva was around. And sunshine! The old place seems like a morgue every time she goes away."

"She worships you, Custer."

"She's a brick!"

He could have voiced no higher praise.

He asked about the fire and especially about the horses. He was delighted when she told him that a man had just come down to say that the fire was practically out and the colonel was coming in shortly; and that the veterinary had been there and found the team not seriously injured.

"I think that fire was incendiary," he said; "but now that Slick Allen is in jail, I don't know who would set it."

"Who is Slick Allen," she asked, "and why should he want to set fire to Ganado?"

He told her, and she was silent for a while, thinking about Allen and the last time she had seen him. She wondered what he would do when he got out of jail. She would hate to be in Wilson Crumb's boots then, for she guessed that Allen was a hard character.

While she was thinking of Allen, Custer mentioned Guy Evans. Instantly, there came to her mind, for the first time since that last evening at the Vista del Paso bungalow, Crumb's conversation with Allen and the latter's account of the disposition of the stolen whisky. His very words returned to her.

"Got a young high-blood at the edge of the valley handling it — a fellow by the name of Evans."

She had not connected Allen or that conversation or the Evans he had mentioned with these people; but now she knew that it was Guy Evans who was disposing of the stolen liquor. She wondered if Allen would return to this part of the country after he was released from jail. If he did and saw her, he would be sure to recognize her, for he must have had her features impressed upon his memory by the fact that she so resembled someone he had known.

If he recognized her, would he expose her? She did not doubt but that he would. The chances were that he would attempt to blackmail her; but, worst of all, he might tell Crumb where she was. That was the thing she dreaded most — seeing Wilson Crumb again or having him discover her whereabouts; for she knew that he would leave no stone unturned and hesitate to stoop to no dishonorable act to get her back again. She shuddered when she thought of him — a man whose love, even, was a dishonorable and dishonoring thing.

Then, she turned her eyes to the face of the man lying there on the bed beside which she sat. He would never love her; but her love for him had already ennobled her.

If the people of her old life did not discover her hiding place, she could remain here on her little grove near Ganado and see Custer often — nearly every day. He would not guess her love — no one would guess it; but she should be happy just to be near him. Even if Grace returned, it would make no difference — even if Grace and Custer were married. Shannon knew that he was not for her — no honorable man was for her, after what she had been — but there was no moral law to be transgressed by her secret love for him.

She felt no jealousy for Grace. He belonged to Grace, and even had she thought she might win him, she would not have attempted it, for she had always held in contempt those who infringed selfishly upon settled affections. It would be hard for her, of course, when Grace returned; but she was determined to like her, even to love her. She would be untrue to this new love that had transfigured her should she fail to love what *he* loved.

Custer moved restlessly. Again he was giving evidence of suffering. She laid a cool palm upon his forehead and stroked it. He opened his eyes and smiled up at her.

"It's bully of you to sit with me," he said; "but you ought to be in bed. You've had a pretty hard day, and you're not as used to it as we are."

"I am not tired," she said, "and I should like to stay — if you would like to have me."

He took her hand from his forehead and kissed it.

"Of course I like to have you here, Shannon — you're just like a sister. It's funny, isn't it, that we should all feel that way about you when we've only known you a few weeks? It must have been because of the way you fitted in. You belonged right from the start — you were just like us."

She turned her head away suddenly, casting her eyes upon the floor and biting her lip to keep back the tears.

"What's the matter?" he asked.

"I am not like you, Custer; but I have tried hard to be."

"Why aren't you like us?" he demanded.

"I — why, I — couldn't ride a horse," she explained lamely.

"Don't make me laugh, please; my face is burned," he pleaded in mock irony. "Do you think that's all we know, or think of, or possess — our horsemanship? We have hearts and minds, such as they are — and souls, I hope. It was of these things that I was thinking. I was thinking, too, that we Penningtons demand a higher standard in women than is customary nowadays. We are a little old-fashioned, I guess. We want the blood of our horses and the minds of our women pure. Here is a case in point — I can tell you, because you don't know the girl and never will. She was the daughter of a friend of Cousin William — our New York cousin. She was spending the winter in Pasadena, and we had her out here on Cousin William's account. She was a pippin of a looker, and I suppose she was alright morally; but she didn't have a clean mind. I discovered it about the first time I talked with her alone; and then Eva asked me a question about something that she couldn't have known about at all except through this girl. I didn't know what to do. She was a girl, and so I couldn't talk about her to anyone, not even my father or mother; but I didn't want her around Eva. I wondered if I was just a narrow prig, and if, after all, there was nothing that anyone need take exception to in the girl. I got to analyzing the thing, and I came to the conclusion that I would be ashamed of mother and Eva if they talked or thought along such lines. Consequently, it wasn't right to expose Eva to that influence. That was what I decided, and I don't just *think* I was right — I *know* I was."

"And what did you do?" Shannon asked in a very small voice.

"I did what under any other circumstances would have been unpardonable. I went to the girl and asked her to make some excuse that would terminate her visit. It was a very hard thing to do; but I would do more than that — I would sacrifice my most cherished friendship — for Eva."

"And the girl — did you tell her why you asked her to go?"

"I didn't want to, but she insisted, and I told her."

"Did she understand?"

"She did not."

They were silent for some time.

"Do you think I did wrong?" he asked.

"No. There is mental virtue as well as physical. It is as much your duty to protect your sister's mind as to protect her body."

"I knew you'd think as I do about it; but let me tell you, it was an awful jolt to the cherished Pennington hospitality. I hope I never have to do it again!"

"I hope you never do."

He commenced to show increasing signs of suffering, presently, and then he asked for morphine.

"I don't want to take it unless I have to," he explained.

"No," she said, "do not take it unless you have to."

She prepared and administered it, but she felt no desire for it herself. Then, Eva came to relieve her, and she bade them goodnight and went up to bed. She awoke about four o'clock in the morning and immediately thought of the little black case; but she only smiled, turned over, and went back to sleep again.

CHAPTER XVIII

IT WAS SEVERAL WEEKS before Custer could ride again, and in the meantime, Shannon had gone down to her own place to live. She came up every day on Baldy, who had been loaned to her until Custer should be able to select a horse for her. She insisted that she would own nothing but a Morgan and that she wanted one of the Apache's brothers.

"You'll have to wait, then, until I can break one for you," Custer told her. "There are a couple of four-year-olds that are saddle-broke and bridle-wise in a way; but I wouldn't want you to ride either of them until they've had the finishing touches. I want to ride them enough to learn their faults, if they have any. In the meantime, you just keep Baldy down there and use him. How's ranching? You look as if it agreed with you. Nobody'd know you for the same girl. You look like an Indian, and how your cheeks have filled out!"

The girl smiled happily.

"I never knew before what it was to live," she said. "I have never been sickly; but on the other hand I never *felt* health before, to know it was a tangible, enjoyable possession that one experienced and was conscious of every moment. People fill themselves with medicines or drugs or liquors to induce temporarily a poor imitation of what they might enjoy constantly if they only would. A man who thinks that a drink is the only thing that can make one feel like shouting and waving one's hat should throw a leg over one of your Morgans before breakfast one of these cool September mornings and give him his head and let him go. Oh, *boy!*" she cried. "*There's* intoxication for you!"

Her cheeks were flushed, her eyes dancing. She was a picture of life and health and happiness; and Custer's eyes were sparkling, too.

"Gee!" he exclaimed. "You're a regular Pennington!"

"I wish I were!" the girl thought to herself. "You honor me," was what she said aloud. Custer laughed.

"That sounded rotten, didn't it? But you know what I meant — it's nice to have people whom we like like the same things we do. It doesn't necessarily mean that we think our likes are the best in the world. I didn't mean to be egotistical."

Eva had just entered the patio.

"Listen to him, the radiant child!" she exclaimed. "Do you know, Shannon, that dear little brother just hates himself!"

She walked over and perched on his knee and kissed him.

"Yes," said Custer, "Brother hates himself. He spends hours powdering his nose. Mother found a lipstick and an eyebrow pencil, or whatever you call it, in his dressing table recently; and when he goes to L.A., he has his eyebrows plucked."

Eva jumped from his knee and stamped her foot.

"I *never* had my eyebrows plucked!" she cried. "They're naturally this way."

"Why the excitement, little one? Did I say you did have them plucked?"

"Well, you tried to make Shannon think so. I got the lipstick and the other things so that if we have any amateur theatricals this winter, I'll have them. Do you know, I think I'll go on the stage or the screen! Wouldn't it be splishous, though? 'Miss Eva Pennington is starring in the new and popular success based on the story by Guy Thackeray Evans, the eminent author!'"

"Eminent! He isn't even imminent," said Custer.

"Oh, Eva!" cried Shannon, genuine concern in her tone. "Surely you wouldn't *think* of the screen, would you? You're not serious?"

"Oh, yes," said Custer. "She's serious — serious is her middle name. Tomorrow she will want to be a painter, and day after tomorrow the world's most celebrated harpist. Eva is nothing if not serious, while her tenacity of purpose is absolutely inspiring. Why, once, for one whole day, she wanted to do the same thing."

Eva was laughing with her brother and Shannon.

"If she were just like everyone else, you wouldn't love your little sister anymore," she said, running her fingers through his hair. "Honestly, ever since I met Wilson Crumb, I have thought I should like to be a movie star."

"Wilson Crumb!" exclaimed Shannon. "What do *you* know of Wilson Crumb?"

"Oh, I've met him," said Eva airily. "Don't you envy me?"

"What do you know about him, Shannon?" asked Custer. "Your tone indicated that you may have heard something about him that wasn't complimentary."

"No — I don't know him. It's only what I've heard. I don't think you'd like him." Shannon almost shuddered at the thought of this dear child even so much as knowing Wilson Crumb.

"Oh, Eva!" she cried impulsively. "You mustn't even think of going into pictures. I lived in Los Angeles long enough to learn that the life is oftentimes a hard one, filled with disappointment, disillusionment, and regrets — principally regrets."

"And Grace is there now," said Custer in a low voice, a worried look in his eyes.

"Can't you persuade her to return?"

He shook his head.

"It wouldn't be fair," he said. "She is trying to succeed, and we ought to encourage her. It is probably hard enough for her at best, without all of us suggesting antagonism to her ambition by constantly urging her to abandon it, so we try to keep our letters cheerful."

"Have you been to see her since she left? No, I know you haven't. If I were you, I'd run down to L.A. It might mean a lot to her, Custer; it might mean more than you can guess."

The girl spoke from a full measure of bitter experience. She realized what it might have meant to her had there been some man like this to come to her when she had needed the strong arm of a clean love to drag her from the verge of the mire. She would have gone away with such a man — gone back home and thanked God for the opportunity. If Grace loved Custer and was encountering the malign forces that had arisen from their own corruption to claw at Shannon's skirts, she would come back with him.

On the other hand, should conditions be what they ought to be and what they are in some studios, Custer would return with a report that would lift a load from the hearts of all of them, while it left Grace encouraged and inspired by the active support of those most dear to her. What it would mean to Shannon, in either event, the girl did not consider. Her soul was above jealousy. She was prompted only by a desire to save another from the anguish she had endured and to bring happiness to the man she loved.

"You really think I ought to go?" Custer asked. "You know she has insisted that none of us should come. She said she wanted to do it all on her own, without any help. Grace is not only very ambitious but very proud. I'm afraid she might not like it."

"I wouldn't care what she liked," said Shannon. "Either you or Guy should run down there and see her. You are the two men most vitally interested in her. No girl should be left alone long in Hollywood without someone to whom she can look for the right sort of guidance and — and — protection."

"I believe I'll do it," said Custer. "I can't get away right now; but I'll run down there before I go on to Chicago with the show herds for the International."

It was shortly after this that Custer began to ride again, and Shannon usually rode with him. Unconsciously, he had come to depend upon her companionship more and more. He had been drinking less on account of it, for it had broken a habit which he had been forming since Grace's departure — that of carrying a flask with him on his lonely rides through the hills.

As a small boy, it had been Custer's duty, as well as his pleasure, to "ride fence." He had continued the custom long after it might have been assigned to an employee, not only because it had meant long, pleasant hours in the saddle with Grace but also to get first-hand knowledge of the condition of the pastures and the herds as well as of the fences. During his enforced idleness while recovering from his burns, the duty had devolved upon Jake.

On the first day that Custer took up the work again, Jake had called his attention to a matter that had long been a subject of discussion and conjecture on the part of the employees.

"There's something funny goin' on back in them hills," said Jake. "I've seen fresh signs every week of horses and burros comin' and goin'. Sometimes they trail through El Camino Largo and again through Corto, and they've even been down through the old goat corral once, plumb through the ranch, an' out the west gate. But what I can't tell for sure is whether they come in an' go out or go out an' come in. Whoever does it is foxy. Their two trails never cross, an' they must be made within a few hours of each other, for I'm not Injun enough to tell which is freshest — the one comin' to Ganado or the one goin' out. An' then, they muss it up by draggin' brush, so it's hard to tell how many they be of 'em. It's got me."

"They head for Jackknife, don't they?" asked Custer.

"Sometimes, an' sometimes they go straight up Sycamore, an' again they head in or out of half a dozen different little barrancos comin' down from the east; but sooner or later, I lose 'em — can't never follow 'em no place in particular. Looks like as if they split up."

"Maybe it's only greasers from the valley coming up after firewood at night."

"Mebbe," said Jake; "but that don't sound reasonable."

"I know it doesn't; but I can't figure out what else it can be. I found a trail up above Jackknife last spring, and maybe that had something to do with it. I've sure got to follow that up. The trouble has been that it doesn't lead where the stock ever goes, and I haven't had time to look into it. Do you think they come up here regularly?"

"We got it doped out that it's always Friday nights. I see the tracks Saturday mornings, and some of the boys say they've heard 'em along around midnight a couple of times."

"What gates do they go out by?"

"They use all four of 'em at different times."

"Hm! Padlock all the gates tomorrow. This is Thursday. Then, we'll see what happens."

They did see, for on the following Saturday when Custer rode fence, he found it cut close by one of the padlocked gates — the gate that opened into the mouth of Horse Camp Cañon. Shannon was with him, and she was much excited at this evidence of mystery so close at home.

"What in the world do you suppose they can be doing?" she asked.

"I don't know; but it's something they shouldn't be doing, or they wouldn't go to so much pains to cover their tracks. They evidently passed in and out at this point, but they've brushed out their tracks on both sides so that you can't tell which way they went last. Look here! On both sides of the fence, the trail splits. It's hard to say which was made first and where they passed through the fence. One track must have been on top of the other, but they've brushed it out."

He had dismounted and was on his knees, examining the spoor beyond the fence.

"I believe," he said presently, "that the fresher trail is the one going toward the hills although the other one is heavier. Here's a rabbit track that lies on top of the track of a horse's hoof pointed toward the valley, and over here a few yards, the same rabbit track is obliterated by the track of horses and burros coming up from the valley. The rabbit must have come across here after they went down, stepping on top of their tracks, and when they came up again they crossed on top of his. That's pretty plain, isn't it?"

"Yes; but the tracks going down are much plainer than those going up. Wouldn't that indicate that they were fresher?"

"That's what I thought until I saw this evidence introduced by Brer Rabbit — and it's conclusive, too. Let's look along here a little farther. I have an idea that I have an idea."

"One of Eva's 'dapper little ideas,' perhaps!"

He bent close above first one trail and then another, following them down toward the valley. Shannon walked beside him, leading Baldy. Sometimes, as they knelt above the evidence imprinted in the dusty soil, their shoulders touched. The contact thrilled the girl with sweet delight, and the fact that it left him cold did not sadden her. She knew that he was not for her. It was enough that she might be near him and love him. She did not want him to love her — that would have been the final tragedy of her life.

For the most part, the trail was obliterated by brush, which seemed to have been dragged behind the last horse; but here and there was the imprint of the hoof of a horse, or, again, of a burro, so that the story that Custer pieced out was reasonably clear — as far as it went.

"I think I've got a line on it," he said presently. "Two men rode along here on horses. One horse was shod, the other was not. One rider went ahead, the other brought up the rear, and between them were several burros. Going down, the burros carried heavy loads; coming back, they carried nothing."

"How do you know all that?" she asked rather incredulously.

"I don't *know* it, but it seems the most logical deduction from these tracks. It is easy to tell the horse tracks from those of the burros and to tell that there were at least two horses because it is plain that a shod horse and an unshod horse passed along here. That one horse — the one with shoes — went first is evident from the fact that you always see the imprints of burro hooves or the hooves of an unshod horse or both superimposed on his. That the other horse brought up the rear in equally plain from the fact that no other tracks lie on top of his. Now, if you will look close and compare several of these horse tracks, you will notice that there is little or no difference in the appearance of those leading into the valley and those leading out; but you can see that the burro tracks leading down are more deeply imprinted than those leading up. To me, that means that those burros carried heavy loads down and came back light. How does it sound?"

"It's wonderful!" she exclaimed. "It is all that I can do to see that anything has been along here."

"It's not wonderful," he replied. "An experienced tracker would tell you how many horses there were, how many burros, how many hours had elapsed since they came down out of the hills, how many since they returned, and the names of the grandmothers of both riders."

Shannon laughed.

"I'm glad you're not an experienced tracker, then," she said, "for now I can believe what you have told me. And I still think it very wonderful, and very delightful, too, to be able to read stories — true stories — in the trampled dust where men and animals have passed."

"There is nothing very remarkable about it. Just look at the Apache's hoofprints, for instance. See how the hind differ from the fore."

Custer pointed to them as he spoke, calling attention to the fact that the Apache's hind shoes were squared off at the toe.

"And now compare them with Baldy's," he said. "See how different the two hoofprints are. Once you know them, you could never confuse one with the other. But the part of the story that would interest me most, I can't read — who they are, what they were packing out of the hills on these burros, where they came from, and where they went. Let's follow down and see where they went in the valley. The trail must pass right by the Evanses' hay barn."

The Evanses hay barn! A great light illuminated Shannon's memory. Allen had said that last night at the bungalow that the contraband whisky was hauled away on a truck, that it was concealed beneath hay, and that a young man named Evans handled it.

What was she to do? She dared not reveal this knowledge to Custer because she could not explain how she came into possession of it. Nor, for the same reason, could she warn Guy Evans, had she thought that necessary — which she was sure it was not since Custer would not expose him. She concluded that all she could do was to let events take their own course.

She followed Custer as he traced the partially obliterated tracks through a field of barley stubble. A hundred yards west of the hay barn the trail entered a macadam road at right angles, and there, it disappeared. There was no telling whether the little caravan had turned east or west, for it left no spoor upon the hard surface of the paved road.

"Well, *Watson!*" said Custer, turning to her with a grin. "What do you make of this?"

"Nothing."

"Nothing? *Watson*, I am surprised. Neither do I." He turned his horse back toward the cut fence. "There's no use looking any farther in this direction. I don't know that it's even worthwhile following the trail back into the hills, for the chances are that they have it well covered. What I'll do is to lay for them next Friday night. Maybe they're not up to any mischief, but it looks suspicious; and if they are, I'd rather catch them here with the goods than follow them up into the hills, where about all I'd accomplish would probably be to warn them that they were being watched. I'm sorry now I had those gates locked, for it will have put them on their guard. We'll just fix up this fence, and then we'll ride about and take all the locks off."

On the way home an hour later, he asked Shannon not to say anything about their discovery or his plan to watch for the mysterious pack train the following Friday.

"It would only excite the folks needlessly," he explained. "The chances are that there'll be some simple explanation when I meet up with these people. As I told Jake, they may be greasers who work all the week and come up here at night for firewood. Still more likely, it's people who don't know they can get permission to gather deadwood for the asking and think they are stealing it. Putting themselves to a lot of trouble for nothing, I'll say!"

"You'll not wait for them alone?" she asked, for she knew what he did not — that they were probably unscrupulous rascals who would not hesitate to commit any crime if they thought themselves in danger of discovery.

"Why not?" he asked. "I only want to ask them what they are doing on Ganado and why they cut our fence."

"Please don't!" she begged. "You don't know who they are or what they have been doing. They might be very desperate men,

The Girl from Hollywood / 149

for all we know."

"All right," he agreed. "I'll take Jake with me."

"Why don't you get Guy to go along, too?" she suggested, for she knew that he would be safer if Guy knew of his intention since then there would be little likelihood of his meeting the men.

"No," he replied. "Guy would have to have a big camp fire, an easy chair, and a package of cigarettes if he was going to sit up that late out in the hills. Jake's the best for that sort of work."

"Guy isn't a bit like you, is he?" she asked. "He's lived right here and led the same sort of life, and yet he doesn't seem to be a part of it, as you are."

"Guy's a dreamer, and he likes to be comfortable all the time," laughed Custer. "They're all that way a little. Mr. Evans was, so father says. He died while we were all kids. Mrs. Evans likes to take it easy, too, and even Grace wasn't much on roughing it, though she could stand more than the others. None of them seemed to take to it the way you do. I never saw any one else but a Pennington such a glutton for a saddle and the outdoors as you are. I don't like 'em any the less for it," he hastened to add. "It's just the way people are, I guess. The taste for such things is inherited. The Evanses, up to this generation, all came from the city; the Penningtons all from the country. Father thinks that horsemen, if not the descendants of a distinct race, at least spring from some common ancestors who inhabited great plains and were the original stock raisers of the human race. He thinks they mingled with the hill and mountain people who also became horsemen through them; but that the forest tribes and the maritime races were separate and distinct. It was the last who built the cities, which the horsemen came in from the plains and conquered."

"But perhaps Guy would like the adventure of it," she insisted. "It might give him material for a story. I'm going to ask him."

"Please don't. The less said about it the better, for if it's talked about, it may get to the men I want to catch. Word travels fast in the country. Just as we don't know who these men are or what they are doing, neither do we know but what some of them may be on friendly terms with our employees, or the Evanses', or yours."

The girl made no reply.

"You won't mention it to him, please?" Custer insisted.

"Not if you don't wish it," she said.

They were silent for a time, each absorbed in his or her own thoughts. The girl was seeking to formulate some plan that would prevent a meeting between Custer and Allen's confederates who she was sure were the owners of the mysterious pack train; while the man indulged in futile conjectures as to their identity and the purpose of their nocturnal expeditions.

"That trail above Jackknife Cañon is the key to the whole business," he declared presently. "I'll just lay low until after next Friday night so as not to arouse their suspicions, and then, no matter what I find out, I'll ride that trail to its finish if it takes me clear to the ocean!"

They had reached the fork in the road, one branch of which led down to Shannon's bungalow, the other to the Ganado saddle-horse stables.

"I thought you were coming up to lunch," said Custer, as Shannon reined her horse into the west road.

"Not today," she said. "I'll come to dinner, if I may, though."

"We all miss you when you're not there," he said.

"How nice! Now I'll surely come."

"And this afternoon — will you ride with me again?"

"I'm going to be very busy this afternoon," she replied.

His face dropped, and then, almost immediately, he laughed.

"I hadn't realized how much of your time I have been demanding. Why, you ride with me every day, and now when you want an afternoon off, I start moping. I'm afraid you've spoiled me; but you mustn't let me be a nuisance."

"I ride with you because I like to," she replied. "I should miss our rides terribly if anything should occur to prevent them."

"Let's hope nothing will prevent them. I'm afraid I'd be lost without you now, Shannon. You can never know what it has meant to me to have you here. I was sort of going to pot after Grace left — blue and discouraged and discontented; and

I was drinking too much. I don't mind telling you, because I know you'll understand — you seem to understand everything. Having you to ride with and talk to pulled me together. I owe you a lot, so don't let me impose on your friendship and your patience. Any time you want an afternoon off," he concluded, laughing, "don't be afraid to ask for it — I'll see that you get it with full pay!"

"I don't *want* any afternoons off because I enjoy the rides as much as you, and they have meant even more to me. I intend to see that nothing prevents them if I can."

She was touched and pleased with Custer's sudden burst of confidence and thankful for whatever had betrayed him into one of those rare revelations of his heart. She wanted to be necessary to him in the sweet and unemotional way of friendship so that they might be together without embarrassment or constraint.

They had been standing at the fork talking, and now, as she started Baldy again in the direction of her own place, Custer reined the Apache to accompany her.

"You needn't come down with me," she said. "It's nearly lunch time now, and it would only make you late."

"But I want to."

"No!" She shook her head. "You go right home."

"Please!"

"This is my afternoon off," she reminded him, "and I'd really rather you wouldn't."

"Alright! I'll drive down in the car early, and we'll have a swim before dinner."

"Not too early — I'll telephone you when I'm ready. Goodbye!"

He waved his hat as she cantered off and then sat the Apache for a moment, watching her. How well she rode! What grace and ease in every motion of that supple body! He shook his head.

"Some girl, Shannon!" he mused aloud as he wheeled the Apache and rode toward the stables.

CHAPTER XIX

SHANNON BURKE did not ride to her home after she left Custer. She turned toward the west at the road above the Evans place, continued on to the mouth of Horse Camp Cañon, and entered the hills. For two miles, she followed the cañon trail to El Camino Largo, and there, turning to the left, she followed this other trail east to Sycamore Cañon. Whatever her mission, it was evident that she did not wish it known to others. Had she not wished to conceal it, she might have ridden directly up Sycamore Cañon from Ganado with a saving of several miles.

Crossing Sycamore, she climbed the low hills skirting its eastern side. There was no trail here, and the brush was thick and oftentimes so dense that she was forced to make numerous detours to find a way upward; but at last, she rode out upon the western rim of the basin meadow above Jackknife. Thence, she picked her way down to more level ground and, putting spurs to Baldy, galloped east, her eyes constantly scanning the ground just ahead of her.

Presently, she found what she sought — a trail running north and south across the basin. She turned Baldy into it and headed him south toward the mountains. She was nervous and inwardly terrified, and a dozen times, she would have turned back had she not been urged on by a power infinitely more potent than self-interest.

Personally, she had all to lose by the venture and naught to gain. The element of physical danger she knew to be far from inconsiderable, while it appalled her to contemplate the after effects in the not inconceivable contingency of the discovery of her act by the Penningtons.

Yet she urged Baldy steadily onward, though she felt her flesh creep as the trail entered a narrow barranco at the southern extremity of the meadow and wound upward through dense chaparral, which shut off her range of vision in all directions for more than a few feet.

At the upper end of the barranco, the trail turned back and ascended a steep hillside, running diagonally upward through heavy brush — without which, she realized, the trail would have appeared an almost impossible one since it clung to a nearly perpendicular cliff. The brush lent a suggestion of safety that was more apparent than real, and at the same time, it hid the sheer descent below.

Baldy, digging his toes into the loose earth, scrambled upward, stepping over gnarled roots and an occasional boulder and finding, almost miraculously, the least precarious footing. There were times when the girl shut her eyes tightly and sat with tensed muscles, her knees pressing her horse's sides until her muscles ached. At last, the doughty Morgan topped the summit of the hogback, and Shannon drew a deep breath of relief — which was alloyed, however, by the realization that in returning she must ride down this frightful trail, which now, as if by magic, disappeared.

The hogback was water-washed and gravel-strewn and as hard-baked beneath the summer's sun as a macadam road. To Shannon's unaccustomed eyes, it gave no clue as to the direction of the trail. She rode up and down in both directions until finally she discovered what appeared to be a trail leading downward into another barranco upon the opposite side of the ridge. The descent seemed less terrifying than that which she had just negotiated, and as it was the only indication of a trail that she could find, she determined to investigate it.

Baldy, descending carefully, suddenly paused and with uppricked ears emitted a shrill neigh. So sudden and so startling was the sound that Shannon's heart all but stood still, gripped by the cold fingers of terror. And then, from below came an answering neigh.

She had found what she sought, but the fear that rode her all but sent her panic-stricken in retreat. It was only the fact that she could not turn Baldy upon that narrow trail that gave her sufficient pause to gain mastery over the chaos of her nerves and drive them again into the fold of reason. It required a supreme effort of will to urge her horse onward again down into that mysterious ravine where she knew there might lurk for her a thing more terrible than death. That she did it bespoke the greatness of the love that inspired her courage.

The ravine below her was both shallower and wider than that upon the opposite side of the ridge so that it presented the appearance of a tiny basin. From her vantage point, she looked out across the tops of spreading oaks to the brush-covered hillside that bounded the basin on the south; but what lay below, what the greenery of the trees concealed from her sight, she could only surmise.

She knew that the Penningtons kept no horses here, so she guessed that the animal that had answered Baldy's neigh belonged to the men she sought. Slowly, she rode downward. What would her reception be? If her conclusions as to the identity of the men camped below were correct, she could imagine them shooting first and investigating later. The idea was not a pleasant one, but nothing could deter her now.

After what seemed a long time she rode out among splendid old oaks in view of a soiled tent and a picket line where three horses and a half dozen burros were tethered. Nowhere was there sign of the actual presence of men, yet she had an uncanny feeling that they were there and that from some place of concealment they were watching her.

She sat quietly upon her horse for a moment, waiting. Then, no one appearing, she called aloud.

"Hello, there! I want to speak with you."

Her voice sounded strange and uncanny in her ears.

For what seemed a long time there was no other sound than the gently moving leaves about her, the birds, and the heavy breathing of Baldy. Then, from the brush behind her came another voice. It came from the direction of the trail down which she had ridden. She realized that she must have passed within a few feet of the man who now spoke.

"What do you want?"

"I have come to warn you. You are being watched."

"You mean you are not alone? There are others with you? Then tell them to go away, for we have our rifles. We have done nothing. We're tending our bees — they're just below the ridge above our camp."

"There is no one with me. I do not mean that others are watching you now, but that others know that you come down out of the hills with something each Friday night, and they want to find out what it is you bring."

There was a rustling in the brush behind her, and she turned to see a man emerge, carrying a rifle ready in his hands. He was a Mexican, swarthy and ill-favored, his face pitted by smallpox.

Almost immediately, two other men stepped from the brush at other points about the camp. The three walked to where Shannon sat upon her mount. All were armed, and all were Mexicans.

"What do you know about what we bring out of the hills? Should we not bring our honey out?" asked the pock-marked one.

"I know what you bring out," she said. "I am not going to expose you. I am here to warn you."

"Why?"

"I know Allen."

Immediately their attitude changed. "You have seen Allen? You bring a message from him?"

"I have not seen him. I bring no message from him; but for reasons of my own I have come to warn you not to bring down another load next Friday night."

CHAPTER XX

THE POCK-MARKED Mexican stepped close to Shannon and took hold of her bridle reins.

"You think," he said in broken English, "we are damn fool? If you do not come from Allen, you come for no good to us. You tell us the truth, damn quick, or you never go back to tell where you find us and bring policemen here!"

His tone was ugly and his manner threatening. There was no harm in telling these men the truth, though it was doubtful whether they would believe her. She realized that she was in a predicament from which it might not be easy to extricate herself. She had told them that she was alone, and if they suspected her motives, they might easily do away with her. She knew how lightly the criminal Mexican esteems life — especially the life of the hated gringo.

"I have come to warn you because a friend of mine is going to watch for you next Friday night. He does not know who you are or what you bring out of the hills. I do, and so I know that rather than be caught, you might kill him, and I do not want him killed. That is all."

"How do you know what we bring out of the hills?"

"Allen told me."

"Allen told you? I do not believe you. Do you know where Allen is?"

"He is in jail in Los Angeles. I heard him telling a man in Los Angeles last July."

"Who is the friend of yours that is going to watch for us?"

"Mr. Pennington."

"You have told him about us?"

"I have told you that he knows nothing about you. All he knows is that someone comes down with burros from the hills and that they cut his fence last Friday night. He wants to catch you and find out what you are doing."

"Why have you not told him?" She hesitated.

"That can make no difference," she said presently.

"It makes a difference to us. I told you to tell the truth, or —"

The Mexican raised his rifle that she might guess the rest.

"I did not want to have to explain how I knew about you. I did not want Mr. Pennington to know that I knew such men as Allen.

"How did you know Allen?"

"That has nothing to do with it at all. I have warned you so that you can take steps to avoid discovery and capture. I shall tell no one else about you. Now, let me go."

She gathered Baldy and tried to rein him about, but the man clung to her bridle.

"Not so much of a hurry, *señorita!* Unless I know how Allen told you so much, I cannot believe that he told you anything. The police have many ways of learning things — sometimes they use women. If you are a friend to Allen, alright. It you are not, you know too damn much for to be very good for your health. You had better tell me all the truth, or you shall not ride away from here — ever!"

"Very well," she said. "I met Allen in a house in Hollywood where he sold his 'snow,' and I heard him telling the man there how you disposed of the whisky that was stolen in New York, brought here to the coast in a ship, and hidden in the mountains."

"What is the name of the man in whose house you met Allen?"

"Crumb."

The man raised his heavy brows. "How long since you been there — in that house in Hollywood?"

"Not since the last of July. I left the house the same time Allen did."

"You know how Allen he get in jail?" the Mexican asked.

The girl saw that a new suspicion had been aroused in the man, and she judged that the safer plan was to be perfectly frank.

"I do not know, for I have seen neither Crumb nor Allen since; but when I read in the paper that he had been arrested that night, I guessed that Crumb had done it. I heard Crumb ask him to deliver some snow to a man in Hollywood. I know that Crumb is a bad man and that he was trying to steal your share of the money from Allen."

The man thought in silence for several minutes, the lines of his heavy face evidencing the travail with which some new idea was being born. Presently, he looked up, the light of cunning gleaming in his evil eyes.

"You go now," he said. "I know you! Allen tell me about you a long time ago. You Crumb's woman, and your name is Gaza. You will not tell anything about us to your rich friends the Penningtons — you bet you won't!"

The Mexican laughed loudly, winking at his companions.

Shannon could feel the burning flush that suffused her face. She closed her eyes in what was almost physical pain, so terrible did the humiliation torture her pride, and then came the nausea of disgust. The man had dropped her reins, and she wheeled Baldy about.

"You will not come Friday night?" she asked, wishing some assurance that her sacrifice had not been entirely unavailing.

"Mr. Pennington will not find us Friday night, and so he will not be shot."

She rode away then; but there was a vague suspicion lurking in her mind that there had been a double meaning in the man's final words.

Custer Pennington, occupied in the office for a couple of hours after lunch, had just come from the house and was standing on the brow of the hill looking out over the ranch toward the mountains. His gaze, wandering idly at first, was suddenly riveted upon a tiny speck moving downward from the mouth of a distant ravine — a moving speck which he recognized, even at that distance, to be a horseman where no horseman should have

The Girl from Hollywood / 159

been. For a moment, he watched it, and then, returning to the house, he brought out a pair of binoculars.

Now the speck had disappeared; but he knew that it was down in the bottom of the basin hidden by the ridge above Jackknife Cañon, and he waited for the time when it would reappear on the crest. For five, 10, 15 minutes, he watched the spot where the rider should come into view once more. Then, he saw a movement in the brush and leveled his glasses upon the spot, following the half seen figure until it emerged into a space clear of chaparral. Now they were clearly revealed by the powerful lenses, the horse and its rider — Baldy and Shannon!

Pennington dropped the glasses at his side, a puzzled expression on his face, as he tried to find some explanation of the fact that the binoculars had revealed. From time to time, he caught glimpses of her again as she rode down the cañon; but when, after a considerable time, she did not emerge upon the road leading to the house, he guessed that she had crossed over El Camino Corto. Why she should do this, he could not even conjecture. It was entirely out of her way and a hilly trail, while the other was a wagon road leading almost directly from Sycamore to her house.

Presently, he walked around the house to the north side of the hill where he had a view of the valley spreading to the east and the west and the north. Toward the west, he could see the road that ran above the Evanses' house all the way to Horse Camp Cañon.

He did not know why he stood there watching for Shannon. It was none of his affair where she rode or when. It seemed strange, though, that she should have ridden alone into the hills after having refused to ride with him. It surprised him and troubled him, too, for it was the first suggestion that Shannon could commit even the most trivial act of underhandedness.

After a while, he saw her emerge from Horse Camp Cañon and follow the road to her own place. Custer ran his fingers through his hair in perplexity. He was troubled not only because Shannon had ridden without him after telling him that she could not ride that afternoon but also because of the direction in which she had ridden — the trail of which he had told her that he thought it led to the solution of the mystery of the nocturnal traffic. He had told her that he would not ride it before Saturday for fear of arousing the suspicions of the men he wished to surprise in whatever activity they might be engaged upon; and within a few hours, she had ridden deliberately up into the mountains on that very trail.

The more Custer considered the matter, the more perplexed he became. At last, he gave it up in sheer disgust. Doubtless, Shannon would tell him all about it when he called for her later in the afternoon. He tried to forget it; but the thing would not be forgotten.

Several times, he realized, with surprise, that he was hurt because she had ridden without him. He tried to argue that he was not hurt, that it made no difference to him, that she had a perfect right to ride with or without him as she saw fit, and that he did not care a straw one way or the other.

No, it was not that that was troubling him — it was something else. He didn't know what it was, but a drink would straighten it out; so, he took a drink. He realized that it was the first he had had in a week and almost decided not to take it; but he changed his mind. After that, he took several more without bothering his conscience to any appreciable extent. When his conscience showed signs of life, he reasoned it back to innocuous desuetude by that unanswerable argument: "What's the use?"

By the time he left to call for Shannon, he was miserably happy and happily miserable; yet he showed no outward sign that he had been drinking, unless it was that he swung the roadster around the curves of the driveway leading down the hill a bit more rapidly than usual.

Shannon was ready and waiting for him. She came out to the car with a smile — a smile that hid a sad and frightened heart; and he greeted her with another that equally belied his inward feelings. As they rode up to the castle on the hill, he gave her every opportunity to mention and explain her ride, principally by long silences, though never by any outward indication that he thought she had ought to explain. If she did not care to have him know about it, she should never know from him that he already knew; but the canker of suspicion was already gnawing at his heart, and he was realizing, perhaps for the first time, how very desirable this new friendship had grown to be.

Again and again, he insisted to himself that what she had done made no difference — that she must have had some excellent reason. Perhaps she had just wanted to be alone. He often had experienced a similar longing. Even when Grace had been there, he had occasionally wanted to ride off into the hills with nothing but his own thoughts for company.

Yet, argue as he would, the fact remained that it had made a difference and that he was considering Shannon now in a new light. Just what the change meant, he probably could not have satisfactorily explained had he tried; but he did not try. He knew that there was a difference and that his heart ached when it should not ache. It made him angry with himself, with the result that he went to his room and had another drink.

Shannon, too, felt the difference. She thought that it was her own guilty conscience, though why she should feel guilt for having risked so much for his sake she did not know. Instinctively, she was honest, and so to deceive one whom she loved, even for a good purpose, troubled her.

Something else troubled her, too. She knew that Custer had been drinking again, and she recalled what he had said to her that morning of the help she had been to him in getting away from his habit. She knew too well herself what it meant to fight for freedom from a settled vice, and she had been glad to have been instrumental in aiding him. She had had to fight her own battle alone; she did not want him to face a similar ordeal.

She wondered why he had been drinking that afternoon. Could it have been because she had not been able to ride with him, and thus, left alone, he had reverted to the old habit? The girl reproached herself, even though she felt, after her interview with the Mexicans, that she had undoubtedly saved Custer's life.

The Evanses, mother and son, were also at the Penningtons' for dinner that night. Shannon had noticed that it was with decreasing frequency that Grace's name was mentioned of late. She knew the reason. Letters had become fewer and fewer from the absent girl. She had practically ceased writing to Custer. Her letters to Mrs. Evans were no longer read to the Penningtons, for there had crept into them a new and unpleasant note that was as foreign as possible to the girl who had gone away months before. They showed a certain carelessness and lack of consideration that had pained them all.

They always asked after the absent girl, but her present life and her career were no longer discussed since the subject brought nothing but sorrow to them all. That she had been disappointed and disillusioned seemed probable since she had obtained only a few minor parts in mediocre pictures; and now, she no longer mentioned her ambition and scarcely ever wrote of her work.

At dinner that night, Eva was unusually quiet until the colonel, noticing it, asked if she was ill.

"There!" she cried. "You all make life miserable for me because I talk too much, and then, when I give you a rest, you ask if I am ill. What shall I do? If I talk, I pain you. If I fail to talk, I pain you; but if you must know, I am too thrilled to talk just now — I am going to be married!"

"All alone?" inquired Custer.

A sickly purplish hue, threatening crimson complications, crept from beneath Guy's collar and enveloped his entire head. He reached for his water goblet and ran the handle of his fork up his sleeve. The ensuing disentanglement added nothing to his equanimity, though it all but overturned the goblet. Custer was eying him with a seraphic expression that boded ill.

"What's the matter, Guy — measles?" he asked with a beatific smile.

Guy grinned sheepishly and was about to venture an explanation when Eva interrupted him. The others at the table were watching the two with amused smiles.

"You see, Momsy," said Eva, addressing her mother, "Guy has sold a story. He got a thousand dollars for it — a thousand!"

"Oh, not a thousand!" expostulated Guy.

"Well, it was nearly a thousand — if it had been 300 dollars more it would have been — and so now that our future is as sured, we are going to be married. I hadn't intended to mention it until Guy had talked with Popsy, but this will be very much nicer, and easier for Guy."

Guy looked up appealingly at the colonel.

"You see, sir, I was summing to key you — I mean I was —"

"You see what it is going to mean to have an author in the family," said Custer. "He's going to talk away above our heads. We won't know what he's talking about half the time. I don't know. Do you, Guy?"

"For pity's sake, Custer, leave the boy alone!" laughed Mrs. Pennington. "You're enough to rattle a stone image. And now, Guy, you know you don't have to feel embarrassed. We have all grown accustomed to the idea that you and Eva would marry, so it is no surprise. It makes us very happy."

"Thank you, Mrs. Pennington," said the boy. "It wasn't that it was hard to tell you. It was the way Eva wanted me to do it — like a book. I was supposed to come and ask the colonel for her hand in a very formal manner, and it made me feel foolish the more I thought of it — and I have been thinking about it all day. So, you see, when Eva blurted it out, I thought of my silly speech and I —"

"It wasn't a silly speech," interrupted Eva. "It was simplimetic gorgeristic. You thought so yourself when you made Bruce Bellinghame ask Hortense's father for her. 'Mr. Le Claire,' he said, squaring his manly shoulders, 'it is with emotions of deepest solemnity and a full realization of my unworthiness that I approach you upon this beautiful day in May —'"

"Oh, for Heaven's sake, Eva, *please!*" begged Guy.

They were all laughing now, including Eva and Guy. The tears were rolling down Custer's cheeks.

"That editor was guilty of grand larceny when he offered you 700 berries for the story. Why, the gem alone is easily worth a thousand. Adieu, Mark Twain! Farewell, Bill Nye! You've got 'em all nailed to the post, Guy Thackeray!"

The colonel wiped his eyes.

"I gather," he said, "that you two children wish to get married. Do I surmise correctly?"

"Oh, Popsy, you're just wonderful!" exclaimed Eva.

"Yes, how did you guess it, father?" asked Custer. "Marvelous deductive faculties for an old gentleman, I'll say!"

"That will be about all from you, Custer," admonished the colonel.

"Any time that I let a chance like this slip!" returned young Pennington. "Do you think I have forgotten how those two imps pestered the life out of Grace and me a few short years ago? Nay, nay!"

"I don't blame Custer a bit," said Mrs. Evans. "Guy and Eva certainly did make life miserable for him and Grace."

"That part of it is alright — it is Guy's affair and Eva's; but did you hear him refer to me as an old gentleman?"

They all laughed.

"But you *are* a gentleman," insisted Custer.

The colonel, his eyes twinkling, turned to Mrs. Evans.

"Times have changed, Mae, since we were children. Imagine speaking thus to our fathers!"

"I'm glad they have changed, Custer. It's terrible to see children afraid of their parents. It has driven so many of them away from home."

"No danger of that here," said the colonel.

"It is more likely to be the other way around," suggested Mrs. Pennington. "In the future, we may hear of parents leaving home because of the exacting tyranny of their children."

"My children shall be brought up properly," announced Eva, "with proper respect for their elders."

"Guided by the shining example of their mother," said Custer.

"And their Uncle Cutie," she retorted.

"Come, now," interrupted the colonel, "let's hear something about your plans. When are you going to be married?"

"Yes," offered Custer. "Now that the 700dollars has assured their future, there is no reason why they shouldn't be married at once and take a suite at the Ambassador. I understand they're as low as 3500 a month."

"Aw, I have more than the 700," said Guy. "I've been saving up for a long time. We'll have plenty to start with."

Shannon noticed that he flushed just a little as he made the statement, and she alone knew why he flushed. It was too bad

The Girl from Hollywood / 165

that Custer's little sister should start her married life on money of that sort!

Shannon felt that, at heart, Guy was a good boy — that he must have been led into this traffic originally without any adequate realization of its criminality. Her own misfortune had made her generously ready to seek excuses for wrongdoing in others; but she dreaded to think what it was going to mean to Eva and the other Penningtons if ever the truth became known. From her knowledge of the sort of men with whom Guy was involved, she was inclined to believe that the menace of exposure or blackmail would hang over him for many years, even if the former did not materialize in the near future; for she was confident that if his confederates were discovered by the authorities, they would immediately involve him and would try to put the full burden of responsibility upon his shoulders.

"I don't want the financial end of matrimony to worry either of you," the colonel was saying. "Guy has chosen a profession in which it may require years of effort to produce substantial returns. All I shall ask of my daughter's husband is that he shall honestly apply himself to his work. If you do your best, Guy, you will succeed, and in the meantime, I'll take care of the finances."

"But we don't want it that way," said Eva. "We don't want to live on charity."

"Do you think that what I give to my little girl would be given in a spirit of charity?" the colonel asked.

"Oh, Popsy, I know you wouldn't feel that it was; but can't you see how Guy would feel? I want him to be independent. I'd rather get along with a little and feel that he had earned it all."

"It may take a long time, Eva," said Custer; "and in the meantime, the best part of your lives would be spent in worry and scrimping. I know how you feel; but there's a way around it that has the backing of established business methods. Let father finance Guy's writing ability just as inventive genius is sometimes financed. When Guy succeeds, he can pay back with interest."

"What a dapper little thought!" exclaimed the girl. "That would fix everything, wouldn't it? You radiant man!"

CHAPTER XXI

ON THE FOLLOWING MONDAY, a pock-marked Mexican appeared at the county jail in Los Angeles during visitors' hours and asked to be permitted to see Slick Allen. The two stood in a corner and conversed in whispers. Allen's face wore an ugly scowl when his visitor told him of young Pennington's interference with their plans.

"It's getting too hot for us around there," said Allen. "We got to move. How much junk you got left?"

"About 60 cases of booze. We got rid of nearly 300 cases on the coast side without sending 'em through Evans. There isn't much of the other junk left — a couple pounds altogether at the outside."

"We got to lose the last of the booze," said Allen; "but we'll get our money's worth out of it. Now you listen, and listen careful, Bartolo."

He proceeded very carefully and explicitly to explain the details of a plan which brought a grin of sinister amusement to the face of the Mexican. It was not an entirely new plan but rather an elaboration and improvement of one that Allen had conceived some time before in the event of a contingency similar to that which had now arisen.

"And what about the girl?" asked Bartolo. "She should pay well to keep the Penningtons from knowing."

"Leave her to me," replied Allen. "I shall not be in jail forever."

During the ensuing days of that late September week, when Shannon and Custer rode together, there was a certain constraint in their relations that was new and depressing. The girl was apprehensive of the outcome of his adventure on the rapidly approaching Friday while he could not rid himself of the haunting memory of her solitary and clandestine ride over the mysterious trail that led into the mountains.

It troubled him that she should have kept the thing a secret, and it troubled him that he should care. What difference could it make to him where Shannon Burke rode? He asked himself that question a hundred times; but though he always answered that it could make no difference, he knew perfectly well that it *had* made a difference.

He often found himself studying her face as if he would find there either an answer to his question or a refutation of the suspicion of trickery and deceit which had arisen in his mind and would not down. What a beautiful face it was — not despite its irregular features, but because of them and because of the character and individuality they imparted to her appearance. Custer could not look upon that face and doubt her.

Several times, she caught him in the act of scrutinizing her thus, and she wondered at it, for in the past, he had never appeared to be consciously studying her. She was aware, too, that he was troubled about something. She wished that she might ask him — that she might invite his confidence, for she knew the pain of unshared sorrows; but he gave her no opening. So, they rode together, often in silence; and though their stirrups touched many a time, yet constantly they rode farther and farther apart just because chance had brought Custer Pennington from the office that Saturday afternoon to look out over the southern hills at the moment when Shannon had ridden down the trail into the meadow above Jackknife Cañon.

At last, Friday came. Neither had reverted since the previous Saturday to the subject that was uppermost in the mind of each; but now Shannon could not refrain from seeking once more to deter Custer from his project. She had not been able to forget the sinister smile of the Mexican or to rid her mind of an intuitive conviction that the man's final statement had concealed a hidden threat.

They were parting at the fork of the road — she had hesitated until the last moment.

"You still intend to try to catch those men tonight?" she asked.

"Yes — why?"

"I had hoped you would give it up. I am afraid something may happen. I — oh, please don't go, Custer!" She wished that she might add: "For my sake."

He laughed shortly.

"I guess there won't be any trouble. If there is, I can take care of myself."

She saw that it was useless to insist further.

"Let me know if everything is alright," she asked. "Light the light in the big cupola on the house when you get back — I can see it from my bedroom window — and then I shall know that nothing has happened. I shall be watching for it."

"Alright," Custer promised, and they parted.

He wondered why she should be so perturbed about his plans for the night. There was something peculiar about that — something that he couldn't understand or explain except in accordance with a single hypothesis — a hypothesis which he scorned to consider yet which rode his thoughts like a veritable *Little Old Man of the Sea*. Had he known the truth, it would all have been quite understandable; but how was he to know that Shannon Burke loved him?

When he reached the house, the ranch bookkeeper came to tell him that the Los Angeles operator had been trying to get him all afternoon.

"Somebody in L.A. wants to talk to you on important business," said the bookkeeper. "You're to call back the minute you get here."

Five minutes later, he had his connection. An unfamiliar voice asked if he were the younger Mr. Pennington.

"I am," he replied.

"Someone cut your fence last Friday. You like to know who he is?"

"What about it? Who are you?"

"Never mind who I am. I was with them. They double-crossed me. You want to catch 'em?"

"I want to know who they are and why they cut my fence and what the devil they're up to back there in the hills."

"You listen to me. You *sabe* Jackknife Cañon?"

"Yes."

"Tonight, they bring down the load just before dark. They do that every Friday and hide the burros until very late. Then, they come down into the valley while everyone is asleep. Tonight, they hide 'em in Jackknife. They tie 'em there an' go away. About 10x o'clock, they come back. You be there nine o'clock, and you catch 'em when they come back. *Sabe?*"

"How many of 'em are there?"

"Only two. You don't have to be afraid — they don't pack no guns. You take gun an' you catch 'em all alone."

"But how do I know that you're not stringing me?"

"You listen. They double-cross me. I get even. You no want to catch 'em, I no care — that's all. Goodbye!"

Custer turned away from the phone, running his fingers through his hair in a characteristic gesture signifying perplexity. What should he do? The message sounded rather fishy, he thought; but it would do no harm to have a look into Jackknife Cañon around nine o'clock. If he was being tricked, the worst he could fear was that they had taken this method of luring him to Jackknife while they brought the loaded burros down from the hills by some other route. If they had done that, it was very clever of them; but he would not be fooled a second time.

Custer Pennington didn't care to be laughed at, and so, if he was going to be hoaxed that night, he had no intention of having a witness to his idiocy. For that reason, he did not take Jake with him but rode alone up Sycamore when all the inmates of the castle on the hill thought him in bed and asleep. It was a clear night. Objects were plainly discernible at short distances, and when he passed the horse pasture, he saw the dim bulks of the brood mares a hundred yards away. A coyote voiced its uncanny cry from a near hill. An owl hooted dismally from a distance; but these sounds, rather than depressing him, had the opposite effect, for they were of the voices of the nights that he had known and loved since childhood.

When he turned into Jackknife, he reined the Apache in and sat for a moment listening. From farther up the cañon, out of sight, there came the shadow of a sound. That would be the tethered burros, he thought, if the whole thing was not a trick; but he was certain that he heard the sound of something moving there.

He rode on again, but he took the precaution of loosening his gun in its holster. There was, of course, the bare possibility of a sinister motive behind the message he had received. As he thought of it now, it occurred to him that his informant was perhaps a trifle too insistent in assuring him that it was safe to come up here alone. Well, the man had put it over cleverly, if that had been his intent.

Now Custer saw a dark mass beneath a sycamore. He rode directly toward it, and in another moment, he saw that it represented half a dozen laden burros tethered to the tree. He moved the Apache close in to examine them. There was no sign of men about.

He examined the packs, leaning over and feeling one. What they contained he could not guess; but it was not firewood. They evidently consisted of six wooden boxes to each burro, three on a side.

He reined the Apache in behind the burros in the darkness of the tree's shade, and there, he waited for the coming of the men. He did not like the look of things at all. What could those boxes contain? There was no legitimate traffic through or out of those hills that could explain the weekly trip of this little pack train; and if the men in charge of it were employed in any illegitimate traffic, they would not be surrendering to a lone man as meekly as his informant had suggested. The days of smuggling through the hills from the ocean was over — or at least, Custer had thought it was over; but this thing commenced to look like a recrudescence of the old-time commerce.

As he sat there waiting, he had ample time to think. He speculated upon the identity and purpose of the mysterious informant who had called him up from Los Angeles. He speculated again upon the contents of the packs. He recalled the whisky that Guy had sold him from time to time and wondered if the packs might not contain liquor. He had gathered from Guy that his supply came from Los Angeles, and he had never given the matter a second thought; but now, he recalled the fact and concluded that if this was whisky, it was not from the same source as Guy's.

All the time, he kept thinking of Shannon and her mysterious excursion into the hills. He recalled her anxiety to prevent him from coming up here tonight, and he tried to find reasonable explanations for it. Of course, it was the obvious explanation that did not occur to him; but several did occur that he tried to put from his mind.

Then, from the mouth of Jackknife, he heard the sound of horses' hooves. The Apache pricked up his ears, and Custer leaned forward and laid a hand upon his nostrils.

"Quiet, boy!" he admonished in a low whisper.

The sounds approached slowly, halting occasionally. Presently, two horsemen rode directly past him on the far side of the cañon. They rode at a brisk trot. Apparently, they did not see the pack train, or, if they saw it, they paid no attention to it. They disappeared in the darkness, and the sound of their horses' hooves ceased. Pennington knew that they had halted. Who could they be? Certainly not the drivers of the pack train, else they would have stopped with the burros.

He listened intently. Presently, he heard horses walking slowly toward him from up the cañon. The two who had passed were coming back — stealthily.

"I sure have got myself in a pretty trap!" he soliloquized a moment later when he heard the movement of mounted men in the cañon below him.

He drew his gun and sat waiting. It was not long that he had to wait. A voice coming from a short distance down the cañon addressed him.

"Ride out into the open and hold up your hands!" it said. "We got you surrounded and covered. If you make a brew, we'll bore you. Come on, now, step lively — and keep your hands up!"

It was the voice of an American.

"Who in thunder are you?" demanded Pennington.

"I am a United States marshal," was the quick reply.

Pennington laughed. There was something convincing in the very tone of the man's voice — possibly because Custer had been expecting to meet Mexicans. Here was a hoax indeed; but evidently as much on the newcomers as on himself. They had expected to find a lawbreaker. They would doubtless be angry when they discovered that they had been duped.

Custer rode slowly out from beneath the tree.

"Hold up your hands, Mr. Pennington!" snapped the marshal.

Custer Pennington was nonplused. They knew who he was, and yet they demanded that he should hold up his hands like a common criminal.

"Hold on there!" he cried. "What's the joke? If you know who I am, what do you want me to hold up my hands for? How do I know you're a marshal?"

"You don't know it; but I know that you're armed and that you're in a mighty bad hole. I don't know what you might do, and I ain't taking no chances. So, stick 'em up, and do it quick. If anybody's going to get bored around here, it'll be you and not none of my men!"

"You're a damned fool," said Pennington succinctly; but he held his hands before his shoulders as he had been directed.

Five men rode from the shadows and surrounded him. One of them dismounted and disarmed him. He lowered his hands and looked about at them.

"Would you mind," he said, "showing me your authority for this and telling me what in hell it's all about?"

One of the men threw back his coat, revealing a silver shield.

"That's my authority," he said; "that, and the goods we got on you."

"What goods?"

"Well, we expect to get 'em when we examine those packs."

"Look here!" said Custer. "You're all wrong. I have nothing to do with that pack train or what it's packing. I came up here to catch the fellows who have been bringing it down through Ganado every Friday night and who cut our fence last week. I don't know any more about what's in those packs than you do — evidently not as much."

"That's all right, Mr. Pennington. You'll probably get a chance to tell all that to a jury. We been laying for you since last spring. We didn't know it was you until one of your gang squealed; but we knew that this stuff was somewhere in the hills above L.A., and we aimed to get it and you sooner or later."

"Me?"

"Well, not you particularly, but whoever was bootlegging it. To tell you the truth, I'm plumb surprised to find who it is. I thought all along it was some gang of cheap greasers; but it don't make no difference who it is to your Uncle Sam."

"You say someone told you it was I?" asked Custer.

"Sure! How else would we know it? It don't pay to double-cross your pals, Mr. Pennington."

"What are you going to do with me?" he asked.

"We're going to take you back to L.A. and get you held to the Federal grand jury."

"Tonight?"

"We're going to take you back tonight"

"Can I stop at the house first?"

"No. We got a warrant to search the place, and we're going to leave a couple of my men here to do it the first thing in the morning. I got an idea you ain't the only one around there that knows something about this business."

As they talked, one of the deputies had taken a case from a pack and opened it.

"Look here!" he called. "It's it, alright!"

"It's what?" asked Custer.

"Oh, pe-ru-na, of course!" replied the deputy facetiously. "What did you think it was? I hope you never thought it none of that hooch stolen from a government bonded warehouse in New York!"

The others laughed at his joke.

"It's too bad," said the marshal, not at all unkindly, "for a decent young fellow like you to get mixed up in a nasty business like this."

"I agree with you," said Pennington.

His mind traveled like lightning, flashing a picture of Shannon Burke riding out of the hills and across the meadow above Jackknife Cañon; of her inquiry that very afternoon as to whether he was coming up here tonight. Had she really wished to dissuade him, or had she only desired to make sure of his intentions? The light would not shine from the big cupola tonight. What message would the darkness carry to Shannon Burke?

CHAPTER XXII

THEY TOOK CUSTER down to the village of Ganado where they had left their cars and obtained horses. Here, they left the animals, including the Apache, with instructions that he should be returned to the Rancho del Ganado in the morning.

The inhabitants of the village, almost to a man, had grown up in neighborly friendship with the Penningtons. When he from whom the officers had obtained their mounts discovered the identity of the prisoner, his surprise was exceeded only by his anger.

"If I'd known who you was after," he said, "you'd never have got no horses from me. I'd 'a' hamstrung 'em first! I've known Cus Pennington since he was knee high to a grasshopper, and whatever you took him for, he never done it. Wait till the colonel hears of this. You won't have no more job than a jackrabbit!"

The marshal turned threateningly toward the speaker.

"Shut up!" he advised. "If Colonel Pennington hears of this before morning, you'll wish to God you was a jackrabbit and could get out of the country in two jumps! Now, you get what I'm telling you — you're to keep your trap closed until morning. Hear me?"

"I ain't deaf, but sometimes I'm a leetle mite dumb." The last he added in a low aside to Pennington, accompanying it with a wink; and aloud: "I'm mighty sorry, Cus — *mighty* sorry. If I'd only knowed it was you! By gosh, I'll never get over this — furnishin' horses to help arrest a friend, and a Pennington!"

"Don't worry about that for a minute, Jim. I haven't done anything. It's just a big mistake."

The officers and their prisoner were in the car ready to start. The marshal pointed a finger at Jim.

"Don't forget what I told you about keeping your mouth shut until morning," he admonished.

They drove off toward Los Angeles. Jim watched them for a moment as the red tail light diminished in the distance. Then, he turned into the office of his feed barn and took the telephone receiver from its hook. "Gimme Ganado No. 1," he said to the sleepy night operator.

It was five minutes before continuous ringing brought the colonel to the extension telephone in his bedroom. He seemed unable to comprehend the meaning of what Jim was trying to tell him, so sure was he that Custer was in bed and asleep in a nearby room; but at last, he was half convinced, for he had known Jim for many years and well knew his stability and his friendship.

"If it was anybody but you, Jim, I'd say you were a damned liar," he commented in characteristic manner; "but what in hell did they take the boy for?"

"They wouldn't say. Just as I told 'em. I don't know what he done, but I know he never done it."

"You're right, Jim — my boy couldn't do a crooked thing!"

"I'm just like you, colonel — I know there ain't a crooked hair in Cus Pennington's head. If there's anything I can do, colonel, you jest let me know."

"You'll bring the Apache up in the morning? Thank you again, Jim, and goodbye."

He hung up the receiver. While he dressed hastily, he explained to his wife the purport of the message he had just received.

"What are you going to do, Custer?" she asked.

"I'm going to Los Angeles, Julia. Unless that marshal's driving a racing car, I'll be waiting for him when he gets there!"

¤

Shortly before breakfast the following morning, two officers, armed with a warrant, searched the castle on the hill. In Custer Pennington's closet, they found something which seemed to fill them with elation — two full bottles of whisky and an empty bottle, each bearing a label identical with those on the bottles they had found in the cases borne by the burros. With this evidence and the laden pack train, they started off toward the village.

Shannon Burke had put in an almost sleepless night. For hours she had lain watching the black silhouette of the big cupola against the clear sky, waiting for the light which would announce that Custer had returned home in safety; but no light had shone to relieve her anxiety. She had strained her ears through the long hours of the night for the sound of shooting from the hills; but only the howling of coyotes and the hooting of owls had disturbed the long silence. She sought to assure herself that all was well — that Custer had returned and forgotten to switch on the cupola light — that he had not forgotten but that the bulb was burned out. She manufactured probable and improbable explanations by the score; but always a disturbing premonition of evil dispersed the cohorts of hope.

She was up early in the morning and in the saddle at the first streak of dawn, riding directly to the stables of the Rancho del Ganado. The stableman was there, saddling the horses while they fed.

"No one has come down yet?" she asked.

"The Apache's gone," he replied. "I don't understand it. He hasn't been in his box all night. I was just thinkin' of goin' up to the house to see if Custer was there. Don't seem likely he'd be ridin' all night, does it?"

"No," she said. Her heart was in her mouth. She could scarcely speak. "I'll ride up for you," she managed to say.

Wheeling Baldy, she put him up the steep hill to the house. The iron gate that closed the patio arch at night was still down, so she rode around to the north side of the house and *coo-hooed* to attract the attention of someone within. Mrs. Pennington, followed by Eva, came to the door. Both were fully dressed. When they saw who it was, they came out and told Shannon what had happened.

He was not injured, then. The sudden sense of relief left her weak, and for a moment, she did not consider the other danger that confronted him. He was safe! That was all she cared about just then. Later, she commenced to realize the gravity of his situation and the innocent part that she had taken in involving him in the toils of the scheme, which her interference must have suggested to those actually responsible for the traffic in stolen liquor, the guilt of which they had now cleverly shifted to the shoulders of an innocent man. Intuitively, she guessed Slick Allen's part in the unhappy contretemps of the previous night; for she knew of the threats he had made against Custer Pennington and of his complicity in the criminal operations of the bootleggers.

How much she knew! More than any other, she knew all the details of the whole tragic affair. She alone could untangle the knotted web, and yet, she dared not until there was no other way. She dared not let them guess that she knew more of the matter than they. She could not admit such knowledge without revealing the source of it and exposing herself to the merited contempt of these people whose high regard had become her obsession, whose friendship was her sole happiness, and the love she had conceived for one of them the secret altar at which she worshiped.

In the last extremity, if there was no alternative, she would sacrifice everything for him. To that, her love committed her; but she would wait until there was no other way. She had suffered so grievously through no fault of her own that she clung with desperation to the brief happiness which had come into her life and which was now threatened once again because of no wrongdoing on her part.

Fate had been consistently unkind to her. Was it fair that she should suffer always for the wickedness of another? She had at least the right to hope and wait.

But there was something that she could do. When she turned Baldy down the hill from the Penningtons', she took the road home that led past the Evanses' ranch and, turning in, dismounted and tied Baldy at the fence. Her knock was answered by Mrs. Evans.

"Is Guy here?" asked Shannon.

Hearing her voice, Guy came from his room, drawing on his coat.

"You're getting as bad as the Penningtons," he said, laughing. "They have no respect for Christian hours!"

"Something has happened," she said, "that I thought you should know about. Custer was arrested last night by government officers and taken to Los Angeles. He was out on the Apache at the time. No one seems to know where he was arrested, or why; but the supposition is that they found him in the hills, for the man who runs the feed barn in the village — Jim — told the colonel that the officers got horses from him and rode up toward the ranch and that it was a couple of hours later that they brought Custer back on the Apache. The stableman just told me that the Apache had not been in his stall all night, and I know — Custer told me not to tell, but it will make no difference now — that he was going up into the hills last night to try to catch the men who have been bringing down loads on burros every Friday night for a long time and who cut his fence last Friday."

She looked straight into Guy's eyes as she spoke; but he dropped his as a flush mounted his cheek.

"I thought," she continued, "that Guy might want to go to Los Angeles and see if he could help Custer in any way. The colonel went last night."

"I'll go now," said Guy. "I guess I can help him."

His voice was suddenly weary, and he turned away with an air of dejection which assured Shannon that he intended to do the only honorable thing that he could do — assume the guilt that had been thrown upon Custer's shoulders no matter what the consequences to himself. She had had little doubt that Guy would do this, for she realized his affection for Custer as well as the impulsive generosity of his nature, which, however marred by weakness, was still fine by instinct.

Half an hour later, after a hasty breakfast, young Evans started for Los Angeles while his mother and Shannon, standing on the porch of the bungalow, waved their goodbyes as his roadster swung through the gate into the county road. Mrs. Evans had only a vague idea as to what her son could do to assist Custer Pennington out of his difficulty; but Shannon Burke knew that Pennington's fate lay in the hands of Guy Evans — unless she chose to tell what she knew.

Colonel Pennington had overtaken the marshal's car before the latter reached Los Angeles, but after a brief parley on the road, he had discovered that he could do nothing to alter the officer's determination to place Custer in the county jail pending his preliminary hearing before a United States commissioner. Neither the colonel's plea that his son should be allowed to accompany him to a hotel for the night nor his assurance that he would be personally responsible for the young man's appearance before the commissioner on the following morning availed to move the obdurate marshal from his stand; nor would he permit the colonel to talk with the prisoner.

This was the last straw. Colonel Pennington had managed to dissemble outward indications of his rising ire, but now an amused smile lighted his son's face as he realized that his father was upon the verge of an explosion. He caught the older man's eye and shook his head.

"It'll only make it worse," he cautioned.

The colonel directed a parting glare at the marshal, muttered something about homeopathic intellects, and turned back to his roadster.

CHAPTER XXIII

DURING THE LONG RIDE to Los Angeles and later in his cell in the county jail, Custer Pennington had devoted many hours to seeking an explanation of the motives underlying the plan to involve him in a crime of which he had no knowledge nor even a suspicion of the identity of its instigators. To his knowledge, he had no enemies whose hostility was sufficiently active to lead them to do him so great a wrong. He had had no trouble with any one recently other than his altercation with Slick Allen several months before; yet it was obvious that he had been deliberately sacrificed for some ulterior purpose. What that purpose was he could only surmise.

The most logical explanation, he finally decided, was that those actually responsible, realizing that discovery was imminent, had sought to divert suspicion from themselves by fastening it upon another. That they had selected him as the victim might easily be explained on the ground that his embarrassing interest in their movements had already centered their attention upon him while it also offered the opportunity for luring him into the trap without arousing his suspicions.

It was, then, just a combination of circumstances that had led him into his present predicament; but there still remained unanswered one question that affected his peace of mind more considerably than all the others combined. Who had divulged to the thieves his plans for the previous night?

Concurrently with that question, there arose before his mind's eye a picture of Shannon Burke and Baldy as they topped the summit above Jackknife from the trail that led across the basin meadow back into the hills, he knew not where.

"I can't believe that it was she," he told himself for the hundredth time. "She could not have done it. I won't believe it! She could explain it all if I could ask her; but I can't ask her. There is a great deal that I cannot understand, and the most inexplicable thing is that she could possibly have had any connection whatever with the affair."

When his father came with an attorney in the morning, the son made no mention of Shannon Burke's ride into the hills or of her anxiety when they parted in the afternoon to learn if he was going to carry out his plan for Friday night.

"Did anyone know of your intention to watch for these men?" asked the attorney.

"No one," he replied; "but they might have become suspicious from the fact that the week before I had all the gates padlocked on Friday. They had to cut the fence that night to get through. They probably figured that it was getting too hot for them and that on the following Friday, I would take some other steps to discover them. Then they made sure of it by sending me that message from Los Angeles. Gee, but I bit like a sucker!"

"It is unfortunate," remarked the attorney, "that you had not discussed your plans with someone before you undertook to carry them out on Friday night. If we could thus definitely establish your motive for going alone into the hills and to the very spot where you were discovered with the pack train, I think it would go much further toward convincing the court that you were there without any criminal intent than your own unsupported testimony to that effect!"

"But haven't you his word for it?" demanded the colonel.

"I am not the court," replied the attorney, smiling.

"Well, if the court isn't a damned fool, it'll know he wouldn't have padlocked the gates the week before to keep himself out," stated the colonel conclusively.

"The government might easily assume that he did that purposely to divert suspicion from himself. At least, it is no proof of innocence."

Colonel Pennington snorted.

"The best thing to do now," said the attorney, "is to see if we can get an immediate hearing and arrange for bail in case he is held to the grand jury."

"I'll go with you," said the colonel.

They had been gone but a short time when Guy Evans was admitted to Custer's cell. The latter looked up and smiled when he saw who his visitor was.

"It was bully of you to come," he said. "Bringing condolences or looking for material, old thing?"

"Don't joke, Cus," exclaimed Evans. "It's too rotten to joke about, and it's all my fault."

"Your fault?"

"I am the guilty one. I've come down to give myself up."

"Guilty! Give yourself up! What are you talking about?"

"God, Cus, I hate to tell you. It didn't seem such an awful thing to do until this happened. Everyone's buying booze or selling booze or making booze. Every one's breaking the damned old 18th Amendment, and it's got so it don't seem like committing a crime or anything like that. You know, Cus, that I wouldn't do anything criminal, and, oh, God, what'll Eva think?"

Guy covered his face with his hands and choked back a sob.

"Just what the devil are you talking about?" inquired Pennington. "Do you mean to tell me that you have been mixed up in — well, what do you know about that?"

A sudden light had dawned upon Custer's understanding.

"That hooch that you've been getting me — that I joked you about — it was really the stuff that was stolen from a bonded warehouse in New York? It wasn't any joke at all?"

"You can see for yourself now how much of a joke it was," replied Evans.

"I'll admit," returned Custer ruefully, "that it does require a considerable sense of humor to see it in this joint!"

"What do you suppose they'll do to me?" asked Guy. "Do you suppose they'll send me to the penitentiary?"

"Tell me the whole thing from the beginning — who got you into it and just what you've done. Don't omit a thing, no matter how much it incriminates you. I don't need to tell you, old man, that I'm for you no matter what you've done."

"I know that, Cus; but I'm afraid no one can help me. I'm in for it. I knew it was stolen from the start. I have been selling it since last May — 7,776 quarts of it — and I made a dollar on every quart. It was what I was going to start housekeeping on. Poor little Eva!"

Again, a sob half choked him.

"It was Slick Allen that started me. First, he sold me some; then, he got me to sell you a bottle and bring him the money. Then, he had me, or at least he made me think so; and he insisted on my handling it for them out in the valley. It wasn't hard to persuade me, for it looked safe, and it didn't seem like such a rotten thing to do, and I wanted the money the worst way. I know they're all bum excuses. I shan't make any excuses — I'll take my medicine; but it's when I think of Eva that it hurts. It's only Eva that counts!"

"Yes," said Pennington, laying his hand affectionately on the other's shoulder. "It is only Eva who counts; and because of Eva, and because you and I love her so much, you cannot go to the penitentiary."

"What do you mean — cannot go?"

"Have you told anyone else what you have just told me?"

"No."

"Don't. Go back home, and keep your mouth shut," said Custer.

"You mean that you will take a chance of going up for what I did? Nothing doing! Do you suppose I'd let you, Cus, the best friend I've got in the world, go to the pen for me — for something I did?"

"It's not for you, Guy. I wouldn't go to the pen for you or any other man; but I'd go to the pen for Eva, and so would you."

"I know it, but I can't let you do it. I'm not rotten, Cus!"

"You and I don't count. To see her unhappy and humiliated would be worse for me than spending a few years in the penitentiary. I'm innocent. No matter if I am convicted, I'll know I'm innocent, and Eva'll know it, and so will all the rest at Ganado; but, Guy, they've got too much on you if they ever suspect you, and the fact that you voluntarily admitted your guilt would convince even my little sister. If you were sent up, it might ruin her life — it *would* ruin it. Things could never be the same for her again; but if I was sentenced for a few years, it would only be the separation from a brother whom she knew to be innocent and in whom she still had undiminished confidence. She wouldn't be humiliated — her life wouldn't be ruined; and when I came back, everything would be just as it was before. If you go, things will not be the same when you come back — they can never be the same again. You cannot go!"

"I cannot let you go and be punished for what I did while I remain free!"

"You've got to — it's the easiest way. We've all got to be punished for what you did — those who love us are always punished for our sins; but let me tell you that I don't think you are going to escape punishment if I go up for this. You're going to suffer more than I. You're going to suffer more than you would if you went up yourself; but it can't be helped. The question is, are you man enough to do this for Eva? It is your sacrifice more than mine."

Evans swallowed hard and tried to speak. It was a moment before he succeeded.

"My God, Cus, I'd rather go myself!"

"I know you would."

"I can never have any self-respect again. I can never look a decent man in the face. Every time I see Eva or your mother or the colonel, I'll think: 'You dirty cur, you let their boy go to the pen for something you did!' Oh, Cus, please don't ask me to do it! There must be some other way. And — and, Cus, think of Grace. We've been forgetting Grace. What'll it mean to Grace if you are sent up?"

"It won't mean anything to Grace, and you know it. None of us mean much to Grace anymore."

Guy looked out of the little barred window and tears came to his eyes.

"I guess you're right," he said.

"You're going to do it, Guy — for Eva?"

"For Eva — yes."

Pennington brightened up as if a great load had been lifted from his shoulders.

"Good!" he cried. "Now the chances are that I'll not be sent up, for they've nothing on me — they can't have; but if I am, you've got to take my place with the folks. You've had your lesson. I know you'll never pull another fool stunt like this again. And quit drinking, Guy. I haven't much excuse for preaching; but you're the sort that can't do it. Leave it alone. Goodbye, now; I'd rather you were not here when father comes back — you might weaken."

Evans took the other's hand.

"I envy you, Cus — on the level, I do!"

"I know it; but don't feel too bad about it. It's one of those things that's done, and it can't be undone. Roosevelt would have called what you've got to do 'grasping the nettle.' Grasp it like a man!"

Evans walked slowly from the jail, entered his car, and drove away. Of the two hearts, his was the heavier; of the two burdens, his the more difficult to bear.

Custer Pennington, appearing before a United States commissioner that afternoon for his preliminary hearing, was held to the Federal grand jury and admitted to bail. The evidence brought by the deputies who had searched the Pennington home taken in connection with the circumstances surrounding his arrest seemed to leave the commissioner no alternative. Even the colonel had to admit that to himself, though he would never have admitted it to another. The case would probably come up before the grand jury on the following Wednesday.

The colonel wanted to employ detectives at once to ferret out those actually responsible for the theft and bootlegging of the stolen whisky; but Custer managed to persuade him not to do so on the ground that it would be a waste of time and money since the government was already engaged upon a similar pursuit.

"Don't worry, father," he said. "They haven't a shred of evidence that I stole the whisky or that I ever sold any. They found me with it — that is all. I can't be hanged for that. Let them do the worrying. I want to get home in time to eat one of Hannah's dinners. I'll say they don't set much of a table in the sheriff's boarding house!"

"Where did you get the three bottles they found in your room?"

"I bought them."

"I asked where, not how."

"I might get someone else mixed up in this if I were to answer that question. I can't do it."

"No," said the colonel, "you can't. When you buy whisky, nowadays, you are usually compounding a felony. It's certainly a rotten condition to obtain in the land of the free; but you've got to protect your accomplices. I shall not ask you again; but they'll ask you in court, my boy."

"All the good it'll do them!"

"I suppose so; but I'd hate to see my boy sent to the penitentiary."

"You'd hate to be in court and hear him divulge the name of a man who had trusted him sufficiently to sell him whisky."

"I'd rather see you go to the penitentiary!" the colonel said.

That night at dinner, Custer made light of the charge against him, yet at the same time he prepared them for what might happen, for the proceedings before the commissioner had impressed him with the gravity of his case as had also the talk he had had with his attorney afterward.

"No matter what happens," he said to them all, "I shall know that you know I am not guilty."

"My boy's word is all I need," replied his mother.

Eva came and put her arms about him.

"They wouldn't send you to jail, would they?" she demanded. "It would break my heart!"

"Not if you knew I was innocent."

"N-no, not then, I suppose; but it would be awful. If you were guilty, it would kill me. I'd never want to live if my brother was convicted of a crime and was guilty of it. I'd kill myself first!"

Her brother drew her face down and kissed her tenderly.

"That would be foolish, dear," he said. "No matter what one of us does, such an act would make it all the worse — for those who were left."

"I can't help it," she said. "It isn't just because I have had the honor of the Penningtons preached to me all my life. It's because it's in me — the Pennington honor. It's a part of me just as it's a part of you and Mother and Father. It's a part of the price we have to pay for being Penningtons. I have always been proud of it, Custer, even if I am only a silly girl."

"I'm proud of it, too, and I haven't jeopardized it; but even if I had, you mustn't think about killing yourself on my account or any one's else."

"Well, I know you're not guilty, so I don't have to."

"Good! Let's talk about something pleasant."

"Why didn't you see Grace while you were in Los Angeles?"

"I tried to. I called up her boarding place from the lawyer's office. I understood the woman who answered the phone to say that she would call her, but she came back in a couple of minutes and said that Grace was out on location."

"Did you leave your name?"

"I told the woman who I was when she answered the phone."

"I'm sorry you didn't see her," said Mrs. Pennington. "I often think that Mrs. Evans or Guy should run down to Los Angeles occasionally and see Grace."

"That's what Shannon says," said Custer. "I'll try to see her next week before I come home."

"Shannon was up nearly all afternoon waiting to hear if we received any word from you. When you telephoned that you had been held to the Federal grand jury, she would scarcely believe it. She said there must be some mistake."

"Did she say anything else?"

"She asked whether Guy got there before you were held, and I told her that you said Guy visited you in the jail. She seems so worried about the affair — just as if she were one of the family. She is such a dear girl! I think I grow to love her more and more every day."

"Yes," said Custer, noncommittally.

"She asked me one rather peculiar question," Eva went on.

"What was that?"

"She asked if I was *sure* that it was *you* who had been held to the grand jury."

"That was odd, wasn't it?"

The Girl from Hollywood / 189

"She's so sure of your innocence — just as sure as we are," said Eva.

"Well, that's very nice of her," remarked Custer.

CHAPTER XXIV

THE NEXT MORNING, he saw Shannon, who came to ride with them, the Penningtons, as had been her custom. She looked tired as if she had spent a sleepless night. She had — she had spent two sleepless nights, and she had had to fight the old fight all over again. It had been very hard, even though she had won, for it had shown her that the battle was not over. She had thought that she had conquered the craving; but that had been when she had had no troubles or unhappiness to worry her mind and nerves. The last two days had been days of suffering for her, and the two sleepless nights had induced a nervous condition that begged for the quieting influence of the little white powder.

Custer noticed immediately that something was amiss. The roses were gone from her cheeks, leaving a suggestion of the old pallor; and though she smiled and greeted him happily, he thought that he detected an expression of wistfulness and pain in her face when she was not conscious that others were observing her.

There was a strange suggestion of change in their relations, which Custer did not attempt to analyze. It was as if he had been gone a long time, and, returning, had found Shannon changed through the natural processes of time and separation. She was not the same girl — she could never be the same again nor could their relations ever be the same.

The careless freedom of their association, which had resembled that of a brother and sister more than any other relationship between a man and a woman, had gone forever. What had replaced it Custer did not know. Sometimes, he thought that it was a suspicion of Shannon that clung to his mind in spite of himself, but again and again, he assured himself that he held no suspicion of her.

He wished, though, that she would explain that which was to him inexplicable. He had the faith to believe that she could explain it satisfactorily; but would she do so? She had had the opportunity before this thing had occurred and had not taken advantage of it. He would give her another opportunity that day, and he prayed that she would avail herself of it. Why he should care so much, he did not try to reason. He did not even realize how much he did care.

Presently, he turned toward her.

"I am going to ride over to the east pasture after breakfast," he said and waited.

"Is that an invitation?"

He smiled and nodded.

"But not if it isn't perfectly convenient," he added.

"I'd love to come with you. You know I always do."

"Fine! And you'll breakfast with us?"

"Not today. I have a couple of letters to write that I want to get off right away; but I'll be up between 8:30 and nine. Is that too late?"

"I'll ride down after breakfast and wait for you — if I won't be in the way."

"Of course, you won't. It will take me only a few minutes to write my letters."

"How are you going to mail them? This is Sunday."

"Mr. Powers is going to drive in to Los Angeles today. He'll mail them in the city."

"Who looks after things when Mr. and Mrs. Powers are away?"

"Who looks after things? Why, I do."

"The chickens, and the sow, and Baldy — you take care of them all?"

"Certainly, and I have more than that now."

"How's that?"

"Nine little pigs! They came yesterday. They're perfect beauties."

The man laughed.

"What are you laughing about?" she demanded.

"The idea of you taking care of chickens and pigs and a horse!"

"I don't see anything funny about it, and it's lot of fun. Did you think I was too stupid?"

"I was just thinking what a change two months have made. What would you have done if you'd been left alone two months ago with a hundred hens, a horse, and 10 pigs to care for?"

"The question then would have been what the hens, the horse, and the pigs would have done; but now, I know pretty well what to do. The two letters I have to write are about the little pigs. I don't know much about them, and so I am writing to Berkeley and Washington for the latest bulletins."

"Why don't you ask *us*?"

"Gracious, but I do! I am forever asking the colonel questions, and the boys at the hog house must hate to see me coming. I've spent hours in the office reading Lovejoy and Colton; but I want something for ready reference. I've an idea that I can raise lots more hogs than I intended by fencing the orchard and growing alfalfa between the rows for pasture. There's something solid and substantial about hogs that suggests a bank balance even in the years when the orange crop may be short or a failure or the market poor."

"You've got the right idea," said Custer. "There isn't a rancher or an orchardist big or little in the valley who couldn't make more money year in and year out if he'd keep a few brood sows."

"What's Cus doing?" asked Eva, who had reined back beside them. "Preaching hog-raising again? That's his idea of a dapper little way to entertain a girl — hogs, Herefords, and horses! Wouldn't he make a hit in society? Regular little tea pointer, I'll say!"

"I knew you were about to say something," remarked her brother. "You've been quiet for all of five minutes."

"I've been thinking," said Eva. "I've been thinking how lonely it will be when you have to go away to jail."

"Why, they can't send me to jail — I haven't done anything," he tried to reassure her.

The Girl from Hollywood / 193

"I'm so afraid, Cus!" The tears came to her eyes. "I lay awake for hours last night thinking about it. Oh, Cus, I just couldn't stand it if they sent you to jail! Do you think the men who did it would let you go for something they did? Could anyone be so wicked? I never hated anyone in my life, but I could hate them if they don't come forward and save you. I could *hate* them, *hate* t hem, *hate* them! Oh, Cus, I believe that I could *kill* the man who would do such a thing to my brother!"

"Come, dear, don't worry about it. The chances are that they'll free me. Even if they don't, you mustn't feel quite so bitterly against the men who are responsible. There may be reasons that you know nothing of that would keep them silent. Let's not talk about it. All we can do now is to wait and see what the grand jury is going to do. In the meantime, I don't intend to worry."

Shannon Burke, her heart heavy with shame and sorrow, listened as might a condemned man to the reading of his death sentence. She felt almost the degradation that might have been hers had she deliberately planned to ensnare Custer Pennington in the toils that had been laid for him.

She determined that she would go before the grand jury and tell all she knew. Then she would go away. She would not have to see the contempt and hatred they must surely feel for her after she had recited the cold facts that she must lay before the jury, unmitigated by any of those extenuating truths that must lie forever hidden in the secret recesses of her soul. They would know only that she might have warned Custer and did not; that she might have cleared him at his preliminary hearing and did not. The fact that she had come to his rescue at the 11th hour would not excuse her in their minds of the guilt of having permitted the Pennington honor to be placed in jeopardy needlessly; nor could it explain her knowledge of the crime or those associations of her past life that had made it possible for her to have gained such knowledge.

No, she could never face them again after the following Wednesday; but until then, she would cling to the brief days of happiness that remained to her before the final catastrophe of her life, for it was thus that she thought of it — the moment and the act that would forever terminate her intercourse with the

Penningtons that would turn the respect of the man she loved to loathing.

She counted the hours before the end. There would be two more morning rides — tomorrow and Tuesday. They would ask her to dinner or to lunch or to breakfast several times in the ensuing three days, and there would be rides with Custer. She would take all the happy memories that she could into the bleak and sunless future.

Their ride that morning was over a loved and familiar trail that led across El Camino Corto over low hills into Horse Camp Cañon, and up Horse Camp to Coyote Springs; then over El Camino Largo to Sycamore Cañon and down beneath the old, old sycamores to the ranch. She felt that she knew each bush and tree and boulder, and they held for her the quiet restfulness of the familiar faces of old friends. She should miss them, but she would carry them in her memory forever.

When they came to the fork in the road, she would not let Custer ride home with her.

"At 8:30, then," he called to her as she urged Baldy into a canter and left them with a gay wave of the hand that gave no token of the heavy sorrow in her heart.

As was her custom, she ate breakfast with Mr. and Mrs. Powers at the little tenant cottage a couple of hundred yards in rear of her own bungalow — a practice which gave her an opportunity to discuss each day's work in advance with her foreman and, at the same time, to add to her store of information concerning matters of ranching and citrus culture. Her knowledge of these things had broadened rapidly and was a constant source of surprise to Powers, who took great pride in bragging about it to his friends; for Shannon had won as great a hold upon the hearts of these two as she had upon all who were fortunate enough to know her well.

After breakfast, as she was returning to her bungalow to write her letters, she saw a Mexican boy on a bicycle turn in at her gate. They met in front of the bungalow.

"Are you Miss Burke?" he asked. "Bartolo says for you to come to his camp in the mountains this morning, sure," he went on, having received an affirmative reply.

"Who is Bartolo?"

"He says you know. You went to his camp a week ago yesterday."

"Tell him I do not know him and will not go."

"He says to tell you that he only wants to talk to you about your friend who is in trouble."

The girl thought for a moment. Possibly, here was a way out of her dilemma. If she could force Bartolo by threats of exposure, he might discover a way to clear Custer Pennington without incriminating himself. She turned to the boy.

"Tell him I will come."

"I do not see him again. He is up in his camp now. He told me this yesterday. He also told me to tell you that he would be watching for you, and if you did not come alone you would not find him."

"Very well," she said and turned into the bungalow.

She wrote her letters, but she was not thinking about them. Then, she took them over to Powers to take to the city for her. After that, she went to the telephone and called the Rancho del Ganado, asking for Custer when she got the connection.

"I'm terribly disappointed," she said when he came to the telephone. "I find I simply can't ride this morning; but if you'll put it off until afternoon —"

"Why, certainly! Come up to lunch and we'll ride afterward," he told her.

"You won't go, then, until afternoon?" she asked.

"I'll ride over to the east pasture this morning, and we'll just take a ride any old place that you want to go this afternoon."

"Alright," she replied.

She had hoped that he would not ride that morning. There was a chance that he might see her even though the east pasture was miles from the trail she would ride, for there were high places on both trails where a horseman would be visible for several miles.

"This noon at lunch, then," he said.

CHAPTER XXV

HALF AN HOUR LATER, Custer Pennington swung into the saddle and headed the Apache up Sycamore Cañon.

The trail to the east pasture led through Jackknife. As he passed the spot where he had been arrested on the previous Friday night, the man made a wry face — more at the recollection of the ease with which he had been duped than because of the fact of his arrest. Being free from any sense of guilt, he could view with a certain lightness of spirit that was almost levity the mere physical aspects of possible duress. The reality of his service to Eva could not but tend to compensate for any sorrow he must feel because of the suffering his conviction and imprisonment might bring to his family, so much greater must be their sorrow should Eva be permitted to learn the truth.

When Shannon had broken their engagement for the morning, he had felt a disappointment entirely out of proportion to its cause — a thing which he had realized himself but had been unable to analyze. Now, in anticipation of seeing her at noon and riding with her after lunch, he experienced a rise in spirits that was equally unaccountable. He liked her very much, and she was excellent company — which, of course, would account for the pleasure he derived from being with her. Today, too, he hoped for an explanation of her ride into the mountains the week before so that there might be no longer any shadow on his friendship for her.

The more he thought about it, the more convinced he was that this afternoon she would explain the whole matter quite satisfactorily, and presently, he found himself whistling as if there were no such places as jails or penitentiaries in the whole wide and beautiful world.

Just then, he reached the summit of the trail leading out of Jackknife Cañon toward the east pasture. As was his wont, the Apache stopped to breathe after the hard climb, and, as seems to be the habit of all horses in like circumstances, he turned around and faced in the opposite direction from that in which his rider had been going.

Below and to Custer's right, the ranch buildings lay dotted about in the dust like children's toys upon a gray rug. Beyond was the castle on the hill, shining in the sun and, farther still, the soft-carpeted valley in grays and browns and greens. Then the young man's glance wandered to the left and out over the basin meadow, and instantly, the joy died out of his heart and the happiness from his eyes. Straight along the mysterious trail loped a horse and rider toward the mountains, and even at that distance, he recognized them as Baldy and Shannon.

The force of the shock was almost equivalent to an unexpected blow in the face. What could it mean? He recalled her questions. She had deliberately sought to learn his plans as she had that other day, and then, as before, she had hastened off to some mysterious rendezvous in the hills.

Suddenly a hot wave of anger surged through him. Quiet and self-controlled as he usually was, there were times when the Pennington temper seized and dominated him so completely that he himself was appalled by the acts it precipitated. Under its spell, a Pennington might commit murder. Now Custer did what was almost as foreign to his nature — he cursed the girl who rode on, unconscious of his burning eyes upon her toward the mountains. He cursed her aloud, searching his memory for opprobrious epithets and anathemas to hurl after her.

This was the end. He was through with her forever. What did he know about her? What did any of them know about her? She had never mentioned her life or associations in the city — he recalled that now. She had known no one whom they knew, and they had taken her in and treated her as a daughter of the house without knowing anything of her; and this was their reward!

She was doubtless a hireling of the gang that had stolen the whisky and disposed of it through Guy. They had sent her here to spy on Guy and to watch the Penningtons. It was she who had set the trap in which he had been caught — not to save Guy but to throw the suspicion of guilt upon Custer.

But for what reason? There was no reason except that he had been selected from the first to be the scapegoat when the government officers were too hot upon their trail. She had watched him carefully. God, but she had been cunning and he credulous! There had been scarce a day that she had not been with him. She had ridden the hills with him, and she had kept him from following the mysterious trail — so he reasoned in his rage, though as a matter of fact, she had done nothing of the sort; but anger and hate are blind, and Custer Pennington was angry and filled with hate. Unreasoning rage consumed him.

He believed that he never had hated before as he hated this girl now, so far to the other extreme had the shock of her duplicity driven his regard for her. He would see her just once more, and he would tell her what he thought of her so that there might be no chance that she would ever again enter the home of the Penningtons. He must see to that before he went away, that Eva might not be exposed to the influence of such a despicable character.

But he could not see her today. He could not trust himself to see her, for even in his anger he remembered that she was a woman and that when he saw her, he must treat her as a woman. If she had been within reach when he first discovered her, a moment since, he could have struck her, choked her.

With the realization, the senseless fury of his anger left him. He turned the Apache away and headed him again toward the east pasture; but deep within his heart was a cold anger that was quite as terrible, though in a different way.

Shannon Burke rode up the trail toward the camp of the smugglers, all unconscious that there looked down upon her from a high ridge behind eyes filled with hate and loathing — the eyes of the man she loved.

She put Baldy up the steep trail that had so filled her with terror when she first scaled it and down upon the other side into the grove of oaks that had hidden the camp; but now, there was no camp there — only the debris that always marks the stopping place of men.

As she reached the foot of the trail, she saw Bartolo standing beneath a great oak, awaiting her. His pony stood with trailing reins beneath the tree. A rifle butt protruded from a boot on the right of the saddle. He came forward as she guided Baldy toward the tree.

"Buenos dias, señorita," he greeted her, twisting his pock-marked face into the semblance of a smile.

"What do you want of me?" Shannon demanded.

"I need money," he said. "You get money from Evans. He got all the money from the hooch we take down two weeks ago. We never get no chance to get it from him."

"I'll get you nothing!"

"You get money now — and whenever I want it," said the Mexican, "or I tell about Crumb. You Crumb's woman. I tell how you peddle dope. I know! You do what I tell you, or you go to the pen. *Sabe?*"

"Now listen to me," said the girl. "I didn't come up here to take orders from you. I came to give you orders."

"What?" exclaimed the Mexican, and then he laughed aloud. "You give me orders? That is damn funny!"

"Yes, it is funny. You will enjoy it immensely when I tell you what you are to do."

"Hurry, then; I have no time to waste."

He was still laughing.

"You are going to find some way to clear Mr. Pennington of the charge against him. I don't care what the way is so long as it does not incriminate any other innocent person. If you can do it without getting yourself in trouble, well and good. I do not care; but you must see that there is evidence given before the grand jury next Wednesday that will prove Mr. Pennington's innocence!"

"Is that all?" inquired Bartolo, grinning broadly.

"That is all."

"And if I don't do it — eh?"

"Then I shall go before the grand jury and tell them about you and Allen — about the opium and the morphine and the cocaine — how you smuggled the stolen booze from the ship off the coast up into the mountains."

"You think you would do that?" he asked. "But how about me? Wouldn't I be telling everything I know about you? Allen would testify, too, and they would make Crumb come and tell how you lived with him. Oh, no, I guess you don't tell the grand jury nothing!"

"I shall tell them everything. Do you think I care about myself? I will tell them all that Allen or Crumb could tell; and listen, Bartolo — I can tell them something more. There used to be five men in your gang. There were three when I came up last week, and Allen is in jail; but where is the other?"

The man's face went black with anger and perhaps with fear, too.

"What you know about that?" he demanded sharply.

"Allen told Crumb the first time he came to the Hollywood bungalow that he was having trouble among his gang, that you were a hard lot to handle, and that already one named Bartolo had killed one named Gracial. How would you like me to tell that to the grand jury?"

"You never tell that to no one!" growled the Mexican. "You know too damn much for your health!"

He had stepped suddenly forward and seized her wrist. She struck at him and at the same time put the spurs to Baldy — in her fear and excitement more severely than she had intended. The high-spirited animal, unused to such treatment, leaped forward past the Mexican, who, clinging to the girl's wrist, dragged her from the saddle. Baldy turned, and feeling himself free, ran for the trail that led toward home.

"You know too damn much!" repeated Bartolo. "You better off up here alongside Gracial!"

The girl had risen to her feet and stood facing him. There was no fear in her eyes. She was very beautiful, and her beauty was not lost upon the Mexican.

"You mean that you would kill me to keep me from telling the truth about you?" she asked.

"Why not? Should I die instead? If you had kept your mouth shut, you would have been alright; but now"— he shrugged sug-

The Girl from Hollywood / 201

gestively — "you better off up here beside Gracial."

"They'll get you and hang you for it," she said.

"Who will know?"

"The boy who brought me the message from you."

"He will not tell. He my son."

"I wrote a note and left it in my desk before I came up here, telling everything for fear of something of this sort," she said.

"You lie!" he accused, correctly; "but for fear you did, I go down and burn your house tonight after I get through with *you*. The ground pretty hard after the hot weather — it take me long time to dig a hole beside Gracial!"

The girl was at her wits' end now. Her pitiful little lie had not availed. She began to realize that nothing would avail. She had made the noose, stuck her head into it, and sprung the trap. It was too late to alter the consequences. The man had the physique of a bull — she could not hope to escape him by recourse to any power other than her wits, and in the first effort along that line, she had failed miserably and put him on his guard.

Her case appeared hopeless. She thought of pleading with him but realized the futility of it. The fact that she did not do so indicated her courage, which had not permitted her to lose her head. She saw that it was either his life or hers as he saw the matter, and that it was going to be hers was obvious.

The man stood facing her, holding her by the wrist. His eyes appraised her boldly.

"You damn good-looking," he said, and pulled the girl toward him. "Before I kill you, I —"

He threw an arm about her roughly, and, leaning far over her as she pulled away, he sought to reach her lips with his.

CHAPTER XXVI

THE APACHE had taken but a few steps on the trail toward the east pasture when Custer reined him in suddenly and wheeled him about.

"I'll settle this thing now," he muttered. "I'll catch her with them. I'll find out who the others are. By God, I've got her now, and I've got them!"

He spurred the Apache into a lope along the steep and dangerous declivity leading downward into the basin. The horse was surprised. Never before had he been allowed to go downhill faster than a walk — his sound forelegs attested the careful horsemanship of his rider.

Where the trail wound around bushes, he took perilous jumps on the steep hillside, for his speed was too great to permit him to make the short turns. He cleared them, and somehow, he stuck to the trail beyond. His iron shoes struck fire from half-embedded boulders.

A rattler crossing the trail ahead coiled, buzzing its warning. The hillside was steep — there was no footing above or below the snake. The Apache could not have stopped in time to save himself from those poisoned fangs. A coward horse would have wheeled and gone over the cliff; but the Morgan is no coward.

The rider saw the danger at the instant the horse did. The animal felt the spurs touch him lightly, he heard a word of encouragement from the man he trusted. As the snake struck, he rose, gathering his four feet close to his belly, and cleared the danger spot far out of reach of the needle-like fangs.

The trail beyond was narrow, rocky, and shelving — the thing could not have happened in a worse place. The Apache lit, stumbled, slipped. His off-hind foot went over the edge. He lunged forward upon his knees.

Only the cool horsemanship of his rider saved them both. A pound of weight thrown in the wrong direction would have toppled the horse to the bottom of the rocky gorge; a heavy hand upon the bit would have accomplished the same result. Pennington sat easily the balanced seat that gave the horse the best chance to regain his footing. His touch upon the bit was only sufficient to impart confidence to his mount, giving the animal's head free play as nature intended as he scrambled back to the trail again.

At last, they reached the safer footing of the basin and were off in a straight line for the ravine into which led the mysterious trail. The Apache knew that there was need for haste — an inclination of his master's body, a closing of the knees against his barrel, the slight raising of the bridle hand had told him this more surely than loud cries of the punishment of steel rowels. He flattened out and flew.

The cold rage that gripped Pennington brooked no delay. He was glad, though, that he was unarmed; for he knew that when he came face to face with the men with whom Shannon Burke had conspired against him, he might again cease to be master of his anger.

They reached the foot of the acclivity terminating at the summit of the ridge beyond which lay the camp of the bootleggers. Again, the man urged his mount to the necessity of speed. The powerful beast leaped upward along the steep trail, digging his toes deep into the sunbaked soil, every muscle in his body strained to the limit of its powers.

At the summit, they met Baldy, head and tail erect, snorting and riderless. The appearance of the horse and his evident fright bespoke something amiss. Custer had seen him just as he was emerging from the upper end of the dim trail leading down the opposite side of the hogback. He turned the Apache into it and headed him down toward the oaks.

Below, Shannon was waging a futile fight against the burly Bartolo. She struck at his face and attempted to push him from her, but he only laughed his crooked laugh and pushed her slowly toward the trampled dust of the abandoned camp.

"Before I kill you..." he repeated again and again, as if it were some huge joke.

He heard the sound of the Apache's hooves upon the trail above, but he thought it the loose horse of the girl. Custer was almost at the bottom of the trail when the Mexican glanced up and saw him. With a curse, he hurled Shannon aside and leaped toward his pony.

At the same instant, the girl saw the Apache and his rider, and in the next, she saw Bartolo seize his rifle and attempt to draw it from its boot. Leaping to her feet, she sprang toward the Mexican, who was cursing frightfully because the rifle had stuck, and he could not readily extricate it from the boot. As she reached him, he succeeded in jerking the weapon free. Swinging about, he threw it to his shoulder and fired at Pennington just as Shannon threw herself upon him, clutching at his arms and dragging the muzzle of the weapon downward. He struck at her face and tried to wrench the rifle from her grasp; but she clung to it with all the desperation that the danger confronting the man she loved engendered.

Custer had thrown himself from the saddle and was running toward them. Bartolo saw that he could not regain the rifle in time to use it. He struck the girl a terrible blow in the face that sent her to the ground. Then, he turned and vaulted into his saddle and was away across the bottom and up the trail on the opposite side before Pennington could reach him and drag him from his pony.

Custer turned to the girl lying motionless upon the ground. He knelt and raised her in his arms. She had fainted, and her face was very white. He looked down into it — the face of the girl he hated. He felt his arms about her, he felt her body against his, and suddenly, a look of horror filled his eyes.

He laid her back upon the ground and stood up. He was trembling violently. As he had held her in his arms, there had swept over him an almost irresistible desire to crush her to him, to cover her eyes and cheeks with kisses, to smother her lips with them — the girl he hated!

A great light had broken upon his mental horizon — a light of understanding that left all his world in the dark shadow of despair. He loved Shannon Burke!

Again he knelt beside her, and very gently he lifted her in his arms until he could support her across one shoulder. Then he whistled to the Apache, who was nibbling the bitter leaves of the live oak. When the horse came to him, he looped the bridle reins about his arm and started on foot up the trail down which he had just ridden, carrying Shannon across his shoulder. At the summit of the ridge he found Baldy grazing upon the sparse, burned grasses of late September.

It was then that Shannon Burke opened her eyes. At first, confused by the rush of returning recollections, she thought that it was the Mexican who was carrying her; but an instant later she recognized the whipcord riding breeches and the familiar boots and spurs of the son of Ganado. Then she stirred upon his shoulder.

"I am alright now," she said. "You may put me down. I can walk."

He lowered her to the ground, but he still supported her as they stood facing each other.

"You came just in time," she said. "He was going to kill me."

"I am glad I came," was all that he said.

She noticed how tired and pinched Custer's face looked as if he had risen from a sick bed after a long period of suffering. He looked older — very much older — and oh, so sad! It wrung her heart; but she did not question him. She was waiting for him to question her, for she knew that he must wonder why she had come here and what the meaning of the encounter he had witnessed; but he did not ask her anything beyond inquiring whether she thought she was strong enough to sit her saddle if he helped her mount.

"I shall be alright now," she assured him.

He caught Baldy and assisted her into the saddle: Then he mounted the Apache and led the way along the trail toward home. They were halfway across the basin meadow before either spoke. It was Shannon who broke the silence.

"You must have wondered what I was doing up there," she said with a backward nod of her head.

"That would not be strange, would it?"

"I will tell you."

"No," he said. "It is bad enough that you went there today and the Saturday before I was arrested. Anything more that you could tell me would only make it worse. Do you remember that girl I told you about — that friend of Cousin William — who visited us?"

"Yes."

"I followed you up here today to tell you the same thing I told her."

"I understand," she said.

"You do not understand," he snapped, almost angrily. "You understand nothing. I only said that I followed to tell you that I have not told you, have I? Well, I don't intend to tell you; but my shame that I don't is enough without you telling me anymore to add to it. There can be no honorable excuse for your having come here that other time, or this time, either. There is no reason in the world why a woman should have any dealings with criminals or any knowledge that would make dealings with them possible. That is the reason I don't want you to tell me more. Oh, Shannon"— his voice broke — "I don't want to hear anything bad about you! ... Please!"

She had been upon the verge of just anger until then. Even now she did not understand — only that he wanted to believe in her, however much he doubted her, and that their friendship had meant more to him than she had imagined.

"But I must tell you, Custer," she insisted. "Now that you have learned this much, I can see that your suspicions wrong me more than I deserve. I came here the Saturday before you were arrested to warn them that you were going to watch for them on the following Friday. Though I did not know the men, I knew what sort they were and that they would kill you the moment they found that they were discovered. It was only to save your life that I came that other time, and this time I came to try to force them to go before the grand jury and clear you of the charge against you; but when I threatened the man, and he found what I knew about him, he said that he would kill me."

"You did not know that I was going to be arrested that night?"

"Oh, Custer, how could you believe that of me?" exclaimed Shannon.

"I didn't want to believe it."

"I came into all this information — about the work of this gang — by accidentally overhearing a conversation in Hollywood, months ago. I know the names of the principals, I know Guy's connection with them. Today, I was trying to keep Guy's name out, too, if that were possible; but he is guilty and you are not. I cannot understand how he could come back from Los Angeles without telling them the truth and removing the suspicion from you."

"I would not let him," said Pennington.

"You would not let him? You would go to the penitentiary for the crime of another?"

"Not for him, but for Eva. Guy and I thrashed it all out. He wanted to give himself up — he almost demanded that I should let him; but it can't be done. Eva must never know."

"But, Custer, you can't go! It wouldn't be fair — it wouldn't be right. I won't let you go! I know enough to clear you, and I shall go before the grand jury on Wednesday and tell all I know."

"No," he said. "You must not. It would involve Guy."

"I won't mention Guy."

"But you will mention others, and they will mention Guy — don't doubt that for a minute." He turned suddenly toward her. "Promise me, Shannon, that you will not go — that you will not mention what you know to a living soul. I would rather go to the pen for 20 years than see Eva's life ruined. You don't know her. She's gay and happy and frivolous on the outside; but deep within, hers is a soul of wondrous sensitiveness and beauty, which is fortified and guarded by her pride and her honor. Strike down one of these, and you will have given her soul a wound from which it may never recover. She can understand neither meanness nor depravity in men and women. Should she ever learn that Guy had been connected with this gang and that the money upon which they were to start their married life was the fruits of his criminality, it would break her heart. I know that Guy isn't criminally inclined and that this will be a lesson that will keep him straight as long as he lives; but she wouldn't look at it that way. Now, do you see why you must not tell what you know?"

"Perhaps you are right, but it seems to me she would not suffer any more if Guy went than if her brother went. She loves you very much."

"But she will know that I am innocent. If Guy went, she would know that he was guilty."

Shannon had no answer to this, and they were silent for a while.

"You will help me to keep this from Eva?" he asked.

"Yes."

She was thinking of the futility of her sacrifice and wondering what explanation he was putting upon her knowledge of the activities of the criminals. He had said that there could be no reason in the world why a woman should have any dealings with such men or any knowledge that would make dealings with them possible. What would he think of her if he knew the truth?

The man's mind was a chaos of conflicting thoughts — the sudden realization of a love that was as impossible as it was unwelcome — recollection of his vows to Grace, which were as binding upon his honor as the marriage vows themselves would have been — doubts as to the character and antecedents of this girl who rode at his side today and whose place in his life had suddenly assumed an importance beyond that of any other.

Then he turned a little, his eyes rested upon her profile, and he found it hard to doubt her.

Shannon felt his eyes upon her and looked up.

"You have been so good to me, Custer, all of you — you can never know how I have valued the friendship of the Penningtons or what it has meant to me or how I have striven to deserve it. I would have done anything to repay a part, at least, of what it has done for me. That was what I was trying to do — that is why I wanted to go before the grand jury no matter what the cost to me; but I failed, and perhaps, I have only made it worse. I do not even know that you believe me."

"I believe you, Shannon," he said. "There is much that I do not understand; but I believe that what you did was done in our interests. There is nothing more that any of us can do now but keep still about what we know, for the moment one of those actually responsible is threatened with exposure, Guy's name will be divulged — you may rest assured of that. They would be only too glad to shift the responsibility to his shoulders."

"But you will make some effort to defend yourself?"

"I shall simply plead not guilty and tell the truth about why I was up there when the officers arrested me."

"You will make no other defense?"

"What other defense can I make that would not risk incriminating Guy?" Custer asked her.

She shook her head. It seemed quite hopeless.

CHAPTER XXVII

FEDERAL OFFICERS searching the hills found the camp above Jackknife Cañon. They collected a number of empty bottles bearing labels identical with those on the bottles in the cases carried by the burros and those found in Custer Pennington's room. That was all they discovered except that the camp was located on the Pennington property.

The district attorney, realizing the paucity of evidence calculated to convict the prisoner on any serious charge, was inclined to drop the prosecution; but the prohibition enforcement agents, backed by a band of women, most of whom had never performed a woman's first duty to the state and society and therefore had ample time to meddle in affairs far beyond the scope of their intellects, seized upon the prominence of the Pennington name to gain notoriety for themselves on the score that the conviction of a member of a prominent family would have an excellent moral effect upon the community at large.

Just how they arrived at this conclusion, it is difficult to discern. Similarly, one might argue that if it could be proved that the Pope was a pickpocket, it would be tremendously effective in regenerating the morals of the world.

Be that as it may, the works of the righteous were not without fruit, for on the 12th of October, Custer Pennington was found guilty and sentenced to six months in the county jail for having had several hundred dollars' worth of stolen whisky in his possession. He was neither surprised nor disheartened. His only concern was for the sensibilities of his family, and these — represented at the trial in the person of his father — seemed far from overwhelmed, for the colonel was unalterably convinced of his son's innocence.

Eva, who had remained at home with her mother, was more deeply affected than the others, though through a sense of injustice rather than of shame. Shannon, depressed by an unwarranted sense of responsibility for the wrong that Custer had suffered and chagrined that force of circumstances should have prevented her from saving the Penningtons from a stain upon their escutcheon, found it increasingly difficult to continue her intimacy with these loved friends. Carrying in her heart the knowledge and the proof of his innocence, she regarded herself as a traitor among them and, in consequence, held herself more and more aloof from their society, first upon one pretext and then upon another.

At a loss to account for her change toward them, Eva, in a moment of depression, attributed it to the disgrace of Custer's imprisonment.

"She is ashamed to associate with the family of a — a — jailbird!" she cried.

"I don't believe anything of the kind," replied the colonel. "Shannon's got too much sense, and she's too loyal. That's all damned poppycock!"

"I'm sure she couldn't feel that way," said Mrs. Pennington. "She has been just as positive in her assertions of Custer's innocence as any of us."

"You might as well think the same about Guy," said the colonel. "He's scarcely been up here since Custer's arrest."

"He's very busy on a new story. Anyway, I asked him about that very thing and offered to break the engagement if he felt our disgrace too keenly to want to marry into the family."

The colonel drew her down to his knee.

"You silly little girl!" he said. "Do you suppose that this has made any difference in the affection that Guy or any other of our real friends feel for us? Not in the slightest. Even if Cus were guilty, they would not change. Those who did, we would be better off not to know. I am rather jealous of the Pennington honor myself, but I have never felt that this affair is any reflection upon it, and you need not."

"But I can't help it, Popsy. My brother, my dear brother, in jail with a lot of thieves and murderers and horrible people like that! It is just too awful! I lie awake at night thinking about it. I am ashamed to go to the village for fear someone will point at me and say, 'There goes the girl whose brother is in jail!'"

"You are taking it much too hard, dear," said her mother. "One would think that our boy was really guilty."

"Oh, if he really were, I should kill myself!"

The only person other than the officious reformers to derive any happiness from young Pennington's fate was Slick Allen. He occupied a cell not far from Custer's, and there were occasions when they were thrown together. Several times, Allen saw fit to fling gibes at his former employer, much to the amusement of his fellows. They were usually indirect.

One day, as Custer was passing, Allen remarked in a loud tone:

"There's a lot more of these damn fox-trottin' dudes that put on airs but ain't nothin' but common thieves!"

Pennington turned and faced him.

"You remember what you got the last time you tried calling me names, Allen? Well, don't think for a minute that just because we're in jail I won't hand you the same thing again someday if you get too funny. The trouble with you, Allen, is that you are laboring under the misapprehension that you are a humorist. You're not, and if I were you, I wouldn't make faces at the only man in this jail who knows about you and Bartolo and — Gracial. Don't forget Gracial!"

Allen paled, and his eyes closed to two very narrow slits. He made no more observations concerning Pennington; but he devoted much thought to him, trying to arrive at some reasonable explanation of the man's silence when it was evident that he must have sufficient knowledge of the guilt of others to clear himself of the charge upon which he had been convicted.

To Allen's hatred of Custer was now added a real fear, for he had been present when Bartolo killed Gracial. The other two witnesses had been Mexicans, and Allen had no doubt but that if Bartolo were accused, the three of them would swear that the American committed the murder.

One of the first things to do when he was released from jail would be to do away with Bartolo. Bartolo disposed of, the other witnesses would join with Allen to lay the guilt upon the departed. Such pleasant thoughts occupied the time and mind of Slick Allen as did also his plans for paying one Wilson Crumb a little debt he felt due this one-time friend.

Nor was Crumb free from apprehension for the time that would see Allen's jail sentence fulfilled. He well knew the nature of the man. It is typical of drug addicts to disregard the effect of their acts further than the immediate serving of their own interests, and the director had encompassed Allen's arrest merely to meet the emergency of the moment. Later, as time gave him the opportunity to consider what must inevitably follow Allen's release, he began to take thought as to means whereby he might escape the just deserts of his treachery.

He knew enough of Allen's activities to send the man to a Federal prison for a long term, but these matters he could not divulge without equally incriminating himself. There was, however, one little item of Allen's past which might be used against him without signal danger to Crumb, and that was the murder of Gracial. It would not be necessary for Crumb to appear in the matter at all. An anonymous letter to the police would suffice to direct suspicion of the crime toward Allen and to insure for Crumb, if not permanent immunity, at least a period of reprieve.

With the natural predilection of the weak for avoiding or delaying the consummation of their intentions, Crumb postponed the writing of this letter of accusation. There was no cause for hurry, he argued, since Allen's time would not expire until the 6th of the following August.

Crumb led a lonely life after the departure of Gaza. His infatuation for the girl had as closely approximated love as a creature of his type could reach. He had come to depend upon her and to look forward to finding her at the Vista del Paso bungalow on his return from the studio. Since her departure, his evenings had been unbearable, and with the passing weeks, he developed a hatred for the place that constantly reminded him of his loss. He had been so confident that she would have to return to him after she had consumed the small quantity of morphine he had allotted her that only after the weeks had run into months did he realize that she had probably gone out of his life forever. How she had accomplished it he could not understand unless she had found means of obtaining the narcotic elsewhere.

Not knowing where she had gone, he had no means of searching for her. In his own mind, however, he was convinced that she must have returned to Los Angeles. Judging others by himself, he could conceive of no existence that would be supportable beyond the limits of a large city where the means for the gratification of his vice might be obtained.

That Gaza de Lure had successfully thrown off the fetters into which he had tricked her never for a moment entered his calculations. Finally, however, it was borne in upon him that there was little likelihood of her returning; and so depressing had become the familiar and suggestive furnishings of the Vista del Paso bungalow that he at last gave it up, stored his furniture, and took a room at a local hotel. He took with him, carefully concealed in a trunk, his supply of narcotics — which he did not find it so easy to dispose of since the departure of his accomplice.

During the first picture in which Grace Evans had worked with him, Crumb had become more and more impressed with her beauty and the subtle charm of her refinement, which appealed to him by contrast with the ordinary surroundings and personalities of the KKS studio. There was a quiet restfulness about her which soothed his diseased nerves, and after Gaza's desertion, he found himself more and more seeking her society. As was his accustomed policy, his attentions were at first so slight and increased by such barely perceptible degrees that, taken in connection with his uniform courtesy, they gave the girl no warning of his ultimate purposes.

The matter of the test had shocked and disgusted her for the moment; but the thing having been done and no harm coming from it, she began to consider even that with less revulsion than formerly. The purpose of it she had never been able to fathom;

but if Crumb had intended it to place him insidiously upon a plane of greater intimacy with the girl, he had succeeded. That the effect was subjective rendered it none the less effective.

Added to these factors in the budding intimacy between the director and the extra girl was the factor which is always most potent in similar associations — the fear that the girl holds of offending a potent ally and the hope of propitiating a power in which lies the potentiality of success upon the screen.

Lunches at Frank's, dinners at the Ship, dances at the Country Club led by easy gradations to more protracted parties at the Sunset Inn and the Green Mill. The purposes of Crumb's shrewdly conceived and carefully executed plan were twofold. Primarily, he sought a companionship to replace that of which Gaza de Lure had robbed him. Secondarily, he needed a new tool to assist in the disposal of the considerable store of narcotics that he had succeeded in tricking Allen and his accomplices into delivering to him with the understanding that he would divide the profits of the sales with them — which, however, Crumb had no intention of doing if he could possibly avoid it.

In much the same manner that he had tricked Gaza de Lure, he tricked Grace Evans into the use of cocaine; and after that, the rest was easy. Renting another and less pretentious bungalow on Circle Terrace, he installed the girl there and transferred the trunk of narcotics to her care, retaining his room at the hotel for himself.

Grace's fall was more easily accomplished than in the case of Gaza and was more complete, for the former had neither the courage nor the strength of character that had enabled the other to withstand the more degrading advances of her tempter. To assume that the girl made no effort to oppose his importunings would be both unfair and unjust, for both heredity and training had endowed her with a love of honor and a horror of the sordidness of vice; but the gradual undermining of her will by the subtle inroads of narcotics rendered her powerless to withstand the final assault upon the citadel of her scruples.

One evening toward the middle of October, they were dining together at the Winter Garden. Crumb had bought an evening paper on the street and was glancing through it as they sat waiting for their dinner to be served. Presently he looked up at the girl seated opposite him.

"Didn't you come from a little jerk-water place up the line called Ganado?" he asked.

She nodded affirmatively.

"Why?"

"Here's a guy from there been sent up for bootlegging — fellow by the name of Pennington."

She half closed her eyes as if in pain.

"I know," she said. "It has been in the newspapers for the last couple of weeks."

"Did you know him?"

"Yes — he has been out to see me since his arrest, and he called up once."

"Did you see him?"

"No — I would be ashamed to see any decent person!"

"Decent!" snorted Crumb. "You don't call a damned bootlegger decent, do you?"

"I don't believe he ever did it," said the girl. "I have known him all my life, and his family. I'm certain that he couldn't have done it."

A sudden light came into Crumb's eye.

"By God!" he exclaimed, bringing his fist down upon the table.

"What is the matter?" Grace inquired.

"Well, wouldn't that get you?" he exclaimed. "I never connected you at all!"

"What do you mean?"

"This fellow Pennington may not be guilty, but I know who is."

"How do you know? I don't understand you. Why do you look at me that way?"

"Well, if that isn't the best ever!" exclaimed the man. "And here you have been handing me a long line of talk about the decent family you came from and how it would kill them if they knew you sniffed a little coke now and then. Well, wouldn't that get you? You certainly are a fine one to preach!"

"I don't understand you," said the girl. "What has this to do with me? I am not related to Mr. Pennington, but it would make no difference if I were, for I know he never did anything of the sort. The idea of a Pennington bootlegging! Why, they have more money than they need and always have had."

"It isn't Pennington who ought to be in jail," he said. "It's your brother."

She looked at him in surprise, and then she laughed.

"You must have been hitting it up strong today, Wilson," she said.

"Oh, no, I haven't; but it's funny I never thought of it before. Allen told me a long while ago that a fellow by the name of Evans was handling the hooch for him. He said he got a job from the Penningtons as stable man in order to be near the camp where they had the stuff cached in the hills. He described Evans as a young blood, so I guess there isn't any doubt about it. You have a brother — I've heard you speak of him."

"I don't believe you," she said.

"It don't make any difference whether you believe me or not. I could put your brother in the pen, and they've only got Pennington in the county jail. All they could get on him, according to this article, was having stolen goods in his possession; but your brother was in on the whole proposition. It was hidden in his hay barn. He delivered it to a fellow who came up there every week, ostensibly to get hay, and your brother collected the money. Gosh, they'd send him up for sure if I ever tipped them off to what I know!"

And thus was fashioned the power he used to force her to his will.

A week later, the bungalow on Circle Terrace was engaged, and Grace Evans took up the work of peddling narcotics, which Shannon Burke had laid down a few months before. With this difference — Gaza de Lure had shared in the profits of the traffic, while Grace Evans got nothing more than her living and what drugs she craved for her personal use.

Her life, her surroundings, every environment of this new and terrible world into which her ambition had introduced her tended rapidly to ravish her beauty. She faded with a rapidity that was surprising even to Crumb — surprising and annoying. He had wanted her for her beauty, and now, she was losing it;

but still, he must keep her because of her value in his nefarious commerce.

As weeks and months went by, he no longer took pleasure in her society and was seldom at the bungalow save when he came to demand an accounting and to collect the proceeds of her sales. Her pleas and reproaches had no other effect upon him than to arouse his anger. One day when she clung to him, begging him not to desert her, he pushed her roughly from him so that she fell, and in falling, she struck the edge of a table and hurt herself.

This happened in April. On the following day, Custer Pennington, his term in the county jail expired, was liberated.

CHAPTER XXVIII

CUSTER'S LONG HOURS of loneliness had often been occupied with plans against the day of his liberation. That Grace had not seen him or communicated with him since his arrest and conviction had been a source of wonder and hurt to him. He recalled many times the circumstance of the telephone call with a growing belief that Grace had been there but had refused to talk with him. Nevertheless, he was determined to see her before he returned to Ganado.

He had asked particularly that none of his family should come to Los Angeles on the day of his release but that the roadster should be sent up on the preceding day and left in a garage for him. He lost no time after quitting the jail in getting his machine and driving out to Hollywood to the house where Grace had boarded.

The woman who answered his ring told him that Grace no longer lived there. At first, she was loath to give him any information as to the girl's whereabouts; but after some persuasion, she gave him a number on Circle Terrace, and in that direction, Pennington turned his car.

As he left his car before the bungalow and approached the building, he could see into the interior through the screen door, for it was a warm day in April and the inner door was open. As he mounted the few steps leading to the porch, he saw a woman cross the living room into which the door opened. She moved hurriedly, disappearing through a doorway opposite and closing the door after her. Though he had but a brief glimpse of her in the darkened interior, he knew that it was Grace, so familiar were every line of her figure and every movement of her carriage.

It was several minutes after Custer rang before a Japanese appeared at the doorway. It was the same Japanese "schoolboy" who had served as general factotum at the Vista del Paso bungalow. He opened the screen door a few inches and looked inquiringly at the caller.

"I wish to see Miss Evans," said Custer.

He took a card case from his pocket and handed a card to the servant, who looked blankly at the card and then at the caller, finally shaking his head stupidly and closing the door.

"No here," he said. "Nobody home."

Pennington recalled once more the affair of the telephone. He knew that he had just seen Grace inside the bungalow. He had come to talk with her, and he intended to do so.

He laid his hand on the handle of the door and jerked it open. The Jap, evidently lacking in discretion, endeavored to prevent him from entering. First, the guardian clawed at the door in an effort to close it, and then, very foolishly, he attempted to push Pennington out on the porch. The results were disastrous to the Jap.

Crossing the living room, Custer rapped on the door through which he had seen Grace go, calling her by name. Receiving no reply, he flung the door open. Facing him was the girl he was engaged to marry.

With her back against the dresser, Grace stood at the opposite end of the room. Her disheveled hair fell about her face, which was overspread with a sickly pallor. Her wild, staring eyes were fixed upon him. Her mouth, drooping at the corners, tremulously depicted a combination of terror and anger.

"Grace!" he exclaimed.

She still stood staring at him for a moment before she spoke.

"What do you mean," she demanded at last, "by breaking into my bedroom? Get out! I don't want to see you. I don't want you here!"

He crossed the room and put a hand upon her shoulder.

"My God, Grace," he cried, "what is the matter? What has happened to you?"

"Nothing has happened," she mumbled. "There is nothing the matter with me. I suppose you want me to go back with the rest of the rubes. I am through with the damned country — and country jakes, too!" she added.

"You mean that you don't want me here, Grace? That you don't love me?" he asked.

"Love you?" She broke into a disagreeable laugh. "Why, you poor rube, I never want to see you again!"

He stood looking at her for a moment longer, and then he turned slowly and walked out of the bungalow and down to his car. When he had gone, the girl threw herself face down upon the bed and burst into uncontrollable sobs. For the moment, she had risen triumphant above the clutches of her sordid vice. For that brief moment, she had played her part to save the man she loved from greater torture and humiliation in the future — at what a price only she could ever know.

Custer found them waiting for him on the east porch as he drove up to the ranch house. The new freedom and the long drive over the beautiful highway through the clear April sunshine with the green hills at his left and the lovely valley spread out upon his right hand to some extent alleviated the depression that had followed the shock of his interview with Grace; and when he alighted from the car, he seemed quite his normal self again.

Eva was the first to reach him. She fairly threw herself upon her brother, laughing and crying in a hysteria of happiness. His mother was smiling through her tears while the colonel blew his nose violently, remarking that it was "a hell of a time of year to have a damned cold!"

Custer joked a little about his imprisonment, but he soon saw that the mere mention of it had a most depressing effect upon Eva; so he did not revert to the subject again in her presence. He confined himself to plying them with a hundred questions about happenings on the ranch during his long absence, the condition of the stock, and the crop outlook for the season.

As he considered the effect his undeserved jail sentence had produced upon the sensibilities of his sister, he was doubly repaid for the long months of confinement that he had suffered in order to save her from the still greater blow of having the man she was to marry justly convicted of a far more serious crime. He saw no reason now why she should ever learn the truth. The temporary disgrace of his incarceration would soon be forgotten in the everyday run of work and pleasure that constituted the life of Ganado, and the specter of her hurt pride would no longer haunt her.

Custer was surprised that Guy and Mrs. Evans had not been of the party that welcomed his return. When he mentioned this, Eva told him that Mrs. Evans thought the Penningtons would want to have him all to themselves for a while and that their neighbors were coming up after dinner. And it was not until dinner that he asked after Shannon.

"We have seen very little of her since you left," explained his mother. "She returned Baldy soon after that and bought the Senator from Mrs. Evans."

"I don't know what is the matter with the child," said the colonel. "She is as sweet as ever when we do see her, and she always asks after you and tells us that she believes in your innocence. She rides a great deal at night but seldom, if ever, in the daytime. I don't think it is safe for a woman to ride alone in the hills at night, and I have told her so; but she says that she is not afraid and that she loves the hills as well by night as by day."

"Eva has missed her company very much," said Mrs. Pennington. "I was afraid that we might have done something to offend her, but none of us could think what it could have been."

"I thought she was ashamed of us," said Eva.

"Nonsense!" exclaimed the colonel.

"Of course, that's nonsense," said Custer. "She knows as well as the rest of you that I was innocent."

He was thinking how much more surely Shannon knew his innocence than any of them.

During dinner, Eva regained her old-time spirit. More than once, the tears came to Mrs. Pennington's eyes as she realized that, once more, their little family was united and that the pall of sorrow that had weighed so heavily upon them for the past six months had at last lifted, revealing again the sunshine of the daughter's heart, which had never been the same since their boy had gone away.

"Oh, Cus!" exclaimed Eva. "The most scrumptious thing is going to happen, and I'm so glad that you are going to be here, too. It's going to be perfectly gorgeristic! There'll be a whole regiment of them, and they're going to be camped right up at the mouth of Jackknife. I can scarcely wait until they come — can you?"

"I think I might manage," said her brother; "at least until you tell me what you are talking about."

"Pictures," exclaimed Eva. "Isn't it simplimetic gorgeristic? And they may be here a whole month!"

"What in the world is the child talking about?" asked Custer, appealing to his mother.

"Your father —" Mrs. Pennington started to explain.

"Oh, don't tell him," cried Eva. "I want to tell him myself."

"You have been explaining for several minutes," said Custer; "but you haven't said anything yet."

"Well, I'll start at the beginning, then. They're going to have Indians, and cowboys, and —"

"That sounds more like the finish," suggested Custer.

"Don't interrupt me! They're going to take a picture on Ganado."

Custer turned toward his father with a look of surprise.

"You needn't blame papa," said Eva. "It was all my fault — or, rather, I should say our good fortune is all due to me. You see, Papa wasn't going to let them come at first, but the cutest man came up to see him — a nice, shorty fat little man, and he rubbed his hands together and said: 'Vell, colonel?' Papa told him that he had never allowed any picture companies on the place; but I happened to be there, and that was all that saved us, for I teased and teased and teased until finally Papa said that they could come provided they didn't take any pictures up around the house. They didn't want to do that, for they're making a Western picture, and they said the scenery at the back of the ranch is just what they want. They're coming up in a few days, and it's going to be perfectly radiant, and maybe I'll get in the pictures!"

"If I thought so," said Custer, "I'd put a can of nitroglycerine under the whole works the moment they drove onto the property!"

He was thinking of what the pictures had done for Grace Evans.

"I am surprised that you permitted it, father," he said, turning to the colonel.

"I'm rather surprised myself," admitted the older Pennington; "but what was I to do, with that suave little location manager rubbing his hands and oiling me on one side and this little rascal here pestering the life out of me on the other? I simply had to give in. I don't imagine any harm will come from it. They've promised to be very careful of all the property, and whenever any of our stock is used, it will be handled by our own men."

"I suppose they are going to pay you handsomely for it," suggested Custer.

The colonel smiled.

"Well, that wasn't exactly mentioned," he said; "but I have a recollection that the location manager said something about presenting us with a fine set of stills of the ranch."

"Generous of them!" said Custer. "They'll camp all over the shop, use our water, burn our firewood, and trample up our pasture, and in return, they'll give us a set of photographs. Their liberality is truly marvelous!"

"Well, to tell you the truth," said the colonel, "after I found how anxious Eva was, I wouldn't have dared mention payment for fear they might refuse to come and this young lady's life might be ruined in consequence!"

"What outfit is it?" asked the son.

"It's a company from the KKS, directed by a man by the name of Crumb."

"Wilson Crumb, the famous actor-director," added Eva. "How perfectly radiant! I danced with him is Los Angeles a year ago."

"Oh, that's the fellow, is it?" said Custer. "I have a hazy recollection that you were mad about him for some 15 minutes after you reached home, but I have never heard you mention him since."

"Well, to tell you the truth," said Eva, "I had forgotten all about him until that perfectly gorgeous little loquacious manager mentioned him."

"Location manager," corrected her father.

"He was both."

"Yes, he was," said the colonel. "I rather hope he comes back. I haven't enjoyed any one so much since the days of Weber and Fields."

It was after eight o'clock when the Evanses arrived. Mrs. Evans was genuinely affected at seeing Custer again, for she was as fond of him as if he had been her own son. In Guy, Custer discovered a great change. The boy that he had left had become suddenly a man, quiet and reserved, with a shadow of sadness in his expression. His lesson had been a hard one, Custer knew, and the price that he had had to pay for it had left its indelible mark upon his sensitive character.

Guy's happiness at having Custer back again was overshadowed to some extent by the shame that he must always feel when he looked into the face of the man who had shouldered his guilt and taken the punishment which should have been his. The true purpose of Pennington's sacrifice could never alter young Evans's realization of the fact that the part he had been forced to take had been that of a coward, a traitor, and a cad.

The first greetings over, Mrs. Evans asked Custer if he had seen Grace before he left Los Angeles.

"I saw her," he said, "and she is not at all well. I think Guy should go up there immediately and try to bring her back. I meant to speak to him about it this evening."

"She is not seriously ill?" exclaimed Mrs. Evans.

"I cannot say," replied Custer. "I doubt if she is seriously ill in a physical sense, but she is not well. I could see that. She has changed a great deal. I think you should lose no time, Guy," he added, turning to Grace's brother, "in going to Los Angeles and getting her. She has been gone almost a year. It is time she knew whether her dreams are to come true or not. From what I saw of her, I doubt if they have materialized."

"I will go tomorrow," said young Evans.

CHAPTER XXIX

THE SIX MONTHS that had just passed had been months of indecision and sadness for Shannon Burke. Constantly moved by a conviction that she should leave the vicinity of Ganado and the Penningtons, she was held there by a force that she had not the power to overcome.

Never before since she had left her mother's home in the Middle West had she experienced the peace and content and happiness that her little orchard on the highway imparted to her life. The friendship of the Penningtons had meant more to her than anything that had hitherto entered her life; and to be near them, even if she saw them but seldom, constituted a constant bulwark against the assaults of her old enemy, which still occasionally assailed the ramparts of her will.

After the departure of Custer, she had conscientiously observed what she considered to be his wishes as expressed in his reference comparing her with the girlfriend of Cousin William, whom he had practically ordered out of the house. She had, as far as possible, avoided Eva's society; and though contemplation of the cause of this avoidance filled her with humiliation and with a sense of the injustice of all that it implied, she nevertheless felt it a duty to the man she loved to respect his every wish, however indirectly suggested.

That she might put herself in Eva's way as seldom as possible, Shannon had formed the habit of riding at those hours at which the Penningtons were not accustomed to ride. The habit of solitude grew upon her, and she loved the loneliness of the hills. They never oppressed her — she never feared them. They drew her to them and soothed her as a mother might have done. There, she forgot her sorrows, and hope was stimulated to new life.

Especially when the old craving seized her did she long for the hills, and it was because of this that she first rode at night — on a night of brilliant moonlight that imparted to familiar scenes the weird beauties of a strange world. The experience was unique. It assumed the proportions of an adventure, and it lured her to other similar excursions.

Even the Senator felt the spell of enchantment. He stepped daintily with uppricked ears and arched neck, peering nervously into the depth of each shadowy bush. He leaped suddenly aside at the movement of a leaf, or halted, trembling and snorting, at the moon-bathed outlines of some jutting rock that he had passed a hundred times, unmoved, by day.

The moonlight rides led Shannon to others on moonless nights so that she was often in the saddle when the valley slept. She invariably followed the same trail on these occasions with the result that both she and the Senator knew every foot of it so well that they had traversed it beneath the blackness of heavy clouds or when low fogs obliterated all but the nearest objects.

Never in the hills could her mind dwell upon depressing thoughts. Only cheerful reflections were her companions of those hours of solitude. She thought of the love that had come into her life, of the beauty of it, and of all that it had done to make life more worth the living; of the Penningtons and the example of red-blooded cleanliness that they set — decency without prudery; of her little orchard and the saving problems it had brought to occupy her mind and hands; of her horse and her horsemanship, two never-failing sources of companionship and pleasure which the Penningtons had taught her to love and enjoy.

On the morning after Custer's return, Guy started early for Los Angeles, while Custer — Shannon not having joined them on their morning ride — re-saddled the Apache after breakfast and rode down to her bungalow. He both longed to see her and dreaded the meeting; for, regardless of Grace's attitude and of the repulse she had given him, his honor bound him to her. Loyalty to the girl had been engendered by long years of association during which friendship had grown into love by so gradual a process that it seemed to each of them that there had never been a time when they had not loved. Such attachments, formed in the heart of youth, hallowed by time, and fortified by the pride and honor of inherited chivalry, become a part of the characters of their possessors and as difficult to uproot as those other habits of thought and action which differentiate one individual from another.

Custer had realized, in that brief interview of the day before, that Grace was not herself. What was the cause of her change he could not guess since he was entirely unacquainted with the symptoms of narcotics. Even had a suspicion of the truth entered his mind, he would have discarded it as a vile slander upon the girl, as he had rejected the involuntary suggestion that she might have been drinking. His position was distressing for a man to whom honor was a fetish since he knew that he still loved Grace while at the same time realizing a still greater love for Shannon.

She saw him coming and came down the driveway to meet him, her face radiant with the joy of his return and with that expression of love that is always patent to all but the object of its concern.

"Oh, Custer!" she cried. "I am so glad that you are home again! It has seemed years and years rather than months to all of us."

"I am glad to be home, Shannon. I have missed you, too. I have missed you all — everything — the hills, the valley, every horse and cow and little pig, the clean air, the smell of flowers and sage — all that is Ganado."

"You like it better than the city?"

"I shall never long for the city again," he said. "Cities are wonderful, of course, with their great buildings, their parks and boulevards, their fine residences, their lawns and gardens. The things that men have accomplished there fill a fellow with admiration; but how pitiful they really are compared with the magnificence that is ours!"

He turned and pointed toward the mountains.

"Just think of those hills, Shannon, and the infinite, unthinkable power that uplifted such mighty monuments. Think of the countless ages that they have endured, and then, compare them with the puny efforts of man. Compare the range of vision of the city dweller with ours. He can see across the street and to the top of some tall building, which may look imposing; but place it beside one of our hills, and see what becomes of it. Place it in a ravine in the high Sierras, and you would have difficulty in finding it; and you cannot even think of it in connection with a mountain fifteen or twenty thousand feet in height. And yet, the city man patronizes us country people, deploring the necessity that compels us to pursue our circumscribed existence."

"Pity him," laughed Shannon. "He is as narrow as his streets. His ideals can reach no higher than the pall of smoke that hangs over the roofs of his buildings. I am so glad, Custer, that you have given up the idea of leaving the country for the city!"

"I never really intended to," he replied. "I couldn't have left on father's account; but now I can remain on my own as well as his and with a greater degree of contentment. You see that my recent experience was a blessing in disguise."

"I am glad if some good came out of it; but it was a wicked injustice, and there were others as innocent as you who suffered fully as much — Eva especially."

"I know," he said. "She has been very lonely since I left, with Grace away, too; and they tell me that you have constantly avoided them. Why? I cannot understand it."

He had dismounted and tied the Apache, and they were walking toward the porch. She stopped and turned to look Custer squarely in the eyes.

"How could I have done otherwise?" she asked.

"I do not understand," he replied.

She could not hold her eyes to his as she explained but looked down, her expression changing from happiness to one of shame and sadness.

"You forget that girl, the friend of Cousin William?" she asked.

"Oh, Shannon!" he cried, laying a hand impulsively upon her arm. "I told you that I wouldn't say that to you. I didn't want you to stay away. I have implicit confidence in you."

"No," she contradicted him. "In your heart you thought it, and perhaps you were right."

"No," he insisted. "Please don't stay away — promise me that you will not! You have hurt them all, and they are all so fond of you!"

"I am sorry, Custer. I would not hurt them. I love them all; but I thought I was doing the thing that you wished. There was so much that you did not understand — that you can never understand — and you were away where you couldn't know what was going on; so, it seemed disloyal to do the thing I thought you would rather I didn't do."

"It's all over now," he said. "Let's start over again, forgetting all that has happened in the last six months and a half."

Again, as his hand lay upon her arm, he was seized with an almost uncontrollable desire to crush her to him. Two things deterred him — his loyalty to Grace and the belief that his love would be unwelcome to Shannon.

CHAPTER XXX

GUY EVANS SWEPT over the broad, smooth highway at a rate that would have won him 10 days in the jail at Santa Ana had his course led him through that village. The impression that Custer's words had implanted in his mind was that Grace was ill, for Pennington had not gone into the details of his unhappy interview with the girl, choosing to leave to her brother a realization of her changed condition, which would have been incredible to him even from the lips of so trusted a friend as Custer.

And so, it was that when he approached the bungalow on Circle Terrace and saw a coupé standing at the curb, he guessed at what it portended; for though there were doubtless hundreds of similar cars in the city, there was that about this one which suggested the profession of its owner. As Guy hurried up the walk to the front door, he was as positive that he would find Grace ill and a doctor in attendance as if someone had already told him so.

There was no response to his ring, and as the inner door was open, he entered. A door on the opposite side of the living room was ajar. As Guy approached it, a man appeared in the doorway, and beyond him, the visitor could see Grace lying, very white and still, upon a bed.

"Who are you — this woman's husband?" demanded the man in curt tones.

"I am her brother. What is the matter? Is she very ill?"

"Did you know of her condition?"

"I heard last night that she was not well, and I hurried up here. I live in the country. Who are you? What has happened? She is not — my God, she is not —"

"Not yet. Perhaps we can save her. I am a doctor. I was called by a Japanese man who said that he was a servant here. He must have left after he called me, for I have not seen him. Her condition is serious and requires an immediate operation — an operation of such a nature that I must learn the name of her own physician and have him present. Where is her husband?"

"Husband! My sister is not —" Guy ceased speaking and went suddenly white. "My God, doctor, you don't mean that she — that my sister — oh, no, not that!"

He seized the other's arm beseechingly. The doctor laid his hand upon the younger man's shoulder.

"She had a fall night before last, and an immediate operation is imperative. Her condition is such that we cannot even take the risk of moving her to a hospital. I have my instruments in my car, but I should have help. Who is her doctor?"

"I do not know."

"I'll get someone. I have given her something to quiet her."

The doctor stepped to the telephone and gave a number. Evans entered the room where his sister lay. She was moving about restlessly and moaning, though it was evident that she was still unconscious.

Changed! Guy wondered that he had known her at all now that he was closer to her. Her face was pinched and drawn. Her beauty was gone — every vestige of it. She looked old and tired and haggard, and there were terrible lines upon her face that stilled her brother's heart and brought the tears to his eyes.

He heard the doctor summoning an assistant and directing him to bring ether. The, he heard him go out of the house by the front door — to get his instruments, doubtless. The brother knelt by the girl's bed.

"Grace!" he whispered and threw an arm about her.

Her lids fluttered, and she opened her eyes.

"Guy!"

She recognized him — she was conscious.

"Who did this?" he demanded. "What is his name?"

She shook her head.

"What is the use?" she asked. "It is done."

"Tell me!"

"You would kill him — and be punished. It would only make it worse — for — you — and Mother. Let it die with me!"

"You are not going to die. Tell me, who is he? Do you love him?"

"I hate him!"

"How were you injured?"

"He threw me — against — a table."

Her voice was growing weaker. Choking back tears of grief and anger, the young man rose and stood beside her.

"Grace, I command you to tell me!"

His voice was low, but it was vibrant with power and authority. The girl tried to speak. Her lips moved, but she uttered no sound. Guy thought that she was dying and taking her secret to the grave.

Her eyes moved to something beyond the foot of the bed, back to his, and back again to whatever she had been looking at, as if she sought to direct his attention to something in that part of the room. He followed the direction of her gaze. There was a dressing table there, and on it a photograph of a man in a silver frame. Guy stepped to the table and picked up the picture.

"This is he?"

His eyes demanded an answer. Her lips moved soundlessly, and weakly, she nodded an affirmative.

"What is his name?"

She was too weak to answer him. She gasped, and her breath came flutteringly. The brother threw himself upon his knees beside the bed and took her in his arms. His tears mingled with his kisses on her cheek. The doctor came then and drew him away.

"She is dead!" said the boy, turning away and covering his face with his hands.

"No," said the doctor, after a brief examination. "She is not dead. Get into the kitchen and get some water to boiling. I'll be getting things ready in here. Another doctor will be here in a few minutes."

Glad of something to do just to help, Guy hastened into the little kitchen. He found a kettle and a large pan and put water in them to boil.

A moment later, the doctor came in. He had removed his coat and vest and rolled up his sleeves. He placed his instruments in the pan of water on the stove, and then, he went to the sink and washed his hands. While he scrubbed, he talked. He was an efficient-looking, businesslike person, and he inspired Guy with confidence and hope.

"She has a fighting chance," he said. "I've seen worse cases pull through. She's had a bad time, though. She must have been lying here for pretty close to 24 hours without any attention. I found her fully dressed on her bed — fully dressed except for what clothes she'd torn off in her pain. If someone had called a doctor yesterday at this time, it might have been alright. It may be alright even now. We'll do the best we can."

The bell rang.

"That's the doctor. Let him in, please."

Guy went to the door and admitted the second physician, who removed his coat and vest and went directly to the kitchen. The first doctor was entering the room where Grace lay. He turned and spoke to his colleague, greeting him; then he disappeared within the adjoining room. The second doctor busied himself about the sink, sterilizing his hands. Guy lighted another burner and put on another vessel with water in it.

A moment later, the first doctor returned to the kitchen.

"It will not be necessary to operate, doctor," he said. "We were too late!"

His tone and manner were still very businesslike and efficient, but there was an expression of compassion in his eyes as he crossed the room and put his arm about Guy's shoulders.

"Come into the other room, my boy. I want to talk to you," he said.

Guy, dry-eyed and walking almost as one in a trance, accompanied him to the little living room.

"You have had a hard blow," said the doctor. "What I am going to tell you may make it harder; but if she had been my sister,

I should have wanted to know about it. She is better off. The chances are that she didn't want to live. She certainly made no fight for life — not since I was called."

"Why should she want to die?" Guy asked dully. "We would have forgiven her. No one would ever have known about it but me."

"There was something else — she was a drug addict. That was probably the reason why she didn't want to live. The morphine I had to give her to quiet her would have killed three ordinary men."

And so, Guy Evans came to know the terrible fate that had robbed his sister of her dreams, of her ambition, and finally of her life. He placed the full responsibility upon the man whose picture had stood in its silver frame upon the girl's dressing table. As he knelt beside the dead girl, he swore to search until he had learned the identity of that man and found him and forced from him the only expiation that could satisfy the honor of a brother.

CHAPTER XXXI

THE DEATH OF GRACE had, of course, its naturally depressing effect upon the circle of relatives and friends at Ganado; but her absence of more than a year, the infrequency of her letters, and the fact that they had already come to feel that she was lost to them mitigated to some degree the keenness of their grief and lessened its outward manifestations. Her pitiful end could not seriously interrupt the tenor of their lives, which had long since grown over the wound of her departure as a tree's growth rolls over the hurt of a severed limb, leaving only a scar as a reminder of its loss.

Mrs. Evans, Guy, and Custer suffered more than the others — Mrs. Evans because of the natural instincts of motherhood and Custer from a sense of loss that seemed to have uprooted and torn away a part of his being even though he realized that his love for Grace had been of a different sort from his hopeless passion for Shannon Burke. It was Guy who suffered most, for hugged to his breast was the gnawing secret of the truth of his sister's life and death. He had told them that Grace had died of pneumonia, and they had not gone behind his assertion to search the records for the truth.

Locked in his desk was the silver frame and the picture of the man whose identity he had been unable to discover. The bungalow had been leased in Grace's name. The Japanese servant had disappeared, and Guy had been unable to obtain any trace of him. The dead girl had had no friends in the neighborhood, and there was no one who could tell him anything that might lead to the discovery of the man he sought.

He did not, however, give up his search. He went often to Hollywood, where he haunted public places and the entrances to studios in the hope that someday he would find the man he sought; but as the passing months brought no success and the duties of his ranch and his literary work demanded more and more of his time, he was gradually compelled to push the furtherance of his vengeance into the background, though without any lessening of his determination to compass it eventually.

To Custer, the direct effect of Grace's death was to revive the habit of drinking more than was good for him — a habit from which he had drifted away during the past year. That it had ever been a habit he would, of course, have been the last to admit. He was one of those men who could drink or leave it alone. The world is full of them — and so are the cemeteries.

Custer avoided Shannon when he could do so without seeming unfriendly. Quite unreasonably, he felt that his love for Shannon was an indication of disloyalty to Grace. The latter's dismissal of him he had never taken as a serious avowal of her heart. He had realized that the woman who had spoken so bitterly had not been the girl he had loved and whose avowals of love he had listened to. Nor had she been the girl upon whose sad, tired face he had looked for the last time in the darkened living room of the Evans home, for then, death had softened the hard lines of dissipation, revealing again, in chastened melancholy, the soul that sin had disguised but not destroyed.

Shannon recognized the change in Custer. She attributed it to his grief and to his increased drinking, which she had sensed almost immediately, as love does sense the slightest change in its object however little apparent to another. She did not realize that she was purposely avoiding her. She was more than ever with Eva now, for Guy, having settled down to the serious occupations of man's estate, no longer had so much leisure to devote to play.

She still occasionally rode at night, for the daytime rides with Custer were less frequent now. Much of his time was occupied closer in around the ranch with the conditioning of the show herds for the coming fall — an activity which gave him a plausible excuse for foregoing his rides with Shannon. The previous year, they had been compelled to cancel their entries because of Custer's imprisonment since the colonel would not make the circuit of the shows himself and did not care to trust the herds to anyone but his son. Now the Morgans, the Percherons, the Herefords, and the Berkshires that were to uphold the fame of Ganado were the center of arduous and painstaking fitting and grooming as the time approached when the finishing touches were to be put upon glossy coat and polished horn and hoof.

May, June, and July had come and gone — it was August again. Guy's futile visits to Los Angeles were now infrequent. The life of Ganado had again assumed the cheerfulness of the past. The heat of summer had brought the swimming pool into renewed demand, and the cool evenings saved the ballroom from desertion. The youth of the foothills and valley, re-enforced by weekend visitors from the city, filled the old house with laughter and happiness. Shannon was always of these parties, for they would not let her remain away.

It was upon the occasion of one of them early in August that Eva announced the date of her wedding to Guy.

"The 2nd of September," she told them. "It comes on a Saturday. We're going to motor to —"

"Hold on!" cautioned Guy. "That's a secret!"

"And when we come back, we're going to start building on Hill 13."

"That's a cow pasture," said Custer.

"Well, it won't be one any more. You must find another cow pasture."

"Certainly, little one," replied her brother. "We'll bring the cows up here in the ballroom. With 5000 acres to pick from, you can't find a bungalow site anywhere except in the best dairy cow pasture on Ganado!"

"With 5000 acres to pick from, I suppose you can't find a cow pasture anywhere but on the best bungalow site in Southern California! You, radiant brother! You wouldn't have your little sister living in the hog pasture, now would you?"

"Heavens, no! Those nine children you aspire to would annoy the brood sows."

"You're hideous!"

"Put on a fox trot, someone," cried Guy. "Dance with your sister, Cus, and you'll let her build bungalows all over Ganado. No one can refuse her anything when they dance with her."

"I'll say they can't," agreed Custer. "Was that how she lured you to your undoing, Guy?"

"What a dapper little idea!" exclaimed Eva.

Guy danced that dance with Mrs. Pennington, and the colonel took out Shannon. As they moved over the smooth floor with the easy dignity that good dancers can impart to the fox trot, the girl's eyes were often on the brother and sister dancing and laughing together.

"How wonderful they are!" she said.

"Who?" inquired the colonel.

"Custer and Eva. Theirs is such a wonderful relationship between brother and sister — the way it ought to be but very seldom is."

"Oh, I don't know that it's unique," replied the colonel. "Guy and Grace were that way and so were my father's children. Possibly it's because we were all raised in the country where children are more dependent upon their sisters and brothers for companionship than children of the city. We all get better acquainted in the country, and we have to learn to find the best that is in each of us, for we haven't the choice of companions here that a city, with its thousands, affords."

"I don't know," said Shannon. "Perhaps that is it; but anyway, it is lovely — really *lovely*, for they are almost like two lovers. At first, when I heard them teasing each other, I used to think there might be some bitterness in their thrusts; but when I came to know you all better, I realized that your affection was so perfect that there could never be any misunderstanding among you."

"That attitude is not peculiar to the Penningtons," replied the colonel. "I know, for instance, of one who so perfectly harmonized with their lives and ideals that, in less than a year, she became practically one of them."

He was smiling down into Shannon's upturned face.

"I know — you mean me," she said. "It is awfully nice of you, and it makes me very proud to hear you say so, for I have really tried to be like you. If I have succeeded the least bit, I am so happy!"

"I don't know that you have succeeded in being like us," he laughed; "but you have certainly succeeded in being liked *by* us. Why, do you know, Shannon, I believe Mrs. Pennington and I discuss you and plan for you fully as much as we do the children. It is almost as if you were our other daughter."

The tears came to her eyes.

"I am so happy!" she said again.

It was later in the evening, after a dance, that she and Custer walked out on the driveway along the north side of the ballroom and stood looking out over the moon-enchanted valley — a vista of loveliness glimpsed between masses of feathery foliage in an opening through the trees on the hillside just below them. They looked out across the acacias and cedars of the lower hill toward the lights of a little village twinkling between two dome-like hills at the upper end of the valley. It was an unusually warm evening, almost too warm to dance.

"I think we'd get a little of the ocean breeze," said Custer, "if we were on the other side of the hill. Let's walk over to the water gardens. There is usually a breeze there, but the building cuts us off from it here."

Side by side, in silence, they walked around the front of the building and along the south drive to the steps leading down through the water gardens to the stables. The steps were narrow, and Custer went ahead — which is always the custom of men in countries where there are rattlesnakes.

As Shannon stepped from the cement steps to the gravel walk above the first pool, her foot came down upon a round stone, turning her ankle and throwing her against Custer. For support, she grasped his arm. Upon such insignificant trifles may the fate of lives depend. It might have been a lizard, a toad, a mouse, or even a rattlesnake that precipitated the moment which, for countless eons, creation had been preparing; but it was none of these. It was just a little round pebble — and it threw Shannon Burke against Custer Pennington, causing her to seize his arm. He felt the contact of those fingers and the warmth of her body and her cheek near his shoulder. He threw an arm about her to support her.

Almost instantly she had regained her footing. Laughingly, she drew away.

"I stepped on a stone," she said in explanation; "but I didn't hurt my ankle."

But still, he kept his arm about her. At first, Shannon did not understand, and, supposing that he still thought her unable to stand alone, she again explained that she was unhurt.

He stood looking down into her face, which was turned up to his. The moon, almost full, revealed her features as clearly as sunlight — how beautiful they were and how close. She had not yet fully realized the significance of his attitude when he suddenly threw his other arm about her and crushed her to him; and then, before she could prevent, he had bent his lips to hers and kissed her full upon the mouth.

With a startled cry she pushed him away.

"Custer!" she said. "What have you done? This is not like you. I do not understand!"

She was really terrified — terrified at the thought that he might have kissed her without love — terrified that he might have kissed her *with* love. She did not know which would be the greater catastrophe.

"I couldn't help it, Shannon," he said. "Blame the pebble, blame the moonlight, blame me — it won't make any difference. I couldn't help it; that is all there is to it. I've fought against it for months. I knew you didn't love me; but, oh, Shannon, I love you! I had to tell you."

He loved her! He had loved her for months! Oh, the horror of it! Her little dream of happiness was shattered. No longer could they go on as they had. There would always be this between them — the knowledge of his love; and he would learn of her love for him, for she would not lie to him if he asked her. Then she would either have to explain or to go away — to explain those hideous months with Crumb. Custer would not believe the truth — no man would believe the truth — that she had come through them undefiled. She herself would not believe it of another woman, and she was too sophisticated to hope that the man who loved her would believe it of her.

He had not let her go. They still stood there — his arms about her.

"Please don't be angry, Shannon," he begged. "You may not want my love, but there's no disgrace in it. Maybe I shouldn't have kissed you, but I couldn't help it, and I'm glad I did. I have that to remember as long as I live. Please don't be angry!"

Angry! She wished to God that he would crush her to him again and kiss her — kiss her — kiss like that now and forever. Why shouldn't he? Why shouldn't she let him? What had she done to deserve eternal punishment? There were countless wives less virtuous than she. Ah, if she could but have the happiness of his love!

She closed her eyes and turned away her head, and for just an instant, she dreamed her beautiful dream. Why not? Why not? Why not? There could be no better wife than she, for there could be no greater love than hers.

He noticed that she no longer drew away. There had been no look of anger in her eyes — only startled questioning; and her face was still so near. Again, his arms closed about her, and again his lips found hers.

This time she did not deny him. She was only human — only a woman — and her love, growing steadily in power for many months, had suddenly burst forth in a consuming fire beneath his burning kisses. He felt her lips move in a fluttering sob beneath his, and then her dear arms stole up about his neck and pressed him closer in complete surrender.

"Shannon! You love me?"

"Ah, dear boy, always!"

He drew her to the lower end of a pool where a rustic seat stood half concealed by the foliage of a drooping umbrella tree.

There, they sat and asked each other the same questions that lovers have asked since prehistoric man first invented speech and that lovers will continue to ask so long as speech exists upon earth; very important questions — by far the most important questions in the world.

They did not know how long they had sat there — to them it seemed but a moment — when they heard voices calling their names from above.

"Shannon! Custer! Where are you?"

It was Eva calling.

"I suppose we'll have to go," he said. "Just one more kiss!"

He took a dozen; and then they rose and walked up the steps to the south drive.

"Shall I tell them?" he asked.

"Not yet, please."

She was not sure that it would last. Such happiness was too sweet to endure.

Eva spied them.

"Where in the world have you two been?" she demanded. "We've been hunting all over for you and shouting until I'm hoarse."

"We've been right down there by the upper pool trying to cool off," replied Custer. "It's too beastly hot to dance."

"You never thought so before," said Eva suspiciously. "Do you know, I believe you two have been off spooning! How perfectly gorgeristic!"

"How perfectly nothing," replied Custer. "Old people, like Shannon and me, don't spoon. That's for you kids."

Eva came closer.

"Shannon, you'd better go and straighten your hair before anyone else sees you." She laughed and pinched the other's arm. "I'd love it," she whispered in Shannon's ear, "if it were true! You'll tell me, won't you?"

"If it ever comes true, dear"— Shannon returned the whisper — "you shall be the first to know about it."

"Scrumptious! But say, I've got the divinest news — what do you think? Popsy has known it all day and never mentioned it

— forgot all about it, he said, until just before he and Mother trotted off to bed. Did you ever hear of anything so outrageous? And now, half the folks have gone home, and I can't tell 'em. Oh, it's too spiffy for words! I've been longing and longing for it for months and months and months, and now it's going to happen — really going to happen — actually going to happen on Monday!"

"For Heaven's sake, little one, unwind and get to the end of the harrowing story. What's going to happen?"

"Why, the KKS company is coming on Monday, and Wilson Crumb is coming with them!"

Shannon staggered almost as from the force of a physical blow. Wilson Crumb coming! Coming to Ganado! Short indeed had been her sweet happiness!

"What's the matter, Shannon?" asked Custer solicitously.

The girl steadied herself quickly.

"Oh, it's nothing," she said, with a nervous laugh. "I just felt a little dizzy for a moment."

"You had better go in the house and lie down," he suggested.

"No, I think I'll go home, if you'll drive me down, Custer. You know 10 o'clock is pretty late for us."

"It's Saturday night," said Eva.

"But I don't want to miss my ride in the morning. You're all going, aren't you?"

"I am," said Custer.

He noticed that she was very quiet as they drove down to her place, and when they parted, she clung to him as if she could not bear to let him go.

It was very wonderful — the miracle of this great love. As he drove back home, he could not think of anything else. He was not egotistical, and it seemed strange that, from all the men she must have known, Shannon had kept her love for him. With Grace, it had been different. Their love had grown up with them from childhood. It had seemed no more remarkable that Grace should love him than that Eva should love him or that he should love Grace; but Shannon had come to him out of a strange world — a world full of men — where, with her beauty and her charm, she must have been an object of admiration to many. Yet, she had brought her heart to him intact; for she had told him that she had never loved another — and she had told him the truth.

CHAPTER XXXII

AFTER CUSTER LEFT HER, Shannon entered the bungalow and sat for a long time before the table on which stood a framed photograph of her mother. Never before had she felt the need of loving counsel so sorely as now. In almost any other emergency, she could have gone to Mrs. Pennington, but in this she dared not. She knew the pride of the Penningtons. She realized the high altar upon which they placed the purity of their women in the sacred temple of their love, and she knew that none but the pure might enter.

In her heart of hearts, she knew that she had the right to stand there beside his mother or his sister; but the pity of it was that she could never prove that right, for who would believe her? Men had been hanged upon circumstantial evidence less damning than that which might be arrayed against her purity. No — if ever they should learn of her association with Wilson Crumb, they would cast her out of their lives as they would put a leper out of their home.

Not even Custer's love could survive such a blow to his honor and his pride. She did not think the less of him because of that, for she was wise enough in the ways of the world to know that pride and virtue are oftentimes uncompromising, even to narrowness.

Her only hope, therefore, lay in avoiding discovery by Wilson Crumb during his stay at Ganado. Her love, and the weakness it had induced, permitted her to accept the happiness from which an unkind fate had hitherto debarred her and to which, even now, her honor told her she had no right.

She wished that Custer had not loved her and that she might have continued to live the life that she had learned to love where she might be near him and might constantly see him in the happy consociation of friendship; but with his arms about her and his kisses on her lips, she had not had the strength to deny him or to dissimulate the great love which had ordered her very existence for many months.

In the brief moments of bliss that had followed the avowal of his love, she had permitted herself to drift without thought of the future; but now that the sudden knowledge of the approaching arrival of Crumb had startled her into recollection of the past and consideration of its bearings upon the future, she realized only too poignantly that the demands of honor required that sooner or later she herself must tell Custer the whole sordid story of those hideous months in Hollywood. There was no other way. She could not mate with a man unless she could match her honor with his. There was no alternative other than to go away forever.

It was midnight before she arose and went to her room. She went deliberately to a drawer which she kept locked, and, finding the key, she opened it. From it she took the little black case, and, turning back the cover, she revealed the phials, the needles, and the tiny syringe that had played so sinister a part in her past.

What she was doing tonight she had done so often in the past year that it had almost assumed the proportions of a rite. It had been her wont to parade her tempters before her that she might have the satisfaction of deriding them and of proving the strength of the new will that her love for Custer Pennington had been so potent a factor in developing. Tonight, she went a little further. She took a bit of cotton, and, placing it in the bowl of a spoon, she dissolved some of the white powder with the aid of a lighted match held beneath the spoon, and then, she drew the liquid into the syringe.

Her nerves were overwrought and unstrung from the stress of the conflicting emotions they had endured that evening and the risk she took was greater than she guessed. And yet, as she looked at the syringe, and realized that its contents held surcease of sorrow, that it held quiet and rest and peace, she felt only repugnance toward it. Not even remotely did she consider the possibility of resorting again to the false happiness of morphine.

She knew now that she was freer from its temptations than one who had never used it; but she felt that after tonight, with the avowal of Pennington's love still in her ears, she must no longer keep in her possession a thing so diametrically opposed to the cleanliness of his life and his character. For months, she had retained it as a part of the system she had conceived for ridding herself of its power. Without it, she might never have known whether she could withstand the temptation of its presence; but now, she had finished with it. She needed it no longer.

With almost fanatical savagery, she destroyed it, crushing the glass phials and the syringe beneath her heel and tearing the little case to shreds. Then, gathering up the fragments, she carried them to the fireplace in the living room and burned them.

On the following day, the horses and several loads of properties from the KKS studio arrived at Ganado, and the men who accompanied them pitched their camp well up in Jackknife Cañon. Eva was very much excited and spent much of her time on horseback, watching their preparations. She tried to get Shannon to accompany her, but the latter found various excuses to remain away, being fearful that even though Crumb had not yet arrived, there might be other employees of the studio who would recognize her.

Crumb and the rest of the company came in the afternoon although they had not been expected until the following day. Eva, who had made Custer ride up again with her in the afternoon, recalled to the actor-director the occasion upon which she had met him, and they had danced together, some year and a half before.

As soon as he met her, Crumb was struck by her beauty, youth, and freshness. He saw in her a possible means of relieving the tedium of his several weeks' enforced absence from

Hollywood — though in the big brother he realized a possible obstacle unless he were able to carry on his purposed gallantries clandestinely.

In the course of conversation, he took occasion to remark that Eva ought to photograph well. "I'll let them take a hundred feet of you," he said, "someday when you're up here while we're working. We might discover an unsung Pickford up here among the hills!"

"She will remain unsung, then," said Custer curtly. "My sister has no desire to go into pictures."

"How do you know I haven't?" asked Eva.

"After Grace?" he asked significantly.

She turned to Crumb.

"I'm afraid I wouldn't make much of an actress," she said; "but it would be perfectly radiant to see myself in pictures just once!"

"Good!" he replied. "We'll get you alright someday that you're up here. I promise your brother that I won't try to persuade you into pictures."

"I hope not," said Custer.

As he and Eva rode back toward the house, he turned to the girl.

"I don't like that fellow Crumb," he said.

"Why?" she asked.

"It's hard to say. He just rubs me the wrong way; but I'd bet almost anything that he's a cad."

"Oh, I think he's perfectly divine!" said Eva with her usual enthusiasm.

Custer grunted.

"The trouble with you," announced Eva, "is that you're jealous of him because he's an actor. That's just like you men!"

Custer laughed.

"Maybe you're right," he said; "but I don't like him, and I hope you'll never go up there alone."

"Well, I'm going to see them take pictures," replied the girl; "and if I can't get anyone to go with me, I'm going alone."

"I don't like the way he looked at you, Eva."

"You're perfectly silly! He didn't look at me any differently than any other man does."

"I don't know about that. I haven't the same keen desire to punch the head of every man I see looking at you as I had in his case."

"Oh, you're prejudiced! I'll bet anything he's just perfectly lovely!"

Next morning, finding no one with the leisure or inclination to ride with her, Eva rode up again to the camp. They had already commenced shooting. Although Crumb was busy, he courteously took the time to explain the scene on which they were working and many of the technical details of picture-making. He had a man hold her horse while she came and squinted through the finder. In fact, he spent so much time with her that he materially delayed the work of the morning. At the same time, the infatuation that had had its birth on the preceding day grew to greater proportions in his diseased mind.

He asked her to stay and lunch with them. When she insisted that she must return home, he begged her to come again in the afternoon. Although she would have been glad to do so, for she found the work that they were doing novel and interesting, she declined his invitation as she already had made arrangements for the afternoon.

He followed her to her horse and walked beside her down the road a short distance from the others.

"If you can't come down this afternoon," he said, "possibly you can come up this evening. We are going to take some night pictures. I hadn't intended inviting any one because the work is going to be rather difficult and dangerous and an audience might distract the attention of the actors; but if you think you could get away alone, I should be very glad to have you come up for a few minutes about nine o'clock. We shall be working in the same place. Don't forget," he repeated as she started to ride away, "that for this particular scene, I really ought not to have any audience at all; so if you come, please don't tell anyone else about it."

"I'll come," she said. "It's awfully good of you to ask me, and I won't tell a soul."

Crumb smiled as he turned back to his waiting company.

Brought up in the atmosphere that had surrounded her since birth, unacquainted with any but honorable men and believing as she did that all men are the chivalrous protectors of all women, Eva did not suspect the guile that lay behind the director's courteous manner and fair words. She looked upon the coming nocturnal visit to the scene of their work as nothing more than a harmless adventure; nor was there, from her experience, any cause for apprehension since the company comprised some 40 or 50 men and women who, like anyone else, would protect her from any harm that lay in their power to avert.

Her conscience did not trouble her in the least, although she regretted that she could not share her good fortune with the other members of her family and deplored the necessity of leaving the house surreptitiously, like a thief in the night. Such things did not appeal to Pennington standards; but Eva satisfied these qualms by promising herself that she would tell them all about it at breakfast the next morning.

After lunch that day, Custer went to his room and, throwing himself on his bed with a book with the intention of reading for half an hour, fell asleep.

Shortly afterward, Shannon Burke, feeling that there would be no danger of meeting any of the KKS people at the Pennington house, rode up on the Senator to keep her appointment with Eva. As she tied her horse upon the north side of the house, Wilson Crumb stopped his car opposite the patio at the south drive. He had come up to see Colonel Pennington for the purpose of arranging for the use of a number of the Ganado Herefords in a scene on the following day.

Not finding Eva in the family sitting room, Shannon passed through the house and out into the patio, just as Wilson Crumb mounted the two steps to the arcade. Before either realized the presence of the other, they were face to face, scarce a yard apart.

Shannon went deathly white as she recognized the man beneath his make-up, while Crumb stood speechless for a moment.

"My God, Gaza. You!" he presently managed to exclaim. "What are you doing here? Thank God I have found you at last!"

"Don't!" she begged. "Please don't speak to me. I am living a decent life here."

He laughed in a disagreeable manner.

"Decent!" he scoffed. "Where you getting the snow? Who's putting up for it?"

"I don't use it anymore," she said.

"The hell you don't! You can't put that over on me! Some other guy is furnishing it. I know you — you can't get along two hours without it. I'm not going to stand or this. There isn't any guy going to steal my girl!"

"Hush, Wilson!" she cautioned. "For God's sake, keep still! Someone might hear you."

"I don't give a damn who hears me. I'm here to tell the world that no one is going to take my girl away from me. I've found you, and you're going back with me, do you understand?"

She came very close to him, her eyes blazing wrathfully.

"I'm not going back with you, Wilson Crumb," she said. "If you tell or if you ever threaten me again in any way, I'll kill you. I managed to escape you, and I have found happiness at last, and no one shall take it away from me!"

"What about my happiness? You lived with me two years. I love you, and, by God, I'm going to have you, if I have to —"

A door slammed behind them, and they both turned to see Custer Pennington standing in the arcade outside his door, looking at them.

"I beg your pardon," he said, his voice chilling. "Did I interrupt?"

"This man is looking for someone, Custer," said Shannon, and turned to reenter the house.

Confronted by a man, Crumb's bravado had vanished. Intuitively, he guessed that he was looking at the man who had stolen Gaza from him; but he was a very big young man with broad shoulders and muscles that his flannel shirt and riding breeches did not conceal. Crumb decided that if he was going to have trouble with this man, it would be safer to commence hostilities at a time when the other was not looking.

"Yes," he said. "I was looking for your father, Mr. Pennington."

"Father is not here. He has driven over to the village. What do you want?"

"I wanted to see if I could arrange for the use of some of your Herefords tomorrow morning."

Pennington was leading the way toward Crumb's car.

"You can find out about that," he said, "or anything else that you may wish to know from the assistant foreman, whom you will usually find up at the other end around the cabin. If he is in doubt about anything, he will consult with us personally; so that it will not be necessary, Mr. Crumb, for you to go to the trouble of coming to the house again."

Custer's voice was level and low. It carried no suggestion of anger, yet there was that about it which convinced Crumb that he was fortunate in not having been kicked off the hill physically rather than verbally — for kicked off he had been, and advised to stay off, into the bargain.

He wondered how much Pennington had overheard of his conversation with Gaza. Shannon Burke, crouching in a big chair in the sitting room, was wondering the same thing.

As a matter of fact, Custer had overheard practically all of the conversation. The noise of Crumb's car had awakened him, but almost immediately he had fallen into a doze through which the spoken words impinged upon his consciousness without any actual, immediate realization of their meaning or of the identity of the speakers. The moment that he became fully awake and found that he was listening to a conversation not intended for his ears, he had risen and gone into the patio.

When finally he came into the sitting room where Shannon was, he made no mention of the occurrence except to say that the visitor had wanted to see his father. It did not seem possible to Shannon that he could have failed to overhear at least a part of their conversation, for they were standing not more than a couple of yards from the open window of his bedroom, and there was no other sound breaking the stillness of the August noon. She was sure that he had heard, and yet his manner indicated that he had not.

She waited a moment to see if he would be the first to broach the subject, but he did not. She determined to tell him then and there all that she had to tell, freeing her soul and her conscience of their burden, whatever the cost might be.

She rose and came to where he was standing and, placing a hand upon his arm, looked up into his eyes.

"Custer," she said. "I have something to tell you. I ought to have told you before, but I have been afraid. Since last night, there is no alternative but to tell you."

"You do not have to tell me anything that you do not want to tell me," he said. "My confidence in you is implicit. I could not both love and distrust at the same time."

"I must tell you," she said. "I only hope —"

"Where in the world have you been, Shannon?" cried Eva, breaking suddenly into the sitting room. "I have been away down to your place looking for you. I thought you were going to play golf with me this afternoon."

"That's what I came up for," said Shannon, turning toward her.

"Well, come on, then! We'll have to hurry if we're going to play 18 holes this afternoon."

Custer Pennington went to his room again after the girls had driven off in the direction of the Country Club. He wondered what it had been that Shannon wished to tell him. Round and round in his mind rang the words of Wilson Crumb:

"You lived with me two years — you lived with me two years — you lived with me two years!"

She had been going to explain that, he was sure; but she did not have to explain it. The girl that he loved could have done no wrong. He trusted her. He was sure of her.

But what place had that soft-faced cad had in her life? It was unthinkable that she had ever known him much less that they had been upon intimate terms.

Custer went to his closet and rummaged around for a bottle. It had been more than two weeks since he had taken a drink. The return to his old intimacy with Shannon and the frequency with which he now saw her had again weaned him from his habit; but today, he felt the need of a drink — of a big drink, stiff and neat.

He swallowed the raw liquor as if it had been so much water. He wished now that he had punched Crumb's head when he had had the chance. The cur! He had spoken to Shannon as if she were a common woman of the streets — Shannon Burke — Custer's Shannon!

Feeling no reaction to the first drink, he took another.

"I'd like to get my fingers on his throat!" he thought. "Before I choked the life out of him, I'd drag him up here and make him kiss the ground at her feet!"

But no, he could not do that. Others would see it, and there would have to be explanations; and how could he explain it without casting reflections on Shannon?

For hours, he sat there in his room, nursing his anger, his jealousy, and his grief; and all the time he drank and drank again. He went to his closet, got his belt and holster, and from his dresser drawer took a big, ugly-looking 45 — a Colt's automatic. For a moment, he stood holding it in his hand, looking at it. Almost caressingly he handled it, and then, he slipped it into the holster at his hip, put on his hat, and started for the door.

CHAPTER XXXIII

CUSTER'S GAIT SHOWED no indication of the amount that he had drunk. He was a Pennington of Virginia, and he could carry his liquor like a gentleman. Even though he was aflame with the heat of vengeance, his movements were slow and deliberate. At the door, he paused, and turning, retraced his steps to the table where stood the bottle and the glass.

The bottle was empty. He went to the closet and got another. Again, he drank, and as he stood there by the table, he commenced to plan again.

There must be some reason for the thing he contemplated. There must be some reason so logical that the discovery of his act could in no way reflect upon Shannon Burke or draw her name into the publicity which must ensue. It required time to think out a feasible plan, and time gave opportunity for additional drinks.

The colonel and Mrs. Pennington were away somewhere down in the valley. Eva and Shannon were the first to return. In passing along the arcade by Custer's open window, Eva saw him lying on his bed. She called to him, but he did not answer. Shannon was at her side.

"What in the world do you suppose is the matter with Custer?" asked Eva.

They saw that he was fully dressed. His hat had fallen forward over his eyes. The two girls entered the room when they could not arouse him by calling him from the outside. The two bottles and the glass upon the table told their own story. What they could not tell Shannon guessed — he had overheard the conversation between Wilson Crumb and herself.

Eva removed the bottles and the glass to the closet,

"Poor Cus!" she said. "I never saw him like this before. I wonder what could have happened! What had we better do?"

"Pull down the shades by his bed," said Shannon, and this she did herself without waiting for Eva. "No one can see him from the patio now. It will be just as well to leave him alone, I think, Eva. He will probably be all right when he wakes up."

They went out of the room, closing the door after them, and a little later, Shannon mounted the Senator and rode away toward home.

Her thoughts were bitter. Wherever Crumb went he brought misery. Whatever he touched he defiled. She wished that he was dead. God, how she wished it! She could have killed him with her own hands for the grief that he had brought to Custer Pennington.

She did not care so much about herself. She was used to suffering because of Wilson Crumb; but that he should bring his foulness into the purity of Ganado was unthinkable. Her brief happiness was over. No indeed was there nothing more in life for her. She was not easily moved to tears, but that night she was still sobbing when she fell asleep.

When the colonel and Mrs. Pennington arrived at the ranch house, just before dinner, Eva told them that Custer was not feeling well and that he had lain down to sleep and had asked not to be disturbed. They did not go to his room at all, and at about half past eight, they retired for the night.

Eva was very much excited. She had never before experienced the thrill of such an adventure as she was about to embark upon. As the time approached, she became more and more perturbed. The realization grew upon her that what she was doing might seem highly objectionable to her family; but as her innocent heart held no suggestion of evil, she considered that her only wrong was the infraction of those unwritten laws of well-regulated homes which forbid their daughters going out alone at night. She would tell about it in the morning and wheedle her father into forgiveness.

Quickly, she changed into riding clothes. Leaving her room, she noiselessly passed through the living room and the east wing to the kitchen and from there to the basement from which a tunnel led beneath the driveway and opened on the hillside above the upper pool of the water gardens. To get her horse and saddle him required but a few moments, for the moon was full and the night almost like day.

Her heart was beating with excitement as she rode up the cañon toward the big sycamore that stood at the junction of Sycamore Cañon and El Camino Largo where Crumb had told her the night scenes would be taken. She walked her horse past the bunkhouse lest some of the men might hear her; but when she was through the east gate beyond the old goat corral, she broke into a canter.

As she passed the mouth of Jackknife, she glanced up the cañon toward the site of the KKS camp, but she could not see any lights as the camp was fairly well hidden from the main cañon by trees. As she approached El Camino Largo, she saw that all was darkness. There was no sign of the artificial lights she imagined they would use for shooting night scenes, nor was there anything to indicate the presence of the actors.

She continued on, however, until presently she saw the outlines of a car beneath the big sycamore. A man stepped out and hailed her.

"Is that you, Miss Pennington?" he asked.

"Yes," she said. "Aren't you going to take the pictures tonight?" She rode up quite close to him. It was Crumb.

"I am just waiting for the others. Won't you dismount?"

As she swung from the saddle, he led her horse to his car and tied him to the spare tire in the rear; then, he returned to the girl. As they talked, he adroitly turned the subject of their conversation toward the possibilities for fame and fortune which lay in pictures for a beautiful and talented girl.

Long practice had made Wilson Crumb an adept in his evil arts. Ordinarily he worked very slowly, considering that weeks or even months were not ill spent if they led toward the consummation of his desires; but in this instance, he realized that he must work quickly. He must take the girl by storm or not at all.

So unsophisticated was Eva and so innocent that she did not realize from his conversation what would have been palpable to one more worldly wise; and because she did not repulse him, Crumb thought that she was not averse to his advances. It was not until he seized her and tried to kiss her that she awoke to a realization of her danger and of the position in which her silly credulity had placed her.

She carried a quirt in her hand, and she was a Pennington. What matter that she was but a slender girl? The honor and the courage of a Pennington were hers.

"How dare you?" she cried, attempting to jerk away.

When he would have persisted, she raised the heavy quirt and struck him across the face.

"My father shall hear of this, and so shall the man I am to marry — Mr. Evans."

"Go slow!" he growled angrily. "Be careful what you tell! Remember that you came up here alone at night to meet a man you have known only a day. How will you square that with your assertions of virtue, eh? And as for Evans — yes, one of your men told me today that you and he were going to be married — as for him, the less you drag him into this the better it'll be for Evans, and you, too!"

She was walking toward her horse. She wheeled suddenly toward him.

"Had I been armed, I would have killed you," she said. "Any Pennington would kill you for what you attempted. My father or my brother will kill you if you are here tomorrow, for I shall tell them what you have done. You had better leave tonight. I am advising you for their sakes — not for yours."

He followed her then, and, when she mounted, he seized her reins.

"Not so damned fast, young lady! I've got something to say about this. You'll keep your mouth shut, or I'll send Evans to the pen where he belongs!"

"Get out my way!" she commanded and put her spurs to her mount.

The horse leaped forward, but Crumb clung to the reins, checking him. Then, she struck Crumb again; but he managed to seize the quirt and hold it.

"Now listen to me," he said. "If you tell what happened here tonight, I'll tell what I know about Evans, and he'll go to the pen as sure as you're a silly little fool!"

"You know nothing about Mr. Evans. You don't even know him."

"Listen — I'll tell you what I know. I know that Evans let your brother, who was innocent, go to the pen for the thing that Evans was guilty of."

The girl shrank back.

"You lie!" she cried.

"No, I don't lie, either. I'm telling you the truth, and I can bring plenty of witnesses to prove what I say. It was young Evans who handled all that stolen booze and sold it to some guy from L.A. It was young Evans who got the money. He was getting rich on it till your brother butted in and crabbed his game, and then, it was young Evans who kept still and let an innocent man do time for him. That's the kind of fellow you're going to marry. If you want the whole world to know about it, you just tell your father or your brother anything about me!"

He saw the girl sink down in her saddle, her head and shoulders drooping like some lovely flower in the path of fire, and he knew that he had won. Then, he let her go.

It was half past nine o'clock when Colonel Pennington was aroused by someone knocking on the north door of his bedroom — the door that opened upon the north porch.

"Who is it?" he asked.

It was the stableman.

"Miss Eva's horse is out, sir," the man said. "I heard a horse pass the bunkhouse about half an hour ago. I dressed and come up here to the stables to see if it was one of ours — somethin' seemed to tell me it was — an' I found her horse out. I thought I'd better tell you about it, sir. You can't tell, sir, with all them pictur' people up the cañon, what might be goin' on. We'll be lucky if we have any horses or tack left if they're here long!"

"Miss Eva's in bed," said the colonel; "but we'll have to look into this at once. Custer's sick tonight, so he can't go along with us; but if you will saddle up my horse and one for yourself, I'll dress and be right down. It can't be the motion-picture people — they're not horse thieves."

While the stableman returned to saddle the horses, the colonel dressed. So sure was he that Eva was in bed that he did not even stop to look into her room. As he left the house, he was buckling on a gun — a thing that he seldom carried, for even in the peaceful days that have settled upon southern California, a horse thief is still a horse thief.

As he was descending the steps to the stable, he saw someone coming up. In the moonlight, there was no difficulty in recognizing the figure of his daughter.

"Eva!" he exclaimed. "Where have you been? What are you doing out at this time of night, alone?"

She did not answer, but threw herself into his arms, sobbing.

"What is it? What has happened, child? Tell me!"

Her sobs choked her, and she could not speak. Putting his arm about her, her father led her up the steps and to her room. There he sat down and held her and tried to comfort her while he endeavored to extract a coherent statement from her. Little by little, word by word, she managed at last to tell him.

"You mustn't cry, dear," he said. "You did a foolish thing to go up there alone, but you did nothing wrong. As for what that fellow told you about Guy, I don't believe it."

"But it's the truth," she sobbed. "I know it is the truth now. Little things that I didn't think of before come back to me, and in the light of what that terrible man told me, I know that it's true. We always knew that Custer was innocent. Think what a change came over Guy from the moment that Custer was arrested. He has been a different man since. And the money — the money that we were to be married on! I never stopped to try to reason it out. He had thousands of dollars. He told me not to tell anybody how much he had; and that was where it came from. It couldn't have come from anything else. Oh, Popsy, it is awful, and I loved him so! To think that he, that Guy Evans, of all men, would have let my brother go to jail for something he did!"

Again, her sobs stifled her.

"Crying will do no good," the colonel said. "Go to bed now, and tomorrow, we will talk it over. Goodnight, little girl. Remember, we'll all stick to Guy no matter what he has done."

He kissed her then and left her, but he did not return to his room. Instead, he went down to the stables and saddled his horse, for the stableman, when Eva came in with the missing animal, had put it in its box and returned to the bunkhouse.

The colonel rode immediately to the sleeping camp in Jackknife Cañon. His calls went unanswered for a time, but presently, a sleepy man stuck his head through the flap of a tent.

"What do you want?" he asked.

"I am looking for Mr. Crumb. Where is he?"

"I don't know. He went away in his car early in the evening and hasn't come back. What's the matter, anyway? You're the second fellow that's been looking for him. Oh, you're Colonel Pennington, aren't you? I didn't recognize you. Why, someone was here a little while ago looking for him — a young fellow on horseback. I think it must have been your son. Anything I can do for you?"

"Yes," said the colonel. "In case I don't see Mr. Crumb, you can tell him or whoever is in charge that you're to break camp in the morning and be off my property by 10 o'clock!"

He wheeled his horse and rode down Jackknife Cañon toward Sycamore.

"Well, what the hell!" ejaculated the sleepy man to himself and withdrew again into his tent.

CHAPTER XXXIV

SHANNON BURKE, after a restless night, rose early in the morning to ride. She always found that the quiet and peace of the hills acted as a tonic on jangling nerves and dispelled, at least for the moment, any cloud of unhappiness that might he hovering over her.

The first person to see her that morning was the flunky from the KKS camp who was rustling wood for the cook's morning fire. So interested was he in her rather remarkable occupation that he stood watching her from behind a bush until she was out of sight. As long as he saw her, she rode slowly, dragging at her side a leafy bough, which she moved to and fro as if sweeping the ground. She constantly looked back as if to note the effect of her work; and once or twice, he saw her go over short stretches of the road a second time, brushing vigorously.

It was quite light by that time, as it was almost five o'clock, and the sun was just rising as she dismounted at the Ganado stables and hurried up the steps toward the house. The iron gate at the patio entrance had not yet been raised, so she went around to the north side of the house and knocked on the colonel's bedroom door.

He came from his dressing room to answer her knock, for he was fully dressed and evidently on the point of leaving for his morning ride. The expression of her face denoted that something was wrong, even before she spoke.

"Colonel," she cried, "Wilson Crumb has been killed. I rode early this morning, and as I came into Sycamore over El Camino Largo, I saw his body lying under the big tree there."

They were both thinking the same thought, which neither dared voice — where was Custer?

"Did you notify the camp?" he asked.

"No — I came directly here."

"You are sure that it is Crumb, and that he is dead?" he asked.

"I am sure that it is Crumb. He was lying on his back, and though I didn't dismount, I am quite positive that he was dead."

Mrs. Pennington had joined them, herself dressed for riding.

"How terrible!" she exclaimed.

"Terrible nothing," exclaimed the colonel. "I'm damned glad he's dead!"

Shannon looked at him in astonishment, but Mrs. Pennington understood, for the colonel had told her all that Eva had told him.

"He was a bad man," said Shannon. "The world will be better off without him."

"You knew him?" Colonel Pennington asked in surprise.

"I knew him in Hollywood," she replied.

She knew now that they must all know sooner or later, for she could not see how she could be kept out of the investigation and the trial that must follow. In her heart, she feared that Custer had killed Crumb. The fact that he had drunk so heavily that afternoon indicated not only that he had overheard but that what he had heard had affected him profoundly — profoundly enough to have suggested the killing of the man whom he believed to have wronged the woman he loved.

"The first thing to do, I suppose," said the colonel, "is to notify the sheriff."

He left the room and went to the telephone. While he was away, Mrs. Pennington and Shannon discussed the tragedy, and the older woman confided to the other the experience that Eva had had with Crumb the previous night.

"The beast!" muttered Shannon. "Death was too good for him!"

Presently the colonel returned to them.

"I think I'll go and see if the children are going to ride with us," he said. "There is no reason why we shouldn't ride as usual."

He went to Eva's door and looked in. Apparently she was still fast asleep. Her hair was down, and her curls lay in soft confusion upon her pillow. Very gently, he closed the door again, glad that she could sleep.

When he entered his son's room, he found Custer lying fully clothed upon his bed, his belt about his waist and his gun at his hip. His suspicions were crystallized into belief.

But why had Custer killed Crumb? He couldn't have known of the man's affront to Eva, for she had seen no member of the family but her father, and in him alone had she confided.

He crossed to the bed and shook Custer by the shoulder. The younger man opened his eyes and sat up on the edge of his bed. He looked first at his father and then at himself — at his boots and spurs and breeches and the gun about his waist.

"What time is it?" he asked.

"Five o'clock."

"I must have fallen asleep. I wish it was dinner time! I'm hungry."

"Dinner time! It's only a matter of a couple of hours to breakfast. It's five o'clock in the morning."

Custer rose to his feet in surprise.

"I must have loaded on more than I knew," he said with a wry smile.

"What do you mean?" asked his father.

"I had a blue streak yesterday afternoon, and I took a few drinks; and here I have slept all the way through to the next morning!"

"You haven't been out of the room since yesterday afternoon?" asked the colonel.

"No, of course not. I thought it was still yesterday afternoon until you told me that it is the next morning," said Custer.

The colonel ran his fingers through his hair.

"I am glad," he said.

Custer didn't know why his father was glad.

"Riding?" he asked.

"Yes."

"I'll be with you in a jiffy. I want to wash up a bit."

He met them at the stables a few minutes later. The effect of the liquor had entirely disappeared. He seemed his normal self again and not at all like a man who had the blood of a new murder on his soul. He was glad to see Shannon and squeezed her hand as he passed her horse to get his own.

In the few moments since his father had awakened him, he had reviewed the happenings of the previous day, and his loyalty to the girl he loved had determined him that he had nothing to grieve about. Whatever had been between her and Crumb, she would explain. Only the fact that Eva had interrupted her had kept him from knowing the whole truth the previous day.

They were mounted and had started out when the colonel reined to Custer's side.

"Shannon just made a gruesome find up in Sycamore," he said and paused.

If he had intended to surprise Custer into any indication of guilty knowledge, he failed.

"Gruesome find!" repeated the younger man. "What was it?"

"Wilson Crumb has been murdered. Shannon found his body."

"The devil!" ejaculated Custer. "Who do you suppose could have done it?"

Then, quite suddenly, his heart came to his mouth as he realized that there was only one present there who had cause to kill Wilson Crumb. He did not dare to look at Shannon for a long time.

They had gone only a hundred yards when Custer pulled up the Apache and dismounted.

"I thought so," he said, looking at the horse's off forefoot. "He's pulled that shoe again. He must have done it in the corral, for it was on when I put him in last night. You folks go ahead. I'll go back and saddle Baldy."

The stableman was still there and helped him.

"That was a new shoe," Custer said. "Look about the corral and the box and see if you can find it. You can tack it back on."

Then, he swung to Baldy's back and cantered off after the others.

A deputy sheriff came from the village of Ganado before they returned from their ride and went up the cañon to take charge of Crumb's body and investigate the scene of the crime.

Eva was still in bed when they were called to breakfast. They insisted upon Shannon's remaining, and the four were passing along the arcade past Eva's room.

"I think I'll go in and waken her," said Mrs. Pennington. "She doesn't like to sleep so late."

The others passed into the living room and were walking toward the dining room when they were startled by a scream.

"Custer! Custer!" Mrs. Pennington called to her husband.

All three turned and hastened back to Eva's room where they found Mrs. Pennington half lying across the bed, her body convulsed with sobs. The colonel was the first to reach her, followed by Custer and Shannon. The bedclothes lay half thrown back where Mrs. Pennington had turned them. The white sheet was stained with blood, and in Eva's hand was clutched a revolver that Custer had given her the previous Christmas.

"My little girl, my little girl!" cried the weeping mother. "Why did you do it?"

The colonel knelt and put his arms about his wife.

He could not speak. Custer Pennington stood like a man turned to stone. The shock seemed to have bereft him of the power to understand what had happened. Finally, he turned dumbly toward Shannon. The tears were running down her cheeks. Gently, she touched his sleeve.

"My poor boy!" she said.

The words broke the spell that had held him. He walked to the opposite side of the bed and bent close to the still, white face of the sister he had worshiped.

"Dear little sister, how could you, when we love you so?" he said.

Gently the colonel drew his wife away, and, kneeling, placed his ear close above Eva's heart. There were no outward indications of life, but presently he lifted his head, an expression of hope relieving that of grim despair which had settled upon his countenance at the first realization of the tragedy.

"She is not dead," he said. "Get Baldwin! Get him at once!" He was addressing Custer. "Then telephone Carruthers in Los Angeles to get down here as soon as God will let him."

Custer hurried from the room to carry out his father's instructions.

It was later while they were waiting for the arrival of the doctor that the colonel told Custer of Eva's experience with Crumb the previous night.

"She wanted to kill herself because of what he told her about Guy," he said. "There was no other reason."

Then the doctor came, and they all stood in tense expectancy and mingled dread and hope while he made his examination. Carefully and deliberately, the old doctor worked, outwardly as calm and unaffected as if he were treating a minor injury to a stranger; yet his heart was as heavy as theirs, for he had brought Eva into the world and had known and loved her all her brief life.

At last, he straightened up to find their questioning eyes upon him.

"She still lives," he said, but there was no hope in his voice.

"I have sent for Carruthers," said the colonel. "He is on his way now. He told Custer that he'll be here in less than three hours."

"I arranged to have a couple of nurses sent out, too," said Custer.

Dr. Baldwin made no reply.

"There is no hope?" asked the colonel.

"There is always hope while there is life," replied the doctor; "but you must not raise yours too high."

They understood him and realized that there was very little hope.

"Can you keep her alive until Carruthers arrives?" asked the colonel.

"I need not tell you that I shall do my best," was the reply.

Guy had come with his mother. He seemed absolutely stunned by the catastrophe that had overwhelmed him. There was a wildness in his demeanor that frightened them all. It was necessary to watch him carefully for fear that he might attempt to destroy himself when he realized at last that Eva was likely to die.

He insisted that they should tell him all the circumstances that had led up to the pitiful tragedy. For a time, they sought to conceal a part of the truth from him; but at last, so great was his insistence, they were compelled to reveal all that they knew.

Of a nervous and excitable temperament and endowed by nature with a character of extreme sensitiveness and comparatively little strength, the shock of the knowledge that it was his own acts that had led Eva to self-destruction proved too much for Guy's overwrought nerves and brain. So violent did he become that Colonel Pennington and Custer together could scarce restrain him, and it became necessary to send for two of the ranch employees.

When the deputy sheriff came to question them about the murder of Crumb, it was evident that Guy's mind was so greatly affected that he did not understand what was taking place around him. He had sunk into a morose silence broken at intervals by fits of raving. Later in the day, at Dr. Baldwin's suggestion, he was removed to a sanatorium outside of Los Angeles.

Guy's mental collapse and the necessity for constantly restraining him had resulted in taking Custer's mind from his own grief, at least for the moment; but when he was not thus occupied, he sat staring straight ahead of him in dumb despair.

It was 11 o'clock when the best surgeon that Los Angeles could furnish arrived, bringing a nurse with him, and Eva was still breathing when he came. Dr. Baldwin was there, and together, the three worked for an hour while the Penningtons and Shannon waited almost hopelessly in the living room, Mrs. Evans having accompanied Guy to Los Angeles.

Finally, after what seemed years, the door of the living room opened, and Dr. Carruthers entered. They scanned his face as he entered but saw nothing there to lighten the burden of their apprehension. The colonel and Custer rose.

"Well?" asked the former, his voice scarcely audible.

"The operation was successful. I found the bullet and removed it."

"She will live, then!" cried Mrs. Pennington, coming quickly toward him.

He took her hands very gently in his.

"My dear madam," he said, "it would be cruel of me to hold out useless hope. She hasn't more than one chance in 100. It is a miracle that she was alive when you found her. Only a splendid constitution resulting from the life that she has led could possibly account for it."

The mother turned away with a low moan.

"There is nothing more that you can do?" asked the colonel.

"I have done all that I can," replied Carruthers.

"She will not last long?"

"It may be a matter of hours, or only minutes," he replied. "She is in excellent hands, however. No one could do more for her than Dr. Baldwin."

The two nurses whom Custer had arranged for had arrived, and when Dr. Carruthers departed, he took his own nurse with him.

It was afternoon when deputies from the sheriff's and coroner's offices arrived from Los Angeles, together with detectives from the district attorney's office. Crumb's body still lay where it had fallen, guarded by a constable from the village of Ganado. It was surrounded by members of his company, villagers, and near-by ranchers, for word of the murder had spread rapidly in the district in that seemingly mysterious way in which news travels in rural communities. Among the crowd was Slick Allen, who had returned to the valley after his release from the county jail.

A partially successful effort had been made to keep the crowd from trampling the ground in the immediate vicinity of the body, but beyond a limited area, whatever possible clues the murderer might have left in the shape of footprints had been entirely obliterated long before the officers arrived from Los Angeles.

When the body was finally lifted from its resting place and placed in the ambulance that had been brought from Los Angeles, one of the detectives picked up a horseshoe that had lain underneath the body. From its appearance, it was evident that it had been upon a horse's hoof very recently and had been torn off by force.

As the detective examined the shoe, several of the crowd pressed forward to look at it. Among them was Allen.

"That's off of young Pennington's horse," he said. "How do you know that?" inquired the detective. "I used to work for them — took care of their saddle horses. This young Pennington's horse forges. They had to shoe him special to keep him from pulling the off fore shoe. I could tell one of his shoes in a million. If they haven't walked all over his tracks, I can tell whether that horse had been up here or not."

He stooped and examined the ground close to where the body had lain.

"There!" he said, pointing. "There's an imprint of one of his hind feet. See how the toe of that shoe is squared off? That was made by the Apache, alright!"

The detective was interested. He studied the hoofprint carefully and searched for others, but this was the only one he could find.

"Looks like someone had been sweeping this place with a broom," he remarked. "There ain't much of anything shows."

A pimply-faced young man spoke up.

"There was some one sweeping the ground this morning," he said. "About five o'clock this morning, I seen a girl dragging the branch of a tree after her and sweeping along the road below here."

"Did you know her?" asked the detective.

"No — I never seen her before."

"Would you know her if you saw her again?"

"Sure, I'd know her! She was a pippin. I'd know her horse, too."

CHAPTER XXXV

EVA WAS STILL BREATHING faintly as the sun dropped behind the western hills. Shannon had not left the house all day. She felt that Custer needed her, that they all needed her, however little she could do to mitigate their grief. There was at least a sense of sharing their burden, and her fine sensibilities told her that this service of love was quite as essential as the more practical help that she would have been glad to offer had it been within her power.

She was standing in the patio with Custer at sunset within call of Eva's room as they had all been during the entire day when a car drove up along the south drive and stopped at the patio entrance. Three of the four men in it alighted and advanced toward them.

"You are Custer Pennington?" one of them asked.

Pennington nodded.

"And you are Miss Burke — Miss Shannon Burke?"

"I am."

"I am a deputy sheriff. I have a warrant here for your arrest."

"Arrest!" exclaimed Custer. "For what?"

He read the warrant to them. It charged them with the murder of Wilson Crumb.

"I am sorry, Mr. Pennington," said the deputy sheriff; "but I have been given these warrants, and there is nothing for me to do but serve them."

"You have to take us away now? Can't you wait — until — my sister is dying in there. Couldn't it be arranged so that I could stay here under arrest as long as she lives?"

The deputy shook his head.

"It would be alright with me," he said; "but I have no authority to let you stay. Ill telephone in, though, and see what I can do. Where is the telephone?"

Pennington told him.

"You two stay here with my men," said the deputy sheriff, "while I telephone."

He was gone about 15 minutes. When he returned, he shook his head.

"Nothing doing," he said. "I have to bring you both in right away."

"May I go to her room and see her again before I leave?" asked Custer.

"Yes," said the deputy; but when Custer turned toward his sister's room, the officer accompanied him.

Dr. Baldwin and one of the nurses were in the room. Young Pennington came and stood beside the bed, looking down on the white face and the tumbled curls upon the pillow. He could not perceive the slightest indication of life, yet they told him that Eva still lived. He knelt and kissed her and then turned away. He tried to say goodbye to her, but his voice broke, and he turned and left the room hurriedly.

Colonel and Mrs. Pennington were in the patio with Shannon and the officers. The colonel and his wife had just learned of this new blow, and both of them were stunned. The colonel seemed to have aged a generation in that single day. He was a tired, hopeless old man. The heart of his boy and that of Shannon Burke went out to him and to the suffering mother from whom their son was to be taken at this moment in their lives when they needed him most. In their compassion for the older Penningtons, they almost forgot the seriousness of their own situation.

At their arraignment, next morning, the preliminary hearing was set for the following Friday. Early in the morning, Custer had received word from Ganado that Eva still lived and that Dr.

Baldwin now believed they might hold some slight hope for her recovery.

At Ganado, despair and anxiety had told heavily upon the Penningtons. The colonel felt that he should be in Los Angeles to assist in the defense of his son; and yet, he knew that his place was with his wife whose need of him was even greater. Nor would his heart permit him to leave the daughter whom he worshiped so long as even a faint spark of life remained in that beloved frame.

Mrs. Evans returned from Los Angeles the following day. She was almost prostrated by this last of a series of tragedies ordered, as it seemed, by some malignant fate for the wrecking of her happiness. She told them that Guy appeared to be hopelessly insane. He did not know his mother nor did he give the slightest indication of any recollection of his past life or of the events that had overthrown his reason.

At 10 o'clock on Wednesday night, Dr. Baldwin came into the living room where the colonel and his wife were sitting with Mrs. Evans. For two days, none of them had been in bed. They were tired and haggard, but not more so than the old doctor, who had remained constantly on duty from the moment when he was summoned. Never had man worked with more indefatigable zeal than he to wrest a young life from the path of the grim reaper. There were deep lines beneath his eyes, and his face was pale and drawn as he entered the room and stood before them; but for the first time in many hours, there was a smile upon his lips.

"I believe," he said, "that we are going to save her."

The others were too much affected to speak. So long had hope been denied that now they dared not even think of hope.

"She regained consciousness a few moments ago. She looked up at me and smiled, and then she fell asleep. She is breathing quite naturally now. She must not be disturbed, though. I think it would be well if you all retired. Mrs. Pennington, you certainly must get some sleep — and you too, Mrs. Evans, or I cannot be responsible for the results. I have left word with the night nurse to call me immediately if necessary, and if you will all go to your rooms, I will lie on the sofa here in the living room. I feel at last that it will be safe for me to leave her in the hands of the nurse, and a little sleep won't hurt me."

The colonel took his old friend by the hand.

"Baldwin," he said, "it is useless to try to thank you. I couldn't, even if there were the words to do it with."

"You don't have to, Pennington. I think I love her as much as you do. There isn't anyone who knows her who doesn't love her and who wouldn't have done as much as I. Now, get off to bed all of you, and I think we'll find something to be very happy about by morning. If there is any change for the worse, I will let you know immediately."

In the county jail in Los Angeles, Custer Pennington and Shannon Burke, awaiting trial on charges of a capital crime, were filled with increasing happiness as the daily reports from Ganado brought word of Eva's steady improvement until at last that she was entirely out of danger.

The tedious preliminaries of selecting a jury were finally concluded. As witness after witness was called, Pennington came to realize for the first time what a web of circumstantial evidence the State had fabricated about him. Even from servants whom he knew to be loyal and friendly, the most damaging evidence was elicited. His mother's second maid testified that she had seen him fully dressed in his room late in the evening before the murder when she had come in, as was her custom, with a pitcher of iced water, not knowing that the young man was there. She had seen him lying upon the bed with his gun in its holster hanging from the belt about his waist. She also testified that the following morning, when she had come into make up his bed, she had discovered that it had not been slept in.

The stableman testified that the Apache had been out on the night of the murder. He had rubbed the animal off earlier in the evening when the defendant had come in from riding. At that time, the two had examined the horse's shoes, the animal having just been re-shod. He said that on the morning after the murder, there were saddle sweat marks on the Apache's back and that the off fore shoe was missing.

One of the KKS employees testified that a young man, whom he partially identified as Custer, had ridden into their camp about nine o'clock on the night of the murder and had inquired concerning the whereabouts of Crumb. He said that the young man seemed excited, and upon being told that Crumb was away, he had ridden off rapidly toward Sycamore Cañon.

Added to all this were the damaging evidence of the detective who had found the Apache's off fore shoe under Crumb's body and the positive identification of the shoe by Allen. The one thing that was lacking — a motive for the crime — was supplied by Allen and the Penningtons' house man.

The latter testified that among his other duties was the care of the hot water heater in the basement of the Pennington home. Upon the evening of Saturday, August 5, he had forgotten to shut off the burner, as was his custom. He had returned about nine o'clock to do so. When he had left the house by the passageway leading from the basement beneath the south drive and opening on the hillside just above the water gardens, he had seen a man standing by the upper pool with his arms about a woman whom he was kissing. It was a bright moonlight night, and the house man had recognized the two as Custer Pennington and Miss Burke. Being embarrassed by having thus accidentally come upon them, he had moved away quietly in the opposite direction among the shadows of the trees and had returned to the bunkhouse.

The connecting link between this evidence and the motive for the crime was elicited from Allen in half an hour of direct examination, which constituted the most harrowing ordeal that Shannon Burke had ever endured; for it laid bare before the world, and before the man she loved, the sordid history of her life with Wilson Crumb. It portrayed her as a drug addict and a wanton; but, more terrible still, it established a motive for the murder of Crumb by Custer Pennington.

Owing to the fact that he had lain in a drunken stupor during the night of the crime, that no one had seen him from the time when the maid entered his room to bring his iced water until his father had found him fully clothed upon his bed at five o'clock the following morning, young Pennington was unable to account for his actions, or to state his whereabouts at the time when the murder was committed.

He realized what the effect of the evidence must be upon the minds of the jurors when he himself was unable to assert positively, even to himself, that he had not left his room that night. Nor was he very anxious to refute the charge against him since in his heart he believed that Shannon Burke had killed Crumb. He did not even take the stand in his own defense.

The evidence against Shannon was less convincing. A motive had been established in Crumb's knowledge of her past life and the malign influence that he had had upon it. The testimony of the camp flunky who had seen her obliterating what evidence the trail might have given in the form of hoofprints constituted practically the only direct evidence that was brought against her. It seemed to Custer that the gravest charge that could justly be brought against her was that of accessory after the fact provided the jury was convinced of his guilt.

Many witnesses testified, giving evidence concerning apparently irrelevant subjects. It was brought out, however, that Crumb died from the effects of a wound inflicted by a 45-caliber pistol, that Custer Pennington possessed such a weapon, and that at the time of his arrest, it had been found in its holster with its cartridge belt thrown carelessly upon his bed.

When Shannon Burke took the stand, all eyes were riveted upon her. They were attracted not only by her youth and beauty but also by the morbid interest which the frequenters of courtrooms would naturally feel in the disclosure of the life she had led at Hollywood. Even to the most sophisticated, it appeared incredible that this refined girl, whose soft, well-modulated voice and quiet manner carried a conviction of innate modesty, could be the woman whom Slick Allen's testimony had revealed in such a role of vice and degradation.

Allen's eyes were fastened upon her with the same intent and searching expression that had marked his attitude upon the occasion of his last visit to the Vista del Paso bungalow, as if he were trying to recall the identity of some half-forgotten face.

Though Shannon gave her evidence in a simple, straightforward manner, it was manifest that she was undergoing an intense nervous strain. The story that she told, coming as it did out of a clear sky, unguessed either by the prosecution or by the defense, proved a veritable bombshell to them both. It came after it had appeared that the last link had been forged in the chain that fixed the guilt upon Custer Pennington. She had asked, then, to be permitted to take the stand and tell her story in her own way.

"I did not see Mr. Crumb," she said, "from the time I left Hollywood on the 30th of July, last year, until the afternoon before he was killed; nor had I communicated with him during that time. What Mr. Allen told you about my having been a drug addict was true, but he did not tell you that Crumb made me what I was, or that after I came to Ganado to live, I overcame the habit. I did not live with Crumb as his wife. He used me to peddle narcotics for him. I was afraid of him and did not want to go back to him. When I left, I did not even let him know where I was going.

"The afternoon before he was killed, I met him accidentally in the patio of Colonel Pennington's home. The Penningtons had no knowledge of my association with Crumb. I knew that they wouldn't have tolerated me had they known what I had been. Crumb demanded that I should return to him and threatened to expose me if I refused. I knew that he was going to be up in the cañon that night. I rode up there and shot him. The next morning, I went back and attempted to obliterate the tracks of my horse, for I had learned from Custer Pennington that it is sometimes easy to recognize individual peculiarities in the tracks of a shod horse. That is all, except that Mr. Pennington had no knowledge of what I did and no part in it."

Momentarily, her statement seemed to overthrow the state's case against Pennington; but that the district attorney was not convinced of its truth was indicated by his cross-examination of her and other witnesses and later by the calling of new witnesses. They could not shake her testimony, but on the other hand, she was unable to prove that she had ever possessed a 45-caliber pistol or to account for what she had done with it after the crime.

During the course of her cross-examination, many apparently unimportant and irrelevant facts were adduced, among them the name of the Middle Western town in which she had been born. This trivial bit of testimony was the only point that seemed to make any impression on Allen. Anyone watching him at the moment would have seen a sudden expression of incredulity and consternation overspread his face, the hard lines of which slowly gave place to what might, in another, have suggested a semblance of grief.

For several minutes, he sat staring intently at Shannon. Then, he crossed to the side of her attorney and whispered a few words in the lawyer's ear. Receiving an assent to whatever his suggestion might have been, he left the court room.

On the following day, the defense introduced a new witness in the person of a Japanese who had been a house servant in the bungalow on the Vista del Paso. His testimony substantiated Shannon Burke's statement that she and Crumb had not lived together as man and wife.

Then, Allen was recalled to the stand. He told of the last evening that he had spent at Crumb's bungalow and of the fact that Miss Burke, who was then known to him as Gaza de Lure, had left the house at the same time he did. He testified that Crumb had asked her why she was going home so early; that she had replied that she wanted to write a letter; that he, Allen, had remarked "I thought you lived here," to which she had replied, "I'm here nearly all day, but I go home nights." The witness added that this conversation took place in Crumb's presence and that the director did not in any way deny the truth of the girl's assertion.

Why Allen should have suddenly espoused her cause was a mystery to Shannon, only to be accounted for upon the presumption that if he could lessen the value of that part of her testimony which had indicated a possible motive for the crime, he might thereby strengthen the case against Pennington toward whom he still felt enmity and whom he had long ago threatened to "get."

The district attorney, in his final argument, drew a convincing picture of the crime from the moment when Custer Pennington saddled his horse at the stables at Ganado. He followed him up the cañon to the camp in Jackknife where he had inquired concerning Crumb and then down to Sycamore again where, at the mouth of Jackknife, the lights of Crumb's car would have been visible up the larger cañon.

He demonstrated clearly that a man familiar with the hills and searching for someone whom sentiments of jealousy and revenge were prompting him to destroy would naturally investigate this automobile light that was shining where no automobile should be. That the prisoner had ridden out with the intention of killing Crumb was apparent from the fact that he had carried a pistol in a country where, under ordinary circumstances, there was no necessity for carrying a weapon for self-defense. He vividly portrayed the very instant of the commission of the crime — how Pennington leaned from his saddle and shot Crumb through the heart; the sudden leap of the murderer's horse as he was startled by the report of the pistol or possibly by the falling body of the murdered man; and how, in so jumping, he had forged and torn off the shoe that had been found beneath Crumb's body.

"And," he said, "this woman knew that he was going to kill Wilson Crumb. She knew it, and she made no effort to prevent it. On the contrary, as soon as it was light enough, she rode directly to the spot where Crumb's body lay, and, as has been conclusively demonstrated by the unimpeachable testimony of an eyewitness, she deliberately sought to expunge all traces of her lover's guilt."

He derided Shannon's confession, which he termed an 11th-hour effort to save a guilty man from the gallows.

"If she killed Wilson Crumb, what did she kill him with?"

He picked up the bullet that had been extracted from Crumb's body.

"Where is the pistol from which this bullet came? Here it is, gentlemen!"

He picked up the weapon that had been taken from Custer's room.

"Compare this bullet with those others that were taken from the clip in the handle of this automatic. They are identical. This pistol did not belong to Shannon Burke. It was never in her possession. No pistol of this character was ever in her possession. Had she had one, she could have told where she obtained it and whether it had been sold to her or to another; and the records of the seller would show whether or not she spoke the truth. Failing to tell us where she procured the weapon, she could at least lead us to the spot where she had disposed of it. She can do neither, and the reason why she cannot is because she never owned a 45-caliber pistol. She never had one in her possession, and therefore, she could not have killed Crumb with one."

When at length the case went to the jury, Custer Pennington's conviction seemed a foregone conclusion while the fate of Shannon Burke was yet in the laps of the gods. The testimony that Allen and the Japanese servant had given in substantiation of Shannon's own statement that her relations with Wilson Crumb had only been those of an accomplice in the disposal of narcotics removed from consideration the principal motive that she might have had for killing Crumb.

And so, there was no great surprise when, several hours later, the jury returned a verdict in accordance with the public opinion of Los Angeles — where, owing to the fact that murder juries are not isolated, such cases are tried largely by the newspapers and the public. They found Custer Pennington, Jr., guilty of murder in the first degree, and Shannon Burke not guilty.

CHAPTER XXXVI

ON THE DAY when Custer was to be sentenced, Colonel Pennington and Shannon Burke were present in the court room. Mrs. Pennington had remained at home with Eva, who was slowly convalescing. Shannon reached the court room before the colonel. When he arrived, he sat down beside her and placed his hand on hers.

"Whatever happens," he said, "we shall still believe in him. No matter what the evidence — and I do not deny that the jury brought in a just verdict in accordance with it — I know that he is innocent. He told me yesterday that he was innocent, and my boy would not lie to me. He thought that you killed Crumb, Shannon. He overheard the conversation between you and Crumb in the patio that day, and he knew that you had good reason to kill the man. He knows now, as we all know, that you did not. Probably, it must always remain a mystery. He would not tell me that he was innocent until after you had been proven so. He loves you very much, my girl!"

"After all that he heard here in court? After what I have been? I thought none of you would ever want to see me again."

The colonel pressed her hand.

"Whatever happens," he said, "you are going back home with me. You tried to give your life for my son. If this were not enough, the fact that he loves you, and that we love you, is enough."

Two tears crept down Shannon's cheeks — the first visible signs of emotion that she had manifested during all the long weeks of the ordeal that she had been through. Nothing had so deeply affected her as the magnanimity of the proud old Pennington, whose pride and honor, while she had always admired them, she had regarded as an indication of a certain puritanical narrowness that could not forgive the transgression of a woman.

When the judge announced the sentence, and they realized that Custer Pennington was to pay the death penalty, although it had been almost a foregone conclusion, the shock left them numb and cold.

Neither the condemned man nor his father gave any outward indication of the effect of the blow. They were Penningtons, and the Pennington pride permitted them no show of weakness before the eyes of strangers. Nor yet was there any bravado in their demeanor. The younger Pennington did not look at his father or Shannon as he was led away toward his cell between two bailiffs.

As Shannon Burke walked from the court room with the colonel, she could think of nothing but the fact that in two months the man she loved was to be hanged. She tried to formulate plans for his release — wild, quixotic plans; but she could not concentrate her mind upon anything but the bewildering thought that in two months they would hang him by the neck until he was dead.

She knew that he was innocent. Who, then, had committed the crime? Who had murdered Wilson Crumb?

Outside the Hall of Justice, she was accosted by Allen, whom she attempted to pass without noticing. The colonel turned angrily on the man. He was in the mood to commit murder himself; but Allen forestalled any outbreak on the old man's part by a pacific gesture of his hands and a quick appeal to Shannon.

"Just a moment, please," he said. "I know you think I had a lot to do with Pennington's conviction. I want to help you now. I can't tell you why. I don't believe he was guilty. I changed my mind recently. If I can see you alone, Miss Burke. I can tell you something that might give you a line on the guilty party."

"Under no conceivable circumstances can you see Miss Burke alone," snapped the colonel.

"I'm not going to hurt her," said Allen. "Just let her talk to me here alone on the sidewalk where no one can overhear."

"Yes," said the girl, who could see no opportunity pass which held the slightest ray of hope for Custer.

The colonel walked away but turned and kept his eyes on the man when he was out of earshot. Allen spoke hurriedly to the girl for 10 or 15 minutes and then turned and left her. When she returned to the colonel, the latter did not question her. When she did not offer to confide in him, he knew that she must have good reasons for her reticence since he realized that her sole interest lay in aiding Custer.

For the next two months, the colonel divided his time between Ganado and San Francisco, that he might be near San Quentin where Custer was held pending the day of execution. Mrs. Pennington, broken in health by the succession of blows that she had sustained, was sorely in need of his companionship and help. Eva was rapidly regaining her strength and some measure of her spirit. She had begun to realize how useless and foolish her attempt at self-destruction had been and to see that the braver and nobler course would have been to give Guy the benefit of her moral support in his time of need.

The colonel, who had wormed from Custer the full story of his conviction upon the liquor charge, was able to convince her that Guy had not played a dishonorable part, and that, of the two, he had suffered more than Custer. Her father did not condone or excuse Guy's wrongdoing, but he tried to make her understand that it was no indication of a criminal inclination but rather the thoughtless act of an undeveloped boy.

During the two months, they saw little or nothing of Shannon. She remained in Los Angeles, and when she made the long trip to San Quentin to see Custer, or when they chanced to see her, they could not but note how thin and drawn she was becoming. The roses had left her cheeks, and there were deep lines beneath her eyes in which there was constantly an expression of haunting fear.

As the day of the execution drew nearer, the gloom that had hovered over Ganado for months settled like a dense pall upon them all. On the day before the execution, the colonel left for San Francisco to say goodbye to his son for the last time. Custer had insisted that his mother and Eva must not come, and they had acceded to his wish.

On the afternoon when the colonel arrived at San Quentin, he was permitted to see his son for the last time. The two conversed in low tones, Custer asking questions about his mother and sister and about the little everyday activities of the ranch. Neither of them referred to the event of the following morning.

"Has Shannon been here today?" the colonel asked.

Custer shook his head.

"I haven't seen her this week," he said. "I suppose she dreaded coming. I don't blame her. I should like to have seen her once more, though!"

Presently they stood in silence for several moments.

"You'd better go, dad," said the boy. "Go back to Mother and Eva. Don't take it too hard. It isn't so bad, after all. I have led a bully life, and I have never forgotten once that I am a Pennington. I shall not forget it tomorrow."

The father could not speak. They clasped hands once, the older man turned away, and the guards led Custer back to the death cell for the last time.

CHAPTER XXXVII

IT WAS MORNING when the colonel reached the ranch. He found his wife and Eva sitting in Custer's room. They knew the hour, and they were waiting there to be as near him as they could. They were weeping quietly.

In the kitchen across the patio, they could hear Hannah sobbing.

They sat there for a long time in silence. Suddenly, they heard a door slam in the patio, and the sound of someone running. "Colonel Pennington! Colonel Pennington!" a voice cried.

The colonel stepped to the door of Custer's room. It was the bookkeeper calling him.

"What is it?" he asked. "Here I am."

"The Governor has granted a stay of execution. There is new evidence. Miss Burke is on her way here now. She has found the man who killed Crumb!"

What more he said, the colonel did not hear, for he had turned back into the room and, collapsing on his son's bed, had broken into tears — he who had gone through those long weeks like a man of iron.

It was nearly noon before Shannon arrived. She had been driven from Los Angeles by an attaché of the district attorney's office. The Penningtons had been standing on the east porch, watching the road with binoculars, so anxious were they for confirmation of their hopes.

She was out of the car before it had stopped and was running toward them. The man who had accompanied her followed and joined them on the porch. Shannon threw her arms around Mrs. Pennington's neck.

"He is safe!" she cried. "Another has confessed and has satisfied the district attorney of his guilt."

"Who was it?" they asked. Shannon turned toward Eva.

"It is going to be another blow to you all," she said; "but wait until I'm through, and you will understand that it could not have been otherwise. It was Guy who killed Wilson Crumb."

"Guy? Why should he have done it?"

"That was it. That was why suspicion was never directed toward him. Only he knew the facts that prompted him to commit the deed. It was Allen who suggested to me the possibility that it might have been Guy. I have spent nearly two months at the sanatorium with this gentleman from the district attorney's office in an effort to awaken Guy's sleeping intellect to a realization of the past and of the present necessity for recalling it. He has been improving steadily, but it was only yesterday that memory returned to him. We worked on the theory that if he could be made to realize that Eva lived, the cause of his mental sickness would be removed. We tried everything, and we had almost given up hope when, almost like a miracle, his memory returned while he was looking at a kodak picture of Eva that I had shown him. The rest was easy, especially after he knew that she had recovered. Instead of the necessity for confession resulting in a further shock, it seemed to inspirit him. His one thought was of Custer, his one hope that we would be in time to save him."

"Why did he kill Crumb?" asked Eva.

"Because Crumb killed Grace. He told me the whole story yesterday."

Very carefully, Shannon related all that Guy had told of Crumb's relations with his sister up to the moment of Grace's death.

"I am glad he killed him!" said Eva. "I would have had no respect for him if he hadn't done it."

"Guy told me that the evening before he killed Crumb, he had been looking over a motion picture magazine, and he had seen there a picture of Crumb which tallied with the photograph he had taken from Grace's dressing table — a portrait of the man who, as she told him, was responsible for her trouble. Guy had never been able to learn this man's identity, but the picture in the magazine, with his name below it, was a reproduction of the same photograph. There was no question as to the man's identity. The scarf-pin and a lock of hair falling in a peculiar way over the forehead marked the pictures as identical. Though Guy had never seen Crumb, he knew from conversations that he had heard here that it was Wilson Crumb who was directing the picture that was to be taken on Ganado. He immediately got his pistol, saddled his horse, and rode up to the camp in search of Crumb. It was he whom one of the witnesses mistook for Custer. He then did what the district attorney attributed to Custer. He rode to the mouth of Jackknife and saw the lights of Crumb's car up near El Camino Largo. While he was in Jackknife, Eva must have ridden down Sycamore from her meeting with Crumb, passing Jackknife before Guy rode back into Sycamore. He rode up to where Crumb was attempting to crank his engine. Evidently the starter had failed to work, for Crumb was standing in front of the car in the glare of the headlights attempting to crank it. Guy accosted him, charged him with the murder of Grace, and shot him. He then started for home by way of El Camino Largo. Half a mile up the trail, he dismounted and hid his pistol and belt in a hollow tree. Then he rode home.

"He told me that while he never for an instant regretted his act, he did not sleep all that night and was in a highly nervous condition when the shock of Eva's supposed death unbalanced his mind; otherwise, he would gladly have assumed the guilt of Crumb's death at the time when Custer and I were accused.

"After we had obtained Guy's confession, Allen gave us further information tending to prove Custer innocent. He said he could not give it before without incriminating himself; and as he had no love for Custer, he did not intend to hang for a crime he had not committed. He knew that he would surely hang if he confessed the part that he had played in formulating the evidence against Custer.

"Crumb had been the means of sending Allen to the county jail after robbing him of several thousand dollars. The day before Crumb was killed, Allen's sentence expired. The first thing he did was to search for Crumb with the intention of killing the man. He learned at the studio where Crumb was, and he followed him immediately. He was hanging around the camp out of sight waiting for Crumb when he heard the shot that killed him. His investigation led him to Crumb's body. He was instantly overcome by the fear induced by his guilty conscience that the crime would be laid at his door. In casting about for some plan by which he might divert suspicion from himself, he discovered an opportunity to turn it against a man whom he hated. The fact that he had been a stableman on Ganado and was familiar with the customs of the ranch made it an easy thing for him to go to the stables, saddle the Apache, and ride him up Sycamore to Crumb's body. Here he deliberately pulled the off fore shoe from the horse and hid it under Crumb's body. Then he rode back to the stable, unsaddled the Apache, and made his way to the village.

"The district attorney said that we need have no fear but that Custer will be exonerated and freed. And, Eva"— she turned to the girl with a happy smile — "I have it very confidentially that there is small likelihood that any jury in Southern California will convict Guy if he bases his defense upon a plea of insanity."

Eva smiled bravely and said:

"One thing I don't understand, Shannon, is what you were doing brushing the road with a bough from a tree on the morning after the killing of Crumb if you weren't trying to obliterate some one's tracks."

"That's just what I was trying to do," said Shannon, "Ever since Custer taught me something about tracking, it has held a certain fascination for me so that I often try to interpret the tracks I see along the trails in the hills. It was because of this, I suppose, that I immediately recognized the Apache's tracks around the body of Crumb. I immediately jumped to the conclusion that Custer had killed him, and I did what I could to remove this evidence. As it turned out, my efforts did more harm than good until Allen's explanation cleared up the matter."

"And why," asked the colonel, "did Allen undergo this sudden change of heart?"

Shannon turned toward him, her face slightly flushed, though she looked him straight in the eyes as she spoke.

"It is a hard thing for me to tell you," she said. "Allen is a bad man — a very bad man; yet in the worst of men, there is a spark of good. Allen told me this morning, in the district attorney's office, what it was that had kindled to life the spark of good in him. He is my father."